Beginning of Arrogance

A Paladin's Journey

Book One

BRYAN COLE

Beginning of Arrogance

A Fat Paladin publication
www.fatpaladin.ca

Tellwell Talent
www.tellwell.ca

ISBN
978-0-2288-6867-5 (Hardcover)
978-0-2288-6866-8 (Paperback)
978-0-2288-6868-2 (eBook)

To my friends, who make everything better;
you know who you are.

And to my wife,
who showed me what a strong woman really is.

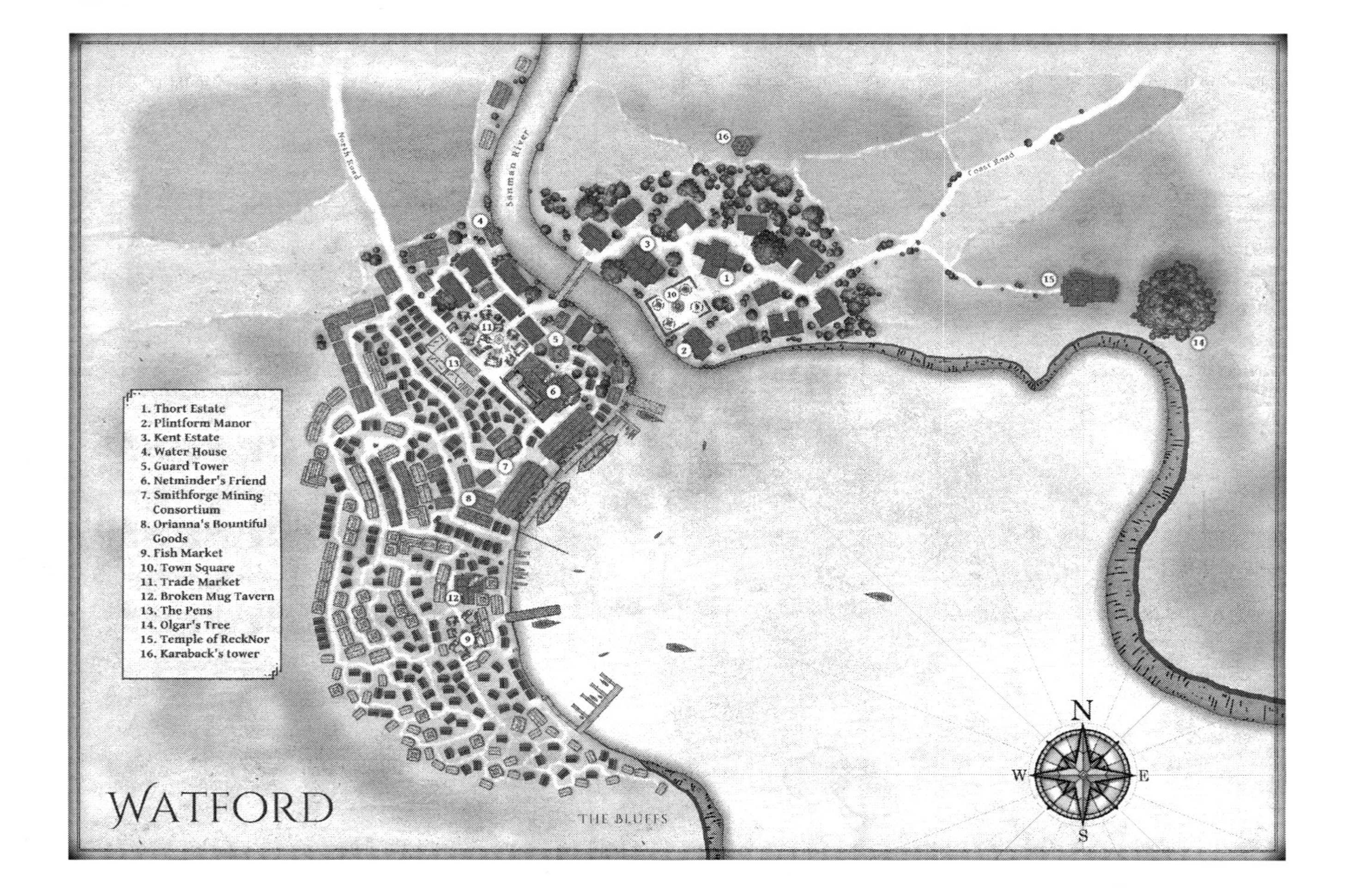
WATFORD
1. Thort Estate
2. Plintform Manor
3. Kent Estate
4. Water House
5. Guard Tower
6. Netminder's Friend
7. Smithforge Mining Consortium
8. Orianna's Bountiful Goods
9. Fish Market
10. Town Square
11. Trade Market
12. Broken Mug Tavern
13. The Pens
14. Olgar's Tree
15. Temple of ReckNor
16. Karaback's tower
North Road
Sanman River
Coast Road
THE BLUFFS
N
W
E
S

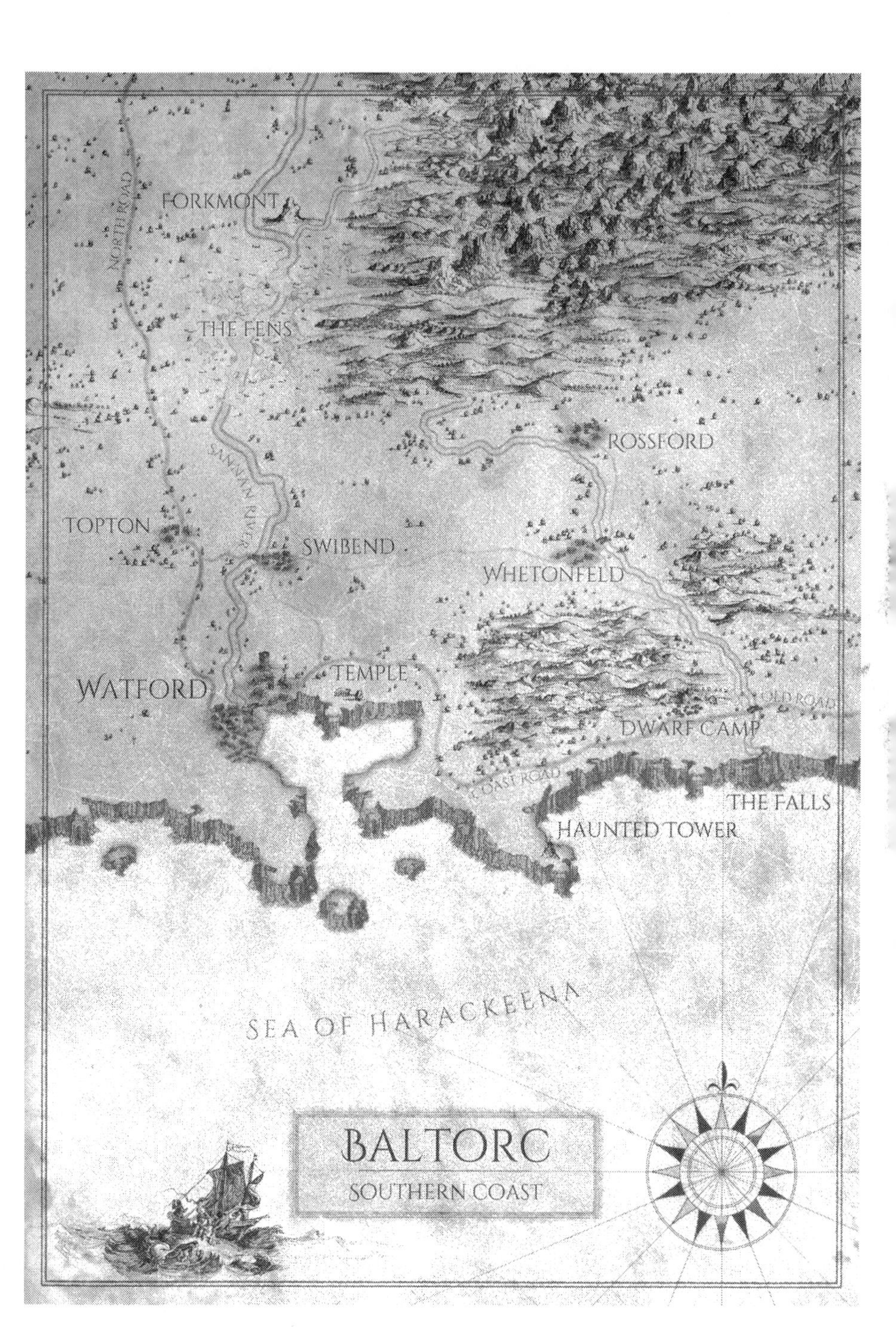
FORKMONT
NORTH ROAD
THE FENS
SANNAN RIVER
ROSSFORD
TOPTON
SWIBEND
WHETONFELD
WATFORD
TEMPLE
OLD ROAD
DWARF CAMP
COAST ROAD
THE FALLS
HAUNTED TOWER
SEA OF HARACKEENA
BALTORC
SOUTHERN COAST

Chapter One

Krell's sword struck the pell.

His heavy breathing couldn't disguise the dull *thunk* from the blade as it hit, bits of wood breaking off. Krell twisted his wrist and pulled, disengaging the blade. He struck again, the blade sliding along the wood, leaving a fresh scar. Once again, he failed to cut through the post.

Krell recovered his stance, his shield raised as Olgar taught him while his sword moved back into proper striking position. His next strike was high and carved another sliver of wood. Without waiting, Krell swung again. The sword hit lower than Krell wanted. He pulled back into the proper stance, and his next strike was on target, carving deep into the wood.

"All right, lad, I think we've seen enough," a voice said from somewhere ahead of him.

Krell took a step back from the pell. An unsteady step, he was forced to admit. The sun was still high in the sky. Sweat ran into his blue eyes, causing him to blink in irritation. He glared at the wooden post. No more than halfway through. His chain mail armor was heavy on his shoulders.

He looked over at the town council, seated at a long table under an awning. They had comfortable chairs for the most part, and were sipping on what looked like cool drinks in the shade. Krell wondered how much attention they were actually paying to this test.

Amra Thort was the leader of the town council, and owner of one of the largest fishing fleets in Watford. She was a formidable-looking woman with steel gray hair, whose hands bore the signs of hard work done many years ago. People in the town respected her, Olgar had told him.

Seated next to her was Daylan Plintform, a wealthy merchant who owned many trading and fishing vessels. His long face was handsome, but he always looked irritated, even when he wasn't. Olgar detested him, but refused to explain why. He was popular in town, since he paid for numerous festivals and banquets when the catch was good.

Daylan and Amra were looking at one another and talking quietly, while the third member of the town council stared at him with rapt attention. Aldrik Kent was young, perhaps only a few years older than Krell himself, and had inherited his father's fishing fleet and trading business. Behind him stood Nathanial, his manservant, a hulking battle-scarred man with bulging arms. Both Aldrik and Nathanial had paid close attention to Krell and his sword work.

The final person at the table was Captain Gijwolf. He was seated on a simple wooden stool at one end of the table, as if ready to leap into battle. He was eyeing Krell critically, taking in the slender youth sweltering in the sun in front of him. His dark skin contrasted sharply against the polished breastplate he wore.

"How do you feel right now?" he asked.

Krell shrugged. Honesty was the best way, Olgar had told him many times. "Hot. A little tired. Thirsty and hungry. Somewhat angry at the pell for still being there."

Captain Gijwolf smiled and stood up. He strode forward, drawing his blade as he went. "Tired? Let's see how tired you really are then. Defend yourself!" Without waiting, he charged.

The first cut came fast and precise. Krell knew he was not in a proper stance, so simply stepped backward to avoid the first stroke. His shield came up a beat before Captain Gijwolf's sword slammed into it, battering it aside. The next strike shoved it completely out of position, but Krell had his sword in hand and used it to deflect the fourth strike. He tried to catch the fifth, but it slid past his guard, rapping him smartly on the shoulder.

Krell counterattacked, his blade cutting low. Captain Gijwolf parried his blade, forcing it upward, and Krell surged forward, hoping to knock the captain backward with his shield to throw him off balance and break his defense.

He didn't even see the next strike, which took him in the leg, leaving a nasty gash. Krell hissed in pain, counterattacking again, aiming for the captain's neck. Captain Gijwolf threaded his arm inside Krell's reach, and the next thing he knew, his arm was locked somehow, his sword wildly out of position. His vision exploded into stars as the captain hammered the pommel of his sword into his face. Without thinking, Krell shoved forward again with the shield, in a last desperate move.

It was like battering a stone wall. The captain simply absorbed the blow from the shield without moving. He then hooked his sword hilt over the shield and pulled, twisting as he did so. Krell was caught completely off guard. He tried to step forward to maintain his balance, but the captain extended a leg and he hit the ground face first. Stunned for a moment, he felt the captain's blade at his throat.

"Good enough, Krell. Get up. Let's see to that leg wound."

The sword withdrew, and Krell rolled over, breathing heavily. Captain Gijwolf kneeled down beside him and tore his leggings open to see the wound, then smiled.

"Well, Olgar wasn't mistaken, and you're no liar. It does look like ReckNor, or some other god, favors you with their grace." As the captain watched, the wound ceased bleeding, then began to slowly mend itself. Then it stopped healing, and a trickle of blood resumed.

"A little favor, at any rate. Can you walk?"

Krell nodded, then clambered to his feet. His leggings were a total loss, torn open and bloody. His leg supported his weight, even though he was growing a little light-headed from the heat and blood loss. Captain Gijwolf nodded at him.

"Come over here and sit. I want to know what you understand about this. What did Olgar tell you?"

Captain Gijwolf led Krell over to the table and shoved him at the stool, then pushed a cup of water to him. Krell took his helmet off and ran a hand through his damp brown hair, and grasped the cup. He drank deeply, emptying it. Without waiting, Captain Gijwolf refilled it and Krell drank again.

"Uh, thank you, Captain. Olgar said that the dwarves nearby have a problem and need some help to look into it. They've sent for their own soldiers, but until they arrive they need warriors to deal with something." Krell gestured at the rest of the town council, who were watching him closely now. "You're putting together a charter for warriors to go to the dwarf mine and figure out what is going on, and deal with it."

Captain Gijwolf nodded.

"He has the skill, Captain?" asked Amra. "He seems capable enough with the blade, even if a bit of a novice with it."

Captain Gijwolf nodded again. "He has the skill required. I'm a strong hand with the blade, and this lad was able to keep me off him far more ably than he should have, considering only Olgar has given him any training. More than that, he's fearless enough to go into some dark hole. Did his best to put me down out there, which is how I ended up dealing that wound to him. Sorry about that, Krell, but you were rushing me with your sword work."

The town councilors looked at one another, then shrugged.

Daylan said, "Why not then? Has he met the others who have arrived?"

Krell looked blankly back at them, then shook his head in the negative. "Others? I thought I'd be going alone."

Captain Gijwolf snorted in laughter. "You are young, aren't you? The things you find out there beyond settled lands, you're never going to want to face them alone. Always bring comrades with you, lest some beast paralyze your will and leave you helpless while it starts to eat you."

THAT WOULD BE A DISAPPOINTING WAY FOR YOU TO DIE.

Krell winced, flinching as the thunder of ReckNor's voice crashed into his thoughts. His sudden movement jostled the table, upsetting some of the drinks. Daylan gave him a disgusted look as his drink toppled over.

Aldrik grinned at Krell. "Well, I like him! He seems like he knows what he's doing, and if Olgar said he was able, and he meets your approval, Captain, then add him to the charter." Aldrik let out a long, wistful sigh. Nathanial began clearing the cups from the table, dumping them out, and placing them into a basket at his feet.

Captain Gijwolf smiled at Aldrik. "He's more than capable enough. Half the guards in town would lose in a duel against him. Well, they're your bones, Krell. If you think you can cut it, an extra sword to venture out with the others cannot do anything but help." Captain Gijwolf clapped him on the shoulder. "If you live, that is. Go clean yourself up and I'll introduce you to the others."

* * *

Krell looked at his leggings, shrugged, and tossed them onto the floor. He pulled on his spare pair from his pack, then set about donning his armor. The chain mail was already showing signs of wear, and the vigorous use he had put it to earlier hadn't helped. It smelled like iron mixed with sweat and mud.

He looked outside and spied Captain Gijwolf standing nearby. Doubtless waiting for him. Looking at the chain mail armor, Krell bundled it up, wrapped his cloak around it to keep it secure, and did his best to stuff it into his pack. Then he put on his boots, buckled on his sword, and stepped into the sunshine.

He'd done it! Olgar had said he was ready, and ReckNor told him he'd be fine. Failing to cut the pell, and then getting beaten by Captain Gijwolf, had done a lot to shatter his confidence. ReckNor was a pressure in his mind, forcing him onward, so he straightened his shoulders. Time to meet these companions who would stand with him at the dwarven mines. The pressure of ReckNor's grace within became colored with laughter.

Captain Gijwolf looked him over as he approached, and nodded. He led Krell from the town market square where the test was administered, toward the Netminder's Friend, the only lodging for travelers here in Watford.

Krell looked with interest at the common room when he stepped inside. The ceiling was high, easily over ten feet, and the floor was made of solid wood that looked reasonably clean. The tables and chairs were a motley collection of mismatched pieces, some of which had clearly been broken and repaired. A bar ran along the wall to his left, and a happily smiling woman with red hair turning to gray walked up.

"Ah, Elias! We don't often see you in here at this hour! Care for a pint or some food?"

Captain Gijwolf shook his head. "Town business, Marlena, perhaps another time for the pint. Yes to the food, though."

Marlena laughed, then turned to Krell. "And young Master Krell! Out without Olgar for the first time! Do you want to partake of my wares?" The emphasis on words left Krell thinking she meant far more than food or drink. He stared at her as a blush crept up his neck. She laughed again. "Always the same, I see! Well, I wager you'll be meeting the others in the back room. Best be on your way!"

Captain Gijwolf smiled at her and walked toward the back. Krell stood staring at her, and she leaned forward, gesturing for him to come closer.

"Best follow the captain," she said in a hushed, sultry voice. "Time enough to get drunk together later!" She laughed, then spun away to a basin filled with water, where she picked up a clay mug and began washing it. She looked over her shoulder at him, then gestured with her head in the captain's direction.

Krell shook his head and looked around. Captain Gijwolf was standing at the back of the tavern next to an open door, looking at him with an expression somewhere between amused at his reaction and irritated at the delay. Krell hurried over and went inside.

A large table surrounded by chairs dominated the room, a private dining room of some sort. Space for ten or more, but what caught Krell's attention at once were the people within.

His new companions.

The fey-touched stood out — he was dashingly handsome, and wearing finery similar to what the council had worn earlier. Fey-touched were always pretty, a remnant of some elven ancestor in their bloodline. He looked at Krell and frowned. A sneering sort of frown that made Krell instantly dislike him for some reason. Krell frowned back, then turned to look at the others.

The orange-tinted orc on the opposite side of the table from the fey-touched slammed his tankard down. He was bare-chested, and his enormous frame was heavily muscled and covered with faint scars. He looked up at Krell.

"Know how to use that?" he asked, gesturing at the sword strapped to Krell's waist.

Krell nodded. A burly green orc sat at the head of the table eating; he nodded in greeting to Captain Gijwolf, and then turned his eyes to him. Where the first orc was bare from the waist up, this one was wearing a breastplate as he ate. A halfling was sitting next to him, and looked up when Kraven spoke.

"Hey, all right, a new face! How you doing? I'm Gerrard!" The halfling hopped down and walked over, extending a hand toward Krell. His grin was infectious, framed by a neatly trimmed beard, and Krell found himself smiling back at him as he took Gerrard's hand and shook.

"There you go. Now your turn, right? That's how this conversation thing works! That's Tristan, he's a fey-touched, and across from him is Kraven, who's got anger issues bigger than his muscles, if you know what I mean. The big green orc at the end is Orca, like the whale. You got a name, or what?"

"Uh, hi. I'm Krell, paladin of ReckNor."

"ReckNor, huh? He's a bit insane for my tastes, but decent enough when not trying to kill everyone with a hurricane! And you said you're a paladin? Didn't think ReckNor called paladins, but you learn something new every day! Wonder how long you'll live?" He grinned and returned to the table. "Come, sit. You wouldn't be here if our dear sponsor, the illustrious Captain Gijwolf, didn't think you could use that sword, so it looks like we've enough to get going with this job! Finally, time for the captain to fill us in, or do you think he's going to wait for more hands to show up?"

Krell sat next to Kraven, a little unsure about where to look. Gerrard certainly commanded a lot of attention. He was now talking about how ReckNor provided food from the sea, and how the other tavern in Watford tried to make alcohol from fish guts.

"So, another brute then?"

Krell looked at Tristan. He was eyeing him with a frown on his face. Krell nodded back.

"I guess you'd say yes. That I'm a brute. If something tries to eat me, I'll feed it my sword first." Krell shrugged, then looked around. He hadn't realized Captain Gijwolf had stepped out of the room until he returned, carrying two bowls and a goblet with practiced ease. He set a bowl in front of Krell, then sat beside him.

"Eat, Krell. I've never known a man your age who wasn't hungry." He set his own bowl down and fished a pair of wooden spoons out of his belt, handing one to Krell. Fish stew by the smell, but the captain was correct. Krell was starving.

Tristan sneered a bit, then said in a tone of voice that instantly irritated Krell, "Where's my food, Captain Gijwolf?"

The captain smiled and gestured toward the door. Tristan subsided into silence, but made no move to get up.

Kraven leaned over and whispered loudly, ensuring Tristan could hear, "Tristan has a big mouth, and is annoying, but he's got lots of power, apparently. He looks too pretty to take into battle, though." Then Kraven grabbed Krell's arm, his hand wrapping almost entirely around, squeezing painfully. "You seem kind of, what's the word? Small? You going to slow us down, little human?"

Krell met his gaze, then at looked at his hand wrapped about his arm, then met his gaze again. He let some anger creep into his voice. "I'm a survivor. If ReckNor wants to take me to glorious service in the afterlife, then I'll die. Not before that. Now, remove your hand so I can eat."

Kraven bellowed out a laugh. "Good enough, Krell! But don't worry, I like you. I'll keep you safe!" He slapped Krell on the back, knocking Krell into the table. Krell grabbed the bowl of stew and his cup before they tipped over. Orca grunted from the end of the table.

"No problem with your reflexes then, and I can see from here the calluses that come from holding weapons. No scars, which means you're likely new to this, so I'll explain a few things. First, ignore Tristan. His tongue is harsh, but he has magic that'll serve to keep us all alive. Second..."

Tristan bristled. "I'll have you know that many people tell me I am quite the elegant speaker, Orca, and that my good vocabulary and success with women are no reason for you to —"

"SECOND," yelled Orca, meeting Tristan's gaze, "I am in charge of this little expedition. Third..."

The room erupted in chaos.

"Who said you were in charge?" Kraven yelled, at the same time Tristan said, "Hardly. I think leadership should fall to the one with the greatest value to add to the team, which is *clearly* me!"

Gerrard looked alarmed. "Hey, whatever, Orca, am I right? No problem if you want to be in charge, but we split the loot evenly, no leadership stakes or other nonsense, right?"

Orca yelled back at Tristan. "I'm in charge because I'm the strongest and smartest one here!"

As they yelled back and forth, Captain Gijwolf calmly ate his bowl of stew. When he noticed Krell watching him, he smiled, gestured with his spoon to continue eating, and then went back to his meal. Krell shrugged and ate.

Whatever he was expecting, this was definitely not it.

* * *

"Now that you've got the yelling out of the way, let me tell you what you're being hired for."

Captain Gijwolf stood at one end of the table, looking at the group of them. Tristan appeared to be pouting, Orca looked angry, Gerrard was listening closely, and Kraven seemed to be paying no attention at all. Krell wondered why Olgar thought he should join these people. They didn't seem to like each other very much.

"The dwarves recently got a commission from our Lord Duke Mavram Hudderly, long may he reign, to dig iron and copper ore out of the hills to the east of Watford. They've established a mining camp, and use the town merchants for food and other supplies, though the ore they have mined is shipped upriver.

"As they dug into the hill, they came across some small caves, not uncommon near the coast, I've been told. They set out to explore these caves cautiously, not knowing what they'd find within.

"Three days ago, a pair of miners went missing. The next day, the search party of eight disappeared down the same hole. They've boarded it up, and set guards as well as they can, but they want someone to go in and recover the bodies. They're pretty sure something is down there and they want it dead and gone so they can continue doing what dwarves do. We put out a call for warriors, and you lot are the ones that have answered so far.

"So, tomorrow morning, you're going to spend a half day walking to the dwarven mining camp, and meet with their leader, Petimus Smithforge. He'll show you to the hole, you go in, find the dwarf bodies, kill whatever killed them, and come out for a reward. Any questions?"

Krell looked around at the others. Tristan raised his hand. "How much is the reward for?"

"Two hundred golden sovereigns, to be split among the survivors. Hopefully, that means you all earn forty. And the gratitude of the dwarves, which may count for something as well."

That number overwhelmed Krell — a month of skilled labor couldn't earn that much coin, and they were going to make it in a day?

"That's it? Hardly a worthwhile use of my time and stupendous talents, wouldn't you say, Captain Gijwolf?" Tristan looked smug. "Perhaps you can sweeten the offer for us? Or at least for me, the one clearly of most value here?"

Captain Gijwolf smiled, then looked at the others. "If it's going to be just the four of you, then the split means you'll end up with fifty coins each, not forty."

"Oh. That's the way it's going to be. Well, I can't leave these poor defenseless brutes to the certain doom that awaits them if I don't come along, so I suppose my gracious nature and incredible generosity will compel me to accept the offer of two hundred coins, to be split among the survivors."

Captain Gijwolf's smile grew wider. "Why thank you, Tristan, for your kind and gracious offer to accompany these new companions of yours and use your formidable might to aid them in the battle that doubtless lies ahead."

He turned to survey the rest of the table. "Any other questions?"

"Yeah, you still paying the bill to sleep here tonight?" Kraven asked.

"The town council is paying, but yes, your room for this evening is paid. After you get your reward, you —"

"Good enough." Kraven stood up. "In the common room, tomorrow, at dawn?"

"Yes," said Orca, also standing. "But we are leaving at dawn, not breaking fast." Orca and Kraven both left.

Gerrard looked around, scooped up a bundle in the corner, and departed the room. As he stepped back into the common room, Krell heard him shout, "Good evening, Watford! You are lucky that Gerrard, a maestro of music with the voice of a songbird, is here to charm and entertain you tonight!"

Tristan also stood up. "Well, I, for one, am excited that you will all get to witness my magical might tomorrow. Pay special attention, Krell, because you're in for a treat!" Tristan left and shut the door, muting the sound of Gerrard's singing and the clapping from the crowd. Even the way Tristan said Krell's name caused a flash of irritation.

GET USED TO HIM, KRELL.

"Do you want a room here, Krell?" Krell turned from staring at the door to Captain Gijwolf. He was looking at him strangely.

"Um, thank you, Captain, but no. I'll walk up to the temple and sleep there tonight. I'm sure Olgar will want to talk to me before tomorrow." He looked around. "Do we leave the plates and things here, or take them somewhere, or clean them ourselves?"

The captain smiled and began collecting the plates, bowls, and spoons left behind. "It speaks well of you that you'd ask that. Most people never realize how a simple common courtesy can earn you gratitude from people. Grab those bowls, and let's make Marlena's life just that much easier."

Krell grabbed the spoons as his stomach rumbled. "Do you think she has more of this stew?"

* * *

Krell walked up the hill alone.

The sun was setting behind him, so the path was well lit. The wind was picking up, and Krell could tell it would rain later. He could smell it on the breeze. Ahead, he saw a small boy leave the temple and run toward him. When he spied Krell he stopped, then ran off the road and went around him in a wide circle, and continued running back to town.

The temple to ReckNor stood on a rocky bluff overlooking both the town of Watford and the Sea of Harackeena. It was modest, as temples go, or so Olgar said to him. The stern visage of ReckNor, the god of the seas and skies, was carved into the front of the temple. Walking from Watford to the temple meant being in his gaze the entire time. Krell assumed there was some symbolism there that he didn't understand.

Olgar was standing at his favorite spot, a rocky outcropping hanging over the sea. It gave an outstanding view of the surrounding area, and incidentally let Olgar see anyone walking from town up to the temple. He was staring west toward the setting sun. His large frame seemed almost perched atop his peg leg, and the symbol of ReckNor hung about his neck, glittering in the sunlight. His graying hair blew wildly in the breeze. He'd doubtless watched Krell walking up the path.

As Krell reached the top, he walked toward the outcropping, coming to stand behind him. Olgar had watched him approach, but now turned his attention to the vista spread out before them. Watford lay below the temple, a small town that was dominated by the docks. Almost everyone who lived there made their living from the sea. The Netminder's Friend was easy to spot, the largest building in Watford, though the large homes of the wealthy were visible surrounding the nearby town square. Beyond, Krell could see the sprawl of the town along the Sanmen River. Krell had never lived in a town before and hadn't really seen much of Watford. He wondered why the buildings kept getting smaller the farther they got from the town square.

The Sanmen River was a sparkling blue color as it entered the town from the north, but became darker and more polluted as it flowed toward the harbor, where it made a muddy smear. The harbor was filled with fishing boats at this hour, each of them doubtless dumping fish guts overboard. Krell knew there was a small set of tunnels under the town to carry clean water to several cisterns for the people living in town. The wealthy had direct connections in their homes. Nobody drank from the river in town. Those who did often died.

He turned his gaze out to sea. As the minutes passed, Krell thought about ReckNor's domain. Never the same, but constant. That was straight out of the book that Olgar made him read. Wild and dangerous, but also the source of life and livelihoods. His thoughts wandered to ReckNor himself, and why he spoke to him so directly.

I SPEAK TO YOU BECAUSE YOU ARE MY PALADIN, KRELL.

"Well, my boy, what did you think of the outside world?"

Krell winced. He wished ReckNor had a voice that sounded less like a roaring thunderstorm. Shaking his head, he looked at Olgar. "You didn't ask if I passed the test the council set for me."

Olgar turned and smiled. "Use that head of yours! If you'd have failed, you would have returned hours ago, and be starving besides. No doubt Captain Gijwolf fed you. He was a young lad once, long ago, just as I was, and we both remember." He walked toward the temple doors, his wooden peg making his gait awkward. "Besides, I was there watching, so I knew you passed when Elias drew his sword on you."

"I didn't see you there," Krell said in surprise. Olgar only made the trek down to town when he needed supplies for the temple, and most of the time, the faithful brought them up when they came up for services.

"You weren't supposed to see me, so you didn't. ReckNor's salty tears, did you think I'd miss the chance to learn firsthand whether you'd embarrassed me or not?" Olgar turned and smiled at him again. "Besides, it's good for me to get down to the town. See some of the faithful who can't or won't make the trek up the hill. I probably don't do that often enough. That hill is hard to climb with this leg, but ReckNor puts challenges in front of all of us. We overcome, or we perish. That is his way. *Our* way. Olgar and Krell, champions of ReckNor!" Olgar swayed unsteadily a bit before recovering his balance.

Krell looked at him closely, then moved forward and breathed in deeply through his nose. "You are drunk. Again."

"Ease off lad, or I'll thump you! I'm an old man, and my days of adventure on the seas are behind me. You can lecture me on my habits when you've had the same sort of experiences I have. I'd wager you'll be doing so from the bottom of a cup, just like me!"

Olgar let out a belch.

"Though, you're much more stubborn that I was, and a paladin besides. Likely you're going to be dead before long, and that'll be a shame, by ReckNor's beard it will, because I like you, my boy! Pleased me greatly when you washed up on the docks here in Watford!" Olgar hobbled over to the doorway and threw open the double doors.

The sunlight filtered through the large window in the back, which was cut to look like ReckNor himself, with his trident and beard prominently displayed. Every column was adorned with his symbol, a trident piercing a wave.

For Krell, it was the first real home he could remember.

"Help me in lad, my flask is empty and I think I want to vomit."

Krell jerked him back away from the temple and supported his weight as he walked Olgar around to the graveyard. "I'm not keen to clean up inside again. Is it urgent, or can you make it to Plintform?" asked Krell. Spread before them was a graveyard, filled with hundreds of markers.

"Nay lad, not so urgent that I can't hold it in. Let's go pay the jackass a visit."

Krell held Olgar's bulk up as best he could, staggering through the cemetery to a large stone monument. Olgar leaned against it, then noisily threw up.

"You ever going to tell me what Daylan Plintform's father did to make you so angry at him, even after all this time?"

Olgar looked at Krell with bleary eyes and shook his head. "No lad, I am not. Help me up, I need a drink."

Krell sighed and heaved Olgar's weight back onto his shoulder, and together they wobbled back to the temple. Once inside, Krell helped Olgar to sit on one of the many benches the faithful used when he called a service. Olgar leaned down and rubbed at his knee and leg.

"Did I ever tell you how the sea devils took my leg?"

Krell smiled. "Yes, Olgar, many times, and always whenever you're drunk. It's a good story, though, so I don't mind."

Olgar gave him a threatening look.

"Never mind then, you condescending little shit. Tell me about the others and fetch my flask from the pulpit up there."

Krell walked up, admiring the simplicity of the temple. Simple benches hand carved from driftwood that washed ashore, and a single pulpit. No books, no curtains, no carpet. Bare stone throughout. Plain. Simple. Harsh. *Pure.*

The pulpit was a simple wooden stand, mostly used by Olgar as a makeshift cane, while he talked to the people who trudged up for prayers. A simple drawer held three flasks inside. Krell shrugged and grabbed all three.

"Ah, smart thinking, lad. Now you won't have to go back up for more later. Stop being stubborn and tell me about the other idiots who answered the call put out by our illustrious town council."

"Well, there's two orcs, Kraven and Orca. They're big and covered in muscles. I think Orca doesn't like me already for some reason, kept shouting he was in charge. Kraven thinks I'm weak." Krell paused for a moment. "No, that isn't it. It's that he thinks I'm scrawny, like I wouldn't be able to lift a sword." Krell thought about them. As orcs, they were substantially larger than most humans, with arms as big around as his legs.

"Gerrard seems really friendly and fun, but it makes me think there must be something wrong with him, because he wants to dive into a dark hole that swallowed up some dwarves. He seems like he's a singer at heart. That part doesn't make sense to me."

Olgar snorted. "Never underestimate what fools will do for coin."

"There's also this fey-touched named Tristan who has magic power."

"I know him!" Olgar shouted. "Karaback's lackey. He does errands for him from time to time. Not an apprentice, as such, but whenever Karaback is too lazy to do it himself, he sends out Tristan. Pretty, but arrogant." Olgar let out a belch. "But not unwarranted, from what I hear. Try your best not to make him angry. May ReckNor aid you there, my boy! You're going to need all the help you can get on that front!" Olgar started laughing.

Krell wondered about that. There was something about Tristan that made him want to grind his teeth, and he didn't understand why.

"Karaback, he's the wizard who lives in town, right?" asked Krell.

"Yeah, and he's self-important and pompous. Don't anger him, or he'll threaten to obliterate you without ever actually doing anything about it. Who else?"

Krell shook his head. "That's all of them. We are leaving tomorrow at dawn from the Netminder's Friend."

"To visit the dwarves," said Olgar. Krell nodded.

"Dwarves are a stubborn folk, but react well to polite words. You'll find out soon enough if you like them or not. Lots of people don't. If you ever want something made of stone or metal, get a dwarf to do it. You'll never see better work than dwarf work."

Olgar took a long drink from his flask, then pulled Krell close. "Now, you listen to me, Krell. People who yell and boast about their strength or magic or whatever, those people are often afraid. Afraid, and possibly unsure. ReckNor, for whatever reason, has picked you to be one of his paladins. A holy warrior going out to work his will on the world."

Olgar pulled Krell even closer, so that he was practically talking directly into his ear.

"ReckNor is wild and tempestuous, like the sea. One minute it's calm and gives you fish to feed your family, the next it washes them all out to sea and drowns them. Lots of others see him as insane, and will tell you that. Learn to control that temper of yours, or you're gonna have nothing but enemies. ReckNor himself speaks to you, though I doubt he has anything useful to say. Don't count on him for aid. Even if he listens and sends help, never count on it. Just this!" And with that, Olgar slapped Krell on his sword arm.

"You're seen as smaller and weaker than others. But I know you, my boy. I know the *will* that sits inside that thick skull of yours, the courage that beats in your heart. ReckNor will tell you to do things. Mostly, if what I've learned is true, you're going to be left alone. Make good choices, because paladins often die young. And stupidly."

Olgar leaned forward, putting more weight on Krell. A minute passed in silence before Olgar let out a small snore. He had fallen asleep. With a heavy sigh, Krell began the effort of getting him into his bed.

Chapter Two

Krell woke, leaping to his feet and groping for a sword that was not there.

He looked around the temple, which was filled with the sound of Olgar's snores. Something had awakened him, a sense of *wrongness.* It was there, grating on his senses. Krell uttered a mild curse and wandered outside to relieve himself, and try to figure out what time it was.

He walked to Olgar's favorite spot, at the edge of the cliff where he could see Watford. The town was still and lifeless. He could see only a single pair of torches, likely a pair of town guards, walking a patrol. The foulness grated on his senses.

He stood there, at the edge of the cliff, watching the sea. The smell of the wind promised rain tomorrow. The sound of the waves was a soothing contrast to the stench in his thoughts. Turning, he saw that the sky had not even begun to lighten. He breathed in deeply, and a strange smell of rotting fish mixed with the stench of a swamp came to his nose.

What had awakened him? Something was wrong, and Krell didn't know what. He suddenly realized he was standing in the open, knowing something, possibly something dangerous, was near, and he'd left his sword inside the temple, along with his armor. Hadn't Olgar just told him that paladins often die stupidly?

He went back inside and found everything the same. Olgar seemed ready to sleep through the day, though Krell knew from long association he would be up and ready to greet the dawn. It was a habit that Krell had learned alone on the island, and Olgar appreciated the company.

His sword was where he left it. It seemed so foolish, waking up as if ambushed. Yet thinking about closing his eyes left Krell feeling uneasy. The longer he waited, the worse the feeling of wrongness grew. Krell stood up and paced back and forth in front of the benches.

Without realizing what he had done, his sword was in hand and he was staring at the temple doors. No memory of thinking about doing that, it was just action. Something grated on his senses, and Krell felt as if it was outside and moving closer. Confused, Krell decided it was worth the pain, and went to wake Olgar.

His room was plain, set in the back corner of the temple. His room had no windows, so he left the door open every night. Krell padded in quietly and braced himself. He reached out and shook him by the shoulder.

"Olgar, wake up, something is wrong."

There was a flash of pain as Olgar's fist lashed out, but Krell was expecting it, and easily avoided the second blow. Even watching for it, Olgar was fast. For a moment, Krell was worried his jaw might have broken.

"ReckNor's salty beard, Krell! What business do you have waking me at this ungodly hour?" he roared, sitting up. He fumbled around for his wooden peg and began strapping it to the end of his leg. "If you don't have a good reason for this, I'm going to beat you senseless!"

Krell took a moment to massage his jaw. It wasn't broken, but Olgar knew how to throw a punch. The grace of ReckNor was already flowing through him, and the pain was already receding.

"Somethin's outshide. Somethin' bad. Don't know what." He rubbed his jaw again, and it felt better. "Do you really try to kill anyone who wakes you in the middle of the night?" Krell tried to be jovial about it, but that faded away at the intense look Olgar was giving him.

"Bad how?" Olgar was suddenly serious, his anger melting away. He buckled the last of the straps for his peg, then dropping to his good knee, he pulled a small flat trunk from under his bed. He fished a key from his amulet and unlocked it, muttering something under his breath. From the set of cloth-wrapped bundles within, Olgar took out the longest. He unfurled a magnificent trident, its head almost gleaming even in the darkness.

"Olgar, what is that? Where did you get it?" Krell was entranced. It was more than just flawless, it almost called to him to use it. He hesitantly reached out as if to take it.

"I told you, lad, I've had adventures of my own in the past. Later… I'll tell you later. For now, I've learned that when a paladin says something is wrong, you treat it like the warning of deadly peril that it is. So again, and with the voice of ReckNor's authority, *bad how?*"

Krell had never seen Olgar like this. Olgar then chanted something, the words making no sense to Krell but echoing with power. Ghostly plates of armor formed, hovering barely above his skin and clothes. They glowed pale blue, yellowing toward the edges.

The sense of wrongness intruded on his fascination. Krell concentrated.

Whatever it was, it was just outside.

"I don't know. It feels almost rancid, like the taste of rotten meat or spoiled milk, but in my thoughts. I think it's right outside."

Olgar nodded, then strode toward the doors. He barked another word of power, and a pulse of magic washed over Krell. At once, all the sconces in the temple flared to brilliance, almost blinding him. Olgar approached the doorway without any apparent fear, then looked behind him at Krell.

"Keep them off my back and stay behind me. Whatever you do, don't leave the temple itself. Understand?" Krell could only nod. Olgar was acting like a battle captain in the books he had made Krell read. His demeanor was like a distant thunderstorm. Beautiful in its way, but terrifying in its potential for destruction. Krell had known he was a true priest of ReckNor, but this was the first time he had really seen what that meant.

Olgar threw open the doors, and the light from the temple spilled out, illuminating a gray thing crouched on the ground. Humanoid, but the arms were too long, as were the legs. No eyes to speak of, just sockets where they should be, and a mouth entirely too large with a tongue trailing across the ground. Following footsteps from the edge of the cliff back to the door of the temple. Krell's footsteps.

Olgar looked grim as he strode out of the temple. Almost as soon as he stepped outside, he turned and thrust to his left. When he pulled the trident back, he had impaled another of the horrid creatures on his trident. It was making a wet moaning noise. He turned and slammed it to the ground behind him, dislodging it in the doorway. He then brought his trident around like a stroke of lightning, deflecting the claws of the first one as it leapt at him, batting it away from his glowing armor.

Krell did not hesitate. His sword sank into the thing right where the heart should be. The stench of foul earth and rotting flesh cloaked the creature. Krell was surprised when it tried to claw at his leg.

"Don't let the ghoul touch you, Krell! Go for the head to put it down proper. How many more do you sense?" Krell heard Olgar talking, even as he yanked his sword out and drove it into one of the eye holes. The gray creature went rigid, and remained that way.

Krell concentrated, calling on ReckNor for aid, and realized that he could separate them out. Not just a background of foulness, but specific points of it.

"Eighteen, Olgar! Six still coming up the cliff, the rest in the darkness that way!" he shouted, then cut the head from the one in front of him just to be sure. The stench of rot grew stronger as a foul liquid oozed from the neck. Olgar grunted, taking a more defensive posture, letting them crowd in closer to him.

"Olgar, we need to get out of here! There are too many for just us to hold the door!"

Olgar laughed. "Nonsense, my boy! Now, you let me know when all of them are up and over the top. Ow!" he said, as one of the ghouls raked its claws along his arm. "Cursed beastie! These are my night clothes, and now you're getting my own blood all over them!" Olgar had a vicious gash along his left arm, but it didn't seem to impede him in any way. His trident was moving in wide sweeping circles, keeping the creatures back.

Krell cut at one that tried to attack Olgar from the left, perhaps seeking advantage, and it withdrew slightly before slashing at Krell. He dodged back, feeling the air move as the claws swung past his face. He concentrated as his sword moved, cutting a clawed hand. "Two more still over the edge!"

"Keep at it, Krell! You're doing fine! I've known many brave men to panic and run when the undead come for them, especially for the first time! They all feel the same to you, all ghouls? Or are there other undead as well?"

Krell looked at Olgar, momentarily forgetting about the creatures. The undead? Ghouls? Why were undead things here, of all places? That made no sense to Krell. He remembered Olgar teaching him that the undead fear true priests. The final points of *wrongness* moved up over the cliff edge and began approaching.

"They're up! They're all the same, as far as I can tell!" Krell shouted, concentrating fiercely on his sense of them. They were homing in on Olgar and him, drawn to the light or, perhaps, the scent of the living.

Olgar stepped forward and grasped his amulet, a sigil of ReckNor, and held it before him. "By the grace and might of ReckNor, lord of the seas and skies, from whom all life emerges and to whom all life returns, *begone!*"

A pulse of yellowish light flashed from the amulet, washing over Olgar, Krell and the creatures. Krell experienced a feeling of warmth and pleasure as it passed over and through him.

As for the undead things, they simply *ceased.* One moment Olgar was surrounded by the creatures, the next there was nothing but collapsing clouds of ash in the air where they once stood. Krell had known Olgar was a true priest of ReckNor. He had seen him wield magic, and his skill with the trident made Krell realize he had a lot to learn about weapons and combat.

But the wave of power that destroyed the undead was something else entirely.

"I thought you — that priests — that you could only drive the dead away with a god's power?" Krell was looking at Olgar in awe.

"Later, my boy, later. Are there any more about?"

Krell concentrated, then shook his head in the negative. He looked out at the cliff edge and thought he saw something there. When he blinked, there was nothing. Olgar grunted, then kicked the ghoul that Krell had slain aside from the doorway.

"Good enough then. Go into the bell room and pull those ropes. Don't stop till I tell you," Olgar ordered, gesturing behind him as he came back into the temple. Krell nodded and dashed for the small room at the back. The pull ropes connected to the belltower were there. He heard Olgar close the doors and slide the enormous bar home, sealing them shut.

Krell began ringing the bell. He kept at it for more than a half hour before Olgar came in.

"That should be enough, Krell. Well done, my boy! Would have been a bit more exciting for me if they'd made it into my bedroom first! Ha!" He punched Krell on the shoulder, knocking him against the wall. "That was fun! It's been ages since I've had a proper fight, even one so short as that!"

Krell looked at Olgar, who had donned a full suit of plate armor. His shield was emblazoned with the sigil of ReckNor, a trident embossed in gold and silver. The armor itself was magnificent. Krell had never seen anything like it before. Olgar smiled.

"Go ahead, lad, you've earned the right to touch, and to ask your questions."

Krell couldn't stop himself. He traced his fingers over the armor, finding subtle designs worked into the metal, of waves and fish and fields and cattle. "Olgar, this is magnificent armor!"

"Aye, lad, and worth a princely sum to be sure. Just so we're clear, I wouldn't be happy if word of this gets around, hear me? Thieves have an annoying way of taking things that don't belong to them, and armor like this attracts master thieves. Understand me?"

Krell nodded. "Olgar, I don't understand. I thought undead were afraid of true priests?"

"They are. The only way they attack like this is if they're being driven. ReckNor is a mighty god, Krell. He gives me power over them. To destroy, or to *command*. My guess is whatever climbed back over the cliff edge was driving them."

"I didn't imagine that, did I?"

YOU DID NOT.

"No, Krell, it was a spellcaster of some sort. Probably a true priest, to command the undead to attack and not just go dig up the graveyard and feast."

Krell shook his head. "Why would someone command undead to attack you?"

Olgar snorted contemptuously. "Three reasons I could think of. First, they wanted to kill me. Second, they wanted to see how strong I am. Third, they were here for you." His eyes unfocused in thought. "Maybe all three, come to think of it."

He looked back at Krell. "Hungry?" Krell nodded.

"Thought so. It's getting close to dawn, so why don't we get you squared away with a little food and into your own armor, then you can head down to the Netminder's Friend." Olgar gestured, and Krell saw he'd set out some dried meats, a soft cheese and a loaf of bread.

Krell suddenly realized he was starving. His stomach gave an audible rumble.

Olgar laughed. "Young men are all the same! Eat, Krell! Unless you know something I do not, we should be safe enough for now."

Krell ate, and asked many questions.

* * *

Krell sat in the common room, waiting.

Marlena was bustling about, sweeping and tending to the fire in the fireplace. He could hear the cook in the back somewhere, the clatter of metal on metal reaching him here. He glanced through the windows at the sun as it continued its steady climb from behind the sea.

They were supposed to have left already.

Marlena came over, smiling brightly. "Anything for you this morning, Krell?" She eyed him up and down in a strange way, as if sizing him up.

"Uh, no, thank you, Marlena. Wait! Actually, is there food? I'm hungry."

"Olgar didn't feed you?"

Krell blushed. "He did. Just, you know, not enough. I'm hungry again."

She smiled. "A tale as old as time, young man! There's porridge as there is every morning, and sliced pork. I can probably get you some eggs if you'd like. Always have bread and cheese and fish, both dried and fresh. Beer and wine, or tea, if you like it."

"I'll have porridge. And maybe pork. Do you have water to drink?"

Marlena screwed up her face at the mention of water. "Just water? Nothing stronger for you?"

Krell felt overwhelmed. Olgar had given him a few coins, although he thought there'd be little need on such a simple job. His concern must have shown.

"Look, Krell, you're as handsome a lad as I've ever seen, and I know you're in good with Olgar and Elias both, so if you don't have the coin, I'd be happy to feed you, regardless. So you know, porridge is two copper pennies for a bowl, fried pork is a copper penny a slice."

Krell was relieved. He fished out one of the silver coins that Olgar had given him.

"Ah, well, no worries then. Want to spend it all on food?" She laughed as Krell thought about it. "Don't hurt yourself thinking so hard, young man! I'll be back!" She scooped up the silver coin and vanished into the kitchen.

Krell looked around. The room held a collection of mismatched chairs and tables that made it feel comfortable. The walls had pieces of wood with little signs near each one. Krell peered at the one next to him. It read HAVEN'S FALL, 1592. He jumped when she put a bowl of porridge down in front of him.

"Sorry, didn't mean to startle you. Start with this. Pork is being fried up for you in the back. Decide how much you want and I'll bring change if you need it. Though I imagine you won't!" She chuckled as she turned away.

"Marlena, why are you open at this hour? There's nobody here but me, and I've been here since before sunrise." Krell gestured at the room, filled with empty tables and chairs. Marlena turned back toward him.

"Oh, never fear, Krell! The fishers who went out early this morning are due back soon, and you wouldn't find a place to sit in here a half hour from now. ReckNor's tides control my business as surely as they control the sea, and when he lets them that are out there back into harbor, they're going to be hungry and thirsty while their catch gets unloaded. After they eat, they'll be back out again! For myself, I've learned to sleep in the middle of the day, so I can be up late and up early and still look this fantastic!" She twirled, her skirts brushing against Krell. He stared at Marlena, his eyes wide.

"Ha! I like you, Krell!" Grinning, she turned and did a strange walk, exaggerating her hips swishing from side to side. When she got to the bar, she turned and looked back at him. For some reason he was suddenly embarrassed, blushing red. Marlena laughed again and gestured at his food.

Krell had nearly finished the bowl when Orca came down the stairs. Krell was still the only person in the common room, so Orca came over and sat across from him.

"Good, you're here. Where are the others?"

Krell just shrugged.

"I thought I told you we wouldn't have time to break fast in the morning."

BE STRONG, KRELL. SHOW NO WEAKNESS.

Krell gave Orca a flat look. "You also said we'd be leaving right at dawn. Yet here I am, as I have been for nearly the last hour, and the sun has already crept over the horizon and you are just arriving." Krell shook his head. "I don't know where everyone else is. If you're going to issue orders, then not obey them yourself, you're going to find nobody else will obey either." Krell silently thanked Olgar for making him read those books on leadership and tactics.

"Are you questioning me?" Orca said quietly, staring intently at Krell.

HE SEEKS TO THREATEN YOU.

Krell let out a sigh. He looked Orca in the eye. "Yes. Why did you say we would leave at dawn, when you were not ready to leave at dawn?"

They locked eyes, staring at one another. Marlena at one point came over, but on seeing the look of the two of them, turned away.

Krell grew frustrated. "Well, if you're not going to answer my question, I'm going to continue eating." He broke eye contact and picked up his spoon.

"How were we supposed to get a good night of rest when the temple bell rang in the middle of the night for no reason?" Orca snarled. "Of course we wouldn't be leaving promptly."

"Why not?" Krell asked through a mouthful of food. Marlena arrived with a plate piled high with sliced pork, setting it in front of Krell. Orca reached out to grab one, and Krell smacked his finger with his spoon.

"Those are mine. Get your own. And you didn't answer my question. Why shouldn't we leave right at dawn as we planned?"

Orca grinned, rubbing his knuckles. "No issue with your reflexes — good that it wasn't all luck yesterday. Whatever happened at the temple stirred up the whole town. Guards shouting and running about all over the place. Some sort of religious thing that forces the guards to wake everyone in every household to make sure everyone is okay? This town is crazy."

"Huh." Krell paused and looked up in thought. Olgar had ordered him to ring the bells, which signaled the guards. Krell thought about what that might mean.

"You know something, don't you?" Orca stared at Krell.

"Yeah, I guess Olgar was concerned the town was going to come under attack, and that's why he had me ringing the bell." Krell shrugged and went back to eating.

Orca smiled, chewing on the pork he'd taken from Krell's plate. "Not the most observant one in the room, even though you have good reflexes." He looked pointedly at Krell. "Attacked by what? You were at the temple — what happened?"

Krell was staring hard at Orca, at the food he'd taken from his plate. Orca just laughed. "All right, all right, I won't do it again. Relax, young human. Just getting your measure. Overly serious, aren't you?"

Krell nodded. "I am. Don't steal from me. I don't like it. These gray undead creatures attacked the temple. Olgar called them ghouls. Said they climbed up out of the sea. He ordered me to ring the bell, I guess to get the town alerted. Sounds like nothing happened down here, though."

"What's this about ghouls?" said Tristan, as he sat down next to Krell, reaching for the fried pork. Krell shouldered his arm away.

"Those are mine. Marlena! They want to order food!" Krell called out. "As for the ghouls, they attacked the temple last night. Olgar and I destroyed them. Well, Olgar did. I helped." Krell resumed eating.

"Ghouls are a minor annoyance for one of my power, so I imagine it was quite the fight you two had. How many were there? Two, three? Maybe even four? It looks like Olgar must have done all the work, because you're not even injured from what I can tell." Tristan turned his attention to Marlena. "The pork smells wonderful, and perhaps some cheese to go with it?" Tristan flashed a silver coin across his knuckles.

Krell stared. "How did you do that?"

Smiling smugly, Tristan yawned theatrically and said, "Oh, just a simple trick to amuse simple people." Krell stared at him for a moment, then grabbed the last of the pork and put it in his mouth.

Orca snorted. "Looks like we're breaking fast anyway, then. Fine. Marlena! The pork is good! More for this lot! And beer for me!"

Marlena came back with a plate filled with food for Tristan, collecting his coin and Orca's, and then went back to the bar. As she returned with a mug of beer, Kraven came down the stairs and intercepted her.

"Ah, a woman after my own heart! Best way to start the morning!" he said, making a grab for the beer. Marlena easily spun out of his grasp, putting it down in front of Orca, and said, "You want one too, Master Kraven?"

Kraven sat down next to Krell and let out a mighty yawn. “Please. And some of whatever that was,” he said, pointing at Krell’s empty plate and bowl. She nodded and departed.

Kraven looked around. “I don’t know that I like this town. They’re crazy with the middle-of-the-night bell ringing. Anyone know what that was about?”

Tristan sat up straight. “Oh, Krell and Olgar were attacked at the temple by a ghoul or two, and Krell decided to ring the bells to let everyone know about it.” Kraven looked at Krell darkly. “What in the hells, manling? I need my beauty rest to look this good!”

Krell shot Tristan a dark look, then turned to Kraven. “First, it wasn’t one or two ghouls, there were *nineteen* of them. Second, I didn’t ring the bells, Olgar *ordered* me to ring the bells. After witnessing him summoning ReckNor’s might first-hand, I wasn’t going to stop and ask questions when he gave me orders. If he orders you to do something, I’d do it if I were you.”

Tristan smirked. “Well, thank goodness you are not me then!”

Kraven looked at Krell and rubbed at his neck. “Nineteen, huh? Sure they were ghouls?”

Krell shook his head. “I am not, but Olgar seemed certain of it.”

Orca finished his beer just as Marlena arrived, putting plates down in front of him and Kraven, and two additional mugs of beer. “Ah, a good hostess who knows her patrons is a thing to be treasured! My thanks, Marlena!”

She smiled a different smile at Orca than she used on him, Krell noted. Marlena saw him looking at her and her smile changed. Krell blushed.

Tristan laughed. *ReckNor give me strength to endure,* Krell prayed silently.

After fifteen minutes, Orca snarled in frustration and asked Marlena which room Gerrard was in, then left to rouse him.

* * *

ReckNor was going to bless them with rain later this morning.

Krell walked along the path behind Orca and Kraven, listening to Tristan and Gerrard bicker behind him. At first it was Gerrard complaining about the hour, then it was Tristan and Gerrard complaining about breakfast, then Gerrard about the quality of the road, and now Tristan was talking about the weather.

"I am a magic user of great and terrible power, and I do *not* want to be rained upon. This is beneath my dignity and my station!"

Gerrard laughed. "Well, I don't know what to tell you then, Tristan. Maybe you shouldn't be beneath the clouds!"

Krell shook his head and focused on keeping up with the brisk pace that Orca and Kraven had set. The chain mail armor he wore was bearing down on his shoulders, and felt heavier with every step he took. Still, Olgar had trained him well. He knew he could go for days yet before he'd need to take it off.

Orca stopped suddenly. "Time for a rest."

Gerrard veered off the road, dropped his pack on the ground, and sat heavily. He looked tired as he fumbled for a waterskin and drank deeply from it.

Kraven and Krell both walked from the eastward road toward the cliffs to the south, looking out over the sea. Dark clouds were moving toward the road, and the sea was covered in waves.

"See anything out there, Krell?" Kraven asked. "I like looking at the sea. It's always so quiet and peaceful."

Krell gave him an incredulous look and laughed. "Never been shipwrecked during a storm before, huh?"

"Oh, and you have?" he growled, turning to face Krell.

"Yup. Twice."

Kraven looked at him in surprise. "Huh. I wouldn't have guessed that, seeing how young you are. How'd you survive?"

Krell shrugged. "First time, no clue. I was just a child and barely remember anything. Washed up on an island alone. Spent years there, just surviving. Second time was pretty recently. The ship that rescued me sank in a storm. I just grabbed some wood and floated for a few days. Another ship picked me up, and its next port of call was Watford."

"What ship was that?" Kraven asked.

"The one that rescued me was called *Hollow's March*. It wrecked in a storm. If I had to guess, the crew didn't appease ReckNor and mostly died as a result. I had nothing, but even I knew to make an offering. The second one was a fishing vessel out of Watford, called *The Gambling Mermaid*. Found me and another member of the crew, picked us both up, and took us back to Watford."

"When was that?"

"Oh, six months ago, give or take? Olgar was at the docks and, well, I've been in service to ReckNor ever since."

"What did you offer to ReckNor?"

"My sharp rock."

Kraven paused, a grin threatening to break out on his face. "A sharp rock? That was a worthy offering?"

Krell nodded, his face serious. "You appreciate it a lot more when it's the only sharp thing you have. I loved that rock. The offering itself isn't important, it's how much you value it that matters."

Kraven grunted. "Busy life so far."

Krell shrugged. "ReckNor wants something from me. He called me to be a paladin, probably because I'm a survivor. It's easy to forget how great it is to have weapons, or warmth, or food whenever you want it. Until suddenly you don't have *anything*, and the only thing left to you in your cold and hunger and loneliness is prayer." Krell turned to Kraven. "ReckNor demands tribute for the use of his oceans. Propitiate him or suffer the consequences."

Kraven smiled at Krell, then clapped him on the shoulder. "I like you, Krell. You're intense. Even if I don't know what that word means!"

Krell grinned back at him. "Yeah, I like that word too. It means do what ReckNor wants, or else."

Kraven raised an eyebrow. "Or else what?"

Krell shrugged. "You know, shipwrecks, hurricanes, floods, thunderstorms, that sort of thing."

Orca shouted from the road. "Rest is over! Time to go!"

Thunder rumbled in the distance.

* * *

The mining camp stank.

Krell could smell it before the last rise, a combination of burning wood, tar, and something else that reminded Krell of vaguely of rotting food soaked in beer. The sun was directly overhead, but hidden by the rain clouds.

From the top of the hill, the camp seemed almost temporary. Smoke from a dozen chimneys cast a haze in the air, which persisted even in the light rain and brisk wind. As they descended, it became clear they were in a gully, and the wind was being deflected overhead by the surrounding hills. A rhythmic hammering noise could be heard echoing over the hilltops.

"Finally, we get here, and about time. Who had the bright idea to walk through the mud in a rainstorm?" Tristan complained.

Krell was beginning to grow weary of listening to Tristan whine about everything. It seemed that every event that happened was either a slight against him or to be attributed to his greatness.

Gerrard chimed in, "Hey, at least you're way up there with those long legs! Know what I mean, Tristan? Like, I'm down here covered in mud to my tender bits, and you're up there complaining about the clean water!"

Krell looked at Gerrard. The halfling was covered in mud up to his waist, and he was hunched over. "You doing okay, Gerrard? It's been tough in the mud for the last hour. It has to be hard when you're one of the small folk walking through this."

"That's the spirit, Krell! Looking out for others — I like it, know what I mean? Orca, here, he doesn't think about others so much," Gerrard said. Krell noticed he was trembling a little.

Orca glanced backward. "We'll take a short break in the hospitality that the dwarves provide. In warmth and out of the rain. If walking through the mud is too much for you, Gerrard, then quit now. It's going to get worse."

Krell looked down at Gerrard. "Need help?"

"I appreciate the offer, Krell, but Orca there, he's right. Gotta pull my own pack through the mud some days, other days get to sing to beautiful women, right?" Gerrard smiled wanly at Krell, shrugged to adjust the pack he carried, and walked down what was left of the path toward the wooden palisade.

Orca nodded at Gerrard and followed. Kraven and Tristan glared at one another and joined them.

Krell watched them walk for a moment until they were far enough away that they probably wouldn't overhear. Tristan looked unhappy, frowning at the sky as if blaming it for the rain. Orca and Kraven both ignored the rain entirely. Gerrard struggled to keep up, and it was only now that Krell realized that the pace Orca had set meant that Gerrard had been forced into an awkward jog. He'd run nearly all the way from Watford.

Krell's opinion of Gerrard went up a notch. Then he looked up at the sky, letting the rain fall on his face. As good a place for a prayer as any.

"ReckNor, I'm not much for prayers. Olgar taught me the words, but they feel stupid to say them out loud. Thanks for the rain. It made the trip much less pleasant, but cooler. I'm probably going underground into a hole to look for trouble. When I come out again, I'll say something nice about the sky, so it'd be good if it was clear of clouds," said Krell. He thought that the pressure within changed slightly. Maybe that meant ReckNor was pleased with his prayer?

Orca was nearly halfway to the palisade. Krell hurried after the group, catching up to Gerrard and joining the others.

As they approached the palisade, a dwarf stepped out of the covered hut perched over the simple gate. He was taller than Gerrard, but broader than Krell, and had arms the size of Kraven. He was shirtless and heavily muscled. His fiery orange beard was elaborately braided and reached almost to his waist. He shouted something at them in a strange tongue.

"What?" Krell yelled back.

"Oh, human, is it? I asked who is going to here, manling. What business of yours is here?"

Orca gave Krell a dark look, then stepped forward. "The Watford town council offered to help and sent out a call for warriors. Here we are. Let us in and get us somewhere warm. Then you can tell us what's going on." He glanced at Krell again. "ReckNor's rainstorm has clearly frayed all our common sense, as well as our tempers!"

The dwarf dropped out of sight, though they could see him through the holes in the poorly made wooden gate. There was a *thud*, then the dwarf opened the gate inward. "True enough, true enough! Here for Petimus you are, then?"

"Petimus Smithforge, yes, that's who the council told us to contact when we got here," replied Orca as he strode forward into the encampment.

It seemed a dirty place to Krell, with every surface covered in soot and dirt. The rain certainly was not helping, as the entire area was just one big sea of mud. The dwarves had propped the buildings up on wooden supports, leaving plenty of room beneath for water to flow. Their dwarf guide swung the gate shut and lifted a meager bar back in place. "This way then. Be coming this way!"

Where Gerrard struggled through the mud, the dwarf seemed unaffected by it. It was like the mud wasn't important enough to keep him from what he wanted to do. Krell glanced at Gerrard, who smiled back.

"Hey, I know. Dwarves, right? Tough as rocks and just as smart, but I'd trade a lot for that strength just now." Gerrard was watching where he stepped, moving around puddles and trying to keep his footing.

"I suppose. I've never met a dwarf before."

Gerrard shrugged. "We're all just people, all with different gifts, right?" Gerrard sneezed. "Take me, for example. I'm talented, lucky, and a maestro with my instrument," he said, with a meaningful smile on his face, "and the ladies love a man who can use his instrument, if you know what I mean."

"I doubt a normal woman would even feel you between her legs, Gerrard," Tristan said venomously.

"Tristan, just because you're tired, wet and cold, is no reason to be cruel." Krell shook his head. "We're going to be working together, so let's at least pretend to be nice to one another."

"See, that's why I like him," said Kraven, talking to Orca. "He's smoothing things out at the same time he's causing trouble! You're a piece of work, Krell."

"On that I think we can all agree!" said Tristan happily, as they were led through an open doorway into what looked like a mess hall.

Long trestle tables with simple benches lined each side, with a large kitchen area at the far end. Wood-burning stoves were spaced between the tables, providing warmth. Krell looked at the kitchen, then turned to their dwarf guide.

"Why is the kitchen here, instead of in another room or in another building?" he asked.

"Ah, it is a dwarf thing. Why be putting up a wall to separate from us that what we want? This way a dwarf who wants something can be seeing it made, or do the making of it!" He looked around. "Sit yourselves on the benches here, and I go to be finding Petimus. Do not the breaking of things in here, yes?"

The benches were shorter than Krell expected, and he was awkward as he sat. Still, it felt good to get off his feet for the first time since they left Watford. He examined his boots, then made to take them off.

"I wouldn't do that, Krell. Your feet will swell and you'll have trouble getting them back on," Orca warned.

Krell looked at his feet, confused. "Why would they swell?"

The others stared at him like he was a fool. "Uh, the walking maybe?" said Kraven.

Krell smiled. "Oh. I get it. My feet don't do that. It's a paladin thing." Krell took off his boots and set them next to a warm stove, leaning back and propping his feet up in front of the fire. Orca just shook his head.

After a few minutes, the door opened again, and a new dwarf entered. He was wearing an overcoat, which he doffed and hung on a peg by the door, before coming over. His luxurious dark beard was braided with gold, and his hands were both clean and adorned with gem-studded rings.

"Petimus Smithforge, at your service, young warriors! You're the ones Watford has sent to aid us?" Petimus looked at them critically, Krell and Gerrard in particular. "You know there will be no light below, right? I mean no offense, but your kind cannot see in the dark."

Orca grunted. "It will be fine. Torches for the human and the halfling, and to make better light for the rest of us. The charter," he said, sliding a paper across the table to Petimus. He glanced at it.

"Looks official enough, at least for me. Welcome, lads, welcome! We're glad you're here." Petimus sat on a bench so he could see everyone.

"You speak much better than the other dwarf who met us," Krell noted. Gerrard looked scandalized, covering his face with his hand. Orca just rolled his eyes.

"Well, as to that, I'd wager he speaks the common tongue of man much better than you speak the common tongue of dwarves, hmm? Not everyone has a gift for languages, young human, but that is neither relevant nor interesting. What'd the good guard captain tell you?" Petimus leaned toward a nearby stove, sighing in appreciation.

"Only that you discovered a cave system. Some miners went in and didn't come back. A larger search party went in and didn't come back, either. So you boarded it up and called for help," said Orca.

"Well enough then, lads, that's the keystone of the problem. We want to know what happened and recover the remains if possible. If there's a beastie down there, stick those swords in it, eh?" Petimus grinned at them.

Krell frowned, then raised his hand. "Why do you think they're dead?"

Petimus smiled. "We're dwarves. If they weren't dead, they'd have come back by now. Not likely they're gonna get lost down there, is it?"

Krell's frown deepened as he lowered his hand. "Things underground. You'd know lots about them, right?" Petimus nodded and gestured for him to continue. "Did you see any signs or tracks in the caves near the hole you boarded up?" Something about this made little sense to Krell.

Petimus thought for a moment, then said, "Not that I recall hearing about, no. If there were tracks within, we'd likely have done things a little different, and certainly the search party would know to be on their guard. Whatever happened down there, 'twas enough to take a party of eight dwarves, and far enough away from the hole that we heard nothing."

Tristan spoke next. "What if it's some sort of poison gas or something?"

Petimus laughed. "It is a hard thing to poison a dwarf, my new elvish friend! And such perils belowground are known to us dwarves. No, whatever happened, it is something we know nothing about in normal circumstances, which means we want some skilled hands with blade and spell to go in there and learn the truth of things."

Petimus stood up. "Now, I expect you'd be hungry after a long and wet walk. Bide here a time. Feel free to make yourself something to eat, for the sun is high. I'll get the others organized and be back in a turn of the glass." Petimus winked at them, then went back to the door, retrieved and donned his overcoat, and stepped out into the rain.

Chapter Three

Krell immediately understood why Olgar said dwarven skill at building was superior to all others.

The mineshaft they descended was much larger than Krell had thought, easily over ten feet high. The floor was smooth and had a pair of metal rails running along the center. Petimus explained it was for hauling ore up out of the mine. The entire place was well lit, with lanterns that glowed with a purplish red light. There was also somehow a light breeze blowing throughout the corridors, and the air smelled clean.

They had expanded the upper part of the mineshafts into living quarters and workshops. The shoddy look and feel from the poorly made wooden structures above contrasted with the comfortable rooms they could see here.

Petimus noticed Krell gaping. "First time in a dwarfholme, young Master Krell?" he asked kindly.

Krell could only nod in appreciation at the complexity of the stonework. The blocks were all of irregular sizes, yet fit together so cleanly that there was barely a visible seam.

"Aye, lad, if us dwarves know one thing, it's the nature of stone. Meaning no disrespect, but you humans always work it to fit a shape you decided on beforehand. That rough handling weakens it, takes its will and its strength and saps it away. It's why you mortar your stonework, to keep the stones from trying to escape the prison you've bound them in," Petimus said.

Krell didn't know what to make of that. "Are you saying the stones are alive somehow?" he asked. He furrowed his brow in thought.

"No, Master Krell, not in any sense that you'd understand it, but each thing has its own shape and purpose, and with stone, we dwarves know best how to let it keep its shape, but with greater purpose. These stones here, they *want* to be these halls and floors." Petimus smiled at the stone walls, running his hands over them.

Krell shook his head. "I still don't understand."

Tristan snickered and Orca grunted, then said, "Nor will you, because you're not a dwarf. Listen to their explanation, but dwarves know how to work stone in ways no others can. Just leave it at that."

Krell looked thoughtful, then reached out and touched the walls as they walked down the hall. It felt like stone to him.

The hallway ended at a metal grate, which Petimus lifted upward. Within was a metal platform, with a large wheel attached to the wall. As they stepped in, Petimus reached down and did something to the rails, and they retracted a bit. Next, he reached up and pulled a strap, which pulled the metal gate down, sealing them into a stone room. Then he reached over to the wheel and gave it a spin. At once, the platform lurched and descended.

"That's clever," said Kraven, "How does it work?"

Petimus smiled, then said, "I could explain it to you, but you've neither the time nor the interest to listen to me, and frankly, I doubt you've the background in metal and engineering to understand, anyway. Simply, the wheel moves other gears and counterweights, which makes the platform go up and down." He gestured at a lever mounted in the corner. "We use that to adjust the number of counterweights, so if a full mine cart is in here, then it won't take an hour to get up top, if that makes sense." Petimus looked around at the mostly uninterested or confused expressions and sighed.

Their descent abruptly revealed a metal grate similar to the one from above. Petimus spun the wheel again, and as Krell watched, he could see there were dozens of markings on the wheel and on the wall where it attached. The platform slowed, then descended just past the metal grate. Petimus adjusted the wheel, and they rose until there was a slight bump.

Petimus centered the wheel, lifted the grate, and then reached down. Watching closely this time, Krell saw him flip a metal catch and slide a rail out, where it locked into a waiting socket on the other side. He repeated it for the other rail.

The corridor beyond was much more like what Krell was expecting. The lights were fewer and farther between, and the air was not as fresh. The rhythmic sound of hammering reached them, and Petimus set off at once.

"This way, lads!" he said jovially, as he strode down the shaft into a pool of darkness.

Orca and Kraven followed at once. Tristan gave Krell a condescending smile, then followed. Gerrard looked up at him.

"Hey, Krell, you doing all right there?" The look on Krell's face was not reassuring to Gerrard.

Krell shook his head. "Yeah, I'm fine. I don't enjoy being underground, is all. Too far from the sea and sky, I guess. ReckNor, right?" Krell gave Gerrard a smile, then set off after the others.

* * *

The cave was strange.

Krell stared at the slightly glowing mushrooms that clustered in one corner. They provided nowhere near enough light for him to see. Petimus had warned them they were extremely poisonous and would let out a cloud of spores, quickly killing anything that came close.

The air also was strange. In the dwarf tunnels, there was a breeze somehow, through some clever craft the dwarves had done to make the air move. Here, the air was still, and the torch he carried cast a steady light.

Orca grunted as he and Petimus shook hands and then turned to face the rest of them. “Right, one path forward. Avoid the mushrooms. Let’s go.” He lifted his torch and started toward the only path out of the cave.

Gerrard whispered to Krell. “Hey, Krell, my man. We’ll stick together down here, right?” Krell smiled and nodded, tapping his face next to his eyes. Gerrard grinned back. “You understand me perfectly.”

The cave passage was narrow and twisted. It looked like water wearing through the stone made it, but ages ago, and the settling earth had broken parts of it. There was only one way they could go. There were obvious signs of the dwarven search party having passed this way: the chalk markings on the walls, the broken pieces of stone that made the passage easier to navigate, and the numerous footprints in the sand and dust beneath their feet.

They moved forward, though Krell wished they moved more quietly. His chain mail made a rhythmic noise as the metal rang against itself, and Orca was no better in his breastplate, a constant ringing noise as he scraped it across rocks. Between those noises, and the sound and light of the torches, whatever was down here would be aware of them approaching.

The passage opened into a larger space where the floor sloped sharply downward. There was a new smell. Blood.

“Smell that?” Kraven asked.

“Look around,” said Krell. “Let’s see if we can find out what happened in here.”

A quick search found a smear of blood on a rocky outcropping, which turned into a trail leading down the only other exit from the cavern. Krell gestured for everyone to stay back and crept forward, examining the ground intently.

Tristan snorted in contempt. “What does he think he’s doing, exactly, oh illustrious leader?” he asked Orca.

Orca just shrugged. "Dwarves think the missing are dead. No harm in waiting to see. And possibly much good. Keep your eyes open," he said, turning to Tristan, "and your mouth *shut.*" Tristan opened his mouth to say something but thought better of it.

"It looks like the search party went down this passageway," Krell said, gesturing, "and then a single dwarf came running back this way. Whatever was chasing him caught him, dashing him against the stone here, then dragged him back that way. Whatever is down there, it's mobile and aggressive."

Kraven looked over Krell's shoulder, saying, "I can see it as well. The boot prints mostly go that way, but there's that one set widely spaced coming back."

Krell nodded, then pointed.

"There — you can see the drag marks of the body. No other tracks, so they must have been obscured by the dragging. I can't tell if that was intentional or not, but I'm going to guess that it was." Krell turned and looked Kraven directly in the eyes. "They know we're here, and that we're coming. They'll be waiting in ambush for us."

"And how do you know that?" snarled Orca from behind.

Krell gestured with his torch. "The passageway here goes up slightly. You can see the smoke flowing up that path. If they can't see the light, or haven't heard us yet, the smell from the smoke has warned them they're not alone." Krell shrugged. "First step to avoiding an ambush is knowing it's there. Whatever it is, if it's going to jump us, it'll be counting on us being surprised."

Orca and Kraven shared a look, then nodded. "That's enough then. Be ready, and when whatever's down there attacks, react at once and we'll win the day."

"Wait, that's the plan?" asked Tristan, sounding somewhat alarmed. "Wait for something terrible to jump on you, then kill it?"

Orca nodded. "Kraven and I go first. Krell, stay between us and Gerrard and Tristan. You two," — he pointed at Tristan and Gerrard — "stay behind Krell and do what you can from back there. Let's go." Orca and Kraven turned and jostled one another to see which one would get through the passage first.

After a brief walk through the cavern, it opened up into a larger room, this one with a flat, sandy floor strewn with large rocks. The sand was disturbed, with many footsteps and patches of dried blood. Orca stepped boldly into the room, followed by Kraven. Krell stood in the passage itself, blocking access from the room to prevent any foes from reaching Tristan or Gerrard.

Orca and Kraven looked around, standing ready. Nothing happened.

A minute passed.

"Well, this is disappointing," Orca said. "Where do you suppose they are?"

Krell looked at Kraven. "Watch my back and I'll see if I can tell."

As he set out toward the center of the room, Kraven followed close behind.

"It looks like they walked to here and were attacked," Krell said, looking around. "I think that whatever attacked them was on them before they knew it was there. They were clearly surprised by whatever —"

As Krell talked, a part of the boulder next to him seemed to shimmer and detach itself, claws flashing toward his face.

* * *

Krell threw himself backward, the talons narrowly missing his eyes.

Kraven was roaring in anger to his left as he regained his feet. He dropped the torch, hoping it wouldn't go out, and drew his blade barely in time to deflect the next swipe from the claws. His companions were all yelling now, and Krell could hear Tristan speaking words of power.

The thing in front of him was difficult for him to make sense of. It looked like a piece of the rock, but there was a shimmer about it, making it look almost flat. It almost seemed to come into and out of existence as it turned and moved, making it hard to know where it was, like a piece of paper blowing in the wind.

The feel of claws scoring along his armor from behind was all the warning Krell had that there was another behind him, even as a third joined the one in front of him. Sparing a quick glance, he could see Kraven surrounded by at least four, his great-axe swinging in large circles to keep them at bay, while Orca was engaged with at least two.

Since his companions were engaged and unlikely to come to his aid, Krell decided it was best to aid himself. He surged forward, his shield crashing into one of the creatures. It felt solid enough, and it fell to the ground from the force of the blow. He suddenly spun, his sword cutting behind him, and caught the one to his rear across what passed for its chest. It let out a moaning hiss that made Krell think of a boiling kettle.

The original one, unimpeded, struck at Krell and its claws found purchase through his armor. The wound burned like fire in his shoulder, but his arm seemed to work fine despite the damage. Shaking it free, he deflected its next attack. The one on the ground was rising again, although it was hard to see if it was floating or using arms and legs, or something else entirely.

Krell attacked. His sword cut the one in front of him in the arm, and it slashed at him. His shield moved to block it, and he felt claws raking his armor from behind, though they did not penetrate.

Krell raised his shield toward the two in front of him and pivoted, his sword lashing out at the one behind him. He caught it cleanly, cutting a gash in its arm before slamming his blade home into its center. It gurgled, and a blackish purple fluid sprayed out as it collapsed.

The two on him attacked in a fury, but his shield kept them away long enough for him to recover his sword from the corpse and reset his stance. Krell struck again, decapitating one of them.

There was a flash of light, and a loud *thump* in the air that Krell could feel more than hear. The entire cavern shook slightly, and one creature fighting Kraven fell to the ground. A ragged hole had been blasted through the center of it.

"Behold my power!" shouted Tristan, laughing contemptuously.

Krell avoided the claws of the next attack by stepping back slightly, then extended his sword, taking it in the neck. It clutched at his sword, slashing its clawed hands, before falling to the sand. Krell followed it down with his blade, keeping it embedded in its throat.

Kraven was covered in wounds, but they did not seem to bother him as he roared in fury at the two remaining before him. His axe crashed down, cutting deeply into the center of one of the remaining creatures. Its companion raked its claws across Kraven, leaving fresh cuts that looked painful.

Orca took that one from behind. Suddenly, the only sounds were the five of them panting, and the sputtering of the torches that had been dropped. Krell eyed his blade, seeing if the blood of the creatures was harming it, but it didn't appear so.

"Everyone okay?" he asked, as he pulled a rag from his backpack and wiped his blade clean before sheathing it. Orca was doing the same, looking around. He nodded. It looked like Orca was unharmed.

Gerrard came forward, his small blade stained with dark purple blood. "Two of them in the hallway behind us. Not a problem for me, though, right?" Krell handed him the rag, clapped him on the shoulder, then went over to Kraven.

The blood was seeping from his wounds, and they looked shallow. Still, there were dozens of them. Krell shook his head.

"How are you still standing?"

Kraven looked at him in surprise. "What, these little scratches? This is nothing. I barely feel them. Don't worry about me, worry about yourself." He gestured at the blood on Krell's armor.

"Oh yeah," Krell said, moving his arm and feeling no pain. "I think the grace of ReckNor has already dealt with it. I'm fine. Can I try something?" he asked.

Kraven shrugged and nodded. Krell reached out with a hand and put it on Kraven's shoulder.

"ReckNor, lord of the seas and skies, your power is the power of a hurricane! Let that might flow into Kraven and give him strength!" As Krell spoke, there was a soft glow about his hand. Gerrard whistled in appreciation as several of the wounds across Kraven's body visibly healed.

YOU KNOW YOU DON'T NEED TO ASK OUT LOUD. JUST WILL IT AND IT WILL BE SO.

Krell winced, the thunderous voice of ReckNor echoing in his thoughts. He withdrew his hand from Kraven's shoulder.

"Not all of them, though, huh? Do you think it's because ReckNor doesn't like Kraven, or is it because you're incompetent, Krell?"

Krell glanced at Tristan, giving him a dark look. Kraven just laughed.

"Either way, it feels nice! I pray to my god and he does nothing, so incompetent or not, that was better than anything I could do!" Kraven laughed delightedly, moving his arms and shoulders around, then slamming a fist down on Krell's shoulder. "Tell your god, good job!"

Krell grinned and shrugged. He looked up at the ceiling. "Good job." Kraven laughed.

Orca pushed one of the dead creatures over and examined it. "What do you suppose these things are?"

In death, their form became much clearer. They were thin and had mottled skin that resembled stone. Two large granite eyes and a wide mouth filled with needle-like teeth were their only features.

Their arms ended in three claws, with two opposable thumb-like fingers on the opposite side.

"They look different dead, don't they?" Krell said, nudging one with his boot.

"Well, *obviously* they look different," said Tristan. "They're not moving anymore, for example!" He put on a bored look, as if waiting for the nonsense of the others to conclude.

"No, I mean, they looked thinner and more like stone when they were alive. Do you think they were using magic to hide?" Krell looked at the one he'd decapitated. In his memory, it was hard to see: a twisting, almost flat image of the stone with claws slashing at his eyes, and in the next moment, a misshaped body falling to the ground.

Orca shrugged. "Maybe, Krell, maybe. Who can say? The more important questions are, are there more of them, and where are the dwarf bodies?"

* * *

The bodies were hanging from the ceiling. They'd been gutted, with most of their insides removed.

Krell looked up at them, and down at the pool of blood and viscera that had collected below, where several smaller versions of the creatures had been feeding noisily when they entered. They took no notice of Orca as he moved over and slew all of them in short order.

This cave was narrower, but the smell of blood and the drag marks led them within. How the dwarves were suspended was a mystery at the moment, but Gerrard was scaling the rock wall, heading up to find out.

"Well, at least there are ten of them. All dwarves accounted for," said Tristan, gesturing upward. Orca nodded, looking around.

"What do you suppose these things ate before the dwarves opened this cave and walked into their lair?" Krell was looking around at the several other passages that exited the cavern they were in.

Kraven turned to him. "Who cares, so long as we killed a bunch and get the dwarf bodies back down. It's what we're being paid to do, so do that and don't worry about the rest."

"Hey, Kraven, what if there are more of them?" Gerrard said from above. "What if there's, you know, an entire colony of them down these passages, gorging on mushrooms or something?"

Orca snorted. "If there are more, then they'll probably be pretty angry about their dead young here. That no more have arrived makes me think we got them all, but Gerrard is right, we need to explore. Never know what you might find in holes like this."

"Well, right on then. Hey, these dwarves are hung up here by their boots with something that looks like dried-up slime. Krell, my man, can you hold the light up higher?" Gerrard was hanging by one hand and foot, his other foot resting on a dwarf body while he prodded at the boots.

Krell held the torch closer and could kind of make out what Gerrard was talking about. Some sort of hardened yellow goo covered the ceiling, and the dwarven boots were sunk into it.

"Gerrard, can you unbuckle their boots?"

"Good plan, Krell! Let me try." Gerrard reached out with one hand and began loosening the leather through a buckle. Krell readjusted the light and Gerrard grunted in appreciation. Suddenly, the dwarf swung sideways as one foot came free of the boot, knocking into Krell.

Over the course of the next ten minutes, Gerrard freed the dwarven corpses so they fell into the waiting arms of Kraven one by one. Orca wrapped them in blankets he had brought with him, to make them easier bundles to carry. Tristan waited impatiently.

When the last dwarf fell, Gerrard said, "Hey, Krell, can you catch me?"

Krell nodded, then caught Gerrard as he dropped. The halfling was shaking as Krell set him on his feet.

"Well done, Gerrard. How are your arms? I couldn't have held myself up there for that long." Krell was impressed with Gerrard. He had more strength than Krell would have guessed.

Gerrard sat, rubbing his shoulders and rotating them. "Ah, sore and weak, but nothing a moment's rest won't fix!" He began humming a tune that sounded vaguely familiar to Krell. Gerrard looked really happy.

Krell smiled. Orca seemed like he wanted to argue all the time, and Tristan was an ass, but when Krell looked at Gerrard and Kraven, he found himself concerned for their safety. It was a strange thought to him. Before this, he'd really only cared about Olgar.

TRISTAN TOO. HE IS IMPORTANT AND NEEDS TO BE PROTECTED.

Krell flinched, glancing at Tristan, then sighed. When ReckNor spoke, it was always like a crash of thunder. Krell could feel a headache coming on, both from ReckNor's voice and from what those words implied for Krell's future.

* * *

They spent an hour moving the dwarven bodies back to the entrance, handing them over to Petimus and the miners who were acting as guards.

Petimus got the story from Tristan, a tale told in such a way that it was nearly a single-handed victory by magic alone, while the others stood around flailing their weapons uselessly after being stupidly ambushed. Krell couldn't help but notice the tale was told only when both Kraven and Orca were out of earshot.

Petimus looked at Krell at various points, and Krell just shook his head slightly. Eventually, Tristan wound down the tale of his amazing exploits, and Petimus turned to Krell, as Krell lifted a dwarf body up and handed it through the passage to the waiting miners beyond.

"What's your plan now, young Master Krell?" Petimus asked.

"We're going back in to make sure there are no more of them. Probably spend another few hours then return. If there are more tunnels than we can explore, that'll be your problem in the long run, but we want to make sure the area near this hole is cleared out fully."

Petimus nodded. "Appreciate that, and that's a fair statement. We've hired on proper warriors from Talcon, and they'll be here in around two weeks. If there's more we'd like to know, but this close to the ocean I can't imagine the caves are very extensive. The crash of the waves on the cliff shakes the stone, so over time there would have been collapse."

He looked up as Kraven and Orca came in with Gerrard in tow, carrying the tenth corpse they recovered. "Ah, and here's the last of them, then. My thanks to you all for this good service. Krell says you're going back in?" he asked Orca. Orca shot a look at Krell, then nodded.

"Good. Do you need anything first?" he asked.

"Nothing for me. Anyone else?" Krell said, at the same time Orca said, "No."

Orca turned towards Krell, a dark expression on his face.

CONFRONT HIM, KRELL. SUFFER NO INSULT.

Petimus noticed the look on Krell's face, then shrugged. "Right then. We're here, same knocking pattern and we'll open up to let you back in." He retreated back through the hole, and the dwarven miners on the other side — with Petimus aiding them — moved the massive wooden wheel back into place and pushed it into the stone passage, plugging it securely.

Orca looked at Krell. "Did you forget that I am in charge, little human?"

"Ah, you want to do this now. Okay." Krell stood up and walked over to Orca. "No, I did not forget, but I also never agreed to it. I'm fine to let you carry the charter and wave it around, but that doesn't mean you're in charge. I'm fine following your plan, as long as your plan isn't stupid. If it is, then I won't."

Krell leaned even closer to Orca's face. "I am not your vassal, or your minion. My life belongs to ReckNor, and my will is his will. Contest that at your peril, Orca. Any who challenge ReckNor end up dead. Those who don't tend to be fine."

Orca let loose a growl, while Kraven burst out laughing.

"See what I mean?" he said, between chuckles. "Intense!"

* * *

The caves were not that extensive.

Returning to the room where the fight with the creatures had taken place, the passages forked off in three additional directions. One led to where they had discovered the dwarven miners, which also had another exit. That left two other paths, plus that one to explore.

The first one they took sloped downward and led to an open chamber, in the center of which was a large cluster of slightly glowing mushrooms. Wrapped among the fungus was a skeletal humanoid, the armor it was wearing rusted to the point of uselessness, the clothing decayed to ruin — aside from the gleaming longsword that was visible through the remains of the scabbard, and a pair of leather boots that showed no signs of weathering or aging.

The debate was fierce.

"I don't care that the mushrooms are poisonous! I want the blade!" Orca yelled at Gerrard.

"Then get it!" snarled Kraven, "We'll be right over here so we can watch you fall and die!"

Gerrard gestured at the chalk marks on the wall. "Looks like the dwarves were here, but decided against going in."

Krell nodded and glanced at Tristan, who was strangely silent and smiling slightly. Tristan noticed him looking and tilted his head questioningly.

"What are your thoughts, Tristan?" Krell asked.

Everyone turned to look at him, and he grinned. "Well, now that you've finally decided to be smart and ask me what I think, I think *this*!" As he said that, he pointed his hand toward the mushrooms while speaking sharp words of power. A bolt of flame sped across the room, slamming into the mushrooms and igniting them. He did this three more times until the entire cluster was burning.

Orca grunted. "Well, the sword should be fine, but it's a shame about those boots." Tristan smirked at him.

"Well, if you had any knowledge in your head, you'd know that if they really were an item of magical power, then a little burning mushroom wouldn't be likely to cause them any harm. Since you obviously don't have that knowledge, you should listen to me as the true leader of this little troupe." Tristan eyed the patch of burning fungus, and sent another blast of flame into it.

Gerrard looked up nervously. "Uh, Tristan, my main man, I like it, I really do, but, uh, what's the plan for all that smoke up there?"

Tristan looked blankly at Gerrard, and then they all glanced upward. The little cave they were in was rapidly filling with smoke.

"Shit!" Tristan swore.

They retreated up the cave passage and waited. The fire seemed to burn itself out after ten minutes, though a haze of foul-smelling smoke remained. Gerrard crawled back down the passage, returning with the sword and the boots, and a fistful of soot-covered coins he found in the burned remains.

The boots were supple leather and showed no damage from the flame. Gerrard looked inside them and grimaced, turning one boot over and dumping out what looked like foot bones and rotten flesh from it. Then he promptly slipped them on, watching them closely.

Krell's eyes widened as the boots shrank, fitting his feet perfectly. Gerrard's face lit up with pleasure. "Hey, yeah! That's what I'm talking about!" Then he ran around the room, jumping and kicking at the air. He frowned.

"They don't do much for jumping or running. I wonder what they do?"

"Well, I for one know exactly how we are going to find out," Tristan said smugly, watching Orca swing the blade through the air a few times.

Orca turned to him and smiled. "Karaback, right?"

"Oh, so you have been paying attention! Yes, Magister Karaback and I are well acquainted and have a good working relationship. I am most pleased to offer my services bartering for his time and power to investigate the use of these and determine what they do." Tristan glanced at Gerrard, who was hopping up and down while looking at the boots, and sneered at him.

"Were there any other exits from that cave? I didn't see any," Krell said.

Gerrard shook his head. "None that I could see."

"Back the way we came, then." Krell led them back to the chamber where the combat had happened, and they took the only other unexplored path. It led to a deep pool of water, with the surrounding ledges covered in the skeletal remains of fish. A scent of the sea came into this room, and the water sloshed gently. Krell looked around with interest, noting that the walls showed signs of being inundated.

"A tidal pool, and I bet it connects to the sea." Krell inhaled deeply. "Even here, ReckNor can be found." Krell realized he was grinning.

"Listen, if you want to prattle on about your made-up god, that's something you can do when you're alone. The rest of us want to finish exploring this place and get out of here." Tristan had a voice that increasingly irritated Krell when he heard it.

"No other exits from here, and the mystery of what those things ate before dwarves got added to the menu is solved. Wonderful. I'm with Tristan, I don't care," said Orca, "so let's get down to where we found the bodies and make sure this place is empty, then we're done here." He turned and stalked back the way he came.

Gerrard smiled and patted Krell on the elbow, and left to follow. Krell took a deep breath, savoring the scent, then turned and followed the others.

The chamber where the dwarves had gutted smelled foul, and the passage beyond was worse. Large quantities of skeletal remains, mostly fish, but some that could have been the creatures they fought — along with some burrowing animals — layered the floor in increasing frequency.

A grating feeling grew on Krell's senses. It nauseated him for a moment before he realized what was happening.

"Hold up. There are dead things ahead of us," he said, stopping and drawing his sword.

"Gee, Krell. Thanks so much for that keen insight," said Tristan, nudging a fish skeleton aside with his boot. "I'm so glad you're here to tell us these things are dead. However would we have figured this out on our own?"

"No, I mean the *undead*. Let me concentrate."

Orca and Kraven shared a look. "Undead?"

Krell looked at them. "Yes, undead. There are three of them ahead of us. Could be more — I won't be sure until we get closer. Aim for the head to kill them."

Orca and Kraven readied their weapons, and Gerrard drew his shortsword. "Do you think this'll work, Krell?" he asked tentatively.

"Sure, Gerrard. You don't need more than two or three inches of steel to kill something, even if it's already dead. Stab it in the eye and it should stop moving. If not, stab it again until it stops. You'll be fine." Krell smiled down at him. "I remember your blade from before. It was covered in purple blood from those creatures. Don't doubt yourself and you'll have a song to sing back in Watford!"

Kraven chuckled. "Yeah, I like you, Krell. You're so dumb, it's great. Let's go kill some dead things!"

The passage widened, and the sense of the undead ahead of him grew stronger. They moved, coming closer. "They know we're here. They're coming," Krell warned everyone. Then he frowned. The *feel* of the creatures was distinct. The same, yet different from one another.

Ahead, the first of the creatures stepped into the edge of the light from Krell's torch. It might have been human once, but its flesh was now gray and rotting, and the eyes were two points of burning red light. It shambled forward, uttering a chilling moan. The stench of it reached Krell, and his stomach roiled. Behind it was a skeleton, the joints visibly held together with some dark energy. The empty eye sockets stared at Krell as it crowded behind the first creature, a rusty sword in its skeletal hand.

Orca shouted a challenge and strode forward. Tristan muttered under his breath, and a bolt of fire shot from his hands, passing narrowly past Orca, and slammed into the rotting creature. The fire scorched a hole in it, but it didn't seem to notice.

Orca thrust his sword into it, and the skeleton behind stabbed Orca in the arm. Kraven cut into the rotting thing with his axe, knocking it to the ground and allowing Orca to recover his sword. Then it slammed a fist into Kraven's leg, causing him to snarl and hobble backward.

Krell stepped forward and caught the rusty sword on his shield. He thrust his blade into the eyes of the creature on the ground, and it went rigid. Krell watched Orca slam his blade through the ribcage of the skeleton. Several bones broke, but dark energy flowed out, catching the pieces and pulling them back into place.

Then the undead creature on the ground struck Krell, shoving him forward, causing him to crash into the skeleton. His armor absorbed part of the blow, but Krell was off balance. Orca roared and slashed the rotting undead, but Krell was between the skeleton and it now.

Yet Krell did not panic. He could feel ReckNor's attention on him, watching to see what he would do. He could see clearly that this was but a test, to see if he was a worthy tool for ReckNor's hand for whatever purpose he would be put to. Well, if this was a test, best to succeed, thought Krell. He shoved the skeleton off balance with his shield and took the moment to cut the rotting undead in the back.

It turned to face him, and Kraven's axe crushed its skull from behind and it dropped to the ground. Kraven shouted in rage and chopped at it again, as Orca moved forward to stand with Krell. The skeleton thrust the rusty sword at Krell, but Orca intercepted, and between them they broke bones until the dark energy failed and they clattered to the ground.

Panting for breath, Krell concentrated. There were three undead before, and the one that remained was around the corner, waiting in ambush. Orca moved to go forward, but Krell stopped him.

"It's around the corner, waiting. Give me a moment to catch my breath." Krell glanced at his companions. "Kraven, you okay?"

Kraven let out a grunt, then strode forward with a minor limp in his stride. He reached the corner and dove around it, leading with the axe. Orca was right behind him, sword plunging forward.

It was over by the time Krell got there. The last one was a ghoul, looking nearly identical to the ones that had attacked Olgar and him at the temple. Orca was drawing his new sword from the eye socket of the thing, and it came out clean, with no hint of dirt or fluid on the blade.

The passage opened up into a cavern, the floor of which was covered in broken bones. Fresh blood stains and bits of viscera were strewn about the place, though nothing was recognizable. Krell looked back at the ghoul and saw for the first time its distended stomach.

"Well, this is revolting," said Tristan as he stepped forward. He errantly put a blast of fire into the undead remains, severing the arms and legs from the ghoul and igniting it. "I do so detest ghouls. They're really hard to kill sometimes."

Gerrard was scribbling notes into a small book he'd pulled out of his pocket, while Orca and Kraven poked around in the piles of bones for anything of worth. Tristan turned to Krell.

"Are we done here?"

Krell looked around. It seemed to be the end of the passage, and there were no other parts of the cave to explore as far as he could see. The rock creatures were slain, these few undead destroyed, and the dwarf remains had been recovered.

"Yeah, I think we're done in here. Find anything?"

Kraven came out with a small gemstone in his hand, and a pair of copper pennies. "Nothing much, looks like an earing and a few coins."

"Well, let's go get a proper reward then!" said Orca.

Chapter Four

"You're certain you won't stay the night?" Petimus asked, hunched over the charter.

Krell shook his head. "It's a short walk back to Watford, and the council is probably waiting to hear from us quickly. We should be there shortly after sunset." Petimus nodded, then set his quill aside and picked up a candle. He fished a block of red wax from the case he had brought with him, then held the flame to it over the charter.

When a blob of melted wax had formed, Petimus took a ring from his finger. He ran his thumb over it, muttering to himself several times. Krell could make out the cadence of words of power, but hadn't the faintest idea what he was doing. Petimus then pressed the ring into the wax, which glowed briefly for a moment.

Petimus stood and looked at the companions, then reached out his hand to each of them in turn.

"My thanks, then, for the recovery of our fallen, and for slaying the things that attacked and killed them. The clan-speakers will hear the tale of your deeds. Know you've made at least one friend among the dwarves, all of you." Petimus bowed to them, handed the charter to Orca, then led the way toward the gate.

"If you're setting out now, I doubt you'll want to wait around any longer. Rain stopped for the time being, but no clue what condition the road — if you can call it that — will be in. May the

Forge Father guard your path and the Fire Lord light your way!" Petimus slipped the bar from the gate.

Krell grinned. Olgar had taught him many things about arms and armor, but he had much to learn. In his religious training, Olgar had been exceedingly thorough.

"My thanks for the ward of Rold, the Forge Father, and the warmth of Phlogos the Fire Lord's breath. Your hearth and home were warm and kind, and may Rold reward you for being a gracious host! Until we meet again, Petimus Smithforge, and may ReckNor turn his baleful gaze away from you and your kin!" Petimus stood, staring slack-jawed at Krell, as everyone else filed past.

Petimus held out his hand and Krell clasped it. Then he nodded and departed.

Gerrard fell back and walked beside Krell for a moment.

"So, Krell, how do you know about the Forge Father and all that? Never heard you say anything like that before, you know?" Gerrard smiled up at him.

Krell laughed. "It's true enough, Gerrard, that my education could best be described as lacking. Most people say I don't know anything. I grew up alone, you see, so nobody taught me anything useful. I had to learn it all myself."

Gerrard looked at him questioningly. "Alone how? I can't see humans, even as insane as they often are, abandoning a youngling to grow up alone."

"Oh, I had a family. Still might, somewhere, maybe. But I was lost at sea when I was young. Not sure how young. Washed up on an island somewhere and spent a bunch of years surviving." Krell looked up at the sky. "My memories there are… poor. Can't remember much, but I remember the cold, the loneliness, and the hunger. Those stand out in my mind." Krell shook his head and frowned.

"Olgar taught me basically everything I know, aside from how to survive alone. Whatever knowledge I have is thanks to him, and one thing he made sure I knew well was who all the gods and their followers are. Paladins apparently spend a lot of time in conflict with faiths other than their own."

"Ah," said Gerrard, nodding in agreement.

Krell shrugged and looked back at Gerrard. "Whatever else I am, Gerrard, I'm a survivor. Maybe that's why ReckNor chose me to be a paladin. Maybe he wrecked the ship on purpose to see if I had what it took. Maybe he didn't. Either way, I hear the call. My blade is in his service, my will is his will. His voice thunders in my head, making his will known to me."

"Wow. You know, Kraven's right, you are intense!" Gerrard walked along in silence for a few minutes next to him. Then he turned and said, "That sounds really hard, having another voice in your head all the time."

Krell laughed. "Nah, it's really easy. When he tells me something, I do it. When he doesn't say anything, I do whatever I want."

Gerrard frowned. "I thought paladins had all sorts of rules they had to follow."

Krell grinned at him. "You're thinking of followers of Hieron the Honorable, lord of justice. There's a big temple of his in Heaford, just up the coast, where the duke holds court. I've never met one of his followers, but apparently he loves calling paladins, and they're pretty common in that faith. Most paladin stories are about paladins of Hieron."

"Not common in ReckNor's faith, though?"

"Not remotely. Apparently, Olgar can't remember the last time ReckNor called one. He's... well, most people think he's insane, and that if you don't appease him, he'll destroy you. A cult of sailors and the mad. That he's temperamental enough that even *if* you appease him, he *still* might destroy you. Which is all... somewhat true, I'd say."

Ahead, Tristan laughed. "You're telling me you think your god is insane?"

Krell shook his head. "No, but temperamental? Absolutely. Appease him or else, which is how his faith works. Sailors and those who live and work on the sea pay homage, though for many, it is out of fear. He's often thought of as a survival-of-the-fittest sort of god."

Krell noticed they were all looking at him now. Orca looked unhappy, Kraven appeared to be controlling his laughter, and Tristan and Gerrard were looking at him like he was dangerous.

"So… what does ReckNor teach, then?" asked Gerrard.

Krell thought about it, and Tristan looked like he was dreading an explanation. Better to keep things simple for now, he thought.

"Basically two things. The first is that the seas and skies are *his*, so make offerings when you use them and he's happy. The second is that he takes joy in the freedom of choice." Krell went silent, and they walked on for a few moments before anyone said anything.

"I thought you were going to drone on incessantly about your god and how great he is all the time," said Tristan. Krell looked at him and smiled.

"I'm a paladin. If you want that, go talk to Olgar. I'm here to show the faith of ReckNor through action, not through words." Thunder rumbled in the distance as if on cue, adding ominous weight to his words.

Gerrard snorted. "Did ReckNor just add some thunder in the background to make you sound more intimidating or dramatic or something?"

Kraven laughed, and Krell joined him. Orca said, "That's ridiculous!" at the same time Krell said, "Probably!"

* * *

The rain had put Tristan in a foul mood.

"This is outrageous. I'm soaked through, and this slow pace merely ensures that I am going to continue to be soaked through for far longer than necessary!" shouted Tristan. "This is your fault, Krell, you and your insane god. Why we ever brought you with us is beyond me, since clearly you did next to nothing in the caves."

"Tristan, be silent," Orca growled. "None of us are happy at the moment. Just keep walking. Silently."

Gerrard whispered to Krell, "Well, you know I'm happy, right, Krell? A solid story to tell for the next year, a load of coin coming our way, and a warm bed tonight in Watford. Possibly with someone to join me, if I'm lucky!" Gerrard had an infectious grin, and Krell couldn't help but smile back.

The sky had darkened quickly when the storm rolled in, and even though there was still some light, it was as dark as a moonlit night and getting darker by the moment. The road was increasingly difficult for Krell to see and follow, and he and Gerrard were slowing the pace of the others as they picked their way along.

"Just because these two can't see in the dark like the rest of us is no reason for us to wait. Why can't we just go on ahead and let them get to Watford whenever they get there?" Krell was growing increasingly certain that Tristan's voice would only ever sound like he was whining to him.

YET YOU NEED HIM.

Krell winced, then muttered, "I wonder if he has a quiet voice he could try using sometimes."

Gerrard gave him a smile, and said, "Oh, Tristan is just a cheat and a liar, and lazy besides. He's pretty, too, so I bet he has a lot of success with the ladies, which means between magic and personality, his ego is the size of Watford." Gerrard shrugged. "I've met and dealt with far worse, you know what I mean?"

Krell shook his head, grateful that his muttered comment had been taken about Tristan, not ReckNor. Still, Gerrard spoke sense.

"Does the big ego mean he has to be an ass all the time?"

Gerrard laughed. "'Fraid so. It'd be like asking you to be less confident — not something you even know you're doing, right? It's just who you are."

Tristan snorted. "You mean arrogant, not confident, Gerrard."

"Wait, you think I'm arrogant?" Krell asked.

"Oh, gods, yes!" said Tristan. "Are you really that blind? You refuse to show any caution or sense, and you have no respect for me and my needs. You're annoying, Krell."

YOU WILL BE FINE, SO LONG AS YOU SERVE MY WILL.

Krell winced.

"Ah, the truth hurts! Finally, I'm getting through that arrogant skull of yours!" Tristan seemed delighted. Krell did not bother correcting his assumption.

"Quiet," Orca growled. He pointed ahead, where a bobbing light could be seen off toward the south. "What is that?" he asked.

Tristan looked at it, then looked at Orca. "It's a light, Orca," he said with a condescending grin on his face.

Kraven looked ahead and followed the motion. "It's heading off the road, toward the sea. It's nothing but cliffs along here, right? If that's someone walking somewhere, where are they going?"

Tristan looked smug. "Oh, it's not a person, it's probably just the ghosts from the old tower up on the cliff." Everyone stopped and turned to face Tristan. He stopped and looked back at them for a moment, then snickered.

"Karaback told me that more than two centuries ago, a wizard had a tower up on the cliff where he practiced his great and terrible magic. Legend says that he lost control of it and destroyed himself and the tower. There's really just a single ruined lower floor left behind. People in town dare one another to go up and visit it, but nobody really ever does."

Tristan paused dramatically.

"Well, aside from me, that is. I certainly have been up there, and it very likely is haunted, but not by anything dangerous."

Gerrard seemed excited. "We should go check it out!"

"What, now?" Krell was taken aback. "Absolutely not! For two reasons. First, if it is haunted, then we go during the day, not at night. Ghosts are undead, and for whatever reason, undead hate sunlight. Second, our goal is to report to the town council and get our reward, not go looking for other trouble!"

Orca grunted. "Krell is right, as annoying as it is to say that. Let's go get our reward and see if the town council knows anything about this tower."

The light faded away to the south, and they did not see it again.

* * *

"… and then Petimus bid us farewell, and we walked back here," said Orca, reaching the end of the tale.

They were standing in Amra Thort's dining room, which functioned as the town council meeting hall. Orca had just recited a fairly accurate account of the journey. Seated at the table across from them were the town council, along with Karaback, the local wizard, Olgar, and Captain Gijwolf.

"The seal is genuine, Magister Karaback?" asked Daylan. Karaback placed the charter back on the table and nodded.

Aldrik Kent clapped his hands in delight. "Well done, brave warriors! It sounds like you had an easy time dealing with those creatures in the darkness! And fighting undead as well! What a grand story!" He looked over at Karaback, seated off to the side in a comfortable chair. "What do you make of their description of those things in the caves, Magister Karaback?"

Karaback stroked his trimmed beard, making a show of gathering his thoughts. He gestured in the air, and an image formed of a creature, thin and gray, with three-fingered claws. "Were these what you saw in the caverns?" he asked.

Krell nodded at once. "They are, and that is a neat trick! How do you do that?"

Karaback waved his hand, and the illusion disappeared. "I'm a wizard, boy. I do not perform *tricks*, I work *magic* by forcing my will upon the reality of the world. We wizards love our secrets." He smiled, and the lighting changed strangely about his face, making him look dark and mysterious.

Gerrard sighed wistfully. "I wish I could do that with the light, know what I mean? Can you imagine?"

"To answer your question, those are properly called *carpamanro*, though many call them cave wraiths. They are exceedingly rare, and it is unfortunate that you did not think to collect any of their blood." Karaback glanced at Tristan, frowning slightly.

Daylan Plintform looked vaguely annoyed. "Can we please get back to the matter at hand? It would seem these brave warriors have indeed fulfilled the charter, and will no doubt hound us incessantly until they are paid their promised reward."

Amra nodded and gestured to Captain Gijwolf, who stood and went to the back of the room. He retrieved a strongbox and put it in front of Amra. She nodded in thanks as she produced a key and unlocked it, then began counting out golden sovereigns onto the table. They were neatly bundled into groups of ten, which she divided into five piles.

"Your reward, brave warriors, for work excellently done. Petimus is likely to be grateful to the town council. Your success here has further smoothed relations between us and the dwarves. We are pleased with your work."

Kraven walked forward and scooped up a pile of coins, then dumped them into a pouch that he tied to his belt. Krell took his and held them in his hand. For all the songs about gold he had heard, he didn't see what the fuss was about. Sure, it sparkled, but he wondered what good it would be when a dark beast was trying to tear your face off.

Krell turned and handed it to Olgar. Olgar promptly handed three of the rolls back. "That's yours, lad. To do whatever you want with."

Daylan and Amra were discussing the loss of a fishing vessel, the fifth one this month. Orca cleared his throat, and they paused, turning to look at him.

"Yes, Orca, was there something else?" Daylan asked, clearly irritated at the interruption.

"The ruined tower outside town. Is it haunted?"

Daylan snickered into his hand, but Aldrik sat forward. "Many people say so, though there are some who doubt. It's mostly just a ruined old tower from a long time ago. Nobody but kids go up there anymore, and then only on a dare so they can get out of their chores."

Nathanial laughed. "There was a time or two I had to go up and bring you back, young Master Kent. Your father knew where you were, but whenever your mother learned of it, off I went to fetch you back."

"What is your interest in this tower, if I may ask?" Amra asked.

Kraven stepped forward. "We saw a light heading toward it, thought it might be haunted." He paused and shot a look at Tristan. "Though if children are swarming over it all the time, then perhaps not." A sly grin crossed over his face.

"Oh no, it's very haunted," said Amra. "The old wizard who lived there centuries ago blew his own tower apart and is apparently cursed to haunt the place. It's why nobody has repaired it or moved in. Shame too — it has a marvelous view. Thinking of trying to claim the reward?"

Suddenly, everyone was paying sharp attention.

"Reward?" asked Orca.

Amra chuckled, and Daylan looked at the ceiling and muttered something about wasted time.

"Shortly after the tower collapsed, there was a surge of undead. Some priests came in and did something to contain it, and let it be. Or possibly not, since the story has been retold so many times. However, there is an old royal proclamation that anyone who rebuilds and takes residence there will get possession free and clear of all past obligations, though taxes and other fees would need to be paid going forward should you gain the title to the property."

She paused, looking at them all.

"Thinking of making a grab for it?"

Kraven shrugged. "No ships in harbor to take me anywhere else, and nothing else to do tomorrow, so yeah, probably. Have others tried?"

Daylan laughed. "Oh yes, many, and hordes of children as well. You're welcome to walk up there, survey the ruined tower and get scared by the ghost, just like everyone else has been for the last two hundred years. It's pointless. Much like this conversation. If we could move back to *meaningful* town business?" Daylan and Amra began discussing the missing fishing vessels again, and what they could do to replace them. Aldrik interrupted, raising a concern about the Black Theocracy and whether Watford would be blamed if one of their trade ships vanished.

Captain Gijwolf walked up to the group of them, gesturing for them to step outside. Aldrik gave an enthusiastic wave as they departed. The evening air was clean now that the rain had stopped, and Krell breathed in deeply, savoring the smell of the sea.

"Well, gentlemen, your work was done and done well. However, more warriors arrived today looking to join the charter. I sent all but one away and was wondering if you'd like to meet him or not. He's at the Netminder's Friend, so he is likely at your destination, anyway. What say you?"

Krell shrugged while Orca grunted and walked off, heading toward the inn.

"Captain Gijwolf, what can you tell us about the tower?" Krell asked.

He smiled. "That's a tale best told with an ale in hand and a warm fire nearby, don't you think?"

* * *

Most sailors go to bed early.

Krell supposed this made sense, now that he was thinking about it. The common room was largely empty, and Marlena was sweeping mud from the floor into the corner with limited success when they entered. Her smile lit up the room when she saw Captain Gijwolf.

"Elias, to what do I owe the pleasure of this visit? And you're bringing the victorious warriors, or so the tale is spreading in town already, though there are some who are not pleased at all. Come, sit! Gerrard, spin me a tale while I fetch you some ale!" Laughing, she walked toward the bar.

Captain Gijwolf gestured at a spare-looking man seated at the bar, who walked over to join them. "This is Maximus, a warrior monk of Veceyr. Max, these are Kraven, Krell, Tristan, Orca, and Gerrard."

Max gave a curt bow, barely bending at the waist. "Greetings, and apologies. It appears that I missed both the challenge as well as the reward."

Krell studied Max as they sat. He was thin, but his muscles stood in sharp relief. There was no extra fat on him anywhere. His head was shaved bald, and a tattoo on his scalp was an image of a fist, the holy symbol of Veceyr, the Silent One, god of discipline and perfection.

"I greet you, and with wisdom shared, may we both prosper," Krell said formally. "And may ReckNor turn his baleful gaze away from you should you displease him!"

"Ah, yes, I learned there was a temple to ReckNor here in Watford. You are one of his many followers then?"

Kraven slapped Krell on the shoulder. Hard.

"He's a paladin of ReckNor, and I like him! Ah, and like a fiery angel, here arrives Marlena with drinks!" Kraven placed a golden coin on the table. "Keep the cups full and let me know when this runs out!" Kraven then grabbed a mug and took a deep drink.

Captain Gijwolf pushed mugs to all the others and held his up. "A toast to your victory!"

"Praise ReckNor!" said Krell, and he took a drink. The ale was fine, but not something Krell enjoyed. Max merely sipped his and politely set his cup aside. Kraven happily grabbed it.

"So, Captain, you have stories about the tower you can share?" said Orca.

Krell leaned over while and whispered to Max, "If the captain thinks you're all right, then you're welcome to come along with us. We're going to go investigate it tomorrow, see what we can learn about the place. Apparently it's haunted."

Max raised an eyebrow. "Ah, with apologies, but without the reward, I am in need of employment. Such a task sounds perhaps a fitting challenge, but without coin to pay for the needs of the body, my spirit will suffer."

"Well, perhaps I can help then," said Captain Gijwolf, "since there is a reward tied to the place. Or, well, at least property, and you could sell your share of that easily enough to get plenty of coin, I'd wager. Still, it's a risk, since many have tried over the last two centuries, but none have succeeded."

He looked around the common room. "When I was a lad growing up, like most of the children here in town, I went up to the tower. Me and my friends, all boasting and goading one another. Well, the ruin itself is stable. Hasn't shifted in all my years, so I doubt it'll collapse anytime soon. As long as you stay back from the cliff you're not likely to fall, so little danger there either.

"The ghost is real enough, though. Saw it myself. Appears as an elderly man in a robe with a crazily tall pointed hat on his head, meandering about the rooms that are left. Really just the bottom level of the tower, which is the only intact part. When the ghost sees you, though, he transforms into a hideous aspect and lets out a terrible wail. Most people run. Those who stay get a swipe from the ghost, whose touch is deathly cold. Stories from many years past tell how occasionally a person would go missing here or there after climbing the hills up toward the tower, but no bodies were ever found."

The captain took a long pull from his drink, while the others looked at one another.

"Of course, we only went during the day, so we only encountered it inside — never was brave enough to go at night. But every so often I head up and check, and sure enough it's still there, and the place still looks abandoned."

Krell looked confused. "Wait, you just leave a haunted tower near town? And let *children* visit it?"

Captain Gijwolf nodded, grinning. "The world is full of nonsense like this, Krell. You'll see it yourself, I'm sure, once you've outgrown Watford. Two centuries, and no change. It's basically harmless."

"So how do we claim the place?" asked Orca.

"Oh, details are in the proclamation, but basically you've got to move in and take residence, and agree to pay taxes and whatnot. You'd probably need to fix the place up to make it livable. Plus, it's up on a cliff near the ocean. No fresh water, nor is any well going to get you anything but saltwater, so who'd bother? Here in town, the Sanmen River gives us all the fresh water we could need, and a tributary runs by the dwarven mining camp, which is why it is where it is."

"Can you even kill a ghost with an axe?" Kraven asked doubtfully.

"Well, maybe not that axe of yours, but there's bound to be a way. Slim chance you'll find it, though. Lots have come before you looking, and nobody's ever succeeded." Captain Gijwolf looked at

Krell. "Of course, I can't ever remember a paladin bothering to come look, so perhaps there's some chance after all!"

Tristan scoffed. "As if Krell will have anything meaningful to contribute."

Krell gave Tristan a flat look, and then turned to Max, sliding a gold coin to him. "Consider this a kindness. ReckNor takes as much pleasure in the child who wonders at the beauty of the sea as he does in the pirate reaver sailing upon it." Krell looked inward, trying to figure out if ReckNor had anything to say about visiting the tower tomorrow, then shrugged. "If ReckNor has nothing for me to do, then I'm free to make my own choices. I'll go, just to see the view that you talked about, Captain."

Captain Gijwolf nodded. "It's spectacular. You can see the temple, the whole town and harbor, and a long stretch of coast. The sea goes on forever from up there." His eyes unfocused as he talked, clearly remembering. Then they locked back on the group. "Well, one drink is more than enough for me, and I've got to be up early. If you head up there, mind the cliff edge!" He stood, clapped Kraven on the shoulder, and departed.

Kraven grabbed Krell's mug from in front of him. "Since you're not drinking, I'll drink for both of us!"

Krell looked at Orca. "You coming with me tomorrow?"

Orca shrugged, then yawned. "Why not? I'm with the Captain, though. It's been a long day and I'm spent. Kraven, you're an idiot, but a fierce warrior. Sleep sometime soon." He stood up, and that signaled a general dispersal. Max walked outside with Krell, as Kraven yelled, "Wait, nobody else is drinking with me? Marlena! You'll share a pint or nine, won't you?"

Max turned to Krell and offered the coin back. "I cannot accept."

Krell grinned and took Max's fingers, closing them over the coin. "The path to wisdom travels strange roads and often never ends where you think."

Max blinked in surprise. "You know our proverbs?"

"I am a paladin of ReckNor, and I don't know much about the world, but Olgar has learned much of the many religions across these lands, and has driven that knowledge into my head whether I want it or not." Krell's grin turned savage. "And I'll use that knowledge to do whatever my god tells me to do!"

He looked around, breathing in deeply. "And right now, my god says nothing. So I choose to offer a gift, and now I choose to sleep. I will see you in the morning — and offer prayer to ReckNor for better weather than we had today!"

Krell turned, took one step away, and turned back, and gave a short bow, barely bending at the waist. "Until tomorrow, my new friend!"

When Krell arrived back at the temple, he could tell Olgar was sound asleep in his room before he even entered. The snoring reverberated from the walls like the sound of the sea crashing against the cliffs.

Chapter Five

The weather was clear the next day.

Krell walked up the road toward the tower, Kraven striding next to him. He looked no worse for his apparently long night of carousing. Gerrard, on the other hand, looked positively awful this morning. Even now he was panting as he kept pace, with Orca walking alongside to make sure he didn't fall behind.

Or, perhaps, fall asleep.

Tristan suddenly sped up, taking the lead ahead of Krell, and pointed to what looked like an animal trail leading from the road into the sparse forest between them and the cliff edge.

"This is the path that is used to get to the tower. Aren't you grateful that I'm here to show you these things?" He looked expectantly at Krell and Kraven.

"No," Kraven said, barging past him and heading down the path. "You're annoying."

"But not as annoying as Krell is!" he said, walking after Kraven, being mindful of the branches he was bending out of the way, deliberately, so they would snap back into Tristan.

Krell shook his head and looked back. Max was walking behind him, looking both concerned and content at the same time. Their gazes met.

"A question for you. It would seem that Tristan does not like you, nor does Orca. Gerrard seems still to be inebriated. Why do you travel with these companions?" he asked.

"I've spent a lot of time thinking about that over the last two days, Max," he said. "What I've figured out is that for the very first time in my life, aside from Olgar, these people will stand with me. For the very first time, I have a sense of something *more.* It's a little hard for me to explain. But I am not lonely, and that is worth a lot to me."

Max looked at Krell, raising one eyebrow.

Krell shrugged. "I know. It isn't a very good answer. Loneliness is crushing, and I've carried the burden for years and years. Now, finally, it is lifted, and for the first time I feel like I can stand up straight. That isn't it either, really, but I can't describe it better than that. Ask Olgar, maybe he knows." Krell looked toward Gerrard, and then at the path that Tristan had shown everyone. "Shall we?" He left the road just as Gerrard caught up and stepped into the brush.

"Hey Krell, maybe we could, you know, take a break?" Gerrard did sound tired, but before he could answer, he heard Orca grunt. "Okay, okay, I get it. No need to shove me around. I'm going. You can see I'm going, right?"

Krell smiled as he heard them coming into the brush behind him.

Following the path was surprisingly easy, even without Kraven's approach of simply crashing through any branches that impeded his path. Tristan and Kraven could be seen looking around up ahead, and as Krell moved closer to the cliff edge, the trees cleared and he could see the tower.

The remains of the tower, at any rate.

It was a circular stone building, easily forty feet across. The base of the tower seemed to be sound, but the upper floors had only fragments of wall still upright, with the top of the remaining structure covered with broken rock fragments, tree branches and leaves, and what looked like animal nests.

A set of broken stairs led up to the remnants of what was now the roof, although only half of what may have been a doorway was still standing. The stone was dark gray and showed extensive weathering from sun and rain. Krell could see around the base what looked like an alcove or entrance into the covered bottom of the tower.

The view, though, was indeed spectacular.

The cliff edge bulged out from the coast for over a hundred feet, and the tower was built there. Looking west toward Watford, Krell could easily see the entire harbor, the temple to ReckNor, the graveyard, and nearly the entire town from where he stood. The road leading toward the dwarven mining camp and back down into town was easily visible from here, since this portion of the cliff was higher than the surrounding terrain, easily over a hundred feet above the sea.

The sea spread out before him, stretching south as far as he could see. Several fishing boats were visible. It was like he was perched atop a cloud, looking out over the water. Krell turned east and could make out what he thought must be Heaford on the horizon.

"ReckNor be praised, this *is* a terrific view!" Krell exclaimed, a smile lighting up his face.

"It is indeed!" an unfamiliar voice said from behind and above him somewhere.

Krell spun, his blade hissing from his sheath as he turned. A plain-looking human standing atop the platform put his hands up to show they were empty.

"Apologies, friends! Apologies! Had no intention of scaring you!" He looked nervous. Kraven was staring at him, his axe still slung on his back. Orca also had his blade out, and Max was crouched slightly, his hands spread apart from his body.

Gerrard chose this moment to crash through the last of the brush and fall noisily to the ground. "Guh! *Now* can we take a break, please? Some of us are not orcs if you know what I mean, and need a break now and then to account for all the drink consumed the night before. Oh, who's that?" Gerrard asked, noticing everyone staring at the stranger atop the building.

"Hello there! Again, apologies! I'm unarmed! Well, I mean, I have this little dagger, here, on my belt, but certainly no arms and armor like you brave warriors have! Can we just put the swords away?" the man asked, clearly nervous at the display in front of him. He glanced behind him. "I don't like my chances of having to jump into the water, so if we could try talking, please?"

Krell sheathed his sword and walked forward. "I am Krell, paladin of ReckNor. Who are you and what are you doing up here?"

"Ah, a paladin, is it? I heard that there was a new one in town. My name is Cor. I'm a leatherworker by trade, and at the moment I'm working with Adnalor Ralojen, the leatherworker in town. You know Adnalor? Trying to see if he'll take me on, like a provisional job, you know?" Cor smiled, nodding. Krell thought he sounded nervous.

"Anyway, I heard about this tower, and today there was no work for me, so I thought I'd come up to look — learning the town and seeing the sights? Then I heard you come crashing through the trees over there and thought it might be a wild animal, and me with my little dagger, so I hid up here until I heard talking. That's when you drew those swords and gave me such a fright! It's… it's okay if I put my hands down?"

Krell smiled. "Of course. We did not intend to scare you, Cor. Find anything interesting up there? Did you know about the ghost?"

Cor laughed in relief as Orca sheathed his sword and the others relaxed. "Oh, that's just a story drunk locals and children tell one another. There's no such thing as ghosts."

"See, that's where you're wrong, Cor, and why you might not be as safe up here as you think you are," said Tristan in his most condescending tone of voice. "We have it on very good authority that there is indeed a ghost up here, and we're here to see if our so-called paladin can do anything about it. Though I think not." Tristan flashed an overly sweet smile at Krell.

Krell thought about pushing Tristan off the cliff.

DON'T. KEEP HIM ALIVE.

Krell winced, then said, "You know, Tristan, if ReckNor didn't have some plan for you, I'd probably be tempted to just throw you over the edge of the cliff and be done with you." Krell turned and looked directly at Tristan. "Be grateful to ReckNor."

"Oh, I'm quite sure he's aware of my importance to the world and how valuable I am to all of you."

Krell ground his teeth, then climbed the steps up to the top. There was a gap between the stairs and the wall where they had separated, and Krell took a long stride, arriving at the top. He looked over at Cor, who smiled.

"Are you really a paladin? I've heard stories about paladins, but I've never met one before!" Cor seemed really excited.

Krell nodded, at the same time that Tristan hopped up, saying "That's what he claims, anyway."

Krell let out a heavy sigh.

* * *

The top of the tower held nothing of interest.

There were the remains of a stairwell that had descended at some point in the past, but was now choked solid with stone debris, probably from when the tower collapsed. Otherwise, the top was covered in broken and uneven stone, with sporadic bits of rotting vegetation and small bird's nests scattered about.

Something about that bothered Krell.

Orca looked around, then snorted in disgust. "Nothing here. Let's go below." He glanced at Krell. "You okay? Is that fearsome bird nest going to attack us or something?" He gave Krell a toothy grin.

Krell turned to face him, then shook his head slightly. "No, it's nothing. Let's go."

They climbed down the stairs and went around to the side entrance. It looked like a set of doors once stood here, but they had long since collapsed and rotted away. Within, the signs of rain and wind were obvious, with scattered tree branches, leaves and soil scatted across the floor. The rotted remains of barrels and shelves could be made out in the far corners where they had been sheltered from the elements.

"I guess this is the storeroom that Captain Gijwolf was talking about, huh?" said Kraven, looking around. There was a broken doorway off to their left, with two boards connected to a rusted hinge. Dozens of tracks covered the ground.

Krell nodded, then kneeled and removed his pack, retrieving two torches. He lit them and handed one to Gerrard, who nodded in gratitude. The other he handed to Max.

"You plan to venture deep within this place?" Cor asked, startling everyone.

"Cor, are you planning on coming with us? If we encounter the ghost, I can't guarantee your safety," Krell said, looking at him. Cor gave a smile and an elaborate shrug.

"I mean, if you have no issue with me tagging along, I'd love to see a paladin at work!"

Krell looked at Orca, who rolled his eyes and moved deeper into the room, heading to the doorway.

Krell nodded to him. "Keep behind us and out of the way, Cor. We're not here to help you sightsee." Krell paused for a moment, then glanced at Tristan, and back to Cor. "In fact, let's make a few things clear right now. If we find and kill the ghost, then there's a royal proclamation about ownership. You're not getting any part of that. Understand?"

Kraven laughed, and Cor looked taken aback. "Uh, yes, I hear you. I understand," he said to Krell, then turned to Gerrard. "Is he always that intimidating?"

Gerrard nodded very seriously. "Sometimes he's more intimidating. When he's not acting insane, that is." Gerrard turned away from Cor and met Krell's eyes, winking at him, a mirthful expression crossing his face. Krell closed his eyes and breathed deeply for a moment, then followed Orca deeper into the ruined tower.

* * *

The ghost wasted no time.

As soon as Orca entered the ruined storeroom, he spotted it. The apparition was wandering aimlessly from shelf to shelf in the next room, a dimly glowing outline of a man wearing a ridiculous hat, wide brimmed, but rising to a point over two feet high. His wispy form became cloudy below the waist, showing no legs.

Krell watched it, confused. Whenever one of the undead was near, he could *feel* it. It imbued him with a general sense of *wrongness,* warning him of danger. Now, though, observing the ghost not twenty feet away from him, he felt nothing.

"Get back, Krell!" hissed Tristan. Orca stood just inside the room, and Krell stood in the doorway. Krell noted Orca had a tight grip on his sword, his every muscle tense. The sword point did not waver at all, however, staying aimed directly at the ghost.

Krell glanced behind him. Cor was off to the side at an angle, so he couldn't see into the room itself. Tristan was right behind him, his hands raised as if to work his magic. Gerrard and Max were standing farther back, both looking concerned and edging toward the door.

"It's all right," said Krell. "I don't think it's going to hurt us."

He paused and frowned. "No, that isn't it. It *can't* hurt us."

The presence of ReckNor within him became colored with laughter. Krell's frown deepened. "At least, I don't feel anything that suggests danger from it."

"Well, it is clearly a ghost," said Orca, his voice betraying only the slightest nervousness. "What do we do next, then, paladin?"

Krell looked around at his companions. Gerrard shook his head emphatically while Kraven hefted his axe. Tristan gave him an exasperated look, while Max appeared quite calm. Cor didn't seem to realize anything was amiss.

"Krell, get out of the way and I'll blast it!" shouted Tristan. Krell nodded, then stepped back. Without waiting, Tristan uttered some words of power, and a bolt of fire shot from his hand, passed directly through the ghost, and slammed into the rotten wooden shelves behind it. They began burning merrily and collapsed to the floor.

The ghost did not react at all.

Tristan grimaced, then gestured while speaking words of power. A scintillating ball of energy flew from his hands. It hissed through the air, barely missing the ghost, and with a clap of thunder blew a chunk of rock out of the wall.

The ghost didn't seem to notice.

"Enough, Tristan," said Orca, as Tristan launched another sphere, this one on target, passing harmlessly through the ghost and scorching the wall with a burst of lightning that arced to nearby objects. Several wooden barrels and a set of shelves collapsed into shattered pieces.

As Tristan subsided, the burning shelves sputtered out, the decayed wood proving to be poor fuel for the flames. The ghost drifted over to a ruined barrel and made as if to open it. It seemed to be completely ignoring their presence.

Krell still felt *nothing* from the floating creature. He glanced at Orca, who remained focused on the ghost, and said, "Watch, and be ready to pull me back if this goes wrong."

Orca looked at him in surprise as Krell walked forward. Behind him, Tristan said, "Krell, you're an idiot!"

Up close, the ghost was obviously translucent, and Krell could make out the wall and other objects behind it through its spectral form. ReckNor, in his thoughts, was quiet, the feeling of his power almost placid, like the sea on a calm day. Krell gave a mental shrug and reached out.

His hand passed through the ghost with no effect. He felt a slight chill, but it was nothing worse than passing his hand through fog.

"Huh," he said, turning back to the others. "Nothing happened." Krell saw Orca's eyes widen in alarm.

As he spun back, he saw the ghost turn to face him, and its features changed from those of an older human man to a vision of horror. The eyes bulged, the face grew three times larger, and the jaw split apart in multiple directions, showing jagged teeth and multiple tongues reaching out for him, even as the hands elongated into wicked-looking claws. It drifted toward him.

Yet there was no alarm from within. ReckNor's power was calm, doing nothing. There was a trickle of something in his thoughts, though, like a thread of fear. Krell could see it against the glow of ReckNor's grace, and could see it not growing from within as it would if it was his own fear, but being introduced from outside of himself. Even as he saw this, the thread of fear evaporated.

The ghost clawed him. Krell felt slightly chilled, but otherwise was unharmed. The ghost moved right through his body, emerging behind him. He turned and watched it head toward Orca and the others.

Orca's eyes were wide with fear, and he stood there, trembling, his sword point wavering in the air. Tristan turned and ran, as did Gerrard and Kraven. Kraven nearly bowled over Max in his haste to flee. Cor was nowhere to be seen, presumably already outside.

As the ghost approached Orca, his lips parted in a silent snarl. Krell said in a soothing tone of voice, "Orca, whatever this is, it is not a ghost. It's harmless."

Orca's eyes snapped to meet Krell's gaze, then looked him up and down before turning back to the ghost. He swallowed hard and sheathed his sword, then stepped forward with his eyes closed.

The ghost passed through him harmlessly. He shuddered, but then snapped his eyes open and looked. "It's all see-through now. What happened?" he asked, his voice tight.

Krell looked at him, a little confused. "It always looked see-through to me, the whole time. What did you see?"

"A man, all in color, with that ridiculous hat on his head, and he was muttering some nonsense about looking for his book. Then when you touched it, it let out a fearful scream." Orca turned and looked out of the room. "It would seem the others have fled."

"I heard nothing the entire time." Krell was confused. The spectral creature was floating back into the room, having resumed its original shape. It passed out of a ruined doorway and then disappeared from sight.

Orca left, saying, "I'm going to collect the others, assuming they haven't run back to Watford by now." Krell nodded and surveyed the room, thinking.

Whatever the thing was, it was harmless. That made no sense to Krell. Certainly it was fearsome for some, but not everyone would have reacted as Tristan and the rest did over the last two hundred years. And if it was harmless, what was the origin of those stories about people going missing?

As Krell thought about it, the ghost returned. It came into the room, and watching closely, Krell could see its mouth moving as if talking, though it was wispy enough he couldn't make out any of the words by looking at the shape of the lips. Something about it nagged Krell, trying to get his attention. He spent a moment concentrating, trying to figure out what was bothering him before he understood.

It was following exactly the same pattern as it had before, coming into the room and acting as if looking for something.

Krell stepped to the side, and watched intently, trying to remember when, exactly, it turned and became fearsome.

Orca returned, leading the others with him. Krell gestured for them to stay there and to be quiet.

The ghost aimlessly moved around, trying to open barrels that were not there, then retreated from the room, disappearing when it went through the doorway as it had before.

"Well, that didn't work," Krell said. "I thought for sure it would turn and go all fearsome again, but it didn't this time. Wait there, I have another idea I want to test."

Tristan snorted and Kraven said, "You're not afraid? I thought I was going to die! My legs were moving me before I even realized what was happening!" His voice still quavered.

"Yeah, I bet. It was fear all right," Krell said.

"Of course I was afraid!" shouted Kraven.

"No, I mean *fear*, as in magic fear, forced on you unnaturally. You weren't afraid, you were *made* afraid." Krell kept his attention on the doorway, where he expected the spirit to return any moment.

"Oh, hey, Krell! I've heard about this before, in songs. It's a thing that dark wizards do in stories, right?" Gerrard said, somewhat excitedly.

"I should think that ghosts would have that power," said Cor nervously from the exterior doorway. "Shouldn't we get out of here? What if it comes back?"

"I expect it to come back. I, for one, am going to wait for it," Krell said.

* * *

The ghost didn't return for over an hour.

Cor spent that time arguing they should flee. Tristan spent the time whining about being bored, and Kraven spent it threatening Tristan with violence if he didn't shut up. Orca sulked, and Gerrard hummed a song while writing in his little notebook. Max sat on his knees near Krell, his eyes closed, breathing deeply.

"It is called meditation," he said, aware somehow that Krell was watching him. "I focus my thoughts within, to find the impure ones and expunge them. This leads to clarity of purpose, a step toward a perfect mind. This is what Veceyr teaches, that perfection is attainable only through focus and discipline."

"Neat," said Krell. "My god teaches that you should do what you want, and the consequences of that are yours to deal with. Also that the seas and skies are *his*, and you should propitiate him to avoid his baleful gaze." Krell turned his attention back to the doorway. The ghost was beginning to anger him with its absence.

"Your god sounds petty and small," said Max, "always demanding tribute to avoid punishment."

Krell chuckled, turning his attention back to Max. "Yeah, most people would agree with you. What they don't get is that there are many things that are terrible and powerful, that would lay waste to all people everywhere if they could. ReckNor uses the power he gains through worship to protect those who offer him prayers. The beasts of the deep that seek to devour ships are deflected. The storms of vengeance conjured by undead powers seeking to end everything are deflected or undone. ReckNor is ever present, always working to keep us alive. He does this without acknowledgment. He cares not whether you like him. He cares that you honor him, and that he has the power he needs to do his work."

CLOSE, BUT SOMEWHAT INACCURATE.

Krell winced and turned his attention back to the doorway. After a moment, Max said, "I have never thought about ReckNor that way before."

"Yeah, most people pay homage to him asking for nice weather, or out of fear of the consequences of not paying homage. Well, it isn't ReckNor who reaches out to punish if you don't pray. It's that he withdraws his sheltering grace and lets the terrors of the deep have their way." Krell smiled to himself. "I guess I don't get it, why others think ReckNor would want people to die. I mean, the gods need us, need our worship, right?"

Max looked troubled, and Krell noticed the others watching him. "Seems to me that all the gods want us around. You offer prayers to Veceyr, who teaches you to make yourself focused and disciplined, likely because that's the strategy he settled on to keep his followers alive. ReckNor says offer prayers or else, because that's the strategy he settled on. Hieron says just laws benefit everyone, and because his followers all band together and support one another, they all stay alive, that's his strategy. It's all the same, really, just different versions for each of the gods."

Tristan looked at him curiously. "Isn't that, I don't know, blasphemy?"

Krell looked up and grinned. "Maybe. But here's the thing about ReckNor. Where Hieron would care a *lot* about anything that slights his so-called honor, ReckNor couldn't care less. I'm free to make my own choices, because ReckNor believes we're smart enough to keep ourselves alive."

Tristan looked at him doubtfully. "I don't think you're smart enough to stay alive. You're reckless."

Krell laughed. "I'm a paladin, Tristan. I'm not here to supplicate the masses, or entertain people. I've been called to make ReckNor's will happen." He turned to Gerrard. "Lots of stories about paladins, right?"

Gerrard nodded. "Lots. Though mostly they're about paladins of Hieron."

"Yeah," Krell agreed. "Hieron apparently loves calling paladins. Maybe he just enjoys talking to people directly, who can say. I certainly don't know many of those stories, but let me see if I can give you the common thread. Paladins of Hieron are always really good, really noble, have honor, are brave, and follow all sorts of rules about behaving properly around others. That accurate?"

Gerrard nodded.

"And each of those stories ends with the paladin dying gloriously, usually putting some big evil down at the expense of their own lives, right?"

Again, Gerrard nodded.

Krell turned back to Tristan. "This is why ReckNor is best. He doesn't give me stupid rules to follow. He doesn't care about honor or how I behave. He cares that people offer prayer, and that I do what he tells me." Krell smiled, a grin that promised violence. "I will see his will done. If he doesn't tell me what to do, then I do what I want. Most importantly, he doesn't care *how* I work his will, only that it gets done. Hieron cares a lot about the methods. ReckNor cares only for results."

Kraven laughed. "This is all nonsense. It's why I worship Udar, the lord of strength! He's simple. Be strong! That's what he teaches!"

Krell smiled slyly at Max, turning his attention back to the doorway. "Yeah, I guess Udar is okay. Boring, but okay. At least he isn't tedious like Hieron or Veceyr."

Krell spotted the ghost reforming. "Make ready. Here it comes. I'm going to test something. Try not to run. Remember, the fear isn't yours, it's being forced on you. Reject it!"

He turned to Kraven. "Be strong!"

He turned to Max. "Be disciplined!"

He turned to Tristan. "Be, I don't know, less annoying somehow."

The ghost entered the room, and Krell immediately went forward and touched it. At once, it turned toward him, adopting a fearful aspect as before. As before, it passed through him. He turned and saw Max and Kraven standing their ground, and Orca looking at the ghost in confusion. Gerrard, Tristan, and Cor were busy making their way out of the ruin as fast as their feet could carry them.

Krell sighed. "Progress, I suppose. You see it as all wispy and see-through now, right?" Kraven nodded, then strode forward, swinging his axe through it several times. The ghost turned toward him and passed through him harmlessly.

Kraven lowered his brow and frowned. "Someone is playing a trick here."

"I agree, and it makes no sense to me. If this thing is harmless, then what about the people who disappeared over the years? Surely not everyone falls for this trick, do they?" Krell looked around. "Orca, let's go get Tristan and Gerrard. We need to, I don't know, hold them down or something to make them see it's harmless."

Chapter Six

It took three more cycles, but finally everyone could see the ghost was not a danger.

It took hours. Every time the ghost adopted the menacing guise, it reformed almost immediately, then disappeared for over an hour. Krell was annoyed by the time Cor finally saw through it and was no longer afraid. He wondered if maybe people and their friends never figured it out as a group all at once, and there were always one or two in a crowd of children who didn't think it was scary, but when the others ran, they ran with them.

It bothered him, though, that there were still those missing people that had cropped up over the years. How did people go missing if the ghost was harmless? Maybe in their panic they ran off the edge of the cliff? Maybe it was more dangerous at night? Something was tugging at his thoughts, and he couldn't shake the feeling that he needed to figure it out.

The base of the tower contained storerooms, and as they ventured into the next room, they found the remains of the stairwell. Krell held up his torch to inspect it, and found it was choked with debris and completely impassable. These rooms contained rotten barrels and shelves that must once have had preserved foodstuffs, but now nothing remained besides a spongy and revolting mass.

Cor looked around. "Well, this was fascinating. I don't see any other rooms, and that staircase isn't passable at all. I'm guessing that ghost is going to reappear any time now. So… what's next?" He focused on Orca, looking expectantly at him.

Krell wandered around the room, looking at the ruined objects. Something bothered him, a thought he couldn't quite form in his head. Kraven was also looking around, then said, "Why is there no junk in the middle of the floor?"

Krell focused and realized that was what bothered him. It was almost like someone cleared the debris out of the center of the floor area to make it easier to walk around. "Kids, you think? But that doesn't make sense to me. Why would they clear a space in here?" Krell gestured toward the back wall of the room. "It's almost like a path was cleared to get over there."

Kraven nodded, and walked in that direction, Gerrard tagging along behind him.

Cor looked around. "Maybe it was flooding? It looks like a path from that staircase there over to the wall. I guess I don't see what the point of further investigation is." He looked skeptical.

Krell turned to him. "Look Cor, you're free to leave anytime you want. It's a little more than an hour to get back to Watford, and you've a lot of daylight left. Otherwise, be quiet." Krell held his gaze and thought he saw him wilt a bit.

Kraven, from the far wall, chuckled. "He's like a thunderstorm, isn't he?"

"You know it, Kraven, my man! Hey, look at this…" Gerrard stuck his knife between two stones, and the sound of his blade hitting metal could be heard throughout the room. "I think there's a hinge here, or a catch or something."

Kraven kneeled down and looked closely, then started pushing at the stones. Gerrard traced his fingers lightly over other seams, then muttered, "I can feel a draft. There's definitely something back here."

Cor scoffed. "It's probably the wind from outside, nothing more."

Orca shook his head. "No, the tower is flat, but the terrain is not. This side of the tower was more sunken into the ground. Can't be the wind, at least not low to the ground like that."

Gerrard let out a cry of triumph and pushed on one side of a stone set into the wall, which pivoted. With a *click,* a section of the stone wall swung free, and he and Kraven opened it, gazing on a narrow stairway. It descended to a landing just below them.

Kraven clapped Gerrard on the shoulder, nearly knocking him over.

"Good work, Gerrard," said Orca, coming over. "Dark down here."

Krell moved over and looked down, holding his torch in. Immediately, the light illuminated an alcove that contained several dusty tarps and blankets. He gestured.

"Ah, you know what? I'm thinking this is to lay on the floor to keep from making marks or something, know what I mean?" said Gerrard, looking around. "I bet you that there's enough to get from here to the outer room. Keep footprints and drag marks hidden."

"Why would someone want to hide their footprints?" said Tristan, clearly irritated at the hours of time spent standing around doing basically nothing.

Gerrard shrugged. "Something that someone is doing so they don't get caught. You know, like something illegal." Gerrard slowly drew his blade, focused on the stairwell.

"You think there's something down there, Gerrard?" Krell asked.

He nodded. "Not everyone has a great past, know what I mean? Like, some people, if they went to bigger cities, might find themselves wanted criminals. People who find themselves in way-out places like Watford." Gerrard looked a little nervous.

Krell laughed, then rested his hand on his shoulder. "Don't steal from me, and I'll stand with you if someone comes for you. You think smugglers? Or slavers? Or something else?"

"Hey, nobody is coming for me, all right? I'm clean as a bathtub, I am, but I hear stories, okay? This looks like a smuggler hole to me, Krell. Like, it's perfect, know what I mean? The way the cliff edges out from the coast, a ship can approach and Watford won't see it at all. If this staircase goes all the way down, then they could unload, then haul stuff up, right?"

He turned and smiled at Krell. "Then you just walk it out to the road, put it on a cart, and straight to Watford it goes."

Cor looked alarmed. "You're saying that there could be smugglers right below us, right now, as we speak? Presumably *armed* smugglers?"

"Keep your voice down," growled Orca, "and yes, that is exactly what we're saying. Kraven, let's go." Orca waited while Kraven eased through the gap onto the stairs beyond. It was narrow initially, but opened up quickly. Kraven grunted.

"Looks like rope and pulleys in here. Probably to haul goods up from below by using a lift. That's how I'd want to do it, instead of carrying them up all these stairs." There was a pause.

"Shit. There's a metal tube here, probably to carry your voice up from below. Or down from above."

Krell looked at Gerrard. He shrugged. "If they're down there, they'll be waiting for us. It'll be a fight, right?"

Krell nodded, then started down after Kraven and Orca.

* * *

The stairs down were wide and spacious.

This made a certain amount of sense to Krell. If you were smuggling goods, then you'd want easy stairs to climb. At some point, though, the center of the staircase was carved out and a rope and pulley added. The lift was likely at the bottom.

As they descended, they found a set of small chambers. Tristan identified one as being a casting chamber, likely where a magician would work some spells, but it clearly hadn't seen use in ages.

Another room had a pedestal on it, with a rock slab mounted atop it. Glowing runes covered the rock and Tristan and Gerrard studied them.

"With my vast knowledge of magical might and how magic works generally, I am certain that this stone is carved with runes of illusion magic," said Tristan.

Gerrard nodded in agreement. "I think so too, Tristan. I bet it's the ghost thing above, that this is what makes it."

Cor looked nervous. "I think we should leave that alone."

Krell shook his head. "Well, there's a simple way to test whether it makes the ghost or not," he said, walking forward, where he shoved the rock off the pedestal. It crashed to the ground and shattered. There was a bright flash, and Krell grunted in pain. His whole body tingled.

"Krell, you stupid idiot!" Tristan raged at him, "Now I'll never be able to figure out how it was made!"

Orca laughed. "Good. You'd never use that knowledge for anything useful — probably start a fire with it." Krell shook out his arms and clutched at the wall for support. Something wasn't working right with his legs. The sense of ReckNor within him was filled with laughter. Krell frowned and concentrated. ReckNor's grace flowed through him, washing away the after-effects.

Krell looked up. Kraven was supporting him, looking concerned. Max was next to him, also looking anxious. He shook his head as it finally cleared, and said, "I'm fine."

"You did not appear to be fine, Krell. You seemed dizzy and disoriented, as if you had been struck in the head." Max still looked concerned, but less so.

"Probably the magic washing over me. ReckNor's balls! That stung! Over with now, and his grace has washed away the magic." Krell looked at Tristan. "For what it's worth, that hurt. A lot."

Tristan shot him a dark look. "Good."

"How far have we descended, do you think?" asked Max.

Orca paused, thinking. "Maybe forty feet? There's a way to go before we get down to the bottom, that's for sure."

Cor looked even more nervous. "What about the smugglers, then?"

Orca grinned and patted his sword hilt.

* * *

The stairs continued down, but a door distracted them.

"Treasure room, huh?" whispered Kraven, eyeing the heavy steel door that was barred from the outside. A crude splash of paint on the door spelled the words TREASURE ROOM across it. Krell looked at the rest of stairs going down, which opened into a landing area.

"Later," whispered Orca. "If they're down there waiting for us, then let's deal with this after." He drew his sword quietly, and Krell nodded, doing the same.

"What's the plan?" asked Tristan. Krell looked at him, then down below.

"Kraven and I go first. Krell follows behind. They spring out to kill us, and we kill them instead," said Orca quietly. "Simple. Easy."

Tristan rolled his eyes. "This is your idea of a plan?" he asked.

Krell found himself frowning, in the rare position of agreeing with Tristan. "What do you propose instead, Tristan?" he asked, wondering if there was some magic he planned to use.

"I'm glad you're finally seeing sense, Krell, and asking for my opinion as the smartest and most valuable member of the team here. I say we shout down and negotiate with them, see if they'll talk first."

"ReckNor's beard, why?" asked Krell. Orca hissed at him, urging him to be quiet.

"Well, if there's a lot of them, and they're waiting for us to kill us, then I'd rather have a chat and see if we can get out of this without risking our necks for no reward."

"Ah," said Kraven, "you're a coward and you're afraid. Come on, Krell. Let's go down and kill some of them, and see if the rest want to give up or need killing as well." Kraven grinned, hefted his axe, and started to descend the stairs.

Krell looked within, at the grace and power of ReckNor, and didn't get a feeling one way or the other. He shrugged, hefted his sword and shield, and started down after Kraven, gesturing at Gerrard to follow behind, since Gerrard was carrying the torch.

"Idiots," muttered Tristan, as Gerrard, then Orca and Max descended the stairs.

Kraven reached the bottom and looked around. Krell could see two doorways leading from the room they were in. He thought he saw someone peering around the corner to his left and turned to face that direction.

Things happened very quickly after that.

From each doorway, lanterns were uncovered, directing all their light into the room, shadowing the ones standing behind it. The light was dazzlingly bright and Krell squinted, crouching down behind his shield as he moved forward. An arrow crashed off his helmet, and another lodged in the front of his shield.

Krell could hear battle behind him but stayed focused on the doorway ahead. He charged through it, taking a sword blow that was deflected by his helmet and another that his chain mail absorbed. He kicked the lantern over, and it crashed against the far wall of the room, spilling oil and causing a fire.

There were six of them, three of whom were discarding bows and drawing blades. Krell turned to the one to his left, cutting with his sword. There was some resistance, but the sword cut deep into his side and he collapsed, coughing blood. He spun back, but Gerrard had stayed directly behind him and had taken another in the groin.

Krell caught a swipe at Gerrard on his blade and used his shield to turn another as the three archers joined the fray. The fire illuminated the room, and the fresh scent of the sea could be smelled above the smoke and blood.

They came forward, and Krell rushed forward to meet them.

"ReckNor is with me!" he shouted. "Surrender or die!"

They paused for a moment, which Krell used to gut the one attacking Gerrard. Gerrard moved behind him. Hoisting his shield up higher, he stepped forward, catching their attacks on his blade and shield, cutting back when he could, but focused on letting Gerrard get into the fray. His shortsword slid up into the guts of the one hammering at Krell's shield, and he coughed up blood and collapsed.

The other two turned to run. Krell cut one down from behind and dashed after the other.

"I said surrender or die! Not run away!" he shouted, as the survivor, a panicked look on his face, paused his flight to yank open a door. Krell slammed into him shield first, and he crashed into the door he was trying to open. As they rebounded from one another, Krell took him in the neck with his sword.

"Krell!" shouted Gerrard from behind him. Krell spun and took a moment to survey the scene.

Kraven was under attack by two armored warriors, who were working as a team to keep themselves safe. Orca was wounded, facing two more who also wore metal armor. Tristan was retreating up the stairs, and Max was doing his best to defend him, though he was gravely wounded, pursued by at least four smugglers. At least eight bodies were on the ground in this room, but an additional three were attacking Gerrard, their blades flashing as he dodged out of the way.

Krell rushed forward, shouting. Two men turned their attention to him, and Gerrard promptly stabbed one in the back, though he took a cut on the shoulder for his efforts. Krell slammed his shield into the unwounded one and cut, killing the injured one with a slash through the neck. He continued his momentum and crashed into the third, who was cutting at Gerrard, and they both fell to the ground.

Krell rolled, a blade crashing to the ground next to him, then rolled again, avoiding another strike. Krell could hear Kraven yelling in anger as Gerrard leapt forward, stabbing at the man Krell had knocked over.

Abruptly rolling in the other direction, Krell hit the legs of the smuggler chasing him, moving inside his next strike and causing it to miss. He fell on top of Krell, who used his blade to give him a slash as he rolled again, ending up on top of him. Krell drew his sword across his neck, then stood as he writhed on the ground, trying to hold in his blood as he choked to death.

Orca was staggering backward, a massive wound to his leg bleeding profusely. As Krell watched, one of the warriors he faced ran him through. Kraven was also in trouble, though he stood amidst a gruesome pile of bodies. He was bleeding from many cuts across his body. Max was fending off the group attempting to get up the stairs but doing no real harm in return. A bolt of fire streaked from Tristan and slammed into the back of one fighting Kraven, causing him to shriek.

Two from the stairs had come toward Krell and Gerrard, and suddenly there was little time for thought. These smugglers, neither armored, were amateurs and Krell easily killed them both while Gerrard engaged the last of the ones fighting him. An arrow streaked by Krell's head, and he saw an armored warrior discard a bow and draw a sword, then walk across the room toward him.

As if in a dream, Krell saw the warrior look toward the stairs and nod at Cor. Cor nodded back and drew a dagger. All of Cor's protests and attempts to get them to stop searching suddenly made much more sense to Krell. He watched as Cor stepped behind Tristan and stabbed him in the back. With a cry, Tristan fell, pleading for his life. Then the warrior was upon him.

In the first moments, Krell knew he was in trouble. His attacks were parried, and he took several blows where only his armor saved him from harm. The smuggler, a swarthy human, smiled at him and said, "You should never have come here, boy. Time for you to die!"

Krell snarled and said, "ReckNor and his might flow through me! Surrender now, or die!" The warrior laughed and cut at Krell in the opening sequence of a set of attacks Olgar had trained him on — trained him on how to deliver, but not to counter. Krell knew the attacks would simply batter his sword further and further out of position until he reversed, cutting Krell across the neck. Unless he simply missed, Krell was going to die.

His thoughts turned inward, and time seemed to slow down as his thoughts raced. Krell could feel the grace and power of ReckNor within him. It gave him many gifts, as all paladins received, such as stamina and some minor healing of wounds. In the future, Krell knew he would learn to use it for other purposes, to shield him from magic, among other things. But now, *right now*, the grace within him would do nothing to save him.

Krell needed more power.

THERE IS NONE TO BE HAD, KRELL. PITY. I HAD HOPED YOU WERE A SURVIVOR.

"Then give it to me!" Krell yelled. The warrior looked confused, though his strokes did not falter.

POWER IS EARNED, NOT GIVEN.

"Then I will take it!" he raged. Reaching within, Krell took his will and fastened onto the grace of ReckNor, and *pulled.* At first, nothing happened, but then it shattered.

Jagged power flooded into Krell.

WHAT HAVE YOU DONE?

Krell thought that ReckNor would be furious, but his voice was tinged with alarm and… admiration? Pleasure?

Krell had no time to think about it. He took the power within him — just as the last stroke in the pattern knocked his sword from his hand — and gestured, shouting a word of power. A barrier of force appeared over him, deflecting the sword strike that would have cut him in the neck and killed him.

"What?" said the warrior in front of him, off balance as his attack failed.

Krell focused on his need, and a rush of power scraped through him, leaving him feeling raw and bloody within. The power flowed into his hand, and a blade of dark metal formed. It was perfectly sized for his immediate need, and Krell rammed it into the neck of the man in front of him.

The pain within was magnificent, and Krell could feel the shattered grace of ReckNor trying to heal his hurts. As the warrior collapsed, Krell sagged backward, catching himself on the wall and breathing deeply.

He was alive.

And something was terribly wrong within him.

He stared for a moment at the blade of dark metal, but the sound of Kraven yelling, Tristan pleading for his life, and Gerrard shouting his name suddenly brought everything into focus. Time enough to worry about what he had done later.

Krell took the last warrior fighting Gerrard from behind, then rushed to the stairs. Max was nimbly defending himself despite his wounds, standing over Tristan. Krell met Cor's eyes, and Cor flicked his gaze to the warrior bleeding to death on the ground. He looked back at Krell and smiled. He pointed at his eye, then at Krell, and made a motion across his neck. Then he turned and ran up the stairs.

"Ingelnas is down!" one of the smugglers shouted. Kraven and Orca were both too gravely wounded to help Krell.

Krell pointed his dark blade at them. Flickers of blue lightning began to course up and down the edge of the sword. "Surrender or die!" he shouted, then strode forward.

* * *

His companions would survive.

Even Tristan, though Krell was conflicted about that. ReckNor had made it clear that he was to keep Tristan alive, but Krell would have preferred to shove him down a flight of stairs and hear his neck break.

The grace of ReckNor did not flow easily anymore. Krell tried to succor his allies and their wounds, but it was a jagged and unpleasant feeling within him, like shards of glass being dragged over an open wound. Still, what power he could force seemed to work normally, though the scale of the wounds his companions had suffered was substantially greater than anything before.

I AM UNCERTAIN WHAT HAS HAPPENED.

Krell winced. He'd broken the grace and power of ReckNor within himself and seized power from that wreckage. If anything, ReckNor seemed almost pleased at his audacity. He could feel it, this stolen power, writhing like an eel within him. It felt familiar and comforting, but also terrible and painful. The agonizing pleasure of ReckNor's grace bled within him, soothing his wounds even as it scraped at his mind.

He stared at where the dark metal blade had been. After setting it down to aid his companions, it persisted for a minute, then dissipated into a dark mist. Whenever Krell thought about a weapon, he could almost feel it in his hand, and with a focused thought, it materialized. Swords, axes, hammers, daggers, but nothing too large or heavy, and no ranged weapons like a crossbow.

What had he done?

YOU SURVIVED. IN THAT, AT LEAST, I AM PLEASED, KRELL, PALADIN OF RECKNOR.

"Do you think you could talk without yelling?" Krell said.

"I am not yelling, Krell, and when I start yelling at you, you'll know it, you arrogant ass!" yelled Tristan. "We all almost died because you ran off and left me with that traitor on the stairs!"

Orca gave Krell a flat look, then turned back to Tristan. "There are a dozen dead at his hand here today, Tristan. He did more than enough with that dark blade of his." Orca cradled the silver blade, pristine and pure and showing no signs of use, as he sat, exhausted, against one wall, keeping close to their prisoners.

Four of the smugglers had surrendered after Krell cut through their ranks. The dark blade had moved easier and faster in his hand, almost an extension of his will. Krell could feel his arm and shoulder moving the blade, but that almost wasn't relevant. It was his *will* that drove the blade.

NO.* MY *WILL, KRELL.

Krell flinched again and sighed.

Gerrard, his arm in a makeshift sling, his blade in hand, came back in. "Max and I have found something you should see."

Orca looked at Gerrard. "Someone needs to guard the prisoners, and we should look in that treasure room above us."

Kraven waved his arm at them. "I'll stay here with this lot, make sure they do nothing stupid. If they so much as make eye contact, I'll remove all their fingers." He gave a fierce grin at the others, made more menacing since he was still covered with gashes and drenched in blood, and most of it not his. Orca nodded, then started up the stairs. Krell followed Gerrard.

The next chamber, where the armored warriors had entered from, was a makeshift armory of sorts, filled with stacks of weapons. Spears, blades, chain mail armor — there was enough equipment to arm over forty warriors in here.

The room beyond had a door, which opened into a short hall to another door and led to a room piled high with trade goods. Rolls of cloth, barrels, food, and crates labeled with various items were neatly organized on the shelves. Krell had no idea how much worth was in the room, but it had to be significant.

Gerrard gestured. "No taxation marks, you know? They smuggled these goods." Krell looked at him blankly.

Gerrard smiled, gesturing.

"Anything of value gets taxed, right? The Crown always wants a cut of everything, know what I mean?" Gerrard nodded at him encouragingly and Krell nodded back. "So whenever something is made, it gets a mark from the Crown, to show it's been taxed. They do something with those marks using magic, so they can tell if they're fake or not, right? Like Petimus did with the charter?"

Krell shrugged. This was not interesting to him.

Gerrard saw his attention wandering and continued. "Krell, if these things were made somewhere else, and then brought here without being taxed, then you could claim you made them and get the mark, without paying the import tax. Sell it free and clear? It's, like, thousands of gold sovereigns we're talking about."

Krell focused again. "I guess. It doesn't make much sense to me, nor is it interesting. Anything else?"

Tristan snorted from behind Krell. "Thousands of gold sovereigns don't interest you? You're insane!"

Max's voice came to him from an open door at the other end of the room. "Yes, Krell. In here, there is more."

Krell went through the doorway, down a short set of stairs set into the passage. The smell of the sea grew strong in the air, and when Krell turned a corner, he was standing in a natural cavern that had been worked and finished with a flat floor. Near an opening in the opposite wall, he could see Max leaning heavily on the wall. He gestured.

The opening looked down on a sheltered harbor made right into the side of the cliff. It was narrow, with a long dock running the length of one side. An area beyond the dock had piles of equipment and supplies.

Max gestured at a doorway on the wall to Krell's right. "Through there, Krell."

Within, Krell found an office of some sort, filled with papers. It looked like Gerrard and Max had been here already.

"Those two on the top, there, are the important ones we found, Krell." said Gerrard from behind him. "They talk about a ship that's coming back to dock tomorrow night, and about the cargo it's carrying. Cor was with the smugglers, right? Probably keeping watch up top. He got away, but unless he's got magic, there's no way for him to warn the ship. They're likely to sail right into this harbor and dock, right?"

Krell looked down and grinned. Gerrard was grinning back. "You think we should take it?"

Gerrard nodded. "A ship, Krell. A real ship, right? We could go anywhere, do anything! We'd need to hire a crew, you know what I mean? But think about it! Your ReckNor would have to be pleased with that, right?" Gerrard was nodding in encouragement, almost willing Krell to agree.

"I don't know, let me check."

Krell looked inward at the painful fractured grace of ReckNor. It was tinged with outrage, admiration and worry, but as he thought about taking the ship, pleasure and excitement as well. Krell shrugged. Good enough for him.

"Yeah, ReckNor seems on board with the idea. Let's take the prisoners back to Watford and get the town council to help. That fight up there nearly ended us, and I'd just as soon have more swords at our disposal when the ship docks." Krell grinned savagely at Gerrard. "Know what I mean?"

Gerrard laughed, then crashed his fist on Krell's shield in triumph. They started collecting papers.

Chapter Seven

"... and that is why their reckless behavior cannot be tolerated, and they should be arrested at once!" shouted Daylan Plintform.

This was proceeding exactly as Krell had anticipated.

It surprised Captain Gijwolf when Orca and Kraven marched their four tight-lipped prisoners into the stone tower that was used to house the town guard. He listened to their story, then sent runners off to find and convene the council, and escorted Krell and his companions to Amra's house himself.

To say that Daylan Plintform was not pleased was putting it mildly. He had moved from demanding their immediate execution to merely their arrest, but he was clearly outraged at the carnage atop the cliff.

Amra Thort made a calming gesture at him, but he was unimpressed. "They have committed murder, destruction of property, and slavery, all punishable by death! Certainly any claim on the cliff and the structure beneath it should be forfeited at once!"

Krell was pretty certain that Daylan Plintform didn't like him.

"Oh, and I suppose you think this is funny, do you, Krell, so-called paladin of ReckNor?" he screamed.

"Daylan, enough!" shouted Aldrik, who was clearly growing tired of this. "They're heroes, not criminals!"

Daylan turned to Aldrik. "And if they came barging into your home without warning, brandishing weapons, then attacked you and your house staff, you'd still expect them to be called heroes?" he shouted incredulously.

Amra leaned over and whispered something to Captain Gijwolf, while Aldrik yelled back, "My home is not a den of smugglers and thieves hiding behind a magic illusion in order to avoid paying thousands in taxes! There is no comparison here!"

"Enough!" shouted Amra, leaning back on her roots as a deckhand on a fishing vessel. "Enough, Daylan! You've made your case, but the council decides, not you!"

"In that case," said Aldrik, "I vote they receive rewards and spoils as befit their actions! And that we honor the royal proclamation!"

Daylan turned to Amra. "So, then it falls to you. I vote that they be imprisoned, tried by a magistrate from the duke's court, and then hanged until they are dead, their bodies burned and the ashes spread to the sea!"

Amra sighed, then turned to observe the group of them.

"This is outrageous!" shouted Tristan. "This is all Orca and Krell's fault anyway, since it was their plan to charge in and start swinging their swords!"

Kraven turned to Tristan. "Shut your mouth, Tristan, or I'll shut it for you!"

Gerrard was trying very hard to remain small and out of sight, almost disappearing behind Kraven and Orca. Max was sitting calmly, his eyes closed but his posture attentive. Krell envied him that apparent calm.

"To answer your question, Master Plintform," he began, "I would say that those criminals struck first when they shot arrows at us. Since it's obvious you don't like us, I guess I don't have anything else to say to you. Besides, ReckNor controls my fate, not you. If he decides you should kill me because you're angry, then I'll die. Otherwise I'm walking out of here."

Captain Gijwolf put his hand on his brow and shook his head in a despairing fashion. Amra looked surprised.

"You think ReckNor would save you if we — if *I* — decide we should hang you?" she asked.

Krell smiled. "I suspect ReckNor would have a lot to say to me if you were going to do that. But since you're not, I guess it doesn't really matter, does it?"

"Oh, and how do you know I'm not?" she said, her countenance darkening as she glared at Krell.

"Because you would have already, instead of listening to all this yelling."

A silence descended over the room for a minute. Krell could feel Tristan and Orca gazing at him in fury, though Aldrik looked absolutely thrilled at his bravado.

Amra sighed and sat down. "Maybe ReckNor does work to protect you. The matter of the proclamation is held in abeyance for now, to be decided on in the future after officers of the Crown have made a proper assessment. They will assess the goods recovered, and a salvage fee paid to the group of you equivalent to four percent of their assessed worth."

"What?" Daylan exploded in fury. "Full salvage rights on that wealth will be hundreds, if not thousands of coins!"

Amra nodded, almost serenely. "Yes, Daylan, it will, and I will issue no payment until the Crown has properly assessed those goods, and they are sold at fair market value. From those funds we will pay their salvage rights out, and the rest goes straight into the town coffer."

She smiled at the group of them. "You've paid for probably two years of expenses to run this town in one day of effort. Some reward should come from that." She glanced at Daylan, who sat back in his chair, seething in fury. "As should some consequences.

"Your charter is now dissolved. The carrying of arms and armor in town is prohibited for you now, as it is for any normal citizen not under charter. You must also pay a fine of five golden sovereigns for each death, both for costs of recovering and interring the bodies, as well as fines for their reckless behavior."

"That barely diminishes the reward they will receive!" shouted Daylan.

"Daylan, enough. Aldrik and I voted to reward them, and you voted to punish. This is the course through the storm they've set, and they're coming out the other side." Daylan subsided under her glare, and she looked back at the rest of them.

"Now, to the matter of the continued smuggling operations, notably the ship that is arriving shortly. Captain Gijwolf will lead a team to seize it in the name of Watford. Captain, assemble a team as you see fit for this purpose," she said.

Captain Gijwolf smiled. "Very well, Mistress Thort. I will put together a charter for warriors and recruit those who have capably demonstrated their value to the town and are willing to serve further." He turned and grinned at Orca, who let out a laugh.

"This is outrageous!" shouted Daylan as he stormed from the room.

"Ha! Well played, Amra!" said Aldrik, clearly pleased with the outcome.

Amra smiled at Aldrik, a sly look on her face. "Remember, you have much to learn, young Master Kent. I concluded this emergency meeting of the council." She winked at Krell, then rose from the table.

I LIKE THAT ONE.

Krell stood up, and looked at Amra. "Yeah, me too," he said.

Everyone gave him a strange look.

* * *

Captain Gijwolf gathered them all at the guard barracks and wrote out a new charter.

"We limited this one in scope to the raid on the smugglers, and it closes afterwards. Daylan Plintform wouldn't tolerate another open-ended one, so we'll see how things go after this, shall we?"

Krell inspected the document. It outlined that the council of Watford was seeking warriors to work with the town guard to apprehend smugglers, seize their ship and impound any goods recovered. Daylan's handiwork was obvious. There was a simple reward of two hundred gold coins being offered for service, to be split among the survivors. Multiple sections followed, outlining how any weapons, armor, goods, or other equipment, including any water vessels, was to become the property of the town and not subject to seizure or salvage.

"This one is really closed off. He doesn't like us much, huh?" said Krell, reading through the pages and pages of specific exceptions.

"No, he does not. I think he's outraged that the town will pay you a vast sum of money for the recovered salvage at the ruined tower already." Captain Gijwolf looked at all of them. "It's likely you're wealthy as it is — no reason to venture into further danger if coin is what you're after."

Krell snorted.

"Well, I for one know precisely how valuable my time and services are, and am most unwilling to cooperate with this endeavor," said Tristan.

CONVINCE HIM.

"Tristan," began Krell, tentatively, "what if I offered you my share of the gold for this to have you join us?"

Everyone turned to look at Krell.

"Well, now, it isn't about the gold, but that admission that you need me, Krell —that you are as helpless as a babe in the woods without me around to keep the wolves away. *That* is something of value to me! You all heard him! He'll give me his share to take part in this little adventure!" Tristan looked insufferably smug.

"Seriously, Krell, you're insane, you know that, right?" said Kraven.

Krell took the charter, signed it, and slid it over to Tristan. He looked him in the eye and said, "By ReckNor's promise of fury, I will give you my share of this charter if you aid us in these upcoming battles."

Orca shook his head. "More ReckNor nonsense, but whatever. I'll be happy to have Tristan and his magic to aid us."

As everyone signed their name to the charter, Krell looked at Captain Gijwolf. "I have a question," he said.

"What's your question?"

"Cor, the smuggler that escaped. He was up on the ruined tower, waiting for us."

Captain Gijwolf nodded, his face blank.

"My question is, why was he there?"

There was a long pause. Captain Gijwolf nodded, then looked at the rest of them. "Any thoughts? I have my suspicions, but I would learn what you think first."

"He was just a guard, right?" said Tristan. "There to keep people from investigating too closely?"

Orca looked at Krell thoughtfully. "No, that makes no sense. If children were running up there to look at the ghost all the time, they can't have had a permanent guard up there."

"That's what's bothering me about it," said Krell. "If there was a guard up there all the time, then someone would have noticed. If they don't post one all the time, what was Cor doing there?"

"Shit," said Kraven. Krell looked at him.

"They've got spies in town." Kraven looked around, then grinned. "It's what I would do. They need to unload all those smuggled goods, right? That means they know people here in town."

Krell nodded. "We talked about visiting the next day in the Netminder's Friend." He frowned. "They put Cor there to convince us to leave. When that didn't work, to take us from behind."

Orca nodded. "Looks that way. We walked into a trap, it would seem."

Captain Gijwolf nodded to them. "That's my conclusion as well." He leaned back and sighed. Then he gestured, and a guard stepped forward with some markings on the bracers he wore.

"Back to the matter of the ship. This is Corporal Hilam Himmeir, who is in charge of the morning watch here in town. He'll be my second for this operation. Hilam, you're in charge of this group and will lead the strike team that assaults the ship when it docks." Captain Gijwolf looked at them, gesturing. "This is the strike team. I won't have you in the assault, Hilam. You're there to coordinate and command, not fight."

"No problem, Captain. I'm getting too old to want to risk my skin any more than I have to. Pleasure," he said, turning to the group. "Tristan and Gerrard are easy, and you're Krell, and you must be Max then. Which of you is Orca, and which is Kraven?" he asked.

As the others introduced themselves, Gijwolf smiled. "As to other news, the original charter is expired, but a few stragglers still arrive, hoping to sign onto it. If you're interested, there is one who would join you on this, though if they do they'll receive a split of the reward, just as you will."

Krell nodded. "If there is a ship full of smugglers, then I have no issue splitting this reward more ways if it means more swords to join the fight." Orca nodded, as did Gerrard. Tristan looked like he was going to object, but said nothing when Kraven growled his agreement.

Captain Gijwolf nodded, then took the charter, organized the pages into a neat bundle, and stood. "Come with me then, and we'll head over to Marlena's. I'll introduce you to Dorn."

* * *

Krell sat, sipping his wine, while Orca berated him.

The Netminder's Friend was busy that evening, since it was still early and the fishers were swarming in from the afternoon catch. Gerrard was in his element, standing on a chair at one end of the room, recounting the tale of their assault on the haunted tower outside town. The room laughed as he told them of his panicked flight when confronted with the ghost.

"Are you even listening to me?" snarled Orca.

"Not really," said Krell, letting his gaze wander around the room. Tristan sat at a table with three other people, recounting his own version of events, Dorn sitting next to him, listening. Kraven and Max had gone to the temple of ReckNor at Krell's insistence, since their wounds were still severe, and Olgar would do a healing on them.

Of Cor, there was no sign. Just as well, since Krell would probably murder him if he saw him.

Dorn was a surprise to Krell. He was dwarven, armed and armored, but a devout follower of ReckNor. A true priest. He'd arrived in town looking to sign the charter, saying that ReckNor had told him he was needed here, though he didn't know why. Or care, apparently. Dorn seemed to move with the freedom of the tides, without worrying about where that might take him. The other dwarves wanted little to do with him, since they largely viewed him as insane.

Krell liked him immediately.

Orca leaned in toward Krell. "I said you nearly got us all hung today!" he said, his voice filled with menace.

Krell turned his attention back to Orca. "I did not. We were in no danger, despite what Plintform was yelling," said Krell calmly. "If we were, ReckNor would have said something."

"Your mad god isn't what I'm talking about here, Krell! I'm talking about you deliberately antagonizing one of the council members while we were on the hook for crimes that would see us hung!" Orca waved his arms in agitation.

Krell met his eyes, then deliberately took a sip of wine. It was much better than ale, though he supposed he didn't really like it much, either. Still, it seemed a celebratory thing to do. He then deliberately, slowly, set the wine down on the table, keeping his eyes locked on Orca's the entire time.

"We were in no danger," Krell said, with emphasis on each word, "because among the papers that Gerrard and I recovered, I found proof that Daylan Plintform was involved up to his eyeballs with those smugglers. In fact, this may be an enormous source of wealth for him. Which we've choked off."

Orca stared at him for a long moment. Then his face revealed his anger. "You didn't tell us any of this!" he yelled. Others in the common room turned to look at them. Krell waved and smiled, and they turned their attention back to Gerrard. He looked back at Orca.

"Correct. Because you'd have tried to use it to blackmail him, or sink him on the council. This way, we can do as we please, and if he threatens us again, we can *destroy him*. Do you understand?" Krell leaned back slightly, watching Orca.

"No! Why not just cast the cad out of the council and get him arrested then, instead of leaving him in power?" Orca's anger was steadily changing to confusion as Krell watched.

"It's a trick, really. I've met Daylan, seen him, and he's a coward at heart. Replace him with who? I enjoy having a known coward who we can ruin whenever we want in that role. It means we really only need to keep on the right side of Aldrik and Amra, as opposed to all three. Better this way, I would say." Krell couldn't help himself, and a smug smile crossed his face.

"You play a dangerous game, Krell. What's to stop Plintform from finding those records and having them burned, then turning on us?"

Krell's smile widened. "Olgar."

"What?" The last of Orca's anger melted away, leaving only confusion behind.

"I left most of the records, certainly enough to destroy Daylan Plintform and his business dealings, in the care of Olgar up at the temple. If you think, for one minute, that Olgar will tamely sit by and let someone come in and steal from him, then you've never met him before." Krell grinned. "I almost hope Daylan hires some thugs to try. Olgar might accidentally let a few of them survive, and that would ruin him for sure."

Orca looked at him, as if seeing him for the first time. "Where did this devious streak come from? You've always struck me as simple, before this."

"It's about freedom to choose, Orca. I want to work ReckNor's will on the world, to be free to do that. It's going to happen one way or the other. If the council tried to arrest us, I'd have to kill them, and most of the town guard, and then the soldiers that the Crown sends after me. That would be distracting and take a long time. This way, the town is grateful, and I'm still free to carry a weapon around. Most importantly, ReckNor is pleased with this outcome." Krell sipped his wine again.

"As well he should be!" yelled Kraven, sitting down at the table next to Orca, his fist holding three mugs of ale that he slammed down. "I like Olgar, Krell! He was rude and hit me in the face, but I've never felt better than I do right now!" He let out an enormous belch. "Drink!" he shouted, then hoisted a mug.

"Yes!" bellowed Dorn from across the room, who raised his pitcher of ale and drank. The room roared in approval and hoisted their cups as well.

Krell smiled and held his glass up in a toast, then sipped his wine.

It was much better than ale.

* * *

The town guard filled the smuggler cave. It had taken a day to organize, but Captain Gijwolf had pulled nearly all of them to be part of the ambush. Now they lay in wait for the smuggler ship to arrive.

Krell was skeptical. "You really think this will work, Captain?" he asked.

Captain Gijwolf turned to Krell and smiled. "Yes, yes, I do. Those papers that Olgar sent me, with the signals they'd be expecting to let them know everything is safe, are going to be invaluable. This is a pretty small little inlet in the rock, so I don't imagine the ship is going to be overly large. The best plan is a simple plan."

"Won't they suspect something is wrong if nobody is waiting to handle the lines?"

"Maybe, but by then, who cares? They'll have sailed straight into an enclosed harbor. If they want out, either they'll need to wait for the tide to go out to escape, or use oars against the current. Like I said, it's got to be a small boat, because the current would dash anything large to pieces on the rocks. Once they're in, the archers up there rain arrow fire on the deck, and you, me, and the rest rush out and leap aboard." He grinned at Krell.

Hilam shook his head beside them. "You sure you want to be up front, Captain?"

He nodded. "I should thank you for this. You know that, Krell? I don't get a lot of chances to use my sword in actual battle very often. I'm really looking forward to tonight." He clapped Krell on the shoulder and walked back to make sure the guards were positioned properly on the dock, hidden from view until it was too late.

Hilam gave Krell a look. "He's a really good captain, Krell. Not just competent, but a good leader, and a good man. Keep him safe, okay?" Krell gave him a solemn nod, and Hilam smiled, then walked off to ensure everything was set properly among the guards, as if Captain Gijwolf had not just checked with them.

Krell looked around. Kraven was sprawled out, snoring away on a loose pile of ropes. Tristan was sulking, leaning in a corner of some crates, with Gerrard next to him, writing something in the little notebook he carried with him. Orca was talking with the other guards, smiling and laughing, while Max was quietly sitting, probably in meditation.

Krell had spent the day at the temple, helping Olgar with the letters. He kept a special one with him, folded neatly in between the pages of a new blank journal book he had purchased. It specifically implicated Daylan Plintform in the smuggling operation, and while Olgar kept a mountain of evidence at the temple, Krell wanted some evidence for himself.

Krell sympathized with Olgar and his disdain for the Plintform family.

He wandered over to Max and sat down next to him. The metallic rustling of his chain mail armor betrayed his presence, and Max opened his eyes and regarded him.

"Something troubles you, my friend?" he asked.

"No."

A moment passed in silence.

"Yes."

"Tell me and let us see if a disciplined examination of your thoughts will yield a solution."

Krell thought about it, trying to put his thoughts in order. He gestured. "This whole place. There's something wrong with it."

"Wrong how?"

"It's too big, I guess," Krell said. "I mean, look at these rooms. There's space here for literally tons of cargo, but there is no way a ship large enough to carry it will get in here. So why is it so large?"

Max shrugged. "I confess, I know little of commerce and smuggling. Did you voice your concerns to Gerrard?"

"I don't think Gerrard knows as much as he thinks he does about this. When I mentioned it to Kraven and Orca, they didn't care at all. I think Orca is still angry with me. I said nothing to Tristan, as I hear enough of his voice already without inviting more of it. Captain Gijwolf seems so certain that nothing is amiss. It's almost as if he doesn't want to concern himself with anything beyond the immediate ambush we have planned." He shook his head. "Perhaps I'm overreacting."

Max thought for a moment. "Perhaps, perhaps not. One thing is certain. In hours, you will know if you were right to worry, or not."

"That is a very boring attitude," said Krell, grinning.

Max smiled. "As you have said, the teachings of Veceyr are very boring."

Krell laughed.

One of the town guards rushed in from the chambers that held the staircase and the metal tubes that allowed voices to travel from above. "Logruff says they're here, and he's passing the all-clear signals!"

Captain Gijwolf bellowed, "Make ready, men! Give them a chance to surrender, and if they don't, kill 'em all!"

Max stood easily in a single fluid motion. He held out his hand to Krell. "Come, my friend. It is time to learn the truth of your thoughts."

Krell clasped his arm and was hauled to his feet, taking position just behind a rocky outcropping where he'd be among the first to board the vessel.

He kicked Kraven on the way, waking him up.

Chapter Eight

The boat that came into the harbor was exceptionally small. There were six sailors on it and several bundles of cargo.

Beside him, Captain Gijwolf cursed under his breath. "That's a longboat. It was put into the water by a larger ship, which is doubtless anchored offshore. Hieron's whores, we're not going to get all of them!" Krell looked at Max, who smiled tightly at him and nodded.

Krell nudged Captain Gijwolf. "Follow the plan for now," he whispered, "and when we've taken those six, we can take the longboat back out to the ship. And board it."

"That's exceptionally dangerous, you know that, Krell? If they have armaments aboard, or even just archers, you're as dead as these poor fools," he said, gesturing at the longship rowing up to the dock.

"Be ready, Captain. I'll kick it off, as we agreed." Krell gave him a savage smile. "That ship is using ReckNor's domain. I am not afraid!"

Captain Gijwolf looked at him, then down at his armor. "You probably should be, since you're going to be dragged straight to the bottom with all that steel wrapped around you."

"Only if I fall into the water, Captain!" Krell nodded at him, then looked out. It was almost time. He waited a moment longer, and one of the smugglers jumped out of the boat and took a line, then started to tie it to the dock.

"Hello? Where are you at, Ingelnas?" the sailor shouted. Krell concentrated, and a blade of dark metal formed in his hand. Captain Gijwolf stared at it, then at Krell, who nodded.

Krell stood and strode forward, his blade pointed at the sailor on the dock and the rest in the boat.

"Surrender or die!" he yelled, advancing on them.

They started in surprise, drawing their weapons. With a clatter, the archers positioned in the overlook above and behind the boat rose and drew, training their arrows on them, and the rest of his companions came forward, along with Captain Gijwolf.

They looked around, then back at Krell. With an effort of will, Krell made lightning course from the tip of the blade down its length, its bluish-white light illuminating the sword.

As one, the smugglers threw their weapons down and raised their hands in surrender.

"Udar's balls, that's unfair!" shouted Kraven. "I wanted a fight! Now what am I supposed to do?"

* * *

The sea was relatively calm.

Krell sat very still, in the longboat's centerline, while Orca and Kraven rowed, and Hilam manned the tiller. The rest of his companions were watching the sea, staring at the ship in the distance.

Krell didn't know a lot about ships, but this one looked fast. It was long, with two masts and a deck that was raised at the front and the back. He could see a single light on the ship, probably a covered lantern pointing at the shore. Otherwise, they could just make out the shape of it in the moonlight.

ReckNor's grace smelled of happiness, even though the jagged shards of that grace still raked at Krell. Still, Krell could feel the power leaking out of the fractured connection to ReckNor, and he was becoming accustomed to the pain within.

In the darkness, Hilam set his course to swing wide around to the far side of the ship. It was thought that the smugglers would recognize a boat full of strangers and be wary, so best to sneak up from the seaward side. Though if there were any elves, fey-touched, dwarves, orcs, tieflings, gnomes, or countless other creatures that could see in the dark aboard, they'd be spotted, and this would end badly for them.

The prisoners, however, had been given a choice. Imprisonment for information, or death by hanging. Some of them told Captain Gijwolf that there were only humans aboard. Hence the plan.

There was a fresh feeling through the power of ReckNor within Krell, almost one of sadness. Krell wondered what that meant, but didn't want to ask. Captain Gijwolf made it very clear to all of them that voices on a calm sea carried much farther than anyone realized, and any sound would betray their presence.

I AM ALWAYS A LITTLE SAD WHEN MY TRUE FOLLOWERS FIGHT ONE ANOTHER.

Krell focused, remaining still. He didn't want to flinch in surprise and accidentally make a noise. Since Krell only knew three such followers — himself, Olgar, and Dorn — and was unlikely to fight them, he guessed that meant there was a true priest aboard the ship.

YES, HALPAS. SPARE HIM IF YOU CAN.

Krell nodded to himself. So, there was a priest aboard, and if he knew ReckNor, then that priest would have the full might and power that ReckNor could bring to bear. Krell wondered how the others would react to him fighting another priest of his faith. The presence of ReckNor within him bubbled with laughter and affirmation.

Krell sighed. It was never easy.

They had passed the ship and circled around to approach from the seaward side. Hilam held up his hand, his fingers splayed apart. Five minutes until they pulled up to the ship. Two boarding ladders sat in the longboat's bottom. They had metal hooks on the top that were jagged underneath, designed to slip over the rails of the ship and bite into the wood, making them difficult to dislodge.

Krell would be among the last to go up. Him and Dorn. They both wore chain mail armor, which made a lot of noise as the metal shifted. The sound was distinctive and would alert those on deck. Orca and Kraven would go first, both because they moved quietly when they wanted to and could see in the dark. By the time Krell and Dorn climbed aboard, the sound of their armor wouldn't matter anymore.

Hilam held up two fingers. Krell could barely see the ship they were approaching. He felt around for the power within him, ReckNor's power that he had stolen. He thought about the depths, and how it was always dark beneath the waves, or so Olgar had told him. If he was ever going to venture into ReckNor's domain, he'd need to see, and a torch wouldn't work for obvious reasons.

THEN USE THAT POWER, KRELL. LIKE THIS.

A thought plunged into Krell's mind, like a harpoon spearing the whale. Krell took that thought and forced the stolen power to flow around it. His eyes began to pain him, a burning sensation that caused him to grimace. He leaned forward, covering his eyes with his hands while choking back a scream, striving to be silent. Max put his hand on his shoulder, sensing his distress, but not saying anything.

The burning sensation subsided even as Krell felt the longboat come alongside the ship, gently bumping into it. Krell was supposed to raise the ladder, and when he opened his eyes, he could see clearly. Clearly, as if it were bright daylight instead of a deep moonless night. The ship stood out, as did Tristan as he squatted down, grasping one side of the ladder, looking questioningly at him. As soon as he met Krell's gaze, his expression changed to one of surprise. Orca and Max had the other ladder and were already raising it. Krell reached down, and they raised the ladder, sliding it neatly over the side of the railing.

Hilam took Kraven's oar, and did his best to steady the longboat, while Kraven and Orca climbed the ladders. Krell could see them both clearly, with no problem.

Tristan was staring into his eyes, an alarmed look on his face.

The presence of ReckNor within him felt satisfied.

* * *

By the time Krell scaled the ladder, battle was well underway.

Kraven and Orca had split, Kraven heading forward, while Orca headed aft. Krell guessed they had cut down three of the smugglers before they were spotted, and the alarm raised. Orca shouted a war cry as he dashed up the steps onto the raised afterdeck.

Max pulled Krell up and over the railing, then darted aft to join Orca. Gerrard was engaged by a hatch to the rear as sailors tried to come up from below decks. Gerrard had killed one in the doorway, and was menacing the others, impeded by the body of their fellow and shouting in alarm. A bolt of fire flew from Tristan's hand and slammed into one sailor on the aft deck, igniting him. With a shriek, he leapt overboard.

Kraven was alone up at the bow, and Krell rushed forward to join him as Dorn finished clambering over the side. "ReckNor has come for you!" Dorn shouted, then launched himself at the doorway where Gerrard was fighting.

Kraven had cut down two, though he'd taken several wounds by the time Krell arrived at his side. His dark blade took another sailor from behind, and several turned to engage him.

"Just the one longboat, lads. We'll gut them and feed them to ReckNor as tribute!" shouted one sailor, and the others gave a ragged cheer. Krell looked at him, identifying a leader. He had a counter-offer ready.

"Surrender or die!" he shouted, then cut at a sailor whose club was entirely too slow to catch Krell's sword. The blade struck home, and with a thunderous *boom* it propelled the sailor backward, his chest a bloody ruin.

"If you surrender, it's the gallows for you, boys! It's victory or death for all of us!" shouted the leader, who slashed at Krell. Krell stepped back, avoiding that strike while parrying another, deflecting a third with his shield and ducking slightly to avoid a fourth. Kraven roared just behind him, and in that moment where the smuggler leader's eyes turned to Kraven, Krell surged forward.

His shield caught him fully across his chest, and he stumbled backward. Unfortunately for him, his legs hit the railing, and he dropped his sword and fell over the edge. Turning, Krell took a strike that cut through his armor, leaving a line of fire across his back, and gutted another of the sailors as his sword swept through his midsection.

Kraven roared again, and Krell turned to see him impaled on a sword, swinging his axe with a mad look on his face. Suddenly, Krell felt a wave of magic washing over him, and his muscles started to lock in place. With an effort of will, Krell shattered the spell attempting to bind him, cut at another sailor, and turned to look.

Another hatch mid-deck had opened, and three sailors had come out, followed by a human wearing a breastplate. The symbol of ReckNor was draped around his neck, and he looked at Krell in consternation as his magic failed.

Halpas. Krell was satisfied to know where he was. A sword ringing off his helmet, leaving a cut on his brow, brought his attention back to the sailors before him. There were seven left on the forward deck, and as Krell watched, the leader he had knocked over the edge climbed back up. Apparently, he had caught himself on the railing.

Krell leapt forward, his blade wreathed in lightning, and with another thunderous *boom* the smuggler leader died as Krell slashed him through the neck, the power of ReckNor ripping it open and dropping him to the deck. Krell took two strikes to his back as he rushed forward, but his armor held the blades away from his body.

Kraven killed another, but took three more wounds in the meantime. He dropped to one knee, spat out some blood, and roared in fury. His axe swept upward, catching one smuggler in the groin. He collapsed to the deck howling, while three others clubbed and stabbed at him. Krell cut a sailor in front of him down and slammed his shield into another, knocking him to the deck, where he kicked him in the face. Five left.

Krell took a cut to his arm, then with a thought, wreathed his blade in lightning again, slashing another. The blast of thunder dazed his opponent, and Krell followed up with another strike, taking his head from his shoulders.

"I said, surrender or die!" he shouted again.

The three attacking Kraven finally dropped him and joined the last one facing Krell. It looked like Kraven might still be alive, but in dire need of help, as blood seemed to be pooling out from his body rhythmically. Krell couldn't do anything about it at the moment, so he strode forward, cutting one sailor down in exchange for a wound to his leg.

The grace of ReckNor was working within him. Krell could feel it trying to salve his wounds and suddenly realized how paladins kept dying all the time. It was closing his wounds, but far slower than he needed. He was growing light-headed from blood loss. Three left.

The sailor farthest from Krell suddenly shrieked and burst into flame as a bolt of fire slammed into his back. The plight of their friend momentarily distracted the others. Krell seized the advantage and leapt forward, his blade plunging into the chest of the one on his right. Krell deflected a strike with his shield.

His blade became stuck in the body. Krell released it at once, deflecting another blow with his shield. The last sailor saw him weaponless and redoubled his attacks. He died surprised when

Krell reformed the blade in his hand and slashed him through the neck.

The deck was slick with blood. Krell stumbled over to Kraven and placed his hand on one of the worst wounds. He did his best to push ReckNor's grace from his body into Kraven, but had no time to ensure that anything useful had been done.

As Krell watched, they cut Orca down on the aft deck, Max standing over his body. Gerrard and Dorn had lost the door, though there were easily eight dead smugglers over there. The other priest, Halpas, turned back to Krell, and a pillar of silvery fire slammed into the deck near Krell as he rolled sideways away from it. He grinned at the priest, then leapt down to the main deck and charged him.

That there were three smugglers between him and the priest was something he would have to deal with first, though. They attacked, and Krell could feel ReckNor's blessing guiding their strikes against him. Krell shrugged, and with cold efficiency cut them down one after the other, though another blast of silvery fire caught him, burning his skin and dazing his senses.

These smugglers were not nearly as capable as the ones he had fought on the main deck. Krell spied Tristan, lying on the deck bleeding from a wound, though Krell was certain he saw Tristan watching him as he approached. Deception then, and that meant Krell was not alone in this fight.

Though, well, it was Tristan, so who could say.

Halpas faced him, drawing a longsword. "You cannot defeat me, boy, for ReckNor guides my hand and gives me strength!"

Krell laughed. "Don't worry, Halpas. ReckNor has told me to take you alive if I can. Surrender now, or, well, I guess I'll beat you unconscious!"

"How do you know my name?" Halpas said in alarm, cutting at Krell, who blocked the strike with his shield.

"ReckNor told me." Krell cut Halpas on the leg, then slammed his shield into him, knocking him backward. Krell advanced and

Halpas gestured, calling the silvery fire again. Krell dodged to his right, keeping his shield between him and Halpas.

"Olgar taught me that one, Halpas. You'll need better magic than that to lay me low!" Krell cut again, catching Halpas in the arm, and then slammed his helmet forward. With a wet snap, Krell heard Halpas's nose break. "And in the future, wear a helmet into battle!" he mocked.

Halpas snarled and cut at Krell with his sword, scoring a hit across his shoulder above the shield. Krell hammered his sword down, catching Halpas in the arm. There was a sharp *crack*, and his blade fell from useless fingers. Krell slammed the pommel of his sword into his face and he fell backward onto the deck.

As Halpas pushed himself up, he said, "ReckNor is invincible! You will never defeat —"

Krell kicked him in the face, his armored boot snapping his head backward, thumping it into the deck. Halpas collapsed.

Krell looked at him, then looked upward. "Tell him to stay down and he might yet live."

He charged toward Max, rushing up the stairs. Gerrard was down, but Dorn was standing over him, his shield and rapier flashing back and forth as he cut at the few remaining near him.

Max looked gravely wounded, and Orca appeared to be bleeding out. With a gesture, a figure on the back of the ship sent a conjured arrow made of green energy slamming into Max. There was a bubbling hiss, and Max collapsed — his ribs visible in the bloody mess that was his chest.

Among the many dead atop the deck, Krell saw the spellcaster at the back, two others who looked unremarkable, and one who he guessed must be the captain. He had an elaborate set of sashes made of fine cloth and several gold chains about his neck. While wounded, he stood bravely, presenting himself to Krell. His sword, covered in what Krell guessed was Orca's blood, looked to be of fine quality.

They all turned to face Krell.

Krell glanced at Max, obviously dead, and turned his gaze to the captain. "Surrender or die!" he shouted at them. His dark blade became wreathed in lightning.

"Remember, lads, it's the gallows if you quit!" shouted the captain, who stalked forward, his sword held in a low guard position.

"Aye, Captain!" shouted the two other sailors, while the spellcaster began muttering something and gesturing behind him.

Krell shrugged, saying, "Fine, easier this way!" He stepped forward, and he and the captain traded sword strikes. Krell took a wound from the captain as he cut at one of the other sailors, causing him to hobble backward, bleeding. The spellcaster finished whatever he was doing, and suddenly Krell felt a wave of magic attempting to freeze his muscles in place. With an effort of will, the magic shattered, leaving him free to act.

The other sailor cut at Krell, and he deflected the strike with his shield and parried the attack by the captain. Krell wreathed his blade in lightning and slashed at the captain's leg where he already had a wound, cutting him again. The lightning coursed through him, knocking him backward a bit, but he seemed to shrug off most of the harm.

The spellcaster gestured, and bolts of magical force flung from his hands, streaking toward Krell. He dropped his blade and gestured, and a shield of magical force sprung up around him. The magical darts slammed into it with no effect; at the same time, it deflected a strike from the smuggler who had moved behind him.

Krell grinned at the spellcaster and recreated a blade of dark steel in his hand, with the one that clattered to the deck vanishing in a cloud of mist. He cut at the sailor, catching him under his arm in the ribs, and he dropped, blood pouring from his mouth as he gasped for air.

Krell stepped on his throat as he strode forward, crushing it, and caught the last of the smugglers in the neck with an extended thrust. He used his shield to deflect the captain's attack and then turned to face him.

"Your crew is dead, and your ship is lost. Even now, forces from Watford are rowing out to reinforce us. There is no escape for either of you. Surrender, and you may yet live. Otherwise, die here!" said Krell.

"I've not lost yet, and while you've killed many of my crew, you're running out of your own strength too, *boy*. I'm not about to surrender to an arrogant young pup like you!" The spellcaster in the back gestured, and a ray of blue energy leapt from his hands. Krell raised his shield, intercepting it, and a rime of frost enveloped it.

"So be it!" Krell yelled as he surged forward. While Krell had talked, the grace of ReckNor had been working and his strength had been trickling back. Krell slammed his shield into the captain, knocking him backward. His wounded leg gave out, and he lost his sword as he collapsed. Without waiting, Krell kicked the blade overboard, then cut at him. He rolled away from Krell and grasped a blade from one of the dead smugglers littering the deck, then rose to face Krell.

Krell was not there. He had taken two quick steps, crashing into the spellcaster at the aft rail where he gutted him with his sword. As he collapsed to his knees, Krell met the captain's eyes. He stepped behind the spellcaster, then grabbed him by the hair, put his blade across his throat and slashed, cutting him to his spine. Krell threw him forward onto the deck, where a pool of blood began spreading from his twitching form.

The captain looked at Krell advancing toward him, and his face fell.

"Who are you?" he asked, wondering if they were among his last words.

"I am Krell, paladin of ReckNor!"

"I'll remember that. That offer of surrender still good?"

Krell gave him a flat look.

"No."

With that, Krell summoned lightning about his blade and struck at the captain's sword, knocking it aside. Krell followed it up with his shield, shoving the captain into the ship's wheel. The captain moved to parry Krell's next strike, but the elaborate sashes he wore caught on the wheel, and his arm didn't come around in time.

Krell took his head from his shoulders.

With a contented sigh, Krell closed his eyes and breathed in. The scent of blood, but also of the sea, flooded his senses. The sound of combat still rang out on the lower deck. Krell looked forward, seeing Dorn engaged with three smugglers. Possibly the last three aboard. Max was dead. Kraven was down, possibly dead. Orca was down, possibly dead. Gerrard was on the deck, bleeding, just behind Dorn. Tristan was lying next to the rail, not moving.

Krell stepped up onto the railing and leapt from the top deck toward the three remaining smugglers still fighting Dorn. He landed on one, knocking him down but falling to the deck himself. He stabbed upward, catching the second one in the gut, then rolled atop the one he knocked down. Krell lost his grip on his sword and grabbed the smuggler's sword arm while his shield pinned him to the deck. They struggled for a moment over who would gain control of the sword, the smuggler with his grip, or Krell with his leverage.

Then Dorn stabbed the sailor in the neck, and Krell knew the fight was over.

* * *

Max was dead, and there was a question of whether Orca or Kraven would live.

Gerrard lay on the deck, breathing heavily, trying not to move as Tristan attempted to bandage his wounds. Dorn was on the aft deck, trying to save Orca's life.

Krell was suddenly so exhausted he could barely move. He sat, leaning against the doorway that was choked with dead smugglers, his eyes closed, concentrating on his breathing.

It reminded him of Max.

OTHERS MAY FALL, KRELL. I CHOSE YOU BECAUSE YOU ARE A SURVIVOR.

"Oh, shut up for now," Krell said irritably.

The memory of Max lying dead on the deck above him made mockery of the victory they had won. Krell had liked Max.

Dorn settled down on the deck next to him. "Well, Orca will live. ReckNor let me heal him. He's up and talking. Probably angry. Kraven will live too, though I think that's your doing." Dorn ran his fingers through his dark beard. They came away bloody.

"I need a bath," he said, with a wry grin on his face.

Krell looked at himself. His armor dripped blood whenever he moved. His shield was dented and splintered and would need to be replaced soon. His helmet had a jagged dent he barely remembered receiving, and he was covered in cuts. Even as Dorn watched, the cut on his brow continued to knit itself closed. Very slowly.

"ReckNor's salty balls, that's a useful bit of power right there!" said Dorn in admiration. "I can only call forth healing by using up the power he gives me each day. Run out of power, and no more healing. You, though, you seem to just pour it out non-stop."

Krell grinned tiredly. "It probably looks a lot better than it feels," he said.

Dorn laughed, and then groaned, clutching at his side. "Do you think there are more of them below decks?"

"I don't know. I expect we'll have to go find out here shortly." Krell waved his arm vaguely at the forward hatches. "Nobody came out of the door over there, only out of this one. Whatever is through that door, it probably isn't crew."

Dorn sighed, and Krell noticed a trickle of blood running onto the deck. He reached over and put his hand on Dorn's shoulder.

ReckNor's grace flowed through him, smoothly this time, without the jagged pain, and Dorn drew in a sharp breath.

"Oh, that's much better! Thanks for that, Krell," he said, smiling.

Krell leaned back against the door frame and closed his eyes. "Not me, Dorn. ReckNor. It is to him you owe thanks. I'm just here to do what he wants." Krell opened one eye and glanced over at him. "Besides, he clearly likes you for some reason or other," he said, smiling.

DWARVES RARELY HEAR MY CALL TO SERVE.

"Would you stop yelling?" Krell said.

"Uh, what?" said Dorn. Krell shook his head and waved his hand.

"Never mind. ReckNor sounds like crashing thunder and the roar of a breaking wave all at once whenever he talks to me." Krell leaned his head back and closed his eyes again.

"Must be nice, having him talk directly to you," said Dorn thoughtfully.

"I feel like there isn't enough room in my head for myself whenever he speaks. Not sure he can talk without yelling."

Dorn laughed, then grunted in surprise. "Hey, you healed me!" He lifted his arm and bent at the waist, then shot a grin at Krell.

"Yeah, it was easier with you than it is with others. Probably because you worship ReckNor, and that lets the healing flow like water."

Krell heard Orca came down the steps. It sounded like he was limping slightly as he stood over Krell.

Without opening his eyes, Krell said, "What?"

"What are you doing?"

"I am guarding the passageway to below decks," said Krell, still sitting with his eyes closed. "I am also resting, because I am tired."

"We have to clear the rest of the ship."

"I know," said Krell, "but I also know that I prefer resting here a moment longer, recovering my strength, before we venture below." Krell waved vaguely at the forward section of the ship. "Whatever is in there has not come out, and unless it does, I want to wait until Kraven can come with us."

Orca let out a grunt, then squatted down next to Krell.

"You're making decisions now, is that it?" he said with quiet menace.

Krell nodded. "Looks that way, Orca. I take orders from one source, ReckNor himself. At the moment, I want to rest here, feeling the grace of ReckNor flow back into me, filling me with his majesty and might." Krell opened his eyes and looked at Orca. "That means I'm staying here for the next ten minutes. After that, I'm going to open that door over there and see what is inside. Probably the same as here."

Krell gestured at the open doorway he was sitting against. On the other side lay a wooden hallway with a staircase leading downward and four additional doors, all of which were shut.

"Though I might start here." Krell pointed at the door farthest aft. "Seem to remember the captain always takes the aft cabin, does he not?"

Orca nodded, then stood. "The wind blows the ship forward, which means only the smell of the ocean from behind. None of the ship smells. I'm going to find Kraven."

He paused, then looked at the unconscious form of Halpas lying on the deck. "What do we do with him?"

"He's a true priest of ReckNor," said Krell. "I think I'll threaten him a bit, then take his armor and throw him overboard. If ReckNor wants him to live, then he'll swim to shore." Krell shrugged. "If not, then ReckNor will call him to service in the afterlife."

Orca nodded, then walked off.

Krell leaned back against the door frame. The grace of ReckNor continued to trickle in.

It hurt the entire time, as that jagged and broken power saturated his being.

Chapter Nine

Kraven was unhappy.

"So you're saying you left me lying on the deck, unconscious, while you went off and had all the fun?"

Krell shook his head. Leave it to Kraven to suggest a fight that nearly saw all of them dead was a type of fun. He gave him a grin.

"Kraven, my man, you had already killed, like, ten, you know?" said Gerrard, working at the door in front of them. Krell had healed him as much as he could and Gerrard was in high spirits as a result. "You were probably due for a nap!"

"How many did Orca or Krell kill then, huh?" he snarled. "I'm going to fall behind!"

Krell looked at him and snorted. "Let's say I only killed one and move on, shall we?"

Orca shook his head. "More than a dozen, Krell. Hard to say for sure, but definitely more than a dozen."

Kraven growled.

They were standing before the doorway to the forward section, which was locked shut. Gerrard looked up from the door. "I think it's barred on the other side."

Krell nodded, then let his weapon dissipate into mist. He then conjured a long, thin blade, which he slid between the door and the frame, and lifted. He could feel it when he hit the bottom of the bar on the other side, and as he lifted it up further, he felt it slide. With a jerk upward, he heard the bar clatter to the floor.

"Krell, my man, that is a handy bit of magic!" Gerrard looked at the blade enviously. "I could use magic like that." Krell let the thin blade go and conjured the longsword he was most familiar with. He gestured at the door.

Gerrard nodded and opened it. As Krell guessed, there was a short hallway, with a set of stairs descending downward. Five doors lined this hallway, two on each side with one facing them at the end.

"What is that smell?" Kraven asked. "I've never smelled anything like that before." A strange smell had greeted them when the door opened. Something musty that smelled vaguely of rotting vegetation in the sea. It tugged at Krell's memory. He'd smelled this before.

Krell shrugged and Orca stepped forward, first peering down the stairs, then moving to the nearest door on his left. "Can't hear anything from belowdecks. Looks like the whole crew came up." Orca stopped, staring at the door in front of him.

"Huh. They barred this one from the outside."

"Prisoners, do you think? Slaves? We should rescue them, to be seen as heroes!" said Tristan. Tristan had been unconscious near the railing for the end of the fight, apparently from a wound to his head. Before that, he had slain no fewer than six of the smugglers with blasts of fire. Happily, he hadn't torched the ship while they were still on it.

Orca said, "Only one way to find out." He reached down and lifted the bar, casting it aside, and opened the door.

The scent grew stronger, whatever it was. The room was dark beyond.

"Some sort of guest suite, I think, and… uh… what is that?" Orca began backing away from the door.

A strange guttural sound, mixed with hisses, came from the room as Orca retreated outside with the others. The creature that stepped out was tall, easily over seven feet. It had skin that was mottled in shades of blue, and long limbs that ended in jagged claws and talons. Its face was bestial and its mouth was enormous, reminding Krell of a shark. It glared at them, then repeated its hissing and croaking noises.

"I think it's trying to talk to us," said Kraven.

"Well, of course it is, you dullard," said Tristan, earning himself a menacing look from Kraven.

The creature gestured, then paused. It sniffed visibly at the air, and as Krell watched, its eyes dilated and saliva ran from its jaws as it began breathing heavily.

Then it leapt forward, claws extended, snarling.

There was no warning, but Orca, closest to it, was not caught off guard. His sword came around, deflecting the claws, but the creature plowed into him and bit at his face. Orca jerked his head back, costing him his balance, and he fell to the deck.

Kraven roared and swung his axe, even as Krell stepped forward with his blade, Gerrard close behind him. The creature caught Kraven's axe by the haft in one hand, and bit him on the shoulder. It jerked its body, causing its teeth to savage Kraven. He let out a howl of anger and pain.

Krell slashed it across what passed for its back, but bony spines sticking out caught his blade, fouling his strike. Without looking, the beast flung its other arm out, catching Krell in the face and knocking him away. Gerrard, right behind him, upset his balance and Krell fell overtop of him, causing them to crash onto the deck.

Tristan uttered some words of power as Dorn struck with his blade, leaving a wound that bled green. A bolt of fire slammed into the creature, causing it to hiss in pain, but also to release its jaws from Kraven.

Its arms were longer than they looked, and it raked Tristan with its claws, causing him to cry out and stumble backward, a cut on his face bleeding into his eyes.

Krell rolled off of Gerrard and they both stood. The creature slashed at Dorn with its free hand, while wrenching the axe from Kraven's grasp and trying to bite him at the same time. Krell and Gerrard rushed forward next to Dorn, and both cut at the creature. The arm fouled Krell's attack, batting his blade aside. That left Gerrard free, and he struck true, his blade sliding into its torso.

The beast shoved Kraven away, then hurled the axe at Gerrard. It was a poor throw, but the axe was large and the haft caught Gerrard, knocking him down. The beast bit at Krell and slashed at him with its free hand.

Krell blocked with his shield, and it came apart, shattering into splinters of wood. The hand closed around his forearm and yanked him forward. Krell instinctively ducked his head, and the teeth slammed into the helmet instead of his face.

"ReckNor's tits! Just die, you stupid beast!" shouted Dorn, who cut it on the arm. Gerrard jerked his sword free and stabbed it again.

Its grip was like iron. Krell tried to break its hold on him, but the pressure on his neck was enormous. He could feel himself being pressed downward, and instead of falling, he dropped to one knee.

Then the pressure was gone. Krell stood up and stepped back, his ruined shield dragging at his arm. Orca had beheaded the beast, and it had fallen still, a putrid green blood pumping from its neck to cover the deck.

"ReckNor be merciful… what was that?" Krell asked, shaken. The stench of its breath was still strong on him, like rotten fish. He yanked the helmet from his head, breathing deeply. Tristan was lying on the deck, his hands covered in his own blood and pressed to his face. Krell stepped over.

"Let go, Tristan. Let me see," he said.

Tristan made no noises, which surprised Krell. Part of him was ashamed that he thought Tristan should be mewling like a sick dog from the pain, but mostly he was impressed. The claw had caught Tristan on his forehead and skipped right over his eye, cutting open his cheek below.

"Well, this is what you said, so do it," said Krell, looking up. He placed his hand on Tristan's face and tried to marshal ReckNor's grace.

IT IS. YOU WILL NEED HIM.

Krell flinched even as he felt the grace of ReckNor flow from his hands, soothing yet jagged, and the wound knitted shut. Tristan grimaced in pain, but again said nothing.

As ReckNor's grace healed Tristan, Krell found it was almost bubbling with laughter. He got the sense that it was enough, and when he pulled his hand away from Tristan's face, a vivid scar remained.

"ReckNor must like you, Tristan," Krell said, smiling down at him. "That scar is going to earn you a lot of free drinks!"

Tristan looked at him in horror, then frantically dug through his pack and pulled out a polished steel mirror.

"Oh bloody hell, Krell, you stupid ass! How could you do this to me?"

Krell looked upward and sighed.

* * *

The ship was full of cargo.

Krell looked around the lower deck, seeing it strung with bunk beds above dozens of crates, boxes, barrels, and bundles of goods: carpet, foodstuffs, spices, rare woods, musical instruments, paintings, and countless other objects.

And weapons. Vast quantities of weapons.

Krell listened at a locked door, trying to hear over the sound of Kraven roughly prying open a crate. He heard nothing inside. Shrugging, Krell stood back and kicked the door next to the handle. It refused to budge. He kicked it again.

"Step aside, Krell. Let me show you how it's done!" said Kraven, as he shoved Krell to one side.

When he kicked the door, the frame shattered, as did the door around the lock, which clattered to the floor. Kraven gave him a toothy smile and looked into the room beyond.

Krell saw additional crates and boxes, and a tarp hanging from the ceiling.

It gave a crackling, purring noise that sounded almost questioning.

Kraven had his axe in hand almost instantly and cautiously entered the room.

"There's no danger here, Kraven. Relax," said Krell. ReckNor's grace was tinged with an almost happy curiosity that made little sense to Krell.

"Then what in Udar's name made that noise?" he growled menacingly.

"Whatever is under the tarp, I suppose. Watch my back." Krell strode past Kraven and took the covering off the object.

Beneath was a metal cage made of blackened iron. It had thick bars set closely together, each easily as big around as two of Krell's fingers. Within the cage was what looked like a dragon, squeezed into a prison almost too small to contain it.

"Dragon!" roared Kraven, whose axe swung over Krell's head, slamming into the cage and knocking it from the ceiling. It crashed into the corner of the room. Krell tackled Kraven as he tried to sweep forward to strike it again.

"Kraven, no! It's a prisoner!" Kraven looked back at Krell, then at the dragon in the cage, who was staring at Kraven with ferocious intent.

"Look at it, Krell, it's going to attack me!" he shouted.

Krell looked. "No, Kraven, it's scared of you. Look at it! It can barely turn around in that cage, let alone attack you. The poor thing is probably hurt as well." Krell glared at Kraven. "So put that axe away and start using your head!"

Kraven shoved Krell off him, and he fell backward, landing hard and striking his head on the wooden wall of the room.

Kraven glared back, then growled something under his breath and left the room, shooting a distrustful gaze at the dragon as he left.

Krell shook his head to clear his thoughts and then crawled over to the cage.

"Hey there, little one. I'm going to set you free, okay?" The dragon in the cage stared at Krell, though he couldn't make any sense of what its thoughts might be.

Now that Krell was closer, and the dragon was still, he could clearly see it. Not much larger than a house cat, the creature had a red, scaly body, with purple-hued wings. Its jaws featured prominent teeth, and two black horns topped its head with a ridge of black spikes running the length of its body along its spine. It had a large, bulbous tail, with a protruding sharp spike on the end.

Krell had never seen anything so magnificent before.

Its wing was also clearly broken, whether before or during the crash of Kraven's axe, Krell could not tell. The dragon focused on him with a disturbing intensity.

"I'm going to pick the cage up and take you up to the sky, okay? From there, I'm going to open the cage and let you go. I'm going to try to heal your wing, but I'll need to touch you to do that." Krell was speaking in a calm and soothing voice, trying to convince the dragon to avoid using its claws or teeth on him.

It let out a small hiss, but was otherwise quiet.

Krell took the cage in his hands. The dragon moved to put as much distance between itself and his hands as possible, which wasn't much. As Krell walked out of the room, Kraven glared at him.

"This is a stupid idea, Krell. That thing is dangerous."

Krell glanced at him. Kraven was completely on guard, his axe in hand. Krell carefully walked up the steps to the hallway, and from there out onto the deck itself. He set the cage down, listening to Kraven coming up behind him. Krell also heard the bump of the boat returning and saw the ladders they had left in place shift.

"Okay, I'm going to open the cage now," he said to the dragon.

The cage itself was latched shut and seemed to be locked somehow. Krell looked at the mechanism, which looked simple enough for him to open. He conjured a small knife in his hand, and the dragon hissed in alarm. Krell slid it into the lock and pressed upward, and with a *click,* it disengaged. Holding the knife in place, Krell opened the latch.

The dragon was very still for a moment, then tentatively it stepped out of the cage, and stood next to Krell, looking at him.

"Oh my, that's a dragon!" said Tristan. "Quick, Krell, grab it! It's worth thousands of coins!" The dragon visibly tensed.

"No, I'm not going to do that. I'm going to touch you now, so don't bite me, okay?" Krell said, never taking his eyes off the dragon standing before him. He could hear Tristan coming closer and turned to look at him. Tristan stopped when he met Krell's gaze.

"That is treasure, Krell, and you're letting it go! I'm going to make sure that Captain Gijwolf hears about this!"

"Hears about what? It's so dark I can barely see!" said the captain, as he climbed up over the side.

Krell looked back at the dragon and reached out a finger, gently pressing it against its head. Krell reached in and asked ReckNor's grace to flow out of his fingertip, and this time, there was no jagged pain with the act. Krell wished he understood why it hurt sometimes and not others.

The little dragon hissed at Krell, but he was unsure whether it was a hostile noise. Krell could see the wing bones align and fuse properly. As soon as they did, it flapped hard, and with a gust of wind it was in the sky, heading toward the shore.

Krell watched it go until he lost sight of it, while Tristan explained to Captain Gijwolf what he had done.

* * *

Captain Gijwolf and Krell stood over Halpas.

"He's a priest, is he?"

Krell nodded. "A true priest. I felt the power of ReckNor being used against me."

Captain Gijwolf looked at Krell, and then back down at Halpas. "How does ReckNor feel about that, do you think?"

Krell gave him a tight smile. "I think ReckNor is all about the freedom to choose. A less well understood part of my faith is that the consequences of that choice are yours to own. Here, Halpas tried to fight his own god by striking at a paladin of his god. That was a bad choice."

Captain Gijwolf snorted. "See, this is why I'm grateful I never settled on one god over the other. That would confuse me."

"Well, I'm sure it is for gods who have tons of rules, like Hieron. For ReckNor, it's pretty simple. I did what I wanted, he did what he wanted, and one of us was better." Krell nudged him with his foot. "I'm going to threaten him a bunch, then set him free."

"He's committed a crime, Krell."

"Mostly, he just defended himself and made some terrible choices about who he spends time with. I think he's got more of ReckNor's power than Dorn does, but don't tell Dorn that. He's the sort that would take that poorly, I think."

Krell reached down, and with the captain's help, removed the armored breastplate that Halpas was wearing. Krell looked at it and set it aside. He then roughly searched him, looking for weapons, finding two daggers tucked away in secret sheaths, one on his arm and another in his boots. Krell also took his boots, just to be sure, along with his belt pouch and two rings.

Captain Gijwolf tied his hands with a leather cord, while Krell examined the items he'd taken. The rings looked cheap, as did the boots. The bag also looked plain, but when Krell reached in, his arm went in all the way to the elbow before Krell realized it was magical.

Captain Gijwolf let out a whistle. "A bag of holding, unless I miss my guess. Feel anything in there?"

Krell nodded, then began pulling items out of the bag, stacking them on the deck. A bundle of rope, several sets of clothing, a pair of boots, a set of lock picks, and dozens of other items all came out of the bag. Krell was delighted and tied the bag to his belt.

The captain nodded. "I'll pretend I didn't see that. Wake him."

Krell leaned down and rested a hand on Halpas's shoulder. ReckNor's grace flowed through him, jagged and painful.

Halpas stirred and opened his eyes. He focused on Krell first, looming over him, then looked up at Captain Gijwolf. He tried to move his arms, then grimaced and slumped down.

"Well, it appears I am scuppered."

"Indeed," said Krell. "You're in a great deal of trouble here, Halpas. Want a way out of it?" Krell wondered if he would be smart enough to take the opportunity or not. He hoped he would, but for reasons he didn't really understand. ReckNor's grace within him was quiet, giving him no hint.

"I suppose this is one of those *or else* sort of offers. Yes, I'll take what you give me," he said, a wry smile crossing his features. "State your terms, and I pre-emptively accept."

Captain Gijwolf snorted, and Krell smiled. "Okay. I'm going to cut you loose. Literally. I'm going to free your hands, then toss you overboard. You think you can swim to shore?"

Halpas craned his head around, looking through the railing at the distant shore, then back at Krell. "I'm not sure."

Krell shrugged. "Here's the thing, Halpas. You're a true follower of ReckNor, so I don't want to kill you out of hand. Nor does the captain of the Watford town guard here mind if I cut you loose. Having said that, if either of us ever sees you again, you're probably going to regret that. Swim and pray to ReckNor and live. Or die here." Krell called forth an elongated dagger in his hand. He looked down at Halpas, a stern look on his face.

"Ah, well then, cut my bonds, and I'll be on my way... and I'll pray to ReckNor that our paths never cross again!" Halpas looked at the distant shore and grimaced.

Captain Gijwolf hauled him to his feet, spun him around, and undid the leather cord binding his wrists. Halpas rubbed his hands over them, restoring circulation.

"You going to jump, or want us to push?" asked the captain.

Halpas looked at him, then back at Krell. "It's strange, but I'm glad to have met you, paladin of ReckNor. What's your name?"

"Krell."

"Well, Krell, paladin of ReckNor, I'll remember and do my best to avoid you. Assuming I don't drown, that is." Halpas gave them a weak smile, then climbed onto the railing and leapt feet first into the water below. Krell looked over the side. After a moment, Halpas surfaced, then started swimming toward shore at a steady pace.

"You think he's going to make it, Krell?"

Krell looked within at the grace of ReckNor. It lay quiet within him, but there was a thread of pleasure in those jagged edges he could feel.

"He's a priest of ReckNor, in ReckNor's domain. Of course he's going to make it."

* * *

One downside to the deaths of all the smugglers was that nobody was left alive who knew how to sail the ship.

Orca turned out to have quite a bit of knowledge, and would be a capable member of a crew on a vessel that they had just seized, except that he would be one of many. Krell and the others, along with Captain Gijwolf and several guards, did their best to obey his orders.

Getting the ship in motion proved easy enough.

Stopping was proving to be a great deal more challenging.

As Orca steered the ship into the harbor at Watford, he began shouting orders. Krell was aloft, having removed his armor to allow climbing to be easier.

"Trim the sails!" shouted Orca from below.

"What does that even mean?" yelled Krell.

"It means we need less sail!" shouted Orca.

Krell looked around. There were dozens and dozens of ropes attached to the mast he clung to, and he hadn't the faintest idea how to trim the sails.

"How do I do that?" he yelled back. Orca swore.

Captain Gijwolf, from the bow, shouted, "I think we're going too fast!"

Krell looked out over the harbor. Sure enough, several fishing vessels were scattering out of the way. The official town of Watford harbor pilot boat was approaching, but it too was veering off, several people aboard waving their arms angrily at them. Krell thought about what it meant that all those other boats were getting out of their way as quick as they could.

It was not a pleasant conclusion.

"Stop daydreaming and get the sails down!" shouted Orca,

They had waited until sunrise, so that everyone could see clearly what they were doing. The wind was brisk and blowing westward, which was convenient since they didn't need to adjust the angle of the sails. Krell wasn't certain what that meant, but Orca made it sound like that was easier. Orca had shown them how to untie ropes to lower the sails, and Krell was up top trying to remember how to do that. He thought the sails needed to be pulled up, but he didn't see how that could be done.

"Krell! Pull the sails in or I'll have Tristan burn them!" shouted Orca, a bit of panic edging his voice. "Do it now or we're going to wreck!"

Krell inhaled deeply and drew his will together, conjuring a dagger of dark metal. He crawled out along the wooden beam that held up the sail, cutting every rope he could find. The sail sagged, then collapsed.

Of course, Krell only went to one side, which meant that the beam he was on pivoted as the weight changed. The ship also changed direction as the wind began pushing it unevenly. Krell moved as quickly as he could, trying not to listen to Orca and Captain Gijwolf yelling at one another.

Krell reached the end of the wooden beam, and with a tearing sound it tore, falling to the deck below, leaving only a wisp of sail behind. Krell didn't know any better, so he continued out, cutting the rest of the sail free.

The ship lurched as Orca spun the wheel, and it slowed quickly — just not quickly enough. With a *boom*, the bow crashed against one of the stone piers, although Orca had turned the ship so that they hit on an angle, deflecting the ship instead of wrecking it. Nearly everyone aboard was knocked from their feet as the ship abruptly changed direction and slowed.

It was too much for Krell and he lost his already tenuous grip. Fortunately, he had climbed far out, so when he fell, he hit the water instead of the deck. The force was stunning, and he needed a moment to remember why he should be swimming.

The grace of ReckNor within him bubbled with laughter.

When Krell surfaced, he could see the ship had come to a stop, angled poorly and almost wedged in between two stone piers. Kraven was on the deck looking in his direction and pointed at him when he surfaced.

Krell swam for the dock. Not a great start to the day.

* * *

"… and that concludes my report," said Captain Gijwolf, who then stepped aside and sat down in the chair closest to him.

Amra looked at Daylan and Aldrik and raised an eyebrow.

"Well, it would seem that the ship was recovered, if not intact, then mostly intact. Certainly, the goods aboard, none of which bear a proper royal taxation mark, are forfeit to the Crown, as is the ship itself. The magistrate should be here tomorrow to examine everything and assess its worth. In the meantime, are there questions for those who held charter to seize the vessel?"

Daylan cleared his throat and rose. "Captain, you said that there was a beast aboard the ship?"

Captain Gijwolf nodded. "I saw its body. Orca, Kraven, and the rest fought it and may be able to give a better account than I."

"And where is the body of this beast now?" Daylan asked.

"Still aboard the ship, I would hope, unless it's been moved for some reason. I gave orders it should not, at least until the council heard and decided what should be done." Captain Gijwolf looked somewhat unhappy at delivering this news.

"I see. Well, perhaps an expert could be brought in to examine it, so we can learn more about what it… what is going on out there?" Daylan turned as a loud clatter came from the front hall of Amra's house.

Then the doors to the dining room, which served double duty as the city council chambers, were thrust open. Nathanial backpedaled in, propelled by Olgar.

"I said, are you daft or deaf? I need to speak to the council! Ah, there you are, you worthless sacks of shit. Hey there, Daylan. Still an annoying little jackass?" Olgar looked around, and his eyes fastened on Captain Gijwolf.

"I request permission to address the council!" he bellowed.

Krell wondered if he was drunk or not. It was rare in the mornings, but not unheard of.

"What business do you have for the council, Olgar? We're in the middle of something here," Captain Gijwolf said, in a tone of voice somewhere between anger and resignation at the interruption.

"It's related, you codfish! Settle your bones and shut your mouth!" Olgar turned, looking around. "Ah, good, Krell. Bring your chair over here for me."

Krell stood at once, grabbed his chair, and moved it in front of the council so Olgar could sit. Daylan cleared his throat. "It is customary for those addressing the council to stand, Olgar," he said in a severe tone of voice.

Olgar sat down in the chair with a heavy sigh and rubbed at his knee where the peg attached. "Yeah, and it's customary for people to have two full legs, so I guess there's boatloads of disappointment to go around, isn't there, you festering boil?"

Aldrik looked positively scandalized. "This is not the proper way to address the council!" he shouted.

Amra, Krell noted, was trying to contain her laughter.

"Not seen you up at the temple since your parents died, young Aldrik. ReckNor not important enough for you to make the trip once in a while?" Olgar furrowed his brow. "Bad things often happen to people who spurn the gods. Unless you've found another and not told anyone?"

Aldrik sputtered, unable to form a thought, and Amra interrupted.

"You have something of importance for us, Olgar? You don't make the trip into town lightly, nor do you like talking to the council, so it must be important."

"Ah, see, this one at least has some sense!" shouted Olgar. "Well, I went to that pretty ship that the lads crashed in the harbor and looked at the beastie myself. No doubt in my mind. It's a sea devil, sure as I'm a priest of ReckNor."

"Impossible," said Daylan, rising to his feet. "The smugglers would never have had one aboard!"

Olgar gave him a menacing grin. "Careful there, Plintform. You come close to admitting things you don't want admitted, and *perilously* close to calling me a liar." As Olgar talked, his eyes lightened and small blue arcs of lightning began forming about them. "You'd not appreciate getting ReckNor angry at you. Nobody in this town would."

Amra laughed. "Stop the theatrics, Olgar. We both know you love this place and care for many of the people here as if they were your own children. Stop trying to scare Daylan with empty threats."

Olgar looked at her, then smiled. "Empty? Hmm, we'll have to see about that should he ever really make me angry." He turned to Krell and Orca. "You fought the beast, right?" he asked.

Krell nodded and Orca said, "We did, and it was terribly strong. It threw both Kraven and me around like we weighed nothing."

"It attacked you?"

"Yes," said Krell, "though we had to open the door to the room it had been given. It tried to talk to us, but we couldn't understand it. I thought it might be a prisoner, but they would have restrained it if it were. It smelled familiar, somehow."

"It tried to *talk* to you?" Olgar asked, emphasizing his words.

Krell nodded, at the same time Kraven and Orca did as well. Tristan looked bored, almost like he was not paying attention, and Gerrard was trying to make himself disappear by hiding behind Kraven.

"Smelled familiar?" asked Amra.

Krell nodded at her. "I know I've smelled something like it before. But I can't..." Krell's voice trailed off. He turned to look at Olgar.

"On the cliff. I smelled it on the cliff, before the ghouls attacked."

"Did you, now? That... makes a lot of sense to me."

"It does?" said Orca,

"Describe to me the moments right before it attacked," said Olgar, changing the subject abruptly.

"It was talking at us, though we couldn't understand it. Then it stopped, and after a moment it charged, swinging its claws and biting with that enormous jaw. I thought for sure Krell was dead when it bit him in the head, but his helmet saved him," said Orca.

"Any more details?" said Olgar. "No matter how small you might think it is, it matters. More than you know."

Krell thought. "Just before it attacked, it sniffed the air a bit. Then its eyes widened, like where the black part gets bigger? Then it leapt at us."

"Were any of you wounded at the time, or covered in blood?"

"Olgar, all of us were wounded, and the deck was running red with blood, some of it ours," said Kraven.

"Ah, I knew it. As soon as it smelled the blood, it lost all reason, becoming a murderous beast. Like I said, my dear council, a sea devil. I'm certain of it." Olgar paused, absently groping at his waist where he often kept a flask. "Though, I'll be candid. I've not seen one that large before."

Amra looked troubled, as did Daylan. Aldrik, for the most part, just looked confused. "What is a sea devil?"

Olgar looked at Amra, who gestured at him to continue. He cleared his throat.

"Sea devils are a race of creatures that live beneath the waves. Properly, they're called the sahuagin, but most people call them sea devils. They're shark-like, often found with the beasts in the waves, since they have a gift for controlling them. Like sharks, they're predators, living only to feed. They're kept in check by many of the things that live in the deep, but mostly by themselves. They don't hesitate to eat one another, you see."

Olgar reached out and took Amra's cup from in front of her. He raised it in a salute before drinking it down and replacing the cup.

"Where was I? Oh yeah, they're hunters. They come looking for prey, and take it whenever they can. Usually ships at sea. They sneak aboard in the dead of night, and kill as many as they can, as quickly and quietly as they can. More than one crew has woken from a good night's slumber to find the deck covered in blood and the night watch gone."

Olgar looked thoughtful.

"Better that you go down fighting. Being captured is often worse than death. They have these mask things, some sort of jellyfish, that they slap on your face. You can breathe underwater, but you can't see, and the thing poisons you the whole time. Eventually, the poison kills you, but it rots you out on the inside something awful first. Apparently this is a delicacy among their kind."

Olgar looked at Aldrik. "You're too young to remember, but there was a town between us and the ducal palace, long may he reign, called Swamp Hold, around ten miles up the coast. One night the sea devils came ashore, and when they left, only the stone tower that the guard used was standing. Everything else had been burned, and all the people were gone. By the bloodstains found, many had died, but there were no bodies. The beasts made off with all of them."

Orca interrupted. "I've heard stories about these things, that they're barely more than sharks themselves, cunning, but not capable of real plans. How is this possible?"

Olgar nodded at him. "Those stories are true, to a point. Like sharks, a sea devil starts small, but grows larger over time. Ever larger. The older it is, the bigger it is. Well, as they get bigger, they get smarter too, whether through experience or some other means. Eventually one gets so big he takes over a whole school of these things. Us surface dwellers call those underkings, though who knows what words they use themselves for such a leader."

Olgar looked at the council sternly. "Unless I miss my guess, such a one has grown into power, and now they're coming again. Explains the attack on the temple. If Krell smelled one, then those ghouls were being commanded to attack. Probably trying to kill me."

Amra looked pale. "It's been thirty years, I had hoped they were gone." Daylan almost looked like he was going to cry.

Aldrik looked around, alarmed at the reactions he was seeing from Amra and Daylan. "So, how do you know these things are coming?"

Olgar snorted, and Amra put her head in her hands.

There was a long pause, then Daylan answered. "Because, Aldrik, aside from the fact that it looks like they tried to kill Olgar, we've lost five fishing boats in the last month. No storms to account for it. None of the boats were so poorly maintained they would have sunk on their own." He snorted. "As if they'd sink! Boats are made of wood. Nothing washed up on shore. They were just… gone."

Daylan turned to look at Olgar. "Now we know why."

Olgar nodded to him. "Aye, lad, we do. Like a bloody wave, they're coming to crash into Watford. What worries me more is that you found one with the smugglers."

Amra raised her head, looking at Olgar. "Why?"

"Well, it was big and smart enough to talk. Not a prisoner, but they were wise enough to keep it away from the crew. And the ship's hold was filled with weapons, as was that cave. Weapons for who?" Olgar paused a moment to let them think.

Captain Gijwolf got it first. "You can't be serious."

Olgar grimaced. "Find me another explanation."

"You think these smugglers were going to *arm* the sea devils?"

"That there is the bone hook stuck in my throat, Elias. In the past, when they waged war, they used bone and stone weapons. Sharp and dangerous, sure, but they tend to shatter on steel. Now, if that underking is clever and has done this before, he'd know that. Which might mean he'd be keen to get his vile clawed hands on some steel weapons."

"Impossible!" shouted Daylan. "No fool would deal with the sea devils and expect to live!"

Krell looked at Olgar. “Never underestimate what fools will do for coin, right, Olgar?”

Olgar looked at Krell and smiled. “Exactly that, my boy. Exactly that.” He turned, looking back at the council, his smile disappearing. “You’ve a big problem, and sometime in the next year it’s coming ashore. When it does, if you’re not ready, then everyone in Watford will die.”

Chapter Ten

The magistrate arrived with quite a lot of fanfare.

Krell was standing in the courtyard of the guard post, breathing heavily. He'd just finished a training session with several of the town guard who finished their morning watch. Hilam was happy to allow him to participate in the drill alongside the others, but Krell found it frustrating more than anything else. He kept bumping into others and falling out of formation.

As Hilam dismissed the guards and was speaking with Captain Gijwolf, there was a shout from the harbor. Captain Gijwolf climbed onto the observation platform and looked out to sea.

Krell could see the tops of the masts of a massive ship that was sailing into Watford's small harbor. Three masts, at least, with multiple sails on each one. Even without seeing the body of the ship, Krell thought it might be able to take the one they had captured as cargo within it.

Captain Gijwolf walked up. "Well then, looks like the magistrate is here. Come with me Krell, let's go meet him properly at the dock. If it's still Callodan Koramir, he's sensible enough and doesn't like delays." He ordered four of the guards nearby to accompany them and sent three others into town to search for the council members. The remaining four formed up around Hilam.

Krell looked down at his armor. He had spent most of last night and this morning cleaning it, and any dust and sweat he'd worked into it today would hopefully go unnoticed.

Captain Gijwolf led Hilam, Krell, and the four other guards down to the docks. Krell couldn't help but gawk at the enormous vessel. It practically filled the harbor, and glowing runes on the side of the ship spoke to the magical protections woven into it.

"Oi, that sure is a beaut, eh, Captain?" said one of the guards.

"It sure is, Jarmins, it sure is. I bet it handles like a barn in a storm, though."

The one named Jarmins whistled. "Still, though, that would be a treat, to serve on a ship like that!"

The captain turned to him and smiled. "All you'd need to do is join His Majesty's levies, figure out how to avoid the infantry and get into the marines, then be good enough to be posted there. Still interested, Jarmins?"

"You saying I can't do it?"

"No, lad, I'm saying I'll write you a letter of recommendation today. But just so you know, it might not work out. Think about it and let me know." He looked back over at the ship. "Ah, they're lowering a boat."

Krell could see a longboat being lowered down the side of the ship, with almost a dozen people aboard. Once the boat was in the water, the rowers pushed away from the side of the ship and made swift progress toward the dock, where Captain Gijwolf and his party waited.

They expertly maneuvered the boat against the dock, and two of the armed soldiers within climbed nimbly out of the boat, tying it off. One reached down to help a spare man in plain clothing, but adorned with a sash of rich material, in stepping from the boat up onto the dock. He looked at the group.

"Captain Gijwolf?" he said.

The captain stepped forward and bowed. "I am, my lord. We have met before, and it pleases me to welcome you to Watford.

I have assembled these guards to act as honorable escort for you and have sent runners to locate the council and assemble them as soon as your ship was spotted. The council meets in the dining room of Councilor Amra Thort's residence, and we may proceed there at once."

"Excellent, Captain. Excellent," said the magistrate. "I apologize, but I have no memory of you. You were party to the events I am here to adjudicate?"

"I was, my lord, as were several of these guards here, and this young man, who was under charter from the town. This is Krell, a paladin of ReckNor. Krell, this is Lord Magistrate Callodan Koramir, appointed by His Grace the Lord Duke Mavram Hudderly, long may he reign, a loyal steward of His Majesty King Fideon the Second." Krell looked at the man and gave a clumsy bow.

"A paladin of ReckNor, you say? How intriguing! ReckNor so rarely calls paladins that you shall stand out in my memory, young Krell. Come, tell me your version of events as we walk to the council." At once, Callodan began walking off, his guards forming around him and leaving Krell no choice but to walk with him.

* * *

Callodan Koramir sat at the head of the table, reading in silence.

Krell stood in the corner of Amra's dining room. He was growing very familiar with this room and the hallway beyond. Amra's butler, Godun CloudSurge, was a friendly sort, and Krell was beginning to like him. He sipped at the water, flavored with pieces of fruit. Krell quite liked this flavored water.

His companions stood restlessly next to him. Callodan had heard their tales, each individually, and now read through the copious papers recovered from the smugglers' vessel. News of the sea devils had changed the tone of his visit entirely, and he had displaced Amra from her residence after announcing he planned to stay for several days.

Amra, Daylan, and Aldrik sat at the other end of the table, notes and ledgers ready in front of them. Callodan would sometimes look up and ask a question, and they promptly searched their notes and papers for the relevant details. He then went back to reading.

The strangest addition to the table was Petimus Smithforge, who sat among the councilors at the end of the table. He sat patiently, almost unmoving. He reminded Krell of a stone.

Krell was terribly bored and growing hungry. He had been standing here for hours. His stomach rumbled.

"Where is Olgar? I would like to speak with him," Callodan said, looking up from the page he was reading. Krell could tell from this distance that it was written in Olgar's strong and blocky hand.

Amra cleared her throat. "With apologies, my lord, he sent word back with the guards sent to retrieve him that if your august presence wanted to see him, then you'd need to walk up to the temple to do so." She looked uncomfortable delivering this message.

Callodan smiled. "Yes, that sounds like Olgar. I mean, it sounds like how Olgar would behave. Someone has doubtless softened the message from the words he would have used. Well, it has been some time and, based on the noise in here, I suspect some of you are hungry. Let us refresh ourselves, then I will conclude some of the business that was the purpose of my trip. This news," he said, tapping Olgar's letter, "requires additional inspection, but my other duties cannot be neglected."

At once, Godun stepped forward. "My lord, refreshments have been prepared and can be brought at once." Callodan looked at Amra and smiled.

"My compliments, Amra, on your well-run household. Please Godun, let us eat." Callodan began organizing the papers into neat piles, setting them aside, as Godun left, then promptly returned, pushing a small cart piled high with meat, cheese, bread, and fruit. From the bottom, he fetched plates and set them before those seated at the table. From the center of the cart he opened a panel, from which he removed warmed pastries. He set the food in the center of the table, then proceeded to serve.

Amra looked at Krell and the others. "You're free to go, but return here in half a glass if you would. Try not to get drunk," she said severely, looking at Kraven and Orca in particular. Krell's face fell and Amra noticed. She gave him a smile.

"I don't have food enough to feed all of you here, Krell, but Marlena certainly does!"

Krell nodded and departed with the others, heading to the Netminder's Friend.

* * *

Krell was blushing.

Kraven and Orca had been teasing him as they returned to Amra's dining room. Marlena had, after serving them food, sat next to Krell. In Krell's mind, it was uncomfortably close.

"I can't believe you don't realize she wants to sleep with you!" Kraven roared with laughter.

"Why? I'm nobody special!" said Krell, in a tone of voice that to his ear sounded disturbingly like Tristan's voice.

Orca just laughed, and Gerrard giggled next to him.

"Hey Krell, you know, you're awesome and all, but you have no clue how people work, do you?" Gerrard said, laughing. "You're a handsome man — don't let these others convince you otherwise — and you're a proven warrior. *And* you're going to be rich. No question in my mind why she would want to sleep with you. It's a question of why she *wouldn't*, you know what I mean?"

Krell blushed harder. Kraven roared with laughter again.

"Maybe you should get a scar across your face to get people to leave you alone," said Tristan bitterly.

Krell felt a trickle of anger. "ReckNor healed you, Tristan. The scar will fade, and I would wager that you can use it to convince women to bed you easily enough. It's just red for now." He looked Tristan in the eye. "It makes you look like a warrior."

GOOD, KRELL. GOOD.

"Oh, shut up!" said Krell, looking at the sky. Kraven laughed again, while Orca gave him a strange look.

They all quieted a bit as they walked back in. Godun met them at the door and escorted them to the dining room.

"My lord. Orca, Kraven, Krell, Gerrard, Dorn and Tristan have returned."

"Excellent, come in, brave warriors. Come in! It is time to discuss your rewards." Callodan had several pieces of paper resting in front of him, the rest in a neat pile.

Callodan looked them over, and then picked up a piece of paper. "To the matter of the ended charter for aid to the dwarven mining encampment, you have received your compensation, correct?"

Krell and the others nodded, and Orca said, "Correct, my lord."

Callodan set that paper aside, then selected the next one. "As part of that charter, you had spied the ruins of the Tower of Burchard, located atop the cliffs near Watford, correct?"

"That is correct, my lord."

Callodan turned to Amra, Daylan, and Aldrik. "You, as the town council, overtly suggested that they investigate the tower. Is this correct?"

Daylan frowned, shaking his head, as Amra said, "Yes, my lord."

"Why?"

Amra looked surprised at the question. "We thought nothing of it, My Lord. Children have ventured up to the tower for many years to gaze upon the ghost that haunted the ruins. That they were successful, beyond any expectation, is a surprise to us here."

"I see." Callodan steepled his fingers before him and rested his chin on his fingertips. "You then promised them salvage rights to the contents of the smugglers' den they uncovered?"

Amra nodded. "We did, my lord, though that decision was not unanimous."

"Yet that was the decision of the council, was it not?" Aldrik started to look anxious about this line of questioning. Amra looked resigned.

"It was, my lord."

"I wonder if that was wise," said Callodan flatly. He let the words hang in the air for a moment. "Well, the damage has been done, and I see no reason to undo it." Daylan looked unhappy. "I will uphold the salvage for the contents of the smugglers' den. The material goods are listed here." Callodan turned to look at Krell and his companions. "Do you need an account of these goods, or is the word of the royal magistrate sufficient for you?"

Krell sensed the danger, and almost as one, they all spoke.

"It is, my lord."

"That's fine, my lord."

"No need for an accounting, my lord."

Callodan nodded. "Very well. I have assessed the contents of the goods as worth twenty-seven thousand, four hundred and sixty golden sovereigns. Salvage rights account for four percent of the value of these goods, which comes to one thousand ninety-eight golden sovereigns and four silver ducats. I assess fines and fees for body recovery and the acts of violence outside the scope of the charter at ninety golden sovereigns. Since Dorn was not party to the original charter, he receives no share of this. Split among the five survivors, you are each awarded two hundred and one golden sovereigns, six silver ducats, and eight copper pennies." Callodan noted the numbers on the paper, then handed it to one of his guards, who promptly walked over to Amra and handed it to her.

"Review this, please, Amra, on behalf of the council. If you find it in order, then all survivors who originally signed the charter should sign this document." Amra read through it, then looked up.

"It appears to be correct in all respects, my lord."

"Very well." He turned to the rest of them. "Sign, please, and my thanks on behalf of the Crown and King Fideon for your service and recovery of smuggled goods, and putting an end to their ongoing activities."

Krell waited until everyone else had signed, then scrawled his name at the bottom: *Krell, paladin of ReckNor.* Looking at his signature made him wonder who else would see this paper, and know that ReckNor had called a paladin.

Callodan retrieved the document, setting it into a pile next to him.

"Now, as to the matter of the subsequent charter to apprehend the sailing vessel. They have not compensated you for that charter at this time, correct?" Callodan eyed the group of them again.

"That is correct, my lord," said Orca. Krell couldn't remember ever seeing him so polite before.

"Very well, then. I hold this charter successfully fulfilled. The payment of two hundred golden sovereigns to be distributed at once among the survivors." He looked up. "Less five golden sovereigns to pay for recovery and proper treatment of the remains of your companion who did not survive."

Krell nodded, at the same time Tristan opened his mouth to argue, then decided against it.

Amra pulled a small lock box from the floor under the table and opened it. Within, she pulled out six leather pouches that made that distinctive noise coins made when they clashed against one another. She opened each pouch and removed a single golden coin from each one. She set five of them aside, then put the remaining gold coin into the lockbox, after which she retrieved a fistful of silver ducats and put two in each pouch, then retied them. She then handed the pouches to Orca, who turned and handed them to everyone else.

As soon as Krell got his, he turned to Tristan, handing him the pouch. "As promised, Tristan." He looked insufferably smug as he took the pouch, giving Krell a condescending smile.

Callodan raised an eyebrow at seeing that. Then he set the paper aside. "The charter is completed and dissolved."

"I will offer surety for their weapons, my lord," said Captain Gijwolf, "until such time as they can be properly stowed."

"Entirely acceptable, Captain. Now, as to the matter of the goods recovered aboard the ship, and the ship itself, they are now possessions of the Crown and King Fideon. They have been assessed and their value calculated, which is not a matter of importance. I remand the vessel to the authority of the Watford town council."

Gerrard frowned, and Krell put his hand on his shoulder in consolation.

Callodan continued. "The council is to supply crew for the vessel, to use in service of the royal proclamation I shall address shortly. This matter is closed." Callodan set the papers aside, then retrieved the next one from the stack.

"As to the previous royal proclamation issued over two centuries ago by Magistrate Theodric Saghaza, the terms were clear. Removal of the infesting spirits and establishment of a residence. No residence has been built. Is this correct?"

Krell nodded as Amra and Daylan both said, "That is correct, my lord." They glared at one another.

"Very well then. The property is held by royal decree and remanded to the town council of Watford until one of the survivors of the dwarven mining camp charter, who announce now in my presence their intention to take residence atop the cliff outside of town, does indeed establish a residence deemed livable by the town council." Callodan turned to the group of them, who shifted their feet.

"Orca of no surname, do you intend to establish a residence atop the cliff, becoming a resident of Watford and becoming responsible for all taxes and duties that such residency implies?"

"No, my lord. I have no interest in a broken tower outside of town."

"Very well. Strike Orca's name from the eligible candidates. Kraven Atka, do you intend to establish a residence atop the cliff? Same question," said Callodan, looking at Kraven, who was standing next to Orca.

"No."

After a pause, Callodan furrowed his brow, then turned to Amra. "Very well. Strike Kraven's name from the eligible candidates. Dorn Ironbrow of Talcon, you were not a signatory of the original charter, correct?"

"That's correct, my lord Magistrate."

Callodan nodded. "Krell, paladin of ReckNor, do you intend to establish a residence? Same question."

Krell looked at Callodan. "I think yes, I do. My lord," said Krell, belatedly.

"Very well. Gerrard Riverhopper, same question."

"Uh, no thanks, Your Lordship."

Callodan nodded. "Very well. Strike Gerrard's name from the eligible candidates. Tristan of no surname, same question."

"Yes, I believe I will, my lord," said Tristan, with a sly look at Krell.

Krell rolled his eyes and sighed.

* * *

"This brings us to the matter of the dwarves," said Callodan.

Petimus stirred and looked back at him. "Has something changed with the commission issued by your duke?" Petimus looked concerned. "We've invested substantially in time, money and lives for the encampment's construction."

Callodan smiled, making a calming gesture. "No, Master Smithforge, nothing is amiss. Our lord duke, long may he reign, would wish to expand the scope of your involvement, based solely on the reports here of the sahuagin menace."

Callodan looked at the town council. "Our gracious duke may overrule me, long may he reign, but in the interim, I would extend your commission to include the town of Watford itself. Specifically, the construction of stone buildings and defenses to prepare for an attack from the sea."

Petimus let out a breath, smiling in relief. "Ah, that's good then. Would you seek to provide compensation via funds, or a grant of citizenship?"

"Citizenship, if it pleases you to accept. The township of Watford's borders would be increased to include the coast up to and for several miles past the dwarven mining encampment. Any dwarves there may remain citizens of Talcon, as I am sure they would regardless of promises made to the Crown of Baltorc, but may also become citizens of Watford. They would be subject to all the duties and responsibilities that entails, which they are mostly already burdened by, but would gain the benefits of formal protection from the Crown, including but not limited to the protection of the guard, based here in Watford."

"Of course," Callodan continued, "this would also involve the expansion of the town council, and I would ask that you, Petimus Smithforge, join the council and become involved in the affairs of the town. A plot of land, graciously sold to the Crown by Daylan Plintform, has been set aside for the creation of a mining headquarters here in Watford, which will double as a residence for you and any additional dwarves you deem necessary to bring with you."

Petimus leaned back in his chair, thinking. A minute passed, and Krell grew anxious, as did Aldrik Kent.

"Master Smithforge? Are you going to answer?" Aldrik asked cautiously.

"I will, young Master Kent, when I have my thoughts in order. Abide a moment longer, please."

Callodan smiled at Aldrik. "Fear not, Aldrik. Dwarves are rarely prone to rash or hasty decisions. Their long lives lead them to think of the long-term consequences, and their idea of long-term can often be longer than you or I will be alive. He'll need some time to think. Best to wait patiently. If it consoles you, elves are far worse."

Aldrik muttered something that sounded suspiciously like "I hate waiting" under his breath.

Krell grew bored waiting. Dorn seemed almost as irritated at the delay as the rest of them. Finally, after several long minutes of silence, Petimus stirred.

"We, as citizens, would be subject to forming a militia in the event of war, regardless of where the enemies of Baltorc lay, correct?" Petimus asked, looking at Callodan.

"Correct, Master Smithforge."

"Any who did not wish to fight could renounce their citizenship, immediately returning to Talcon, could they not?"

"That is also correct, for unless I miss my guess, your king would uphold them as citizens and allow them back into the dwarfholme, though those that did so would not be welcome for some time in Baltorc afterwards." Callodan looked calm about the questions.

"Yes, for a human generation or two, more than likely. Very well, I accept."

Daylan and Amra both looked like they swallowed something foul.

"Excellent. This pleases me greatly, Master Smithforge. I will draw up formal articles of citizenship for you and any number of additional copies for dwarves you wish to include. We would like construction to begin quickly, though I am no expert and bow to your wisdom in this process." Callodan turned to Amra and Daylan.

"I also understand your concern, that now the council can become deadlocked. Should this happen with any frequency, I will appoint a royal representative to join the council, providing a fifth vote to break ties. If it never becomes an issue, then I will not have to take that action." Krell thought that sounded vaguely like a threat. Daylan certainly seemed to feel that it was, if the look on his face was any indication.

Callodan turned next to Captain Gijwolf. "Captain, you are to begin recruiting additional guards at once, such that you can ably patrol the road from here to the dwarven mining encampment and beyond. Our lord duke, long may he reign, through his representative, which is me, understands that this will necessitate the increase of funding to the town. His Grace commands you, through his representative, which is me, to begin preparations at once to both defend the town, and in the event we can locate the strongholds of the sea devils, to assault and drive them out."

Callodan held his hand up as Captain Gijwolf made ready to speak. "Additional magical support from His Majesty King Fideon and the royal mages will be made available if such fortresses can be located. We are well aware they will likely be under the waves."

"Very well, my lord, I will begin at once." Captain Gijwolf looked at Krell and the companions, nodded and rose. "May I be dismissed, to begin the work set for me?"

"Of course, Captain. Of course. Be on your way, we will speak again tomorrow."

Callodan turned back to the group of them.

"Now, you are able warriors, having already faced the smugglers in open battle. More than that, you have confronted and successfully slain a sahuagin, a large example of its kind, I am told, based on these reports. This concerns His Grace, long may he reign, and through him His Majesty King Fideon. Baltorc has a long and proud tradition of defending its people."

Callodan stared at them.

"To that end, there must be information gathered, to learn details about this latest threat posed by the sahuagin and any allies they have mustered. I would create a royal charter for you, to investigate these claims."

Daylan stood at once. "My lord, no, I beg you! We can, as part of the council, provide a charter! To issue a royal charter would be most dangerous for this group!"

Callodan raised an eyebrow and gestured with his hand. "Please, explain."

Daylan looked at the group of them, and then at Amra and Aldrik. Aldrik's face was tight with anger, but Amra had a studiously blank expression. Krell did not understand what was happening.

"We issued a charter to aid the dwarves, and on the back of that charter, they uncovered the smugglers and their base of operations. They then assaulted this operation and put nearly everyone to the sword! With the power of a royal charter, I fear you would find them in all corners of the kingdom, in other duchies, causing mischief and chaos, leaving a trail of dead bodies behind them. Dead bodies that will lead back to His Grace, long may he reign, and a decision to grant a royal charter!" Daylan looked genuinely concerned about this prospect.

"I guess I do not understand," said Krell. "Why is a royal charter so different?"

Amra looked at him. "The charter we created allowed you to carry arms and wear armor, to use magic, generally for a limited purpose. A *royal* charter, on the other hand, is far more broad, and usually only requires you to act in defense of the Crown. With a royal charter that was vague, you could enter a town, declare the council corrupt, and execute them. You would have the legal authority to do that, and only one of the dukes could gainsay that and revoke the charter. Or King Fideon himself, long may he reign!"

She shook her head and turned to Callodan. "I must agree with Daylan, my lord. These warriors have served bravely and well, but they are young, and prone to rash action as all young people are. To entrust them with a royal charter is, perhaps, unwise at this time."

"I see," said Callodan. He looked at Aldrik. "I can see your thoughts on your sleeve, young Aldrik. What do you think, for the record?" He seemed almost amused.

"They're heroes, and have acted bravely in defense of the town so far!" he said, with a rising passion in his voice. "We should grant them such an honor! My lord." Aldrik blushed and slumped in his chair.

"And you, Master Smithforge, what do you say?"

"I agree with Mistress Thort and Master Plintform here, my lord. They have served the dwarven mining encampment well, and have done other deeds worthy of song, but a royal charter may be more power than a young hand would know how to wield wisely." Petimus glanced at Dorn meaningfully.

"Very well, I will bow to the wisdom of the council in this. As it is, it is becoming late, and I would still speak with Olgar. Let us resume tomorrow morning after breaking fast." Callodan looked at Krell. "I understand you often stay at the temple. Perhaps you would be so kind as to walk there with me?"

Krell looked around. Orca was fuming. Kraven and Gerrard seemed calm, and Tristan looked completely expressionless. Dorn merely looked upset at Petimus and was glaring at him.

He turned back to Callodan. "Of course, my lord. It would be my pleasure."

Chapter Eleven

"Are you honest, Krell?"

The question surprised Krell. They had been walking for two minutes in silence. Krell thought it would be a quiet walk.

"Yes," he said, looking at Callodan, then back to the path leading up to the temple.

"Hmm. Both an honest man and a liar would answer the same way," said Callodan, not making eye contact. Krell glanced at the guards who were following behind them, easily able to overhear the conversation.

"Oh, I trust them. More than I trust the council of this shitty little town." Krell snapped his gaze to Callodan. He smiled without looking at him.

"Don't get me wrong, it's a nice enough town, but unremarkable, save perhaps for the extent of the smuggling operations and how thoroughly they dealt with it. Daylan is, of course, guilty. You know this, though, don't you?" Callodan was watching the trail, ensuring he didn't lose his footing.

Krell thought about how best to answer, then gave up. Whatever game he was playing was beyond him.

"Yes, I know he's guilty. I found evidence that proves it."

Callodan glanced at him, then back to the path.

"Yet you did not come forward with this evidence... as an honest man might. Tell me why." It was not a question, but an order. Krell had heard the tone from Olgar often enough to recognize it.

"If he tries to stab me or my companions in the back, it is good to know I can ruin him in response." Krell shrugged. "I'd rather the snake I know about in front of me where I can see it, than a snake I haven't seen. At least when I get bit, I'll be able to see it coming and strike back."

"I see," said Callodan. They walked in silence for another minute.

"Why are you here, Krell?"

The question was so unexpected that Krell nearly tripped over his own feet. He looked at Callodan, who'd stopped walking and was meeting his gaze levelly.

"What do you mean, why am I here?"

"You're a paladin, are you not?"

"I am."

"Then, assuming that is true, why *are you here?*" Callodan asked, an edge in his voice.

"I don't know what you want to hear. I was lost at sea as a child and washed ashore on a deserted island. Around six months ago, I was rescued and the ship that saved me brought me here. Olgar was at the docks, which is totally unusual for him, and he took me into service at the temple. He spent a lot of time building my strength, teaching me about the gods, and then in the last three months, drilling me with weapons." Krell met Callodan's eyes, knowing a contest of wills was occurring, but not understanding why.

"Honestly, I don't have anywhere else to go."

They stood there, staring at one another. A minute passed, then Callodan smiled.

"Well, let me be frank with you then, Krell, *paladin* of ReckNor," Callodan said, a strange emphasis on the word *paladin* that Krell found distasteful and vaguely alarming. "Paladins go where their god tells them to. Hieron adores paladins and seems to call one every month. But all gods call paladins. Paladins, no matter which god they serve, disrupt and destroy plans. Paladins have caused more wars than you would probably guess." He shook his head. "Paladins are nothing but trouble. I'm half tempted to have Gurk murder you here and now on the road. It would probably be easier for everyone if I did."

Krell smiled. "It wouldn't be easier for me."

Callodan looked away from him, toward the temple. "You don't seem nervous about the fact that I am openly discussing whether to have my guard murder you."

Krell chuckled. "Not remotely, my lord, for two reasons. First, if you had decided to have me killed by these trained warriors of yours here, you'd have done it. You certainly wouldn't discuss it with me. Second, ReckNor would have a thing or two to say about that, and you came in a ship." Krell shrugged. "You'd probably be lost at sea on the way back to Heaford."

Callodan laughed, a genuine laugh from the belly. It was not the reaction Krell was expecting.

"Oh, Krell, you are going to ruin everything, aren't you? We have this tentative peace with the Black Theocracy, and even some trade. That's all about to explode in our face, isn't it?" Callodan wiped tears of laughter from his eyes.

"Not to sound like the uneducated peasant that I really am, but what are you talking about? What is the Black Theocracy? I've heard that mentioned in council before, but I don't know what it means." Krell looked at Callodan, who regarded him, then snorted, and resumed walking up to the temple.

"Olgar can tell you all about it, if you ask him. A more pressing concern is the sahuagin menace, which is what I want to talk to Olgar about. He's still a bastard, I see, making me walk all the way up to talk to him."

"You speak as if you know him."

"Oh, Olgar and I go way back. He never mentioned me in his stories?" Krell looked at him blankly. "I thought not. He only ever tells the one, about how he lost his leg. Surely you've heard it?"

Krell nodded. "Probably more than a hundred times."

"Well, I was there when it happened, and I was the one who pulled him back into the boat, minus part of his leg, and fended off two sea devils while he prayed to ReckNor to keep him alive. He cut me from the story years later, when the Crown suppressed the church of ReckNor. We found ourselves on opposite sides of the battlefield. I don't think he's ever forgiven me for that."

Callodan stopped and looked at Krell, the jovial attitude dropping away. "So when I discuss having you murdered, Krell, I am not attempting to intimidate you with an idle threat. I've stymied ReckNor's will before. I can always just walk back to Heaford." He turned and continued walking up the hill.

Krell was suddenly a little afraid of Callodan Koramir. He stood watching him walk for a moment, until one guard gave him a gentle shove, getting him moving again.

* * *

Olgar was waiting for them, seated on the bench nearest to the door.

He grunted when Callodan walked in. "Thought it was you, with the ridiculous size of that ship down there."

"Hello Olgar, and it is great to see you too. Yes, my children are fine, thank you for asking. Why no, no trouble with the weather getting here, thanks be to ReckNor. How's your leg?" said Callodan in an exasperated tone of voice.

"Missing, same as the last time we saw one another." Olgar gave Callodan a hard look.

Callodan let out a long sigh and sat on the bench across from Olgar. "I had hoped we'd moved beyond this, but apparently not. When your mentor decided to kill Mavram, there would be consequences. There had to be. You know that, Olgar. What was done to that army he raised, that you so foolishly joined, was not personal, nor was it a slight against ReckNor. The idiot tried to murder a duke and failed."

Callodan grimaced. "I'm not arguing that things would not have been better if he had succeeded, but the simple truth is he didn't. So here I am, and I want to talk. Are you going to talk to me, or did I waste a lovely climb threatening your young paladin for no reason?"

Olgar snorted. "I warn you, Callodan, Krell is possibly more stubborn and arrogant than I am."

Callodan chuckled in contempt. "Nobody is more arrogant than you, Olgar. And yes, I am aware of my reputation and the towering hypocrisy that I skirt the edge of."

"You might try to kill him, only to find yourself spitted on the end of his blade."

Callodan smiled. "I know paladins are uniquely dangerous warriors. You think I was not aware of that possibility? That he was carrying no blade was partly the reason I made those threats."

Olgar laughed. "You… I… ReckNor's balls, you're here calling me arrogant?" Olgar leaned back on the bench, laughing, then gestured at Krell. "Show him, my boy."

Krell shrugged and held out his hand. A black mist formed and coalesced into a dark metal longsword held firmly in his hand. Callodan stared at it, then turned a hard gaze at Krell.

"You're no paladin. How did you do that?" he said.

THIS PLEASES ME. CALLODAN IS ALWAYS SO CONFIDENT. LET HIM KNOW DOUBT.

Krell smiled. "ReckNor disagrees with you about me not being a paladin. As for how I did it, I willed the sword to be, and so here it is." Krell shrugged, then tossed the sword away into the temple. It dissipated into mist before it struck anything.

"ReckNor called me, Callodan. I am not deceiving you. I am a barely educated peasant who knows nothing of the world. But I survived being shipwrecked, twice. ReckNor called me because I am a survivor. At least, that's what he tells me."

Krell glanced at the guards standing in the entryway. "It would have been a shame to come to blows with them. They seem nice enough and certainly look competent. I'd have hated to have had to kill them because you were stupid or afraid." The guards looked at one another, then shifted position slightly. Olgar grinned.

"Oh relax, boys. Callodan is playing nice, and Krell won't have to learn that you've a decade of sword experience on him and that you'd gut him as easily as you would a house cat." Olgar turned to Callodan. "We done playing around, or do you have some more confidence you want to have wrung out of you first?"

Callodan sighed, then gave Olgar a small salute with his hand.

"Tell me about the sahuagin."

"You read my notes. The simple truth is, Callodan, that I looked at it. It was big enough on its own to be an underking. Smart enough, if it could talk. But it wasn't an underking, was it? An underking would never travel without its school, or it would disperse. This one was walking among the humans without killing them. *Gathering weapons.* It was a smart, powerful herald. If this isn't a precursor to war and invasion, then I don't know what is."

Olgar turned and looked directly at Krell.

"And ReckNor called a paladin. *Here,* in Watford. Possibly that is a coincidence, but if you believe that, then you believe Mavram deserves to be duke."

"Olgar, you speak treason. Please stop, for the sake of my guards, if nothing else." Olgar waved his hand vaguely in apology, and took a long pull from his flask. He handed it to Callodan, who raised it in a toast, then took a drink. His face relaxed with pleasure.

"Well, at least you continue to drink quality, even if you're still a drunkard wasted in a meaningless little town."

"Meaning is where you find it, Callodan. More importantly, ReckNor guided me here, and then put Krell here for me to find. He's always been sparing of visions and prophecy, since he values choice so much, but I've caught some glimpses." He gestured with his head toward Krell. "I see that one standing against sea devils. Lots of them." Olgar let out a belch.

"Wait, you're saying ReckNor called me because the sea devils are coming?" said Krell.

ESSENTIALLY CORRECT, BUT THERE IS MORE TO IT THAN THAT.

"What do you mean, more to it than that?"

"Ah," said Callodan, "so he is a paladin after all." Olgar nodded, then took his flask back and took a drink.

Krell felt the grace of ReckNor within him, tinged with focus and awareness. ReckNor was watching and listening. And something else. Krell concentrated, tracing that feeling. ReckNor was also *amused.*

"I think ReckNor wants to know what you're going to do, Callodan." Krell turned to face him. "As do I."

* * *

They talked long into the evening.

"I still don't understand," Krell said. "Why can't I tell anyone else about my charter?"

Callodan sighed. "Because it is a royal charter, Krell. This little piece of paper that I just signed and sealed means you could, if you chose, arrest the entire council of Watford and take over rulership yourself. But I think I've got your measure and I am wagering, at very high stakes, that you won't abuse it. In fact, I doubt it will bear how you act."

Callodan gave him a smile. "Think of it more like a peace offering from the Crown, represented by me, to ReckNor, represented by you. You're going to do what you're going to do. Instead of having ReckNor furious at the kingdom of Baltorc and King Fideon the second, long may he reign, because you've been arrested, now you can wave a little piece of paper and get yourself out of prison. At least, here in Baltorc. It's worthless — and possibly deadly to have — in other places. Keep that in mind, and by Veceyr's stutter, be discreet."

Callodan looked down at his hands, muttering, "When paladins come, they bring change."

"We do?" said Krell.

Callodan looked up at him and smiled. "History is replete with stories of paladins arriving, dragging some dark secret out into the light and upending everything. It's usually pretty good for the followers of that paladin's god, followers of ReckNor, in your case. The ones who suffer most are usually those already in power. I was not exaggerating when I said paladins have started wars. *Many* wars."

Callodan waved his arm toward Watford. "Let's look at Daylan Plintform as an example. His smuggling operations have been not just disrupted, but utterly destroyed. You and Tristan are now eligible to take the base he was using here in Watford away from him entirely. How long ago did you turn him loose, Olgar?"

"Been about a week, I suppose." Olgar was slurring his words a little.

Callodan shook his head while Krell thought about it. "How is that going to make things better for followers of ReckNor?" Krell asked, trying to piece together what was going on.

Callodan shrugged. "How am I supposed to know? Prices on some goods are about to go up, while other goods should come down. Maybe there is some long-term plan that is beyond mortal understanding. Maybe ReckNor is bored, and wanted to see what a worthless nobody like you would do to the people who currently rule. As one of those people who rule, it's frustrating and dangerous to have a paladin around. Change is never good for people like me who already have everything."

Callodan shrugged, then rubbed his hand through his hair. "A word of caution, Krell. Paladins often die young, and stupidly. Many in power will seek to control you, or if they can't, kill you.

The many stories about paladins — mostly Hieron's paladins to be sure, but paladins regardless — usually end with them tipping the balance of power and getting killed for it."

Callodan looked seriously at Krell. "Tipping over power structures often causes them to collapse. That's how wars start."

Callodan stood and gestured at his guards, who stepped outside. "Olgar, as always, you're an irascible and arrogant jackass. It pleases me to see you again. Krell, try not to die stupidly." He nodded to both of them, then left. Krell could hear him speaking with his guards as he walked down the hill toward Watford.

Olgar gave Krell a look, then shook his head, standing and heading outside. "Get the wooden practice swords out and come with me. I feel like I need to hit something."

* * *

Krell tried to keep his balance and failed.

Turning his backward stumble into a roll, he avoided Olgar's next strike. He rolled again, approaching the cliff edge. Olgar's wooden leg slowed him down, and Krell was able to get his feet under him before Olgar's wooden practice blade crashed into his helmet.

Krell retaliated, striking at Olgar's head, which he parried. Krell grinned as he dropped low, his leg sweeping out, catching Olgar's peg. The leather straps slipped off, and the peg dangled, caught in his clothing, but no longer capable of supporting his weight.

Of course, Olgar clubbed Krell across his head and back when he dropped. Caught under the hammer blow, Krell tried to open the distance between them, knowing Olgar could not keep up. Instead, Olgar dropped on top of him. They wrestled, rolling on the ground for a moment, before Olgar used his bulk to pin Krell on the ground.

He began choking him.

Krell couldn't move Olgar's hands. His grip was like iron, so instead, Krell punched him in the face. Olgar grunted, and the next time Krell punched him, he lowered his head, taking it on the skull instead of his cheek.

Krell's vision began to swim.

He hammered at Olgar's arms, to no effect. He tried kneeing him in the groin, but Olgar chuckled and kept the pressure on.

As his vision blackened, Krell conjured a dagger and slashed Olgar's arm. The pressure on his throat eased slightly as one hand released his throat. Then Olgar's fist slammed into Krell's face, his head snapping back and crashing into the ground. Dazed, Krell was only vaguely aware that the pressure on his throat resumed.

It felt like he was sinking into deep water. The grace and power of ReckNor was there, but was not welcoming or pleased. It was both disappointed and amused. He descended into the depths, and darkness overwhelmed him.

The next thing Krell felt was cold water. He gasped in a breath, coughing and sitting up. He looked up at Olgar, who held an empty bucket.

"Better, lad. You're getting better. Why'd you wait so long to make a blade and cut me with it? And why didn't you go for the throat?"

Krell coughed, doubling over even as the grace of ReckNor, feeling like shards of jagged glass being drawn across his skin, healed the damage to his throat and head. After a moment, his coughing subsided, and he looked up. Of the cut Krell had dealt Olgar, the only sign was the torn and bloody sleeve of his shirt.

Krell shook his head. "I was holding back because I don't want to hurt you."

Olgar laughed, a deep resonant laughter that echoed over the hilltop in front of the temple. He reached down to help Krell up.

"Oh, Krell, you can't be this dense. Do you think I'd still spar with you if you had any chance of winning against me?" He shook his head, still chortling under his breath. "You've got to learn to fight dirty. People will hear the word *paladin* and automatically assume you're a stuck-up moron like all the ones Hieron calls. Use that against them." His expression became serious. "Use it to kill them."

Then Olgar grinned. "Still, you're getting better. Kicking my leg out was new — and a good move. Find the weakness in your enemy and exploit them. Just do it more competently next time?" He looked around, breathing in the night air, then shook his extended hand at Krell. "Come on, I'm hungry."

Krell took his hand, and Olgar hauled him to his feet easily. Once standing, Olgar clapped him on the shoulder and started back into the temple.

"Olgar, how long was I out?" Krell asked. The wooden practice swords were nowhere to be seen, nor did Krell remember a bucket of water anywhere nearby. Olgar had also reattached his peg.

"I let you doze peacefully for around ten minutes, I figure. How's your head?"

Krell thought about it, but couldn't feel anything wrong.

"Seems fine."

"Good. Come in, let's eat."

Olgar had pulled a basket out, filled with cured fish, cheeses, and bread. Krell's stomach rumbled, and Olgar laughed.

"Did you know that working magic takes a toll on the body?" Krell looked at him blankly. "It's true. ReckNor gives us power and guidance, and we channel it through our bodies. You more easily than I, but with more limited options." Olgar took a chunk of dried fish and pulled a dagger from his belt, expertly slicing it.

"Well, the act of the power moving through us takes our own power. People often think that the gods choose their priests and paladins, and that it could be anyone if only you're devout enough." Olgar chewed in silence for a moment, while Krell conjured a dagger and sliced cheese and fish for himself.

"Handy trick, that is. Anyway, I disagree, at least in part. I think there are those who can channel the power, and the gods look for them and try to recruit them. I think people like us are pretty common, relatively speaking. Maybe one in ten people? That seems about right, as far as I can tell."

"Olgar, why are you telling me this?"

"It's important, Krell, for you to know, to *really know* deep down in who you are, that you can be replaced." Olgar looked at him, and the look in his eyes was pitiless but not cruel. "The gods use us mortals, Krell. They *use* us. Whatever ReckNor called you for, remember that he teaches the freedom of choice. If he tells you to do something stupid that will get you killed, refuse."

Krell looked at Olgar, surprised. "Wait, are you telling me to *defy* ReckNor?"

HE IS TELLING YOU HE LOVES YOU IN HIS OWN WAY. HE WANTS YOU TO LIVE, AND TRIUMPH, AND PROSPER. HE IS QUITE RIGHT, AS WAS CALLODAN. PALADINS OFTEN DIE YOUNG, THROUGH EITHER ARROGANCE OR STUPIDITY. ALSO, IT IS MUCH CLOSER TO ONE OUT OF EVERY FIVE HUMANS, THOUGH SO FEW UNDERSTAND OR HAVE THE OPPORTUNITY TO LEARN.

"No, lad, I'm telling you that when he tells you what he wants, figure out how to do that without listening to him tell you *how*." Olgar went back to chewing, observing Krell intently.

Krell struggled with the thoughts in his head. "Olgar, I'm confused. How am I supposed to choose what to do for myself if ReckNor is talking directly to me, telling me what to do?"

Olgar shrugged. "I suspect many paladins do not figure that out, and end up dead as a result. Think about it, Krell." He looked him in the eye. "Think hard. I believe your life depends on the answer to that question." Olgar then smiled. "I'm also trying to tell you to never pass up an opportunity to eat. You'll need the strength to channel ReckNor's power."

Krell shook his head as if to clear it.

"What is the Black Theocracy?"

Olgar's smile faded as he looked at him. "Where'd you hear the term?"

"Aldrik mentioned it in the town council a few days ago, and then Callodan brought it up as we walked up here. He told me to ask you."

Olgar was silent for a bit, chewing thoughtfully.

Krell waited. Then he looked up and said "What is the Black Theocracy?"

DAZGUROTH GREW WEARY OF THE INCOMPETENCE OF HIS FOLLOWERS, AND HAS TAKEN A DIRECT HAND. HE HAS TAKEN MORTAL FORM AND RULES HIS KINGDOM, WHICH HE CALLS THE BLACK THEOCRACY. IT IS A PROBLEM FOR THE REST OF THE GODS. WE ARE UNSURE HOW TO REACT, SO WE OBSERVE FOR NOW.

"Oh. *That* one." Krell looked at Olgar. "How direct a hand has Dazguroth taken?"

Olgar looked at him, then snorted. "Paladins. So easy to forget that their god talks directly to them. Okay, brief history. Dazguroth is an ass. He's a megalomaniacal tyrant who seeks total dominion over everything. People do as he commands, or they perish. For those that obey, he offers protection with his fiendish and undead legions."

Olgar leaned back. "That's his duality. He wants everyone to obey and will protect those that do. He'll destroy anything and everything else, both to eliminate threats and to encourage others to submit. He tells his followers to go out and take over. To rule all that can be ruled."

Olgar smiled. "To say they have a long history of failure is putting it mildly. Some successes here and there in the history texts, but mostly whenever they try to take over, they fail. Spectacularly. And then there's retaliation, and Dazguroth loses followers, since many of them get put to the sword. Following me so far?"

"Like what happened to the followers of ReckNor here, in Baltorc?"

Olgar grimaced. "That cuts close to the heart, Krell, but yes. Exactly like that. There's a reason you haven't met many priests of ReckNor hereabouts."

Krell nodded. It made a twisted sense, he supposed, how Dazguroth's strategy worked to keep his followers alive.

"Well, as near as we can tell, Dazguroth cheated, somehow. Gods are magic, I guess is the way to describe it. Divine beings who gain power through worship. Yet Dazguroth is *here*, in the world, in mortal form. Solid and real. Nobody, not even the gods, seem to know how that is possible. Lots of people thought it was a charlatan or a pretender. Maybe a high priest or something. But it's been over three centuries, and the only conclusion is that Dazguroth is really here."

Olgar looked at Krell. "This is where that track record of failure comes to a halt. He mobilized his followers, organized them in a way that terrifies anyone who has bothered to pay attention. He conquered Galeran, and put about half the population to death. They mostly made his armies of those dead, bound in service and led by fiends. Mortal armies need to be fed, need to sleep, need to have a hope of victory. The armies of the Black Theocracy need none of those things. Kill a fiend? It reforms in the dark pits of the various hells that Dazguroth rules over, and he brings it back. Pitched battle with his army? Unless you win and burn all the remains, he just grows stronger. If one of his armies is victorious, then all the dead on the losing side join the ranks of the winning side."

Olgar looked upward, deep in thought. "There's a genuine worry he's unstoppable."

He smiled and went back to eating. "But the good news is that Baltorc is a long way away from his cursed lands far to the north. The bad news is that the elves, dwarves, and gnomes all agree he *is* coming. Just a matter of time. Those longer-lived races spend a lot of time and effort trying to convince humans to stand up and fight."

"Do you think that's why ReckNor called me?" asked Krell.

Olgar snorted. "Better paladins than you have tried to take Dazguroth and failed. I doubt it. At some point, the other gods will figure out what they want to do about the Black Theocracy, and will let us mortals know. Until then?" Olgar shrugged. "Until then I suspect we've a school of sea devils to kill."

"It's never easy, is it?" said Krell.

"You're a paladin, lad," said Olgar. "Your entire life is difficulty, pain, and challenge. That's what paladins are for, to see clearly and to strike the enemies of their gods down." Olgar grinned at him. "ReckNor, though, is an easy god to worship. He doesn't really ask for much, other than payment for the use of his seas. It will be interesting to see what you do with your life. I suspect, unlike Hieron, ReckNor has no plan for you at all."

"Then why would he call me?" asked Krell.

Olgar shrugged, his grin widening. "Maybe he was bored?"

Krell could feel ReckNor's amusement roiling within him.

Chapter Twelve

Three days later, Callodan Koramir departed.

Petimus had already begun construction in town, several dwarves erecting a squat stone building, then putting up a sign proclaiming the Smithforge Mining Consortium. They began selling metal tools and offering blacksmithing services, which outraged the other smith in town.

Ugly rumors circulated that the dwarves were secretly here to take over. Most dwarves thought this was hilarious, bursting into laughter whenever they heard it. They pointed out that trying to dig a proper home this close to the water was a great way to get a flood, but people didn't seem to want to listen.

The following week, Krell was in the Netminder's Friend, eating lunch. Marlena was busy, and there were several fresh faces in the room. She saw him and wandered over, still swaying her hips at him.

"Busy day today! Have everything you need, Krell?" she asked. She gave him a smile that made Krell feel uncomfortable, and she leaned forward. Krell concentrated very hard on ensuring his eyes stayed on her face. Her voice became husky. "*Anything* I can do for you?"

Krell blushed at the way she emphasized the word *anything* and looked back at his food. "No, Marlena, I'm good, thank you." He reached for his cup and nearly knocked it over. He stared at his hand. Why was it shaking like that?

Marlena laughed and sat down next to him. Right next to him. Her leg and hip pressed up against his. She looked around and smiled. "The rainy season is coming to an end. Dry season is starting already. You missed it last year. I seem to remember you arriving right near the end, then Olgar kept you up at the temple for a while. With the dry season comes dry roads, and lots of caravan traffic." She looked at him, still smiling. "Lots of new faces for me to tease."

She put her hand on his leg. Krell hit his cup awkwardly, catching it before it spilled. She gave a low chuckle that made his heart race. He wasn't sure if he was excited or panicked. He felt a blush creeping up his neck.

She stood up and spun away. Krell watched her go and then realized she was watching him as he watched her. His blush deepened.

Kraven sat down at the table suddenly, looked at Krell and burst out laughing. "She still teasing you, Krell?"

Krell nodded. "What have you been up to?"

"Getting drunk, mostly. Just sleep with her, already. She's rebuffed me often enough." He leaned back and waved to Marlena, who held up a mug and tilted her head questioningly. He nodded.

"The other tavern in town, The Broken Mug, has this drink they make from fish guts. Makes my eyes water! You should try it sometime," he said, giving Krell a look that suggested Kraven would enjoy the experience much more than he would.

"Thanks, I'll pass. I like it here, and I like Salatan's food." The cook rarely ventured out of the kitchen, but that hadn't stopped Krell from learning his name or striking up a conversation with him. Krell glanced at Kraven. He was staring at the door. There was a trickle of unease from the grace of ReckNor, and Krell belatedly realized that the common room had fallen silent. He turned to look in the direction Kraven was staring.

There was a tiefling standing in the doorway.

Tieflings were rare, speaking to a family history that involved some female ancestor of theirs coupling with a fiend, and giving birth to a half-fiend. That half-fiend's children were often, but not always, tieflings. The trait stayed in the family bloodline, cropping up irregularly.

Tieflings were also rare because they tended to be killed shortly after birth by superstitious parents who believed that the child was cursed, particularly if they had other children who appeared normal. Still, the trait was in the bloodline and would surface again.

Olgar hadn't talked much about tieflings, other than to tell Krell they were usually no better or worse than anyone else, but that nobody gave them a fair shake because of their looks.

The one standing in the doorway, looking over the room, was stunning.

She had a figure that was at once both lithe and buxom, and wore a tight-fitting black leather bodysuit that only emphasized her considerable assets. Her skin was a pale blue, her hair a brilliant white, and two black horns protruded from her head in a way that only accentuated her beauty. Her long tail, ending in a flattened spike, swished through the air behind her.

Her gaze drifted across the room, clearly reveling in the attention, as Marlena walked over, looking wary, almost hunching, as if to hide some deformity. The sense of danger from ReckNor's grace grew a little stronger.

"Orianna, we don't often see you, uh, outside your workplace. Is there something I can help you with?" Marlena seemed almost tentative and ashamed to be speaking to her.

Orianna walked over to Marlena, and reached out a finger, caressing Marlena down the side of her face and then lifting her chin gently. Krell felt vaguely embarrassed to watch it happen, though from the growl that Kraven let loose, he clearly enjoyed it.

"No, thank you, Marlena. It is actually a social call that brings me from my lair," she said coyly. Her voice was melodic and sweet, although Krell could see now that her eyes were strange, almost totally white. Orianna turned and focused her attention on Krell.

Then she walked over.

Krell had thought that Marlena was attractive when she walked, swaying her hips in a way that made him desire her, but that also felt embarrassing and uncomfortable. When Orianna walked, however, Krell couldn't take his eyes off her. It was a hypnotic presentation of sexuality that was wholly outside his experience. Something tugged at his attention, but it was hard to focus.

She came over, and her voice washed over him and Kraven both. "May I join you?"

Kraven nodded, almost leaping up from the bench to pull out a chair in a display of chivalry that was completely out of character. As Orianna sat, her tail curled around the chair, adjusting it to her body — even the act of sitting down was laden with promise.

Krell realized he was staring. He also knew he could do nothing about it. There was another distant tug at his attention.

"So, Krell, paladin of ReckNor. Why have you never come to pay me a visit here in town, I wonder?"

Krell stared at her for a moment before he was able to answer. "I don't know who you are or what you do here in Watford." It seemed impossible for a person this beautiful to have escaped his notice.

She laughed, and Krell couldn't help but smile at the same time. Kraven laughed along with her, and her smile lit up the room in an almost literal sense.

"I run a business here in town, Orianna's Bountiful Goods. I am a factor, mainly buying a large portion of the catch every day, then curing it so it will not spoil. From there, I pack it into ships that come every week and ship it back to my homeland." She smiled at Krell and leaned forward slightly. The scent of her filled Krell's nose, a delightful perfume he couldn't place.

Something tugged at his attention, more urgently this time.

"Why I have come to speak to you, Krell, and to you, Kraven, is that these vessels move in both directions and many strange and wonderful items come into my possession. Perhaps you should come by my business and inspect my *assets*." The phrasing was so loaded with innuendo that Krell lost his train of thought. Kraven reached for her, then caught himself, his hand retreating.

She smiled and reached out to take Kraven's hand. Suddenly ReckNor's power burst within him, and Krell could feel the shattered remains of a spell being washed away from his thoughts. The grace of ReckNor gave him a vague feeling of amused alarm, but nothing particularly dangerous, which confused him.

Krell looked at Orianna, and realized she had put a glamor on herself, and it had just broken for him. He could see that she was still beautiful, exceptionally so, but not so flawlessly perfect as he had initially believed. His heart was still racing through, watching her flirt with Kraven.

"Why do you glamor yourself?" he asked.

Orianna turned her head toward him, then cocked it sideways as if seeing him for the first time. She smiled in delight.

"I've never met a paladin before. How did you see through it?"

Kraven had a confused look on his face.

"What are you two talking about?" he asked.

"You're beautiful and you know it. Why hide what you are behind the image of what you think others want you to be?"

Orianna's smile faded, and she looked at him. "Women, Krell, have a hard road. When you have power, you can forge your own path, but all too often some *man* comes along and tries to possess you, or instruct you, or hurt you." Krell could feel her fury beating against his senses. Kraven snatched his hand back, recoiling from her.

"Denied rulership, denied ownership, denied even control over ourselves, our own bodies, just because of our gender. Am I weaker than you? Less intelligent? Less capable in any way, because of these?" she said, gesturing at her breasts.

"No. But then, the only things I know about you are that you're beautiful, have magic, run a business, and are much stronger than you appear," said Krell, looking her in the eyes. "I would say that I have never judged someone based on their gender, but I don't know if that's true or not."

She made a dismissive gesture. "That's neither here nor there, Krell. I'm past that. I'll forge my own destiny, and if that means I use glamors to make men so befuddled that they can't think straight, then so be it. *However*, that's not why I came in here today, as delightful as this conversation has been. For now, I am here to offer you and your companions," — she glanced at Kraven suggestively — "something of value."

"I like what I see already," said Kraven, eyeing her shamelessly. She gave him a smile, then turned back to Krell. "As I said, the boats that carry food from here to my homeland must return to pick up food. There has been some, let us say, *strife*, in my homeland over the past years, and many items of interest, such as art and items of magical power, can be made available to me. If you have an interest in such things, I can procure nearly anything for you."

"You mentioned your homeland. Where is that?" asked Krell.

"Bruwaehan."

Krell thought about that, but drew a blank. Kraven though, recoiled as if burned.

"Bruwaehan no longer exists. The Black Theocracy overran and destroyed it a decade ago!" he snarled. "Which means you work for Dazguroth!"

"Just because my homeland has been conquered does not mean that the people there no longer need to eat, Kraven. Try to remember that I am not smuggling, nor do I deal in the bulk trade of weapons or poison or anything distasteful. I buy fish, here in Watford, and send it to my homeland so the people there can eat. Is that evil?" Orianna gave him a challenging and condescending look.

A minute passed in stony silence. She sighed.

"Well, I see you may have to think about my offer. If you decide you are interested, please come by. I live above my business, so I am always available, should you *desire* me." The suggestion in her language was not lost on either of them.

She stood and left. Every eye in the room tracked her as she walked out. Conversation resumed, though now everyone was looking at — and clearly talking about — Krell and Kraven.

Marlena came over. She seemed subdued. Krell looked at her and smiled in relief.

"Marlena. I can honestly say it is a real pleasure to see you after that one!"

For the first time, Marlena was the one who blushed.

* * *

Dorn had joined them, and bereft of other tasks, he and Kraven decided to get drunk.

Krell couldn't help but notice they got louder as they drank more and the crowd thickened as evening approached, with fishers coming in and talking about their day. There were unfamiliar faces, dusty from the road, and Marlena seemed to be everywhere at once. Krell could make out the story of Orianna's visit earlier that afternoon circling around the common room whenever someone new came in.

It was strange to Krell, this freedom. Before, he'd always had an immediate task. Whether it was survival as a child, or instruction from Olgar, or more recently, battle with the creatures in the mines or the smugglers, there was always something. But for the last few days, neither the town council, Olgar, nor ReckNor had anything for him to do.

Krell watched Dorn and Kraven argue about who would pass out first. He spent the first part of every morning at the temple, cleaning and trying to help Olgar with his impromptu services for whoever showed up. He always adamantly refused any assistance. The rest of the morning before lunch, he spent training. Since he had no charter, he was not allowed to wear armor or carry weapons. The weapons did not bother him any longer, but being without armor left him feeling unprotected.

Krell did not like being without armor.

The door opened and a man staggered in, looking like he was already drunk. The room was full, and he looked around. One of the few tables with available chairs was the table Krell and his companions were sitting at. He staggered over.

As he got closer, Krell could see he looked like a sailor, with his hands showing signs of hard work but faded as if that work occurred in the past. He pulled out the chair and sat without being invited, and belched.

"Hey!" said Dorn. "Shove off!"

"I know you!" he said, focusing on Dorn. "You're that insane dwarf priest of ReckNor! I'll have you know, my little friend, I'm a loyal and true follower, I am, and maybe I need some priestly advice!"

"Do I look like I want to be giving you priestly advice? I said shove off!" Dorn followed with action, literally shoving him out of his chair. "And don't call me 'little'!"

Krell reached out and caught him before he fell, though the chair crashed over. Krell stood, and shoved him into his chair, then righted the other.

"I'm Krell. Tell me what you need."

"Oh, you're that handsome paladin all the girls talk about, are you?" He squinted at Krell, looking him over. "Yup, reckon they're right. You are a handsome one! ReckNor's teats, I need a drink." He rubbed his face with his hands, then leaned his elbows on the table and started to cry.

Krell looked at Dorn and Kraven, who both turned away and studiously ignored what was happening. Krell thought that was deeply uncharitable, since he had no idea what to do about the man crying into his hands. And what did he mean, all the girls were talking about him?

"Let's start with something simple, then. What's your name?"

The man looked up. His eyes were bloodshot, and his face was splotchy. Krell reached out to steady him. ReckNor's grace surged within him and crashed into the man. He sucked in a deep breath, his face clearing of his drunkenness, his bloodshot eyes returning to normal.

The healing he just administered surprised Krell. Normally, he asked for healing, or demanded it. It had never just flowed on its own like this before.

ONE OF MY FOLLOWERS REQUIRES AID. PALADINS ARE OFTEN SEEN AS AID.

"ReckNor's balls, boy! I worked hard to get that drunk. Why'd you have to go ruin it for me?" he shouted.

"Not me!" Krell protested. "That was ReckNor. You're definitely a follower, and he likes you for some reason. I bet you prayed for aid, huh? Now, you know who I am. Who are you?"

He let out a long sigh. "My name is Voss. Until recently, *Captain* Voss, of the merchant ship *Sylph's Tears*. Now, I'm an out-of-work sailor with barely a penny to his name, and probably about to be arrested besides."

"Just Voss then?" asked Krell.

"Kardma Voss, if you must know, but most everyone calls me Voss. Or, until recently, Captain." He shook his head. "I worked hard for that drunken haze, boy! Why'd you have to ruin it so?"

Krell sighed. "If I need to extract every piece of this story one bit at a time, we'll be here all night. Why don't you be more helpful and tell me why you'd be looking for a priest of ReckNor."

Voss glared at Krell, then ran his hand through his hair. "Fine, fine. May as well, since a perfectly good drunken haze has been wasted!

"Until recently, I was employed as master of the *Sylph's Tears*, a ship owned by our illustrious Daylan Plintform, until three days ago, when we put into Heaford. There, local factors came aboard, handed me papers of ownership to inspect, then ordered me and the crew to debark at once. Backed up by the duke's men, they were! I barely had time to clear out my cabin before they took my ship from me!" He looked close to tears again.

"Fourteen years I served, first as crew, then as a mate, and then as captain. And for what? To be dumped in Heaford without a word of warning? Who sells a ship and doesn't tell the captain?" He shook his head. "As if that weren't bad enough, we paid out of pocket for passage back to Watford, and when we arrived to tell Plintform what had happened, he accused us of losing his ship! Forfeited my savings, he did, took every penny I'd saved! Me *and* the crew! So we did what good sailors do and got drunk."

He looked at Krell. "Couldn't pay, of course. Crew always carries coin around, but I was the captain. Now I'm likely to be thrown in jail and sent to a work camp, or forced into the levies. Great way to end a life spent on the sea! Probably have to work the mines with the dwarves!" He grabbed Krell's cup and drank, then shot him a dirty look. "Water, lad? Really?"

The door opened, and Logruff and another guard Krell did not know entered. They looked around, spotted Voss, and walked directly over. Krell stood, then hauled him to his feet. Voss saw the guards and let out a sigh, his shoulders slumping.

"Logruff, well met," said Krell, clasping arms with him. He looked expectantly at the other guard.

"Krell, good to see you following the rules around town. Torvald, this is Krell. Krell, Torvald, my partner. Always walk patrol in pairs. At least, that's the rule the captain drums into us." Logruff nodded toward Voss. "He tell you why we're here?"

"I'll come along peacefully, gents, no worries from me. This young bastard here was cruel enough to take away my drunken stupor, so no stupidity from me tonight. Shame it is, too. I might have lucked out, and you two fine lads might have killed me instead."

Voss looked at Krell. "If ReckNor likes you, best keep out of my way. I'd have sooner died tonight than deal with what's in store for me."

Logruff rolled his eyes, and Torvald took Voss by the elbow and began escorting him out. Krell reached out, grabbing Logruff by the arm.

"A moment, Logruff. What happens to him now?" he asked, nodding toward Voss.

"Why do you care?"

"He's a true follower of ReckNor, Logruff. I'm his paladin as much as I am for anyone else," said Krell quietly.

"Huh. Well, he's in the cell tonight, and doubtless Captain Gijwolf will assess fines and punishment tomorrow morning. If he can't pay, then he'll be forced into the levies till his debt is cleared. From what I heard at the Broken Mug, it'd only be a month or two." Logruff looked at Krell's hand on his arm, then met Krell's eyes again. "Anything else?"

Krell released him, thinking. "No, thank you, Logruff. I think ReckNor intervened tonight to save his life, but I'm not sure about that, or why he'd bother."

Logruff laughed lightly and clapped Krell on the shoulder. "Who can ever understand the will of the gods?"

Krell grinned and sat back down, a plan forming in his head.

* * *

Nathanial opened the door, an angry look on his face.

"Do you know what time it is? What do you want, Krell?"

"Is Aldrik up? I'd like to speak with him."

"*Master Kent* is preparing for bed and reading. Unless this is an emergency, go away." Nathanial closed the door in Krell's face.

"Well, that didn't work," said Krell.

"Yeah, I noticed," said Dorn, standing next to him. "Is there a reason you insisted I come?"

Krell looked down at him and smiled. “In case I end up killing anyone, it’d be nice to have a witness to say it was all in self defense.”

Dorn laughed. “And if it wasn’t self defense?”

Krell’s smile became sly. “I never said anything about you telling the truth, I was talking about you *saying* it was self defense.”

“Well, it’s not likely to matter, since Nathanial there slammed the door in our faces.”

The grace of ReckNor within Krell was pressing on him. It was a strange feeling. A pressure to wait and do nothing.

“It would be nice if you gave clearer instructions,” Krell muttered.

“Huh? You asked me here, remember?” said Dorn, looking at him with concern.

A minute passed before the door opened and Aldrik stood there, a magical lamp in hand.

“Ah, good, you’re still here! Of course I’m happy to talk, Krell. Nathanial is only being protective of me and my time. You’ve no idea how often people come to me asking for things.” He stepped back and gestured. “Come in, come in!”

The foyer was pleasant, if spartan compared to Amra’s home. Aldrik led them into a small sitting room, furnished with six comfortable chairs arranged around a low table. Aldrik sat in one with a comfortable ease and waved for Krell and Dorn to seat themselves.

“What brings the champions of ReckNor to my door this evening?” he asked, his eyes bright. Krell suspected he might be a little drunk.

“Captain Voss. Do you know him?” asked Krell.

“Ah, no, cannot say that I do. What of him?”

“He was arrested today. He’s a follower of ReckNor, and I would intervene on his behalf.”

Aldrik focused on Krell. “Arrested for what? It is very clear that the Crown plays no favorites among the gods, lest one take affront. This is a direct command from His Majesty King Fideon. No special treatment or extra punishment to any based on their religious beliefs. That is not a law I will consider breaking, Krell."

Krell was taken aback. Aldrik had always seemed so young in every encounter before, but suddenly it was clear that he was no pretender to his role on the town council. The fact that he was several years older than Krell made him feel at once both out of place and uncomfortable.

PROCEED. YOU'RE DOING FINE.

Krell winced slightly, striving to hide it. "He was, well, it's a long story, but he's broke and ran up a debt at the Broken Mug today. If the fine were paid, would he be free to go?"

Aldrik sat back and looked at Krell. His eyes were bright, but not with drink. It was intelligence Krell saw there, only realizing for the first time how out of his depth he really was here.

"No. Money may not buy justice. In this, Hieron and the Crown are in agreement. If he has done wrong, then he must be punished as not only an example to others, but for his own well-being. No man may break the law, they may only break themselves upon it."

"You're no follower of Hieron, though. Those aren't his words," said Dorn. "Uldall?"

Aldrik smiled, pleased. "Indeed, yes, the lawgiver is probably my favorite of the gods." He looked at Krell. "Punishment, however, can take many forms, and you probably have something in mind."

Krell nodded. "I'll let Olgar know, so he stops harassing you about attending services. What do you plan to do with the smuggler vessel?"

"Rename it, and then put it into service for the benefit of Watford. We have not decided as a council yet what that service might be."

"So the ship sits idle then, in harbor?" asked Krell.

"It does. Captain Gijwolf has assigned guards, of course, who take shifts keeping watch on it, lest some villain make off with it. However, that would be challenging since I believe someone deliberately ruined most of the rigging for the mainsail."

Aldrik grinned at Krell, who suddenly realized he was talking about him.

"I thought it better than wrecking it and fouling the harbor," he said somewhat defensively.

Aldrik laughed. "Indeed, and ruining the rigging was a better outcome than smashing a dock and sinking the ship, but still, you could have left it anchored where it was and waited for competent sailors to join you." He waved his hand. Krell realized he was entirely correct. Looking back, the decision to take the ship into Watford seemed incredibly stupid.

"However, what was done is done and cannot be undone. You have a plan for the ship, then?"

"Fishing vessels are going missing." Krell waited until Aldrik nodded. "Where?"

"So far, the ones that venture past the horizon. Several of the larger boats head out for two days or more, but we have yet to find any sort of debris washed ashore. We've sent parties riding up and down the coast and sent messages to Heaford, but nothing has been spotted. For a boat to vanish so completely, well, that is unfortunate, but possible. For *five* boats to vanish? In the space of a month? That is extremely unlikely. With the sea devil you killed, well, we have a good idea of what happened now."

"What do you plan to do about it?" asked Krell.

Aldrik shrugged. "As the magistrate suggested, continue reinforcing defenses for the town to prepare for assault. Otherwise, telling fishers not to fish is a fool's errand. We've explained the danger, and certainly the boats owned by my family have been ordered to stay closer to Watford. Cuts profit, but improves safety. Otherwise, there is nothing to be done."

"Give us a charter, the ship, a crew, and a captain, and let us go and see what we can learn," said Krell.

Aldrik sat forward. "Ah, I see your plan now. You want this Voss to captain the vessel under your command, as part of a charter from the town. To what end?"

Dorn spoke up. "Seems to me that wood floats."

Aldrik gave him a confused look. After a moment of silence, he shrugged. "And?"

"Well, if nothing washed ashore, then the boats are still out there. Wood floats, so they'll be on the surface more than likely. So if we sail out, maybe we find one. See what we can learn." Dorn looked intently at Aldrik. "It would be a shame to find out that the sea devils have a boat and pack it full of their kind, then sail right into the harbor and unload directly onto the docks, now wouldn't it?"

Aldrik laughed, reclining into his chair. "You think we'd not notice a boat trying to come in at night? Or if they try it during the day, that we'd not know the difference between people and the sea devils?"

Krell leaned forward. "They've already worked with people once. Why not again?"

Aldrik stopped laughing and stared at Krell in horror. "That would be madness!"

Krell shrugged. "As Olgar is fond of telling me, never underestimate what fools will do for coin."

* * *

Krell waited with the others.

They were standing in the foyer of Amra's home. Tristan and Gerrard occupied the single bench. They were speculating on the reason for them being called to the council session, then not let into the dining room as they had been on previous occasions. Orca and Kraven were standing close, talking quietly in a tongue Krell did not recognize. Dorn stood next to him.

"How much longer do you think, Krell?" he asked, for at least the fifth time.

"I have no idea, Dorn." Krell let out a long sigh. "I expect they'll call us when they're ready and not before."

"I'm bored."

Krell nodded. "I gathered that, my friend, yet there is nothing I can do, other than to tell you, again, that they'll take as long as they take."

"Krell, my man, you know what this is about, don't you?" said Gerrard.

Krell smiled at him.

"Oh bloody hells, Krell, what have you done now?" said Tristan. His voice really annoyed Krell today. Possibly the way the grace of ReckNor felt inside him, like shards of broken glass being dragged across his eyes, was exacerbating his annoyance.

Krell thought about that, ignoring his companions as they began rampant speculation about what Krell had done. Why did some days feel like broken glass, and other days not? The power within him was quiet, offering no clue or direction to these thoughts. *Thanks a lot*, thought Krell.

I DO NOT TELL YOU WHAT TO DO AT EVERY MOMENT. I TELL YOU MY WILL AND EXPECT YOU TO FULFILL IT.

Krell winced. ReckNor sounded almost angry. Then the enormity of what just happened hit Krell like a crashing wave.

Wait, I can talk to you in my thoughts?

INDEED. USING YOUR THOUGHTS MAKES YOU LOOK MUCH LESS INSANE TO OTHERS, DOES IT NOT?

Krell thought about that and decided it didn't really matter what others thought. The grace of ReckNor within him took on a distinctly pleased feeling laced with approval.

The door opened, and Godun stepped into the foyer. "The council is ready for you, gentlemen."

As Krell entered, he noted a few changes. The table was moved, making more room to stand before the council, but making the room less functional for dining. Petimus was seated at the table, a pile of papers set in front of him. Krell could see several of them were precise drawings of buildings and walls, but didn't know what they were for.

Aldrik looked smug, while Daylan looked angry. Amra was controlling her emotions, revealing nothing as they filed in. Captain Gijwolf was seated at one end of the table, present, but separate. Karaback was at the opposite end of the table, looking bored.

"Why is Karaback here?" Tristan whispered to Gerrard.

Amra cleared her throat. "We are now moving to the matter of the captured smuggler vessel. Aldrik, your proposal, please."

Aldrik stood, shot Krell and Dorn a grin, and began speaking.

"Since the vessel has been captured, and the lord magistrate made it the property of the town to be used in its defense, we should put it to work. To that end, I propose a new charter for these warriors who have served the town ably and well in the past. They will take the vessel and search for the lost fishing vessels. Should they encounter sea devils, they will gather what intelligence they can and report back to us."

Aldrik turned to Orca. "While you have some skill and knowledge related to the use and function of such a vessel, Orca, your companions most assuredly do not, in light of the damage it sustained when it nearly wrecked. To that end, a crew will be assembled, and a captain provided to both adhere to the council's wishes and to ensure that the vessel is capably operated."

He turned back to the council, looking at Daylan. "It has come to my attention that a former ship captain of yours has recently departed your service, Daylan, and committed a crime here in Watford. Captain Gijwolf can provide details. Captain?" Aldrik gestured and then sat down.

Captain Gijwolf stood up and stepped forward. "Yesterday, a former captain of the Plintform Shipping Company, Kardma Voss, was arrested for assault and robbery. Notably, for striking a patron at the Broken Mug, and then leaving without settling his — by that time considerable — bill. He was apprehended at the Netminder's Friend without incident. I have assessed his punishment, based on levy rates to pay his debt and fines for the assault, as seven weeks of forced labor. He has been remanded to the custody of the Crown. Which, of course, means nothing special, because we only have the one jail here in Watford." Captain Gijwolf went back to his stool and sat. He winked at Krell as he did so.

Aldrik stood at once. "Thank you, Captain Gijwolf. It would seem we have an opportunity here! I looked at the records you were asked to bring Daylan, and we can all agree that Kardma Voss was an able ship captain for many years, yes?"

Amra and Petimus nodded, but Daylan said, "He was, until I fired him for incompetence."

"Yes, an interesting charge. I've written to the lord magistrate, Callodan Koramir, to ask him to investigate, on your behalf," said Amra.

"You *what?*" Daylan leapt to his feet, yelling.

"Oh, be quiet, Daylan. You know as well as I do you covered your tracks well. This creates a proper look and feel to the whole sordid mess you caused and still lets you get away with it." Amra gave him a stern look. Daylan paled and sat down.

"Now, thank you, Aldrik, for bringing this matter before us. We have discussed the merits of this plan and have agreed to issue a new charter to you all." She slid a small stack of papers across the table toward them. "There are six copies in there, one for each of you to read."

Orca grabbed them, then handed them out. He deliberately passed by Krell, ensuring he got his copy last.

As Krell read, it was much as he surmised. The scope of the charter was to investigate the outer range of the fishing fleet, to ascertain where the missing boats were lost, and to return with information related to the sea devils, if possible. It spelled out that there would likely be a need for several journeys, each lasting days, and that the charter would be reassessed at the conclusion of each journey.

Krell looked at the copy Amra had on the table.

"Those who wish may sign. Those who do not have our thanks for your past service," said Amra.

Krell was the first to step forward and sign.

Chapter Thirteen

"I don't know how to thank you, my lord," said Captain Voss.

Krell smiled at him. "Well, since I'm an uneducated peasant who doesn't know anything, the first thing you can do is teach me how to be a sailor. Seems fitting to me that if I'm going to be crossing the waves in ReckNor's name aboard a ship, then I should know how it works!"

Captain Voss laughed, then turned and yelled, "Herbert! That is not how you make a rope fast! Where's Serda? Serda! See to Herbert!"

Another sailor looked up from where he was coiling ropes and went over to a young man who was trying to get a rope tied off. He had looped it through the railing.

"A few new hands at this, my lord, but they'll learn the ropes soon enough. Most of the rest served with me on the *Sylph*, so they're a solid lot." Captain Voss turned to Krell. "If you really want to learn, you'll fit in fine. Could do with a worse teacher to start with than Serda, but I think I'll pair you up with Artur for now."

Krell nodded, adjusting his breastplate. The captain looked at him, then frowned, shaking his head.

"That metal plate is going to pull you down if you fall in, my lord."

"Stop that," said Krell. "I'm no lord."

"Gotta call you something, and you'll find the rest of the crew will fall into line if I call you 'my lord,' while at the same time you learn the trade. Makes you one of them, but also keeps you separate. Good way to earn respect, bad way to make friends. Follow?"

"Not really, but I trust you know what you're doing. How long until repairs are completed?"

Captain Voss snorted. "Well, my lord, you and your friends did a number on the forward hull. Cracked several beams. With no drydock, we're forced to patch the hard way. Dorn has some of the magic we need to do it proper, though. Should be seaworthy in another two days, maybe three."

Krell frowned. "Any way to be out sooner?"

"Ha! No chance, my lord. At least, not unless you want to risk sinking if we hit a patch of ReckNor's displeasure. Unless you can tell ReckNor to keep storms away, we'd be scuppered. Better to fix it properly while we have a chance." He looked appraisingly at Krell. "I've been paying homage to ReckNor for longer than you've been alive, my lord. Never discount how small and petty he can be."

THAT IS WISE, EVEN IF IT IS UNFAIR.

"ReckNor says you're being unfair," said Krell.

"He really talks to you?"

Krell nodded. "Just now, yes. I'm pretty sure he hears everything I hear, and sees everything I see."

"Of course he does, my lord. He's a god, and we're in his domain. I've not sailed the waves for as long as I have to still have any fear of him. I've seen those who don't give proper offerings die on a calm day, and seen those that do come through storms that should have ended them, but didn't. ReckNor doesn't hate us. If anything, he protects and saves us." He leaned forward, whispering so only Krell could hear. "Most people say I'm mad, and that you appease ReckNor to keep him from causing harm.

I think it's more that you pay ReckNor for protection." He gave Krell a grin. "Like a guild of thieves, but for the ocean!"

He leaned back and spoke normally. "So you let me know, my lord, whether he has anything to say about that!"

Voss looked out over the deck, as the crew worked on tying and weaving ropes. He gestured.

"That one is Artur Clellend. He's one of the best aboard, knows ships almost as well as I do. Go learn how to make rigging, and spend the afternoon getting your hands cut up, earn a few scars. My lord." He gave Krell a brief bow, then a playful shove.

Krell grinned and headed over to Artur.

* * *

Captain Voss was wrong about one thing, at least. The power of ReckNor healed the cuts on his hands before they could leave any scars.

Krell was walking up toward the temple, the setting sun making the sea glow. Krell slowed, admiring the view, and relished the scent of the clean air. He shifted the breastplate he was wearing, unfamiliar with the solid feel of it. Olgar had trained him in chain mail armor, which always shifted.

There was a rustle from the trees behind him, and Krell spun. A blade formed in his hand. His eyes flicked across the trees and brush, but he saw nothing. Yet the rustle was wrong for merely the wind.

Krell knew a lot about surviving. He still wasn't certain how long he spent on that island by himself, but it was probably close to a decade. It was such a blur, for the most part, that constant battle for survival. Finding food, finding drinkable water. How he managed to do it, especially early on when he knew nothing, was a mystery to him.

He suspected ReckNor helped.

He watched the trees and bushes, his senses telling him that something had moved in the brush, making a noise that did not fit. After a minute, he gave up. Whatever it was, it must have been small, and had since left.

Still, it bothered him. Something was watching him, and the only reason he knew it was there was because it made a noise. If what Olgar had said was true, then he was on a quick path to a stupid death. If anything could just sneak up on him, how was he supposed to avoid it?

He wondered if maybe he wasn't supposed to avoid anything. Paladins were made for sharp conflict, not skulking around in the shadows. Krell smiled to himself. He'd spent a lot of time learning to move silently, so he could either avoid predators or hunt prey in the never-ending quest for food. It still surprised him that whenever he was hungry now, there was always food available.

His most poignant memories of his time on the island were of hunger. Hunger and cold and loneliness.

The carved image of ReckNor glared down at him from the temple door. Krell nearly stepped on the dead rat that had been left on the front step.

"Olgar! Why is there a dead rat out here?"

Krell heard a crashing noise from inside. Drunk again, he wagered with himself. Olgar came to the door and opened it, looked at the rat, and then glared at Krell.

"ReckNor's tits, boy, what am I supposed to do with a dead rat?"

"ReckNor doesn't have tits, Olgar," said Krell, grinning.

"He does if he wants to! Now, get rid of that, and tell me about Voss." Olgar took a drink from his flask, stumbling back inside.

Krell squatted next to the rat, examining it. It looked like it died without fighting back. Its throat had a set of neat parallel cuts, which looked fatal. Krell couldn't see any other wounds.

"Krell! Throw it over the cliff already!" shouted Olgar.

Krell conjured a dagger and used the dark metal to gently move the rat, flipping it over. The other side of its neck had an identical set of parallel cuts, which made no sense to Krell. He also spotted something on its flank, what looked like a puncture wound.

Krell readjusted the dagger, turning it into a stiletto, and inserted it into the wound. It went in without resistance. Something had stabbed the rat, then slit its throat.

Krell shrugged, then reached down, grabbed the rat by the tail, and walked toward the edge. He threw it underhanded, and it flew over the edge and vanished from sight.

There was a hiss behind Krell.

He spun, a longsword of dark metal springing into existence as he did. His eyes darted over the temple, then to the graveyard. Nothing moved. He turned, looking at the large tree near the temple that Olgar often dozed under when the weather was clear. The branches swayed in the breeze, but otherwise, nothing.

"I didn't imagine that hiss, did I?" he asked.

NO, YOU DID NOT. AT THE TOP OF THE TEMPLE.

Krell looked up, realizing that he was getting better at not flinching when ReckNor's voice crashed like a thunderstorm into his thoughts. At first he saw nothing different, but as he watched, a portion of the stonework shifted slightly.

A draconic head rose and looked back at him. They made eye contact with one another, Krell recognizing the little dragon he had set free the week before on the smuggler vessel. Then it was gone, retreating over the roof and out of his sight.

Krell felt a little sad, watching it disappear.

"Krell!" shouted Olgar. "I know you're hungry, boy! Get in here already!"

Krell let his blade disappear and went into the temple to tell Olgar about Captain Voss.

When he rose the next morning, there was a dead bird on the front step.

* * *

A gentle rain was falling.

Krell took it as a good omen as he walked into the Netminder's Friend. It was crowded, with dozens of new faces, including a few dwarves. He spied Gerrard, Orca, Kraven, and Dorn all seated around the larger table in the rear of the common room, and headed in their direction.

"Hey, Krell, my man! How are things with ReckNor?" Gerrard seemed in high spirits. "Think it's going to rain tomorrow? I'd love the first trip out to be clear, not miserable like this!"

"You look like a drowned rat!" said Dorn, laughing. "Take a room here! Unless you can't anymore, I guess. Place is filling up with all the caravan traffic starting. Start of the dry season, I hear, so dry roads for wagons and weak storms for ships."

Krell took off his cloak and shook it, deliberately spraying water onto Dorn.

"Jackass paladins, always thinking they can do anything they want!"

Krell and Dorn grinned at one another as Krell shoved him over on the bench and sat next to him. Marlena appeared, setting four steaming pies down in front of everyone.

"Ah, Krell. Fish pies today, if you're interested?"

Krell nodded and flashed a smile at her, which she met. Something had changed since Orianna had paid a visit. Krell wasn't so intimidated anymore, and she was less overt with her flirting.

It didn't mean he wasn't watching her as she walked away. She looked over her shoulder, making eye contact with him, and smiled. Krell blushed and averted his eyes, looking over the room. Kraven and Dorn both chuckled.

A group of dwarves stood out to Krell, because many others in the room were glaring at them and murmuring to one another. The dwarves seemed oblivious to what was happening. The more Krell watched, the more he realized people were glaring at Dorn as well.

Apparently, the local fishers did not like the dwarves moving into Watford.

A well-dressed dwarf was moving from table to table and getting a poor response. Mostly, people were rude and turned away, though a few engaged him in conversation that left both sides appearing angry. Marlena returned, setting a pie down next to him, along with a cup. Krell glanced at it. It looked like water.

"Marlena, why are people angry at the dwarves?"

She let out a sharp breath. "Stupidity, mostly. There's talk that the dwarves are here to take over the town, displacing all the humans and sending them inland. Doesn't matter how often Master Smithforge says that no dwarf would ever want to build a proper home in Watford." She shook her head, then looked at the group of them. "Can I count on you lads to help if trouble starts?"

"What about the guard?" said Orca. "Surely they're aware of the tension?"

"Oh, they are, but they're busy enough guarding the dwarf building and keeping people from making stupid choices. They swing by pretty often, but that'll be small consolation to my furniture if things go bad." She shrugged and wandered off as someone called her name.

The well-dressed dwarf came toward their table as Krell turned to his food. He had brilliant blue eyes that stood out as remarkable. His bright blue jacket was adorned with a red sash and gold buttons. His boots were glossy, though speckled with mud, and his beard was elegantly braided with gold rings — unlike Dorn's, who kept his beard well brushed but otherwise plain. He wondered if this was a dwarf thing related to age. Krell thought of Petimus, looking at him.

"Greetings, I am Vormaeg Frostpike of Talcon. May I have a moment of your time?"

Dorn gave him a shrug. "Dorn Ironbrow. I know the Frostpikes. What brings you to Watford?"

"I search for my daughter, who has gone missing. Have you seen a dwarf maid recently?"

Krell shook his head, looking at his companions. They were already eating again.

"I have not, Master Frostpike," said Krell. "Do you need some help? Wait!" Krell looked upward. "Do you know where she is?"

I AM NOT ALL KNOWING, KRELL. NOR AM I YOUR PERSONAL VALET. SOLVE YOUR OWN PROBLEMS.

"If I knew where she was, young human, I would not be searching for her, now would I?" Vormaeg looked vaguely angry.

Dorn pointed at Krell with his spoon. "Paladin," he muttered, through a mouthful of food.

Vormaeg looked back at him. "My apologies. May I have the courtesy of your name?"

"Krell, paladin of ReckNor."

Vormaeg raised an eyebrow. "ReckNor? I had not heard that ReckNor called paladins."

As he spoke, the door opened, and a group carrying weapons and wearing armor came in, three men and a woman. They moved to a table with two people seated at it and displaced them. There was some objection, but these newcomers were armed and the locals were not.

Krell turned back to Vormaeg. "ReckNor does not know where your daughter is. Do you need help?"

Vormaeg shook his head. "It's my search, Paladin Krell of ReckNor. I'll find her on my own. No offense, but your god has little interest in, or power over, dwarves."

Dorn let out a mocking laugh, then deliberately glared at Vormaeg as he took a drink.

Vormaeg grimaced, then turned and walked away.

"May the Fire Lord light your path, Vormaeg Frostpike," said Krell.

A young halfling woman came into the common room. She was wearing a worn dress for clothing, which was completely soaked through. She looked around and walked over to the table of armed warriors that had entered just before her.

Krell couldn't hear the conversation, but the woman looked suddenly disgusted, while two of the men began to argue with one another.

"Kraven, Orca. Come with me," said Krell, rising from the bench. Kraven looked at Krell, nodding.

Orca looked at him, then deliberately went back to eating his food.

Krell glared at him for a moment, then turned and headed toward the other armed group. The two arguing were yelling now, the little halfling woman cowering behind a chair. Marlena gave him a grateful look as he walked over.

They noticed him coming and turned to face him. "You the guard of this town?"

Krell shook his head. "Nope. Just locals who don't want you to wreck the place."

The larger one was wearing a metal breastplate similar to Krell's. He was taller and weighed more than Krell. If it came to a fight, Krell would have to cheat and use a blade.

Of course, that was why he brought Kraven with him. Kraven, as if on cue, let out a growl.

"You don't scare me, orc! The little lady here is a whore, and I'm inclined to take her for a ride. So go away and mind your own business before I break you in half!"

Krell looked down at the halfling. There was something in her eyes, a hardness, that gave Krell pause.

"What is your name?" he asked her.

"Lily."

"Tell me Lily, is this what you want?"

She shook her head. "No, Great One, it is not, but I have no coin for food or clothing." She grimaced. "It is all that I have left to me, at the moment."

"Well, that's stupid," said Krell. "Here, let me, at the least, offer you employment, with an advance on your salary."

"Hey! Mind your business and leave me to mine!" shouted the man.

She looked at Krell, her eyes widening. "You can't be serious."

The large human shoved Krell, forcing him back a step. "Hey, I said back off, little boy, before I break you in half!"

Kraven shoved him back. "Pick on someone your own size, tough guy."

Krell experienced a moment of panic. This was going to escalate, and quickly. The woman in their group had the same look, as did the other two warriors. Suddenly everyone was moving backward, away from Kraven and the large warrior. Krell grabbed Lily by the arm. She shot him a venomous look, and he released her at once.

The man started by throwing a punch, his fist hitting Kraven in the cheek. Kraven barely moved. Then he roared in a combination of rage and joy and slammed a fist into the man's breastplate. They grappled for a moment before Kraven plowed his head into the man's face. Then it was back to fists.

Krell looked at the woman warrior from their group and held out his hand in an exasperated gesture. He then grabbed Dorn, hauling him backward to stand next to him.

"What, we're not going to help?" shouted Dorn, clearly excited.

"No. The goal is to keep the Netminder's Friend intact. Watch Lily," said Krell, as he moved to intercept a group of fishers who were rising from their table, looking at the group of dwarves. He caught one on the shoulder, forcing him down into his chair again, and glared at the rest.

"Marlena likes this place. I like this place too. *Sit. Down.*"

They took one look at Krell, eyeing his armor, and their anger was replaced with fear.

"Meant no trouble, wasn't going to start nothing," said the one Krell still held by the shoulder.

"Good. Enjoy your drink."

Krell heard them call him a dwarf lover as he walked away.

Kraven, meanwhile, was shouting in joyous outrage as he pummeled the human. The man lowered himself, then slammed his fist directly into Kraven's groin.

"Ha, stupid orc! You should wear armor!"

Kraven laughed and punched him in the face.

"What the…? That normally works!" He hit Kraven in the face, then kneed him in the groin, throwing his full weight into it.

Kraven grunted, then grabbed him by the shoulders and hurled the man at the door. He crashed into it and fell to the floor. Dazed, but still moving, he was already rising to his feet.

Krell made eye contact with the woman from their group and made a negating gesture. She nodded and reached out to steady one of the other men who was going to aid his friend.

"A golden sovereign on the orange orc!" Dorn shouted.

"I'll take that bet!" said the woman, more to defuse the tension than anything else.

Suddenly most of the people in the room were making side bets with one another, as Kraven was rammed face first into the doorframe. There was an audible crack from the wood as he hit, but he stood straight back up afterwards, laughing.

"This usually works!" said the man Kraven was fighting, as he punched him in the face again. Kraven blocked the next one, then punched him back. The man began to wobble.

"What in the hells are you?" he said.

"I'm Kraven!"

Orca came up and stood next to Krell, folding his arms over his chest. "This is your idea of keeping things calm?"

Krell laughed. "Best I could do with that hothead and Kraven in the same room." Orca nodded.

Kraven was on the verge of winning, or so Krell thought, when Captain Gijwolf and the guard arrived.

* * *

"... and that is when Kraven began beating the stuffing out of the man who pushed me," said Krell.

Captain Gijwolf pinched the bridge of his nose and shook his head. There was a long pause, and he looked up at Krell.

"Okay," he said. Krell thought he looked disappointed. He turned and walked back into the Netminder's Friend. The rain had stopped, but the air was still heavy with moisture.

The doorway was largely intact. Dorn had used magic that ReckNor graced him with to effect repairs to the cracks in the door frame, and aside from Kraven and the other man, nobody else was involved. There was some general discontent that the guard had arrived and stopped the fight before it could be resolved, leaving many wagers incomplete, and one chair was nothing but unrecoverable splinters.

Still, no other furniture was damaged, and Lily was safe. Krell looked at her and wondered if he had caused this whole mess himself or not. He pondered that and decided it didn't matter. He felt confident that what he did was right, even if he didn't understand why. ReckNor was silent within him.

That was fair, thought Krell. If he wanted him to solve his own problems, then he had no business being upset with him about how he went about doing it.

PERHAPS THIS IS WHY HIERON HAS SO MANY RULES TO OBEY.

Krell winced, then let out a heavy sigh. ReckNor was confusing to him. He turned to Lily.

"Walk with me. Let's talk about your employment, shall we?"

She gave him a look that he did not understand, and together they began walking through town. Meandering, really, since Krell had no specific destination in mind.

"Where are we going?" she asked.

Krell gestured vaguely. "Nowhere in particular. Tell me, Lily, how did you end up here?"

"Well, I'm from one of the little halfling communities up in the hills." She gestured inland. Krell hadn't known there were other villages near Watford.

She took in a deep breath. "My sister is evil. She stole my fiancé from me and drove me out. I had nothing, so I was trying to find something to eat, but nobody would feed me."

Krell avoided looking at her. She sounded so angry and bitter that it made him feel hurt inside. His eyes tracked around, realizing they had wandered from the area near the town square toward the outskirts of Watford. Krell had seen that the buildings got smaller, but the squalor made Krell pause. The roads became paths, still muddy from the rain earlier in the day. The dwellings themselves seemed almost haphazardly assembled, and people were looking at him, many with hostile eyes.

Krell wondered at this. The docks in Watford were always busy and well organized. The town square was always clean and surrounded by large estates. Shops and pleasant homes lined the road leading to the temple.

This part of Watford was neither pleasant nor clean.

YET AMONG THEM ARE THOSE THAT ARE FAITHFUL.

Krell winced.

"Are you listening to me?" asked Lily.

"Hmm?" said Krell. "I was thinking about something else. What did you just say?" He looked at her, realizing she was restraining a young boy. He was kneeling on the ground, his arm around his back, held painfully in place. Her other hand had grasped his hair, bending his neck backward at an awkward angle.

"I *said*, this kid tried to rob you. Why did you even bring me here?"

"Release him," said Krell. There was a strange feeling inside him he didn't understand. He was looking at the boy now, who was perhaps ten years of age. He was dirty and thin. Painfully thin.

Krell looked at him and saw himself at that age. Hungry. Alone. Cold. *Desperate.*

"Are you hungry?" he asked the boy. Lily rolled her eyes.

The boy said nothing as Lily released him. He took one look at both of them and then ran into a darkened alleyway. Krell could see him clearly as he ran through the darkness, before he turned a corner and vanished from sight.

Krell looked around and noticed that there were probably a dozen children in eyesight who all looked the same.

They looked exactly like his memories of himself.

"I wasn't paying attention to where we were walking."

"You look like you're seeing this part of town for the first time. How is that possible?" she said, rapping her knuckles on his armor.

"I don't know. How is this allowed?" Krell asked, gesturing at the squalid surroundings.

Lily laughed. Her laughter was ugly and cruel to Krell's ears.

"Everywhere is the same, Krell. All people, no matter who, are made up of the haves and the have-nots. Watford is no different. How often does the council walk through here? How often do these people see a guard? Unless I miss my guess, these people are constantly scrounging for food and warmth, all the while fending off those who would steal from them. They're *me*, in a lot of ways. They have basically nothing." Lily gave him a look filled with such contempt that Krell almost took a step away from her. There was a palpable hatred radiating off Lily as they talked, grating on his senses.

Krell shook his head. There were those faithful to ReckNor who lived here. He wondered why Olgar did nothing about this.

"Let's go to the temple. I want to learn more about you, and you seem capable enough to keep thieves off me. If I'm going to give you a job so I can give you money, what can you do?" Krell began walking through the town, heading toward the temple perched on the hill. He never realized you could see it from basically anywhere in Watford.

"You've got a charter, right? To wear that armor?" asked Lily. Krell nodded.

"Then hire me as a soldier. I'm a butcher, Krell." She looked at him, her eyes hard and merciless. "I kill things. Give me weapons and I'll kill for you. I'm also going to kill my sister for what she did to me. You need to know that before you decide whether to hire me."

Krell grinned at her. "Lily, we venture out to fight monsters. If you have no issue killing them, that is enough for me. I'll find out how it works, with the charter, to take you on. If you're half as good in battle as you are at intimidating would-be thieves, it'll be coin well spent."

"You don't mind that I plan to kill my sister? I thought paladins had all sorts of rules they had to follow," she said, looking a little confused.

Krell laughed. "Paladins of Hieron, maybe. I worship ReckNor, lord of the seas and skies. He doesn't ask for much. He wants us to propitiate him for the use of his seas and to ask for good weather. He expects you to deal with the consequences of your choices, but he really wants you to choose." Krell gave a shrug. "I'm not some judgmental avatar sent to the world to uphold some special virtue. If I were, I might go kill the town council for what I saw back there. How is allowing that to persist any different from you murdering your sister?"

Lily looked at him and smiled.

Chapter Fourteen

Lily looked good in her new leather jerkin. Strong and competent.

"Really, Krell? You're bringing her with us?" asked Tristan, looking critically at Lily.

Krell nodded.

"Well, she's your problem then! I'm certainly not going out of my way to help her if she needs it." Tristan stalked off. Krell wondered if he was upset about something else.

Three days had passed. As the sun began to light the horizon, the newly renamed *ReckNor's Bounty* was about to set sail for the first time. Krell frowned. Not the first time, obviously, but the first time since it got its new name.

Kraven slapped Krell on the shoulder, the breastplate absorbing the blow better than the chain mail armor ever did. "Don't worry, Krell. She can just do what Gerrard does, and run and hide when trouble starts!"

Gerrard looked incensed. "Hey, Kraven, you know that's unfair, right? Am I right, Krell?"

Krell nodded seriously at him, then turned to Kraven. "Gerrard has fought valiantly and well in every battle. His blade is always covered with the blood of our enemies. He may not be as large as you, but neither does he run and hide. Do not diminish him."

Kraven laughed, a deep rolling laugh that carried across the whole ship.

"Brace up fore and aft!" Captain Voss shouted, and ropes were pulled and undone, or tied up. It was confusing to Krell, but the sails unfurled.

"Weigh anchor!" The crew hauled on other ropes, and the ship began to move. The wind was blowing easterly, yet the ship moved south.

He had a lot to learn if he was going to participate. Artur had been teaching him how to coil ropes properly, and was displeased with how little Krell knew about the tying of knots. When Krell asked about climbing the rigging, Artur laughed at him and shook his head, telling him not for a while yet.

When the ship cleared the harbor, Captain Voss shouted more commands, and more sails unfurled. They began to pick up speed. Krell had been told that it was vital that he watched and paid attention, yet he didn't know anything about what he was seeing. What was clear to him was that the crew knew what they were supposed to do, for the most part, and seemed to work together nearly seamlessly.

"Like I said, my lord, a good crew." Captain Voss came and stood next to Krell. "Don't worry that you understand nothing yet. Tell me, what do you see?"

"They all work together. I see dozens and dozens of ropes, but everyone seems to know which rope does what. I see you shout one or two things, but then the rest of them do twenty things or more."

"Exactly. You're getting what you need from this. They work together. This ship, it's like our body, yes?" Krell gave him a blank look.

"You've hands and feet. How does the foot know how to move so you don't fall when you walk? How does the hand know to hold the grip on the sword when the arm moves to swing it? Like your body, this ship is made of parts that all work together. The crew knows their business, so we sail!"

A few minutes passed while Krell watched. Ropes were pulled on one side and released on another, and the yards — the long wood beams attached to the masts — swung around.

"As far as punishments go, I still can't think how to repay you for the kindness of this one, my lord," said Captain Voss. Lily stirred, looking at them in a little confusion. Krell looked down at her.

"Captain Voss was betrayed by Daylan Plintform, then was robbed by him. Seems to me that a good and true follower of ReckNor deserved better, so here he is." Lily nodded, then leaned back and closed her eyes.

"You really think he betrayed us?" he asked Krell.

Krell nodded. It made sense to him, the description Captain Voss gave of the events. "I guess Daylan sold the ship, hiding how he got the funds for it, then claimed his ship was stolen, probably getting more money from that somehow, and finally blamed you and the crew, and stole your wages and savings." He looked directly at Captain Voss.

"But I have no proof."

Captain Voss nodded slowly, then took a deep breath in.

"Just kill him," said Lily. Captain Voss looked down at her, and shook his head before turning back to watching the crew.

Minutes passed in silence, as Krell watched the crew making nearly constant minute adjustments to ropes all over the ship.

"Think we're going to find trouble, my lord?"

Krell nodded. "I have no doubt, Captain, none at all. Before we return to Watford, there will be sea devil blood on the deck." Krell looked at him. "You know the crew. Who are the ones with skill in battle? I'm not talking sailors brawling here, but actual combat against terrors from the deep."

"Among the officers, all are capable with a blade, but obviously Barduk is a cut above. He'd give you a run for your money with his skill. Among the crew, I'd trust Kingsmill, Porell, Yank, Chardell, and Serda with a blade, though Chardell and Porell are much better with a crossbow than they are with a sword. The rest I'd send below if it comes to a fight."

Krell nodded. That was better than he was expecting. "If we're boarded, the crew knows what to do?"

"They do, my lord. You still want to do weapons drill among the crew?"

"I do, and I still don't think you should call me 'my lord,' Captain."

Tristan's voice carried to them. "I completely agree with Krell, Captain Voss!"

"You don't like him much, do you, my lord?" asked Captain Voss quietly.

Krell looked at Captain Voss, lost in thought. Did he like Tristan? No, certainly not. Even from the first moment they met, they were at odds with one another. Krell knew enough to know that each thought the other was arrogant and rude... and stupid.

Krell smiled. "Yeah, not really. Yet he has some power with his magic. I suspect that in the future he will be a force that will change the world at his whims. ReckNor tells me to keep him around, whether because he thinks I need him to keep me alive, or because I'm supposed to convert him to the worship of ReckNor, or something else."

"Something else?" asked Captain Voss.

Krell nodded. "It has occurred to me that Tristan's whims may be catastrophically bad for me personally, and many others generally. Others, who may be followers of ReckNor." Krell glanced at Lily and winked.

"It may be that ReckNor wants me to keep him around so I can murder him if he gets out of line."

* * *

It was three days of sailing before they found something.

They were half a day's sail south of the farthest point that the fishing boats would travel, according to Captain Voss. Chardell, from the masthead lookout, spotted what looked like a wrecked ship to the south. As they approached, Captain Voss squinted into the distance.

"My lord, we need a looking glass. Expensive, but worth it. I feel helpless without one." He looked up. "Chardell, what news?"

From above, Chardell looked down. "Looks like they've run aground, Captain! I can see reefs and rocks ahead!"

Voss nodded and looked forward. "Foresail, brace to starboard!" he shouted. At once, several of the crew began loosening ropes on one side of the ship, while pulling on the other. The yard holding the sails on the forward part of the ship began to pivot. Cullen spun the wheel, and the ship heeled to starboard.

Krell had learned a lot in three days. Still, Artur told him it would be a long time before anyone trusted him with anything important.

As they approached more closely, Krell could begin to make out details. The vessel was one of the larger ones, and was not moving at all with the motion of the waves. It was a gentle day on the sea, and the wind was mild, so their progress was slow.

"See there, my lord, how the ship does not move at all? It looks low in the water as well. I wager the bottom has been torn out, and she's resting on the reef, wedged hard, I imagine. Next time a good storm comes along, she'll break apart." Krell thought he was beginning to understand Captain Voss and what he was talking about.

"We don't want to take *ReckNor's Bounty* any closer than this, do we?"

"We've a good way to go yet, but no, we'll stand far off from the reefs. No sense risking anything. Charts!" Voss shouted, grabbing the wheel to steady it. Cullen let go, popped open a sea chest and pulled out a leather map. The map and markings looked almost tattooed on the leather.

"Nothing's supposed to be here, Captain," he said. "Not for leagues and leagues. This reef ain't marked."

Captain Voss nodded, then yelled, "Battle stations! Pull in the sails, and set the sea anchor!" Several of the crew scrambled to pull on light chain mail shirts and picked up shields. Krell could see Barduk organizing them in a tight group, while the rest of the crew pulled on ropes to collapse the sails, bundling them in and tying them off. The whole process took nearly five minutes, by Krell's timing, and when done the ship was largely stationary.

The rest of the crew retreated below decks, and Krell could clearly hear the sounds of the doors being barred.

"Well, my lord, we're as ready as we're ever going to be. Shall we lower a boat for you and yours to go investigate?"

"Ugh, enough with the 'my lord' crap, he's just a peasant like the rest of you," said Tristan. "Yes, lower a boat so we can get this over with."

The armed crew, led by Barduk, made the longboat ready and lowered it over the side. Orca climbed down first, followed by Kraven. Krell and Tristan both tried to go at the same time, and Krell allowed himself to be shoved back.

Gerrard gave Krell a look as Tristan climbed down. "You know I know, right? You let him win there, didn't you?"

Krell grinned at Gerrard. "It seems that little escapes you, Gerrard. Have you heard the call of ReckNor? He's always looking for converts with sharp eyes."

"Hey, you know I like you, Krell, and I have no particular issue with ReckNor, but I'm more of a song-and-dance kind of guy, you know what I mean?"

Krell's grin widened. "ReckNor has no issue with song or dance, Gerrard." He looked at Captain Voss. "We'll return shortly. Everyone stays aboard, no matter what. If it looks like we're lost, leave and report back to the council." Krell climbed over the side and descended into the boat.

From above, Lily started to descend.

Krell looked up. "No, Lily, I need you to stay here and help keep the crew alive."

"You sure about that?" she asked.

Krell shook his head. "No. But I have a feeling that tells me that this is not going to be easy. I worry you're going to be needed here." Lily shrugged, then climbed back up and over the rail. Krell noticed she was a nimble and fast climber.

From above, he heard Gerrard say, "Hey, uh, Krell is a little intense, right? And I'm sure he doesn't really mean that, right? About leaving?"

Lily snorted. "Stop being a coward, Gerrard, and get your ass down there."

When Dorn and Gerrard were aboard, Kraven pushed off from the side of the ship, and he and Krell rowed, while Orca manned the tiller. They approached the wrecked ship. As they got closer, Krell could see that the deck was covered in strange brown patches.

As soon as they climbed aboard, it was obvious what they were. Patches of dried blood.

Krell let a blade form in his hand, looking around. "Well, that removes any question about what happened, I suppose."

"Nonsense," said Tristan. "There's any number of things that could have done this. We need real evidence, not just a bloodstain that could have come from a fish."

Krell looked at Tristan, again questioning why ReckNor would have any interest in him, and why he would be subjected to his presence. When he looked within, the grace of ReckNor was humming with anticipation but also contained currents of amusement. Krell suspected ReckNor was enjoying watching him struggle with Tristan.

The ship was considerably smaller than *ReckNor's Bounty*, and there was only a single door forward leading to belowdecks. When they opened it, the blood-spattered hallway did not have the benefit of drying in the sun. The metallic scent of human blood washed over them.

Orca looked at the walls and ran his fingers along four large parallel gouges. "Those things had four claws for hands, right?"

"The sea devils? Yes," said Dorn. He ventured farther in.

The main hold was built to store fish. The fishing vessel wouldn't stay out long, lest the catch begin to spoil, but they would drag nets for some time, starting as soon as they left Watford in some cases. There should have been something, but it was empty.

They listened to the water lapping against the outside of the hull, and the slight sound of wood creaking. Otherwise, it was silent. The hold reeked of fish and blood.

"So, do you think the town council will want to hear that we found a ship, and we suspect, but don't know, there were sea devils involved, or do we stay out here wandering aimlessly for no reason?" asked Tristan.

Krell found a hatch leading down. "That should be the bilge," said Orca. Krell nodded and opened the hatch. The handle was tacky with dried blood.

The bilge was gone. The bottom of the ship had been ripped out, and it was caught on a spear of rock that was holding the ship in place. Captain Voss was right. The first time there was anything approaching rough weather, it would dash this ship to pieces on these rocks.

Krell looked up and closed the hatch. "The ship is holed. No way it's ever going to sail again."

"Any personal effects, clothing or whatever?" asked Kraven.

"In the bilge?"

"No, anywhere."

"There's probably storage at the aft of the boat. This wall doesn't go far enough back to be the stern." Krell looked up and headed back up to the deck. Outside, the clear air washed away the stink of old blood, and he started to head aft.

A tremor in ReckNor's grace warned him a moment before a clawed hand grasped the railing to his left.

* * *

"They're here!" shouted Krell, who stepped away from the door to make room for others.

The sahuagin pulled itself on deck, stark naked, and Krell could see there were several more in the water, swimming toward them. He looked to port and saw several others.

"I count at least twenty!" he shouted, donning his shield and getting his arm strapped in.

The one on deck didn't waste time, stalking toward him and lashing at Krell with its claws. Krell batted them away with his shield and formed a longsword in his hand as Kraven and Orca came on deck.

Kraven roared a battle cry and charged forward, while Orca spotted them coming up on both sides and stood near Krell so they could defend one another. A bolt of fire shot past Krell, igniting the sea devil clawing at him. It let out a burbling shriek and ran to the rail, but Krell cut it down from behind as it fled.

"Smaller! Easier to kill!" shouted Orca, his sword shedding sahuagin blood and reflecting sunlight as it flashed through the air. Krell couldn't help but agree. Their tactics were simple, if effective. They were going to swarm over them, attacking from multiple sides at once.

"Where did they come from?" Krell looked around. It seemed impossible they missed this many of them in the water so close by. With a terrible thought, Krell's eyes darted to *ReckNor's Bounty*, and he could see Chardell on the masthead lookout with his crossbow, shooting down into the water.

"They're attacking the ship! We need to get back!" shouted Krell. Kraven roared as one of the sea devils slashed him. As one, they all seemed to inhale, and then they went mad, rushing forward with slavering jaws. Anything resembling a coordinated attack vanished in their frenzy.

Krell took a wound to his shoulder and another to his brow, though the helmet deflected most of the blow. His sword cut down three of them, and occasionally a sea devil would drag one of their dead back. At first, Krell thought it was to make room for others to stand with sure footing to continue the attack. His gorge rose as he watched them begin feeding, instead.

Another climbed on deck, larger than the others and wearing elaborate bead necklaces and a silvery metal armband. It looked at Kraven and began uttering words of power. At once, Kraven froze in place, his shouts of rage and excitement cut off. The sea devils swarmed him, dealing many grievous wounds to him.

"Orca! Spellcaster!" Krell surged toward Kraven, seeking to buy him time to shrug off the assault. Two of the sahuagin slashed at him, and one clutched at his shield but he cut it down, and crashed on the other sahuagin like a wave. The nearest ones stopped savaging Kraven, though those farther away continued biting and clawing him.

Dorn was at his side and cast a spell. Suddenly Kraven bellowed in rage, and his axe swung around. Dorn's rapier flashed into a sea devil attempting to jump Krell from behind, and Krell spun around as Tristan let out a panicked yell.

Gerrard was down and being savaged while Tristan was surrounded. Krell slapped Dorn on the shoulder to get his attention, then charged toward them, hoping Kraven could persist. Dorn cast a spell into Kraven, and several of his wounds closed and disappeared, only the blood coating his skin to show that there had ever been wounds at all.

Krell cut down two sahuagin that leapt at him, though a third savaged his leg, causing him to limp. He again broke like a wave atop the sahuagin attacking Gerrard. Gerrard looked bad — pale and covered in deep wounds. The sea devils turned from him to attack Krell, and Tristan reached out to another, his hand crackling with energy, and the sea devil went rigid as lightning coursed over its body.

It shook itself and slashed at Tristan, who had retreated into the doorway.

Krell spared a glance at Orca, who was heavily engaged, and at *ReckNor's Bounty*, where the lower deck appeared lost, as the crew marshaled on the rear deck to defend the stairs. Krell could see several sea devils trying to climb the outside of the ship's hull with varying degrees of success.

He turned his attention back to his immediate peril. There were seven of them facing Tristan and himself, though only two were attempting to get at Tristan at the moment. His breastplate shrieked as claws scraped across it, finding no purchase, and he slashed with his blade, beheading the one still befuddled from Tristan's spell, easing the pressure on him.

Krell took two more wounds and cut at another one. Tristan fanned his fingers, his thumbs touching as he shouted words of power. A sheet of flame erupted from his hands, catching most of the sahuagin and stopping just short of Krell. The wave of heat washed over him as the sahuagin croaked in agony.

Then Dorn and Kraven attacked the sea devils from behind and were joined a moment later by Orca. In seconds it was over, and Krell spun around, searching for the sea devil that had cast a spell at Kraven. It was on the deck in a puddle of greenish blood, near where Orca had been fighting. Krell dropped to his knee to try to get ReckNor's grace to heal Gerrard.

He was already dead.

* * *

The crew were scared.

By the time Krell and the others recovered Gerrard's body and rowed back over to the ship, the attack there was over. Nobody aboard *ReckNor's Bounty* had died, but that was more because of the high walls of the ship and Chardell's alert eyes than any skill with blades. His crossbow had seen heavy use, and the sea was discolored with sea devil blood.

Lily was drenched in green ichor. The crew were eyeing her warily. From the carcasses of the sahuagin still scattered across the deck, and the coating of green blood around the aft stairs, it looked like she'd slain twenty sea devils herself.

Captain Voss wasted no time. The rest of the crew came up, some detailed to get buckets to wash the deck of blood, others to get the ship underway. The crew shoved the sahuagin remains overboard.

"We're leaving? Good," said Tristan, slumped down against a rail on the forecastle deck, where no fighting had taken place. ReckNor's grace had healed his shoulder, but blood soaked his clothes. He was holding a necklace he'd taken from the bigger sea devil. He had already clasped the silvery bracer it was wearing to his arm.

He was certain both were items of power.

Krell leaned against the foremast, his eyes watching Captain Voss on the quarterdeck. He was issuing orders quickly, his eyes seeming to take in everything the crew was doing, but also watching the sea warily. Krell couldn't blame him for that.

The crew were looking at them with a combination of fear and respect.

He looked over at Orca, who was wrapping Gerrard in spare sailcloth. "What do you think, Orca? Fifty of them?"

Orca nodded. "About that, I would wager. Much smaller than the one we fought before, down there," he said, gesturing at the main deck where they had first seen a sea devil. "The spellcaster was smaller, but smarter. Still went all crazy when it smelled my blood, though. If it had kept casting spells, we'd have been in trouble."

Orca finished wrapping Gerrard and began affixing a chain.

"When I killed that one, that's when the others began to run. Only reason I think we lived, honestly."

"What are you doing?" Krell asked.

"Weighting the body, so it sinks when we push it overboard. Why do you ask?" Orca looked at Krell, perplexed.

Krell shook his head. "No."

A thunderous expression crossed Orca's face, and he stood and limped toward Krell. They were all badly hurt, and Orca approached to within an inch of Krell's nose and looked at him, his eyes simmering with fury.

"No? Did I hear that right, little human?" he said, his tone filled with menace.

"That's right, Orca, I said no. I'll not throw a free meal to those beasts. Gerrard deserves better than that!" Krell shoved at Orca, who did not budge at all. "Now, get out of my face."

"Bold words from someone who abandoned an ally in battle, Krell," said Orca. His voice carried traces of anger, and his eyes blazed with fury. "You forget that I am in charge here."

"Oh, ReckNor's balls, Orca. You're not in charge any more than I am. Just shut it and get out of my face. I didn't abandon you. I went to save Kraven. And we're not tossing Gerrard overboard."

"Gerrard's corpse, not Gerrard. Gerrard is dead." Orca looked at him a moment longer, glanced at Kraven, then stepped back. "How do you propose we deal with the stench, then, hmm? You think a rotting corpse is going to honor Gerrard more than becoming fish food will?"

Krell sighed, and Dorn intervened. "He won't rot."

Dorn kneeled down beside Gerrard and cast a spell. Then he leaned back, satisfied. "There. He's preserved for days and can't rise and become undead, either. So cease your complaining, you two, and let's get back and report to the council, and see about a reward!"

Dorn looked at Orca. "Krell's right. Gerrard deserves better than being tossed overboard."

The ship lurched as the sea anchor came clear, and Kraven grunted. "Just as well we're moving. The council should know about the trap we just walked into."

Krell, Orca and Tristan all looked sharply at Kraven, who smiled back at them.

"Why do you think this was a trap, Kraven?" asked Tristan.

"There were fifty of them, we think? And they attacked us and the ship at the same time? The weather was clear, the sea gentle, but nobody saw anything? Then *wham*, fifty of them?" He emphasized his point by smacking his fist into his hand.

"If there were that many right close by, then they'd have swarmed us as soon as we were in the boat, away from the ship. Overturn it, and we're meat in the water for them... no, I'd guess they had lookouts, who saw us coming and went and got the assault group we just about massacred." Kraven looked down at Gerrard, then back at the rest of them.

"We got lucky, you know that, right?"

"Gerrard is dead, Kraven," said Tristan. "How is that lucky?"

"Because if they'd just attacked the ship, I doubt they'd have been able to hold it," he said, gesturing at Captain Voss and the crew as the ship gathered speed, leaving the fishing boat behind.

Captain Voss nodded to Kraven. "Only twenty or so made it aboard, though Chardell got a number of them in the water. Without Lily, we'd have lost the deck and our lives." Lily gave him an evil-looking grin.

Tristan looked at him for a moment. "And?" he said.

"I understand," said Krell. "If they'd have taken the ship, then we'd have that longboat as our only means of escape. That means if we tried to leave, they could have done what Kraven said whenever they wanted. Tipped the boat, dumped us in the water. They could also have just taken the longboat and left us on the wreck with no way to escape." Krell shook his head, a rueful expression on his face.

"Kraven's right, we *were* lucky. Or rather, they were stupid. If they'd taken the ship, we'd have had to take it back. And then, assuming we survived, we'd have to sail it ourselves." Krell gave a meaningful look at the two dozen crew on deck. "We've tried that before. It was not quite a disaster, but pretty close."

They all went quiet, thinking about being stranded three days' sail from anything, in seas infested with sea devils. The wind flowed over the deck toward them, bringing with it the scent of blood.

* * *

Watford was a welcome sight.

Captain Voss neatly aligned *ReckNor's Bounty* perpendicular to the end of the dock, ensuring they could be under way quickly again. Krell jumped down with several others and hauled on the lines while they tied the ship off. The gangway was extended, and people began to disembark.

Captain Gijwolf was walking down the dock toward them, and frowned when he saw Kraven carrying a sail-wrapped bundle over his shoulder as he descended to the dock. He looked around, spotted Lily, then looked at Krell.

"Gerrard?"

Krell nodded. "Going to walk with Kraven up to the temple while Orca and Tristan here report to the council. He deserves that much from us, at least," Krell said this with an edge, glancing at Orca as he did so.

Kraven and Krell left, walking toward the temple.

"You gonna keep poking at Orca?" Kraven asked, as he readjusted the sailcloth bundle that held Gerrard's body.

"He keeps telling me he is in charge. He isn't," said Krell.

"Someone needs to be."

"Kraven, every battle is the same for you. You bellow in rage and run forward. Tristan ignores everyone and everything and does whatever he wants. Dorn might listen to guidance, but he seems pretty erratic. Gerrard listened, but he's dead. Orca won't listen because he's certain that no matter who else comes up with a plan, they're wrong and we should use his plan." Krell looked up at the temple as they climbed.

"It's not about someone being in charge. It certainly can't be me. Whatever has pulled us together, and I blame ReckNor for this mostly, we're stuck with one another." Krell reached out a hand, putting it on Gerrard's body. "I just want you to all stay alive."

"You gonna cry? It looks like you're gonna cry!" said Kraven, gleefully.

"A little, yeah." Krell nodded, wiping at his eyes. They walked the rest of the way in silence.

Olgar was waiting for them outside the temple. He looked at them as they approached and walked inside without a word.

Krell was surprised when he entered. A massive stone altar was at one end of the temple. It was over eight feet long, six feet wide, and four feet high. It had to weigh thousands of pounds.

"Olgar, where did this come from?" Krell asked. He walked up to it, running his hand across the stone. It was polished smooth, and the sides were adorned with images of ships at sea, dominated by the symbol of ReckNor in the center.

Olgar smiled, pleased. "It was in the back room. I made it many years ago, so I brought it out here."

Krell gave him a flat look. "You brought it out. Here. From a back room that we don't have." Krell gestured at the altar. "How much does this weigh, Olgar?"

"Seven thousand pounds or so, I'd say," said Olgar. He gave Kraven a sly smile as he said that, then sobered when he saw the bundle again.

"Gerrard, by the size?"

Krell nodded.

"Well, put him on the altar and unwrap him, and let's see what we can see."

They unwrapped Gerrard, and the wounds stood out starkly on his body. While Gerrard was preserved, his clothing had been soaked in both his and the sea devil's blood. The stench from his clothes filled the temple.

Olgar didn't seem to be bothered by the smell. He put his dagger to work, cutting Gerrard's clothes away. Olgar reached the boots and paused.

"There's magic in these, am I right?" He barked out a laugh. "I sounded like Gerrard just now."

"We know, Olgar, he… Olgar?" Krell looked at Olgar in concern. He'd just made a joke about Gerrard, but now his smile faded and his eyes were unfocused.

"He's here, lad."

"Um. Who is here, Olgar?"

"Gerrard."

Kraven and Krell looked at one another. "Yes, Olgar, he's right there," said Kraven, in a gentle tone Krell had never heard him use before.

Olgar's eyes abruptly focused, and he slapped Kraven across the face. Hard.

"Don't patronize me, boy! I know what I'm talking about!" Kraven and Olgar glared at one another, and Kraven broke eye contact first. Olgar gave a slight nod, then turned to Krell.

"Gerrard is here, Krell. I think he's following you around."

"You're going to need to provide a lot more clarity here, Olgar, because I don't understand."

"I mean his spirit, Krell. He's haunting you." Olgar looked around. "When a god blesses a true priest with power, well, that priest has to earn the right to get more. Gods aren't limitless. Their power comes from worship. When they give power to their priests, they are diminished, but the priest is supposed to use that power to get more followers. Understand?"

Kraven nodded. "I get it, Olgar. So why is Gerrard haunting Krell? Some sort of unresolved sex thing between them?"

Krell spun toward Kraven, shocked, but Olgar just laughed. "Doubtful, Kraven. Krell is too stubborn to ever fall in love with anyone, especially someone like Gerrard. No, I've no clue why Gerrard is following Krell around. But since he is, there's a chance I can stuff him back in his body."

Krell's eyes snapped to Olgar. "What?"

Olgar grinned. "Never knew that about me, did you, my boy?"

Krell felt both impressed and afraid of Olgar. Gods favored their priests with power. As Olgar said, the more power granted, the more powerful the priest. Not just that, though. The power had to be *earned* by the priest.

To have earned the power to bring back the dead was exceptionally rare, but not unheard of. Krell had no idea Olgar was that powerful. He suddenly felt very small, like a fishing boat before an oncoming hurricane.

"Now, I don't like to let people know I have that strength, mind you. Haven't used it before. I'd say keep your mouths shut about it, but seeing Gerrard walking around again would make that pointless, wouldn't it?" Olgar looked thoughtfully at Gerrard. "Probably doesn't even matter. I need diamonds to work the spell, and I have none."

"Why diamonds?" asked Krell.

Olgar shrugged. "Magic is magic, my boy. It needs what it needs. I've never put much thought into why this bit of power requires a piece of string, or that bit of magic some fleece from a lamb. Certainly I don't question why waving this symbol of ReckNor around can mean sometimes I don't need those bits, and sometimes I do. Ask Karaback if you want a long-winded answer that still tells you nothing."

"I've only seen him in council," said Krell. Kraven just looked confused, trying to follow the conversation.

"Is that so? Well, he's as boring as dried kelp, so no loss there. I'm sure he understands why better than I do. I just know that if we're going to catch his spirit and jam it back into his body, we need some diamonds to do it. Not emeralds, not rubies, diamonds."

Olgar looked at him, his expression grave.

"Good ones. High-quality diamonds. The lower the quality, the more I need for whatever reason. Two other things. First, the spell is going to eat them up somehow. Don't know why, but they're going to shrink or be destroyed in the process. If there's not enough, we're scuppered."

Olgar frowned. "Second, the magic Dorn used here — it was Dorn, right?" Krell nodded. "Thought so, has this immovable quality to it that shrieks *dwarf* at me. Anyway, unless we do it soon, his spirit is going to go *on,* or he's going to turn into a monstrous nightmare undead that I'll need to obliterate, so he *can* go on. Any hint of who he worships?"

"He never said, but I got the sense he was open to ideas. Felt that ReckNor wasn't for him, though."

"Ha! Well, if you can find diamonds fast enough, then we'll see how he feels about it after I wrench him back into his corpse!" Olgar rubbed his face, then looked around. "ReckNor's salty tears! It's nearly noon and I've had naught to drink. Get down to town, find some diamonds, and then bring me a keg of the good stuff. Marlena knows what I want."

Olgar looked at Kraven, then back at Krell.

"Well? Why are you still here?"

Chapter Fifteen

"Are you sure about this, Krell?"

Krell nodded. "We've spent the last four hours visiting every place we can think of that might have diamonds. The only one we found, Daylan wouldn't sell. I think it was too small, anyway. I bet we need bigger ones."

Krell looked at Kraven and gestured toward Orianna's Bountiful Goods. "So this is the last, and probably best, place to look for something like that."

Krell walked in.

He wasn't sure what he was expecting, but pink wallpaper was not it. Nor was the smell — a strange blend of flowers and sweetness. The floor was a dark wood, polished to a high shine. Two tables he could see were in front of him, with more behind. The first was piled high with children's toys, the other with what smelled like soap. A tinkling bell above the door announced his arrival.

Orianna emerged. Now that Krell knew there was a glamor, he could see through it. Even without it, the sight of her sent his heart racing, and he didn't fully understand why. Today she was wearing a loose-fitting robe that was open at the front from neck to naval, though closed just enough to cover her breasts.

If anything, it was more enticing than the leather outfit she wore when they first met.

Krell shook his head. Where did *that* thought come from?

The grace of ReckNor within him bubbled in laughter.

"Krell, and Kraven." Even the way she said their names sent a thrill of pleasure through him, though it was tinged with danger. Krell wasn't sure if that made things better or worse for him.

Kraven was breathing heavily beside him. Krell realized he was doing the same and sought to master himself.

ReckNor's amusement grew stronger within him.

She smiled at them, turning in a way that made everything about the situation both worse and better, highlighting the curve of her chest as she leaned against the door frame.

"Are you two going to stand there in the entranceway, or come in and tell me what brings you to my home?"

Krell shook himself and walked forward. "Orianna. You mentioned you had the ability to procure things."

"Ah," she said. It was so laden with layers of meaning that Krell couldn't begin to figure out what she meant. "What is it you seek, Krell?"

"Diamonds."

She looked at him blankly, then laughed. "That was, by far, the least likely thing I expected you to say. What sort of diamonds?"

"I don't know, but the higher the quality, the better."

"Well, I have one necklace that has a few diamonds in it, as well as emeralds and peridots, if you're interested in seeing it." She gave him a dubious look. "Though I doubt you can afford it."

"Not jewelry, diamonds. Loose stones."

"Then this isn't a gift for some paramour of yours. That leaves, distressingly, only two possibilities, one of which is much more likely than the other." She looked a little disturbed. "I didn't realize Olgar was that powerful."

Krell stared at Orianna. He was struggling to understand that statement, and his thoughts whirled around until finally they fell into place. It had to have taken him over ten seconds. At least Kraven still looked confused.

"That was, actually, pretty amazing, that you figured that out from what we said. I'm impressed," said Krell. He made a mental note to himself to never underestimate Orianna. She was much smarter than she looked.

AND HOW EXACTLY DOES A SMART PERSON LOOK DIFFERENT FROM OTHERS?

Krell winced. Some days, it was easier to deal with the crashing thunder of that voice. Today was not one of those days.

Orianna grinned at him, then stepped forward — alarmingly, but enticingly — close. She ran a finger over his armor, and ReckNor's power surged. There was a feeling of something breaking and falling away, like the glamor she wore.

"Stop that," said Krell. Orianna laughed and stepped away.

"Very well, paladin, diamonds can be acquired. I suspect I know substantially more about this than both you and Olgar put together. However, I doubt I can procure any for you in anything approaching the timeline you need, unless that wrapped bundle Kraven and you carried up to the temple was not, in fact, Gerrard, as my information says it was. So, I have an alternate offer. One fraught with risk and peril. If you are interested, that is?"

"Will it get me the diamonds I want in time?"

"Perhaps it will, but I cannot be certain."

The grace of ReckNor lay quiet, but Krell could tell that ReckNor was listening intently.

"Very well. Tell me."

Orianna laughed and turned to Kraven. "And you, my burly orc friend, is there something I can help you with?"

Kraven shook his head. "I mean, unless you have an axe that will let me cut things better, no."

"Wait here." With a triumphant smile, Orianna turned and walked into the back room, and returned a moment later with a large object, vaguely axe-shaped, wrapped in cloth. She gestured, and a table along the back wall flew toward them, settling gracefully on the floor in front of her.

Krell couldn't help but be impressed. He made another note in his head about how dangerous she was. He wasn't sure why that made him desire her more as a result.

She set the bundle on the table and unwrapped it — an axe. The haft was made of dark wood, the head made of black metal, though the edge was a gleaming silver. Runes of eldritch power could be seen carved into the axe, and Krell thought they might be glowing with a purple radiance, though it could have been a trick of the eye.

An item of true power. Krell could feel it, the same way he felt about Olgar's trident. He resisted the urge to reach out and grab it.

Kraven made no such effort. Orianna grabbed his wrist as his hand closed about the axe. Krell saw Kraven's arm muscles clench in effort, but he could not free his wrist from her grasp.

Dangerous indeed.

"Master Kraven, did your mother never teach you that we do not touch things that do not belong to us?" She and Kraven made eye contact, and Kraven released his hand from the axe, and she let him go. He massaged his wrist, looking at her with respect.

"Do you follow Udar, Orianna?"

Her laughter still filled Krell with desire, but now it had a mocking edge to it. "No, Kraven, I do not follow Udar's teachings. He's a boring and pedantic god, who stupidly suggests that might makes right." She smiled, an edge to her smile. "I don't tolerate idiocy."

A tense silence descended.

"Now, you want the axe, I can tell, and I can also tell you that, unless I have been wildly misled, you have no possible way to afford it. For this, I would charge you two thousand five hundred golden sovereigns."

Kraven whistled. "Can you hold it for me, against other buyers?"

She laughed. "And who, Master Kraven, in this little town, do you think would possibly be interested in this axe besides you?"

Her smile lost its mocking edge, becoming something pleasant to see. "I should warn you, I am offering it at a substantial discount, since it has been in my possession for some time and nobody is interested in it. If you were to travel to a larger town or city and find someone selling such an item, you would pay far more for it."

"Aren't you concerned about thieves, if you have such wealth and items of such value?" asked Kraven.

Orianna looked at Krell, and her smile became something that made him want to take a step away from her. He wasn't certain, but he thought her eye color changed, becoming almost pink in hue.

"Master Krell here understands why I have no fear of that."

Krell nodded. "I suspect any thief who has broken into your business or residence here has not lived to learn the error of their ways, have they?"

Orianna's smile grew wider, and she looked back at Kraven. "So you see, Master Kraven, there is both no need for me to worry about thieves, nor is there any need for you to worry that someone will swoop in at the last minute and purchase this item from me."

She turned back to Krell. "Now, what will you offer me in exchange for the knowledge I have of where to find at least a few diamonds of worth?"

Krell shrugged. "I don't know what you want. If you had wanted coin, you would have said so, so it must be something else."

She smiled at him. "You have this delightful directness to you, Krell, that is very appealing." She paused, looking at him. "I'll tell you what, I'll do it, in exchange for a favor in the future."

"No deal," said Krell at once.

"That was fast. May I ask why not?"

"My service is to ReckNor, Orianna. I am a paladin. I will not take obligations to others if I think it will interfere with that service. And no offense," Krell said, grinning as he looked at her, "but someone like you? I can't imagine that it wouldn't interfere, probably in ways I wouldn't understand. So, no deal. What else would you want from me?"

"Hm, perhaps you could grant me an hour of your time, then? Upstairs, in my bedroom?"

Krell's heart hammered at his ribcage. Kraven, helpfully, shoved him toward the doorway at the back of the room, saying, "Go, Krell!"

"Uh, Orianna..." Krell could feel his face blushing scarlet. Her eyes widened.

"Oh, by the stars, you've never lain with a woman before, have you?" Her laughter cut at Krell, and his embarrassment turned to anger. She saw it, and her laughter subsided into chuckles.

"Oh, Krell, I'm sorry, I don't mean to laugh. That was pointlessly cruel. You really have no clue, do you? Half the young women in this town talk about you, how they want you to bed them, the stupid little twats. You could have any of them. Probably all of them, if you wanted."

She shook her head. "Never fret, little paladin. I rescind that offer, because, quite frankly, if we're going to tumble in the sheets, I want to enjoy myself, not be forced to teach you what to do. No, something else then."

Kraven was grinning at Krell. His embarrassment returned, and he blushed more. Kraven's grin widened.

"Krell, I want you to get me proof that Daylan Plintform was involved with those smugglers."

Krell started, his blush receding. "Why would you want that?"

She smiled. "None of your concern. But paladins are notorious in the stories for pulling secrets out into the open. So, that is my price. Find and share with me proof of his perfidy, and I will tell you what I know about where to find diamonds. Though, I wonder if you will be able to complete such a task in time, or without compromising your morals."

Krell looked at her. She looked extremely pleased with herself. Krell realized that she was thinking he was like the paladins in the stories, who had dozens of rules they had to follow all the time. He smiled back at her, and hers faded.

"What morals?" said Krell, fishing his blank journal out of his bag, and pulling the letter that proved Daylan Plintform was involved with the smugglers from it. "You can make a copy of this, but I am keeping the original."

Orianna looked at him strangely and gestured. A quill, inkpot, and a piece of paper floated over to the table as she shoved the axe aside. She expertly copied the note, then returned the original to Krell. That strange look persisted.

I BELIEVE SHE MAKES A MENTAL NOTE TO HERSELF, KRELL, THAT YOU ARE DANGEROUS AND NOT TO BE UNDERESTIMATED.

Krell basked in the feeling of ReckNor's pleasure.

* * *

"I don't understand why I had to come," said Tristan for the fifth time.

Krell had located all of his companions, and explained that he knew there was a cave nearby that should contain treasure within it, and that he needed the diamonds, but that all the other treasure could be split among the rest of them if they came and helped.

Tristan had agreed readily enough, but then, that was yesterday, when the weather was clear. Today, it was raining.

A gentle rain, to be sure, but that did not make it any less miserable. Nor did the fact they were heading inland, across terrain with no roads. After the last few months of the rainy season, the ground was carpeted with underbrush and the trees covered in leaves.

"You said, Krell, we'd be going into a cave. This forest is not a cave," Tristan pointed out. Krell sighed and continued to ignore him.

Orca looked at Tristan, then over at Krell. "You know you're just making things worse, right?"

Krell shook his head and ignored Orca as well.

"Arrogant little shit," muttered Orca under his breath.

"Yeah, but I like him," said Kraven.

"I like him too, even though I think he'll get us all killed one day," said Dorn.

"Well, I don't like him at all," said Tristan. "Can't I just burn this stupid forest down so we can move faster?"

"Aren't we in the forest at the moment?" asked Kraven. "Wouldn't that burn us, also?"

"Well, you maybe, but I'm sure I would be fine," said Tristan in a satisfied tone of voice. Krell again questioned why ReckNor had saddled him with Tristan.

QUESTIONS ARE GOOD. ALWAYS ASK QUESTIONS.

"You didn't answer *my* question," muttered Krell.

NO, I DID NOT, DID I?

ReckNor's amusement rippled through Krell.

It was a long day so far. They'd been stumbling around in the woods, as Dorn put it, for the last two hours. Krell knew he was close, since the ground was rising and the terrain becoming rockier. If the map Orianna had literally conjured out of thin air for him to view was accurate, they would arrive at the cave very soon.

Krell walked as the rest of them bickered, and ahead he saw a sliver of darkness between a pile of rocks, just as Orianna described. He held up his hand, but his companions were not paying attention. Kraven walked right into him, forcing Krell to take another step.

"ReckNor's balls, do none of you know how to remain silent? This is open territory, so who knows what lives here?" said Krell, anger ringing in his voice. "You've been whining for the last two hours, Tristan. However, we're here." Krell pointed at the pile of rocks, and Dorn grunted.

"I see it, Krell. The cave entrance. What's within?"

Krell concentrated, but could sense nothing. He shrugged. "If anything is in there, Orianna did not say. What I know for sure is that the diamonds in there are for Olgar. The rest of the treasure, you can all split among yourselves. We're clear on that?"

"Everyone but you gets a share, and you get all the diamonds. Hardly seems fair to me," said Tristan. "What if we find diamonds bigger than our heads?"

"If we do, then I'll buy you a kingdom, Tristan, so you will have other people to talk nonsense at. That's the bargain. Besides, the diamonds aren't for me, they're for Olgar."

Tristan snickered. "I didn't know you felt that way about him, Krell! No wonder you keep turning Marlena down."

Kraven laughed. "No, it's because he — *OW!*" Krell's fist caught Kraven on the jaw. He turned to Krell, looked him in the eye, and burst out laughing again. "Intense! I like it! Fair deal, Krell. Even if there's nothing in there but diamonds, I'm fine. Unless there's nothing in there for my axe to kill, then I'll be sad."

Krell shook his head. "This isn't for me. This is for Gerrard."

"Then Gerrard's share of treasure will be less, since we're giving up on diamonds to bring him back, aren't we?" said Tristan.

"ReckNor's balls, Tristan. There'll be no diamonds unless we can all agree to this, like you did yesterday. The diamonds are for Olgar, everything else is for you. Good?"

"*Fine*, Krell. I agree," said Tristan.

Krell looked, and everyone else nodded. He readied his shield, conjured a longsword of dark metal in his hand, and ventured forward.

As he approached the cave, Krell noted the small bones of dead animals around the entrance. Within, the floor of the cave contained many more sets of bones, almost carpeting the interior. He gestured at them, and Orca nodded, drawing his gleaming longsword.

As Krell and Orca entered the cave, the bones crunched beneath their feet. The only warning Krell had was a rustling noise, then a bat-like creature shot past Orca, its long needle-like beak slamming into his armor.

There was no time for thought, for at least a dozen of the beasts hurtled toward him, stabbing at his face and arms. He deflected several with his shield, and cut one out of the air, but one slammed into his shoulder. He grew light-headed as it drained his blood, but Dorn's blade caught it, and it fell away.

Kraven roared in fury, charging into the room, cutting one of the creatures from the air. Krell watched something different fall toward Kraven, opening like a hideous octopus. Krell shouted a warning, but the thing fell onto Kraven, immediately wrapping itself about Kraven's head, completely covering his face.

Kraven at once dropped his axe and tried to pry the creature from his head. Krell rushed forward, but then dove backward as another of the octopus bats fell toward him. It missed, but then shot back upward. Kraven fell to his knees, trying to pry the hooked fleshy tentacles from his head.

The ceiling was suddenly filled with webbing, trapping several of the flying creatures above him. Tristan let out a yell, and Krell dashed forward. He dropped his longsword, and it dissipated to mist as he called a short dagger. He slashed at the tentacles surrounding Kraven's face. Krell wondered if he could breathe.

As soon as he cut at it, the thing released Kraven, and flew toward the ceiling. Tristan caught it with a blast of flame, which ignited it, and it careened upward into the webbing. With a *whoosh*, the entire mass of webs burst into flame. There was a high-pitched shriek from above, and several burning creatures fell from the webbing as it burned away.

Krell used his dagger to slash two of the bat things that had attached to Kraven, while he gasped for breath. His head and face were covered with cuts, and he was bleeding profusely.

Krell dropped the dagger and reached out. The grace of ReckNor flowed through him like jagged glass, and many of the wounds on his face began to close, the torrent of blood lessening. Orca and Dorn roared battle cries behind him, but it seemed they had weathered the assault from the beasts that lived within the cave.

Tristan was blasting all the stalactites off the ceiling. A shower of rocks and pebbles rained down on Krell and Kraven, battering them.

"ReckNor's beard, Tristan! What are you doing?" he shouted.

"Those things look like the stone, Krell. So I'm destroying anything that might be one of them, because I don't want to be wrapped in a flying death octopus face mask! So why don't you ignore my incredibly clever actions and how I just saved everyone, and point me to where the diamonds are, because I don't see anything in here!"

Tristan had a point, Krell was forced to admit. Whatever these things were, they clearly lived on the ceiling. When Tristan created the webs up there, who knew how many were trapped. When he burned the webs, who knew how many he killed?

Krell hated it, but he knew Tristan was right.

"You know what, Tristan? You're right. You did more to win this fight than the rest of us together." Krell looked around. "I also think you're right about the diamonds."

Dorn pointed to the back of the cave. "What about through there?"

Krell looked at him in confusion. "Back where?"

Dorn peered closely at Krell's eyes. "You know your eyes have gone all black, right? Like two pools of darkness? It's creepy as the hells," he said, then he gestured at the back wall. "That is a false wall, like a secret door. It's done well enough, but it's straight. No cave naturally formed has a straight wall. I wager there's a way through."

Krell and the rest examined the wall at the back of the cave, though they all kept a wary eye on the ceiling. Well, everyone except for Tristan, who neither paid attention to the ceiling, nor helped search the wall for a way to open it.

Dorn looked crestfallen. "Well, maybe there isn't a way through," he said.

Krell grinned, saying, "Oh, I don't know about that." He conjured his weapon in the shape of a maul and handed it to Kraven.

Kraven laughed and swung at the wall, cracking it. When Kraven swung again, he smashed a hole straight through it.

Dorn laughed. "See? I knew there would be a way through!"

* * *

The room beyond was a temple.

Krell knew what he was looking at. It was dominated by a black stone statue of a twenty-foot-high frog-like demonic *thing*, with an open mouth and a stone tongue that was forked. Before it was a black metal altar, carved with images of people prostrating themselves before a five-pointed star atop a circle. It wasn't a pentagram, exactly, for the star was not contained within it. The points of the star protruded, making the image look jagged and dangerous.

It was dangerous indeed. Krell recognized it as the holy symbol of Dazguroth.

"Wow. Orianna told you about this place?" said Dorn, looking at the altar, and coming to the same conclusions as Krell.

"That's Dazguroth, right?" Tristan said.

Krell nodded. "I am pretty sure it is, yes."

Krell examined the statue again. As he walked around, Krell could see that its arms held a bowl in front of its mouth, the tongue nearly descending into it. When he peered into the bowl, he saw that there were ashes in the bottom of it.

Krell sought the grace of ReckNor within himself, but felt no threat or warning.

Most relevantly of all, in the eye sockets of the statue were two diamonds.

Large diamonds.

Krell looked at the statue, wondering how he was going to get up there.

Orca looked nervous. "I have a bad feeling about this. I don't want to make an enemy of Dazguroth here, Krell. We should leave."

Krell shook his head. "No, Orca, not without the diamonds. Besides, ReckNor and Dazguroth don't exactly have competing interests, so who cares? Let's just rob the place and get out of here." Krell made to start climbing up the statue.

Kraven grabbed him and pulled him back. "You're good on a rope ladder, Krell, but let me show you how climbing is supposed to be done."

Orca, in turn, pulled Kraven back. "This is a bad idea. We shouldn't touch it. I don't want anything to do with Dazguroth!"

Krell put a hand on his shoulder and smiled at him. "Orca, I don't sense anything. Whatever is happening here, whoever built this, it's just images. I feel nothing like I do when I'm in the temple to ReckNor. The altar there, it hums with power against my senses. Here, I feel nothing."

Orca shook his head. "That's because it's ReckNor's power, and you're a follower of ReckNor. Dazguroth wants to remain hidden, to work in secret. No wonder you feel nothing."

"I thought you said, Krell, that Orianna worked for Dazguroth. Why would she tell you about this place?" said Tristan.

He paused. "Wait, how would she even know about this place?"

Everyone stopped what they were doing and thought about that.

Krell shrugged. "I have two thoughts."

"Just two? That makes perfect sense to me!" said Tristan.

"First," said Krell, ignoring him, "I think that if Dazguroth is trying to build an altar here, and Orianna told us about it, she might be a little bitter about the conquest of her homeland. Second, we need those diamonds regardless." Krell paused in thought for a moment. "I guess third, I have no problem desecrating an altar to Dazguroth."

Dorn laughed. "That's the spirit! Kraven, go get them!"

Kraven shrugged at Orca and climbed the arm of the statue. He perched precariously on the shoulder and pulled a dagger from his belt. Jamming it into the eye socket, he worked it back and forth, trying to pry the diamond out.

"Pity Gerrard isn't here for this," said Tristan. "He's an excellent thief, like many halflings are." He looked at Krell. "Say, where is Lily, anyway?"

"I asked her to go up to the temple and talk with Olgar about ReckNor. I told her that it would be nice if she didn't offend ReckNor with some blasphemous comments while she's traveling with us," said Krell, watching Kraven intently.

Kraven suddenly pressed hard with his dagger, his arm muscles clenching. The gem popped free, flying from the socket, bouncing on the altar and falling to the ground in front of it. Kraven lost his grip on the statue and dropped the dagger as he fell forward, grabbing at handholds.

He had a hand on one of the ears of the statue, the other gripping the empty eye socket. The dagger fell straight down and landed in the bowl the statue was holding.

A flame burst up from the bowl as soon as the dagger was within it. At the same time, Krell felt the power of this place spring to life, a sense of another god's power grating over his senses.

"Uh-oh," he said.

"I knew this was a bad idea!" shouted Orca, as he backpedaled out of the room. Tristan and Dorn looked at one another, then at Krell.

Kraven reset his balance, getting his legs back up on the statue's shoulder, and leaned out, directly over the bowl. "Krell, I need a dagger!"

Krell conjured his weapon in the form of a dagger and stepped onto the altar, holding the dagger out hilt first. Kraven reached down and grabbed it.

"Ever wonder what this is made of?" he asked.

Krell shook his head. "Not really. ReckNor's power would be my guess."

Kraven dug the blade into the eye socket, perched precariously over the burning bowl. He cut around the inside of the eye socket, trying to dislodge it, and then snarled.

"Same as before then. What do you think happens if the dagger made of ReckNor's power falls into the magic bowl of Dazguroth?" said Kraven, grinning at Krell.

Krell smiled. "Don't worry, won't happen."

Kraven snorted, then shoved the dagger into the eye socket, his arms bunching up in effort once again.

As before, suddenly the diamond popped free. Krell, standing on the altar and waiting for it, grabbed it from the air.

Kraven, as before, lost his balance. The dagger fell, but Krell simply dismissed it, and it turned to mist before hitting the flame.

Kraven's feet dangled down and the flames rose, licking at them.

"Don't fall into the fire!" shouted Tristan.

"Gee, thanks, Tristan! I never would have thought of that!" snarled Kraven in response. He readjusted his grip and swung his legs sideways. Then he let go, falling clear of the statue entirely, but landing hard on the altar, splitting his head open.

The fire flared high as soon as blood hit the altar.

"That's not good," muttered Krell, feeling ReckNor's grace sheltering him from the rising power of this place. Krell leapt off it at once, and grabbed Kraven, dragging him to the hole in the wall they'd made.

"Dorn!" he shouted, as soon as he thought he was far enough away.

Dorn muttered some words of power, his hands waving in an elaborate gesture. Then he thrust his hand forward and clenched his fist. A thunderous boom echoed in the small room and the statue shattered as if blown apart. The altar itself cracked, split almost down the middle.

The feeling of power against his senses did not diminish. Krell looked at Dorn.

"Again! Let's collapse the whole cave!"

"Get clear then!" shouted Dorn, as everyone backpedaled. Orca gave Krell a disgusted look, then reached down and picked up Kraven. He turned to leave the cavern. Tristan was already outside.

"Krell, it's still raining. Can't your stupid god do anything about this?"

As Krell left the cave, the sound of Dorn's magic boomed from within and a cloud of dust billowed from the cave. Several small rocks struck Krell in the back, and he spun around, looking inside, but unable to see because of the dust in the air.

"Dorn!"

"What?" he said, walking through the dust. Then he turned and cast the spell again, and with a shuddering crash, the entire hill sank downward as the cave collapsed.

"There, that should be good enough!" he said, wiping dust that was turning to mud off his face, as the rain continued to fall.

Krell looked back at the ruins of the cave. He reached out with his senses, searching.

The power of Dazguroth was still there, thrumming in anger.

* * *

"Well, this sucks, Krell," said Tristan.

Kraven had recovered once Dorn used some of ReckNor's power to heal his head wound. They were all standing in the rain, arguing about what had just happened.

"This was a disaster, Krell!" shouted Orca, his body tense with anger. "You've brought Dazguroth's attention to us, which is never good! Never!"

"Krell, you said there'd be treasure, and now we've nothing to show for this except being wet," said Tristan.

"Shut it, Tristan, or I'll shut it for you," snarled Kraven, moving menacingly toward Tristan.

Dorn looked at Krell and shrugged. "Tristan's right, it would be better if there was some reward from all this."

Krell stood in the rain, observing all of them silently, concentrating on the sound of the raindrops hitting his helmet. His thoughts turned to trying to find a way to make everyone happy, which he found surprising. He cared about these people, even as they frustrated him.

"Is one diamond enough?" he asked, looking upward.

MORE THAN ENOUGH, KRELL.

"What?" asked Orca. "Are you talking to your god again?"

"Let's go to visit the dwarven mining camp," said Krell, turning and walking in that direction.

"Krell, how do you even know you're going in the right direction?" asked Tristan.

"Why the dwarves?" asked Kraven.

Krell looked back at them. "First, this is the way we came in, so retracing our steps will take us back to the road, eventually, which we can then use to get to the mining camp itself. Second, the dwarves should have something to trade for one of these, so we can split one and get each of you a reward."

Orca looked at Krell. "Just like that, you're going to collapse and give in to their demands?"

Krell looked him in the eye. "Looks that way."

* * *

The dwarven mining encampment looked the same.

They had been ushered into the same dining hall as before, but this time the gate guard who escorted them had to light one of the stoves to start warming the room up. The rain had diminished, but the ground was still muddy.

They sat, clustered around the stove, warming themselves as best they could, when a dwarf walked in. He reminded Krell of Petimus, but younger.

"Ah, welcome to the Smithforge Mining Consortium! My name is Oxton Smithforge, at your service!" He gave them a flamboyant bow, then straightened, looking at them. "Thramnon said that you have some items of wealth to trade. Is this so?"

Dorn uttered some words in a tongue Krell did not know, but guessed to be Dwarvish from the sound. Oxton replied, and they looked at one another and smiled. Oxton then turned to Krell.

"Show me what you have, Master Krell, and let us see if what I have is worth the trade or not."

Krell looked at Dorn, then shrugged. "I think you're going to need to teach me that," he said.

"What, Dwarvish? Sure, I can teach you," said Dorn. Orca just grunted, and Kraven chuckled.

"Who cares. As long as they speak the common tongue, that's good enough, right?" said Tristan. He waved at Krell. "Get on with it. I want to get back to Watford and talk to Karaback about your stupidity."

Krell reached into his magic bag and pulled out two diamonds, setting them on the table next to him. Oxton walked over.

"Forge Father be praised! They're huge, and expertly cut as well!" said Oxton, clearly impressed. "I doubt I have enough to trade for both of these magnificent gems, but if you'll take a promise of future payment, I'd happily take both of them!"

Krell looked at the others. Kraven shrugged, while Orca and Dorn nodded. Tristan gave him a challenging look back in return.

"Oxton, it's a pleasure to meet you. Based solely on the good reputation of the Smithforge name, I am interested in accepting. However, I need to see what you have available right now, for we have need of diamonds for a specific purpose," said Krell.

"Magic, is it? A pity," muttered Oxton. "Always destroys the gems, and that's a right shame indeed." He smiled. "Ah, well, let us see what I have. Abide here a time, and I'll return!"

Oxton donned his cloak and left, returning after five minutes with a small wooden chest. He set it on the table, opened it, and removed a dark cloth, which he spread out. Then he set the two gems they had recovered onto it, at one end, and put a metal-and-glass object to his eye. He leaned down and examined the gems closely.

"These are exquisite stones, my friends, exquisite," he said happily. "I'd love to have them both. Let me show you what I have on hand."

Oxton stood up and returned the metal object to the wooden chest. He lifted a panel and emptied it out. Seven red gemstones were placed onto the black cloth at the other end. He then opened another compartment and pulled out four clear stones, which he added to the collection. Finally, he opened the last compartment and added three blue stones.

All of the gems were cut and polished, and Oxton readily leaned forward.

"Rubies, each worth, as magicians value such things, one hundred fifty golden sovereigns. Sapphires, again, as magicians value such things, worth four hundred eighty golden sovereigns, each. These last, diamonds, valued by magicians as being worth three hundred fifty golden sovereigns, each, except that one, which is worth seven hundred."

Oxton looked at Krell and his companions seriously. "I would wager that these gems you offer in trade are probably worth three thousand golden sovereigns, each. Possibly more if I can find the right buyer for them, but you'll need to trust in the word of the dwarves on this one. The gems here," he said, gesturing to the pile he added, "are worth four thousand two hundred and forty, as magicians reckon such things. I could probably get more. Factoring in some fee for the exchange service I am providing, let us say that this would leave me in your debt for an additional one thousand five hundred golden sovereigns worth of gemstones."

Krell suddenly felt very foolish. "Are those diamonds enough?" he said, looking toward the ceiling.

MORE THAN ENOUGH.

Krell shook his head ruefully. His companions were looking at him strangely. He sighed. "Well, I'm an idiot."

"Obvious to all," murmured Tristan.

Krell grunted. "I made that too easy for you. What I mean is, we went and found these diamonds, at some peril, when Oxton had these ones here the entire time!"

"Yeah, but you didn't know that, right?" said Kraven.

Krell nodded. "But I also didn't even think to ask Petimus, who was in Watford. We talked to nearly everyone, but not Petimus." Krell turned toward Oxton. "He knows you have these?"

Oxton looked like he was trying very hard not to laugh. "Of course."

Orca was glaring at Krell.

Krell glared back at him, then turned to Dorn. "What in the hells, Dorn? You didn't think to suggest talking to Petimus?"

"You never explained, Krell. You said *come help me loot a cave for some diamonds*, not that you needed diamonds! Who am I to take your choice away from you?" shouted Dorn. His face was flushing red in anger.

Krell looked upward and sighed. Tristan snickered.

Oxton was watching them, clearly waiting for them to say something.

"Everyone is fine with this trade?" asked Krell.

"How would we divide those stones up, then?" asked Tristan, eyeing the gemstones.

Kraven shrugged. "Diamonds to Krell, the rest we argue about. I'm not good at numbers. How do we break those into four equal piles?"

Krell looked at Oxton. "We agree, it would seem."

"Humans! I love how quick you are to decide! Done and done, my new friends! I shall try to collect diamonds as the additional one thousand five hundred golden sovereigns of obligation that I have incurred here. Let me write a formal contract for us, that we have clear terms we can abide by. Is one year an acceptable timeframe for repayment of the debt?"

Krell shrugged and nodded. "I have no issue with that." He looked at the others, who nodded agreement.

"Excellent!" said Oxton, who pulled a small drawer out from the bottom of the chest and retrieved several pieces of paper. He began writing.

Krell watched as his companions argued about how to split the other gems. When they asked Oxton if they could move them around, he waved his hand at them, but remained focused on the contract he was documenting.

They ended up with three piles of one sapphire and one ruby, and a final pile of four rubies. Krell tried to calculate the numbers in his head and gave up. Kraven ended up with the four rubies, saying that four was better than two. Tristan smiled smugly and took his share.

Oxton gave the contract to Krell, and it seemed simple enough.

Krell signed, then passed it to Orca. Everyone else signed in turn. Oxton finished writing up a duplicate, and everyone signed again.

"My new friends, excellent that you chose to come and visit me today!" said Oxton, clearly pleased. He put the signed contract and writing tools into the drawer, and closed it shut. Then he grabbed the two large diamonds and put them into the chest and waited while everyone retrieved their gems. Krell looked at the handful of clear diamonds in his hand and put them into his bag.

Oxton rolled up the black cloth, put it into the chest, and closed and latched the lid. Then he smiled. "My friends, unless you would depart at once, I would offer some hospitality to you! Would you care to join me for a drink?"

Krell glanced outside as the sun began to set. Darkness was already creeping at the base of the buildings he could see through the doorway.

"I'd love a drink!" said Kraven.

Krell sighed.

* * *

Dwarven ale did not agree with Krell.

Happily, the grace of ReckNor cleansed the nauseous feeling from his body even as he sputtered. The ale tasted nothing like what was found in Watford. It was thick and dark, with a heady foam. Krell thought it tasted foul.

Kraven and Dorn both drank deeply, and Orca was a little more reserved, but close behind them. Tristan sniffed it and pushed it away. As soon as Dorn and Kraven were finished, they each grabbed at Tristan's mug. Kraven was faster. Dorn shrugged, grabbing Krell's. They drank again.

Krell and Tristan shared a look, and smiled at one another. It was strange, feeling a moment of camaraderie with Tristan.

Orca finished his at the same time as Oxton. "This is excellent, Oxton, just excellent," he said.

Oxton beamed in pleasure. "My thanks! I am, among other trades and skills, brewmaster here at the Consortium, so it pleases me that you enjoyed this!" He glanced outside. "It is getting late, and I wish to be mindful of your human friend here. I would be pleased to offer you accommodations for the evening if you wish to stay."

Oxton looked at Krell. "Even if you leave now, you're likely traveling in darkness for at least two hours."

Krell nodded. "My thanks, Oxton, for the Forge Father's ward, and the warmth of the Phlogos the Fire Lord's breath. Your hearth and home have been warm and kind, and may the Forge Father reward you for being a gracious host! Until we meet again, Oxton Smithforge, and may ReckNor turn his baleful gaze away from you and your kin!"

Oxton grinned. "May ReckNor's grace gift you life from the sea, and may your days be filled with fair winds and sunshine!"

"Ha!" said Krell as he clasped Oxton's outstretched arm. Krell turned to leave, and the others followed. The sky was still cloudy, but Krell thought he could see breaks in the clouds that suggested the weather would be clear tomorrow.

He looked at Dorn. "I think I like dwarves."

Dorn snorted. "Of course you do! Who wouldn't?"

* * *

Olgar was casting the spell. He'd been at it for some time.

Krell was rapidly becoming bored.

It had started interestingly enough, with Olgar inspecting the diamonds, then judging their quality to be good enough, and putting two of the smaller ones on Gerrard's chest. From there, he began beseeching ReckNor for aid and casting an elaborate spell, replete with gestures, walking around, and constant words of power. Krell had never seen a spell of such complexity before.

It kept going.

And going.

It had been a half hour, and Krell was wondering if he shouldn't have left Olgar alone for this. Dorn seemed fascinated, and was paying rapt attention. Krell thought he knew Dorn well enough at this point to see that the respect he held for Olgar had increased.

Krell sighed as quietly as he could.

You busy? He directed this thought inward, toward the power of ReckNor he always felt within him.

I AM ALWAYS BUSY. MANY TENS OF THOUSANDS UTTER MY NAME AT ANY MOMENT, ALL PROVIDING ME STRENGTH. THOSE THAT REQUIRE AID SHOULD RECEIVE IT IF THEY ARE WORTHY.

Is Gerrard worthy? Or is all this a waste of time?

THAT IS A QUESTION FOR GERRARD TO ANSWER. I CARE NOT.

Then why are you letting Olgar cast the spell to bring him back?

BECAUSE OLGAR IS WORTHY, KRELL. I AM NOT A GREEDY GOD, DEMANDING THAT YOU OBEY MANY DOZENS OF CONTRADICTORY RULES. I DEMAND TRIBUTE FOR THE USE OF MY OCEANS. I DEMAND TRIBUTE FOR THE USE OF THE SKY. I DEMAND THAT YOU CHOOSE, FREELY, AND ACCEPT THE CONSEQUENCES OF YOUR CHOICES. THIS IS OLGAR'S CHOICE. IN THIS WAY, HE HONORS ME, EVEN AS I HONOR HIS CHOICES.

Krell immediately developed a throbbing headache.

Do you think you can talk more quietly? You always sound like a thunderstorm.

Krell could feel ReckNor's amusement.

THIS IS ME TALKING QUIETLY, MY PALADIN. I ADVISE YOU TO EITHER GROW ACCUSTOMED TO IT OR TO CEASE ASKING ME FOR IDLE DISCUSSION BECAUSE YOU ARE BORED.

Krell thought about that. It seemed like ReckNor had a point.

I LIKE YOU, KRELL. YOU ARE STUBBORN, AS MOST OF MY FOLLOWERS ARE.

Is being stubborn the trait you look for? asked Krell, thinking about comments others had made to him. Orca called him arrogant. Tristan called him every derogatory term he could imagine.

ARROGANCE AND STUBBORNNESS ARE OFTEN CLOSE FRIENDS.

Krell sighed as quietly as he could and stopped trying to get ReckNor to talk. The headache was at high tide in his head, crashing into his thoughts in waves of pain. ReckNor's amusement was palpable, but he said nothing more.

Olgar continued to cast the spell.

Krell looked at Dorn. His dark beard had been brushed out, as was his long hair. Dorn often let it run wild, becoming a tangled mess. When Krell had asked, he'd said it was important to look good for ReckNor when his might was on full display.

Krell didn't understand that, since ReckNor was always with him. Dorn had spoken with envy of Krell's ability to hear ReckNor directly. Krell wondered how Dorn would react if he explained how grateful he'd be if ReckNor would leave him alone from time to time. The trick wasn't getting ReckNor to talk, it was getting him to shut up.

THAT IS UNCHARITABLE, KRELL. I SPEAK WHEN I HAVE SOMETHING TO SAY.

Krell winced. His headache grew stronger.

IT IS CURIOUS THAT YOU DEVELOP A HEADACHE, EVEN AS QUIETLY AS I WHISPER TO YOU NOW. I UNDERSTAND THAT MY MIGHT AND MAJESTY IS AS THE ROARING OF A HURRICANE TO YOUR MORTAL MIND. YET THIS PAIN YOU FEEL IS NEW. NEVER BEFORE HAS A PALADIN OF MINE HAD THIS.

"Maybe it's because you won't shut up," muttered Krell. Dorn looked at him, as if to demand he be silent. Olgar didn't seem to notice. Krell waved at Dorn apologetically and turned back to Olgar and the spell he was casting.

I SUSPECT IT IS BECAUSE YOU SHATTERED THE GRACE I WAS GIFTING, TO STEAL POWER FROM IT.

When you say it like that, it makes me sound like I did something wrong!

NONSENSE. IN FACT, I AM INTRIGUED. I SPEND POWER ON YOU, KRELL, FOR YOU ARE MY PALADIN. THE FACT THAT YOU STEAL SOME OF IT FROM ME INSTEAD OF RECEIVING IT AS A GIFT DOES NOT CHANGE THAT MY POWER FLOWS TO YOU.

So, you're not angry?

IF ANYTHING, I WOULD SAY I AM CURIOUS. THE POWER THAT YOU STEAL IS DIFFERENT, TRANSFORMED SOMEHOW BY YOUR OWN NATURE. IF YOU WERE SMART, YOU COULD HAVE BEEN A WIZARD. IF YOU WERE WISE, YOU COULD HAVE BEEN A TRUE PRIEST. YOU INSTEAD ARE STUBBORN AND ARROGANT, WHICH MAKES YOU A PALADIN. I HAVE HOPES YOU ARE NOT A TYPICAL PALADIN, IN THAT I HOPE YOU ARE ALSO A SURVIVOR.

Krell thought about his past. He couldn't remember much from his time alone on the island, and nothing from before it. He didn't even know where it was, since the ship that picked him up had been wrecked in a storm, so anyone who knew their position and any ship logs were lost.

Yet Krell knew that if he ever set foot on that island again, he'd remember exactly where the cave he sheltered in would be found, and where the fruit tree grove was, and how to avoid the wild boar that chased him up those trees any number of times. He thought about how young he was, and how utterly unlikely it was that he should have survived.

Do I still have any family left alive somewhere?

IF YOU DO, THEY DO NOT PRAY TO ME.

Krell thought about that, then looked at Dorn, then Olgar and Gerrard. Well, if he didn't have family elsewhere, then he'd make his own family. His thoughts turned to Tristan. Krell was conflicted, because Tristan was such an ass. But even still, he'd do his best to keep him alive. Because Tristan was family, now.

ReckNor's grace seemed to warm him from within, almost like the rays of the sun.

Olgar raised his voice in triumph and reached out as if grabbing something in the air. Then he slammed his fist down on Gerrard's body. Light poured from Gerrard's wounds.

Gerrard gasped in a breath and sat up.

"Why am I naked?" he asked.

Chapter Sixteen

Gerrard was a wreck for the next week.

At first, he barely had the strength to move about on his own. He was uncoordinated and fell down a lot for no reason. That first night he could barely eat, and while he improved substantially after a good night of rest, he still needed help with basic tasks. Dorn helped, as did Kraven, but mostly Krell took care of him.

The weather became drier, and another caravan arrived in Watford.

The next day, Krell was walking down from the temple. His usual morning of being yelled at by Olgar complete, he was hungry. He could see a ship unloading in harbor, one of the waves of traders that were descending on Watford, here to pick up goods from a caravan. Olgar explained that the docking and warehouse fees in Watford were substantially less than in Heaford, but that the harbor was not as deep. Everyone was happy, therefore, because Heaford's harbor could be kept clear of smaller vessels, and Watford flourished.

The gold from the salvage rights was coming in, as the Crown sold off the goods. Aldrik kept a thorough account of the money, which pleased the others. Krell decided that as long as he had enough, he was fine. Though there was a lingering thought about building a home atop the cliff, where the ruins of the tower they had cleared yet remained.

As he walked into the Netminder's Friend, the common room was filled with strangers. He spied Kraven, Gerrard, and Lily at the usual table they used in the corner. He waved to Marlena, who pantomimed eating, then laughed and — without waiting for a response — went into the kitchen.

Krell smiled. An upside, he supposed, to being a regular customer.

"Krell, my friend! You know, I'm feeling much better today, right? Like, I think I've got a song in me waiting to get out, know what I mean?" Gerrard seemed in high spirits.

"That's good, Gerrard. Perhaps you'll sing for us tonight," said Krell. He glanced at Lily, who was sitting in tense silence. "Everything okay, Lily?"

She looked up, and a small smile that did not touch her eyes crossed her face. "The one who tried to whore me, the one Kraven fought, is over there in the other corner."

Krell looked over and spotted him at once. Without his armor on he had a different profile, but it was definitely the same man. Krell looked back at Lily and grinned.

"Thinking about going over there and gutting him?" he asked.

"I might. I'm still thinking about it," said Lily. Krell's smile faded, and he wondered if she was joking or not. Kraven burst out laughing.

"Krell, you're intense! Do you attract people like you everywhere you go, or were you just lucky with her?" He turned to look at Lily. "I like you, little halfling. You're scary!"

The door opened and three young women came in. One blonde, one brunette, and one with dull red hair. They had the look of adventurers, though their gear looked new and untested. Nearly everyone turned to look at them when they walked in. Not only had Krell never seen them in town before, they were all rare beauties. The three of them took one of the few free spots at a small table meant for two near where Krell was sitting. Krell gave a mental shrug and turned his attention back to his companions.

Lily tensed. Krell looked at her, then turned to follow her gaze. The man Kraven had fought here in the common room was heading over. Lily and Kraven locked eyes on him as he moved. He saw Kraven watching, and grinned at him, giving him a salute with his hand, then veered over to the table the young women had sat at.

Marlena arrived and placed a bowl of stew and a basket of bread in front of Krell, and two mugs of ale in front of Kraven. "I'll be back with more, only so many hands," she said, and turned to leave. She paused for a moment, watching the other table with a tightening expression on her face, then went back to the kitchen.

The stew here was always good. Krell ate it nearly every day, mostly because it usually wasn't fish. It was hard to escape eating fish in Watford.

"What do you suppose the stew is today?" asked Krell.

"Mutton," said Kraven, without turning his attention away from the man he'd fought before.

The door opened again, and Captain Gijwolf entered. He spied Krell and his companions and walked over at once.

"To what do we owe the pleasure of your visit, brave Captain Gijwolf?" said Gerrard, giving him an elaborate wave of his hand as he bowed in his seat.

"Work, possibly, if you're interested. You're still under charter to investigate the sea devils, so it makes things easy, if you're up for it." He sat down on the bench next to Lily and gave her a smile. "Lily, good to see you again."

"Captain," she said, then turned back to her meal.

"What's the problem, Captain Gijwolf?" said Kraven, turning to face him.

"A farmer on the outskirts of town had a cow killed by some wild beast. Thought it was a bear, but it wasn't. He ran away while it ate his cow, making a bloody mess, and then knocked his fences down as it left. With the patrols needing to get all the way out to the dwarf mine, I don't have the spares to send on a hunt. Wondering if you're up for it."

Marlena appeared and put mugs of clean water on the table for Krell and Captain Gijwolf. He smiled at her, and she smiled back. Krell looked between them, then turned to look at Gerrard, who gave him a knowing wink.

"Anyway," said the captain, turning back to them, "I'm looking for a team to go out there, find the beast, and kill it."

"What's the pay?" asked Kraven.

"Fifty golden sovereigns, to be split among the survivors."

"So, go find a beast that maybe ran off, that's dangerous enough to take a cow and to have you talking of survivors, for as much gold as you handed me for work well done last week. Is that it?" said Kraven. "Think I'll pass, unless the others are in."

Krell looked at the table with the three young women, where some shouting had broken out. As he watched, the redheaded one, wearing a chain mail shirt, stood and slammed a fist into the man's face.

"I said, don't touch her!" she shouted. Everyone in the room turned to look in their direction.

Captain Gijwolf stood at once. "Rolf! You causing trouble that, in my official capacity as captain of the guard, I need to take note of?"

The man — Rolf — at first looked poised to attack, then relaxed and turned to the captain. "Didn't see you there, Captain Gijwolf. No trouble here, just talking to these beauties, on account of I haven't seen 'em before," he said.

The blonde, her back to Krell, said something to Rolf, and he flushed red with anger. The captain walked over.

Krell went back to his meal.

* * *

As Krell was making ready to leave, the captain returned to their table.

"I may have made a foolish mistake," he said, sitting down.

Krell was immediately attentive. "How so?" he asked.

"Those three over there, they've agreed to take the contract to hunt the beast. Issued them a simple charter, since that redhead seems fiery enough to make an issue of her arms and armor otherwise. Yet, I wonder if they have what it takes? They seem much like you did, Krell, when you first came to Watford. I wasn't comfortable putting you on a charter until after Olgar had beat some skill into you."

Gerrard looked at them. "You know, they're certainly pretty enough to do whatever they like, right? Why risk being a beast hunter, know what I mean?"

Captain Gijwolf shrugged. "They all seem to have something of a chip on their shoulder. Do me a favor and talk to them? See if they'll take some help, or at least advice? Hate for them to all die while only wounding the beast. Next thing, it might get a taste for people, not just cows."

ReckNor's grace lay placid and still within him. Krell gave a mental shrug, then nodded. "Sure, I don't mind."

As he walked over, he looked at the women closely for the first time. Gerrard was wrong. They weren't merely pretty, they were stunning. Krell guessed they were maybe a year older than him. All had fair skin that had seen much sun. Krell was struck by how perfectly arranged their hair was, in complex braids.

The red-haired one was obviously a warrior. Krell could see it in her neck and shoulders, the way she sat, that she would have no trouble using the sword on her hip or the shield that rested against the wall. The brunette was much more slender, and her brown eyes seemed to be watching him approach without looking at him. She was doing her best to try to blend into the back wall, as if attempting to hide. The blonde had her back to Krell, but as he approached, turned to look at him.

"Shit," she said. Her eyes were a startling green color, as were the eyes of the warrior. Her voice was melodic and strange, and Krell found it appealing for reasons he didn't understand, despite the despair that it carried. Her eyes were wide, looking at him. She reached out a hand, and the brunette grasped it, grasping hard enough that their knuckles turned white.

"Uh, hi," said Krell lamely. Something was wrong. They had all become tense as he approached.

"What? Come to proposition us like that lout, Rolf?" asked the red-haired warrior. Her voice was a little deeper but also very appealing, with that same strange melodic cadence to it.

"Huh? No, Captain Gijwolf there asked if I'd help, maybe offer advice or something."

"Oh, so he thinks we need a big strong man to help us?" She stood. Krell realized she was slightly taller than him, and much more heavily muscled.

"I think I'm confused. I'm going to start over. My name is Krell, paladin of ReckNor."

She snorted. "ReckNor doesn't call paladins."

Krell grinned. "It appears you are mistaken, for here I am."

Her eyes flicked over his shoulder, toward the table of his companions, then back to him. "I'm Sheana," she said. "Now, go away."

Sheana was a strange name. He had never heard anything like it before. Suddenly, he felt the grace and power of ReckNor become interested. *Intensely* interested.

"That's new," he said.

THEY HAVE POTENTIAL, ALL OF THEM.

"What's *new*?" Sheana asked, confused.

Krell shook his head. "Nevermind. You are?" he asked, turning to the blonde next to him.

She looked up at him, then gestured. A nearby chair skidded across the floor and bumped into Krell before toppling over.

"Since it is obvious that you are not going to leave us alone, sit. I am tired of looking up at people who harass us." Her tone made Krell feel guilty for some reason he could not understand, but he righted the chair and sat anyway. Sheana gave her a strange look, then sat down in her chair.

"My name is Verbena," she said, then gestured at the brunette. "That is Dahlia. So tell me, Krell, paladin of ReckNor, why did the captain give us a charter to hunt a beast if he was immediately going to second-guess his decision?"

"I don't know," said Krell.

"And what assistance, precisely, would you be trying to provide us, despite none of us asking for any assistance?" Verbena asked.

Krell looked at her and shrugged. "I don't know."

She rolled her eyes, her head rolling with the motion in a way that conveyed both irritation and disgust. Krell felt ReckNor's interest and amusement radiating through him. "Do you, in fact, know anything at all?" she said sarcastically.

Krell was suddenly in familiar territory for him. This was ground he'd trodden many times before with Tristan. He grinned at them.

"Not especially, no, but then, I'm a dumb brute for the most part. ReckNor is in here" — he tapped the side of his head — "and he tells me what to do. When he doesn't, I do whatever I want."

"So you say," Verbena said, sipping at her wine.

"Your voices are strange to my ear," he said.

"We're not from around here," said Dahlia, speaking for the first time. Her voice was lower pitched than Krell would have guessed, but it had the same melodic quality that Verbena's and Sheana's did.

Krell nodded. "I'd have noticed, otherwise," he said. Dahlia's lips quirked into a tiny smile, though Verbena rolled her eyes again.

Sheana laughed. "Well then, paladin, since you don't know anything, what is it you want?"

Krell smiled. "How about my friends and I — the ones at that table over there — simply follow you when you head out? We won't interfere, nor are we making any claim on your charter. You find the beast, you kill it, and we watch and do nothing. But if you need help, then yell, and ReckNor will come to your aid."

"What are the conditions on this aid you would impose?" said Verbena.

"Um, no conditions?" said Krell. "Captain Gijwolf is a pretty honest man, from what I can tell. I think he's just, I don't know, trying to do the right thing."

"Is that what you're trying to do, Krell, paladin of ReckNor?" asked Dahlia.

"Nah, I just take orders from people better than me. That includes Captain Gijwolf at times, but always ReckNor."

Sheana grinned at him. "ReckNor, huh? You trying to convert us to the worship of your god?"

Krell's smile widened. "Absolutely."

Sheana giggled. Verbena rolled her eyes yet again.

* * *

"This is stupid, Krell," said Tristan.

It was the next day. The three young women had departed for the farm early. Krell, on leaving the temple, found a dead bird on the front step. He looked around, but hadn't been able to spot anything. Kraven, Gerrard, Tristan, Lily, and Dorn were waiting in the common room, and they were all there when the three young women descended. Orca was nowhere to be seen, and Marlena hadn't answered him when he asked about him.

Verbena had given them a condescending look, and they left without saying anything. Krell and his companions had been following them ever since.

They were competent enough at tracking. They went straight to the farm, talked to the farmer for a bit, and then followed the tracks. At first, it was easy, because the beast was covered in cow blood. Now, on the forested hillside, Dahlia was stopping and examining the ground and trees, looking for signs of its passage.

She was going about it exactly the way Krell would have. Krell shook his head in irritation.

"Then walk back to town, Tristan! ReckNor's salty beard, there's no reward or opportunity here, so just leave if you don't want to be here!" said Krell, snapping. Dahlia turned and looked at Krell, then went back to examining the ground.

"Well, if I returned to town, you'd all probably die, and then where would I be?" he said. "It's well known by now that, without me, you're all helpless and weak, doomed to an ignoble death in obscurity."

Kraven growled.

"Oh no, big scary Kraven!" said Tristan, in mock alarm. "Whatever will I do if the big scary warrior tries to come for me!"

Krell sighed. "By ReckNor's trident, you're annoying Tristan. Kraven, don't hurt him. We're here to provide assistance if they ask, nothing more."

"Krell, you know, I like you and all, and I'm with you, right?" said Gerrard. "I'd be fish food otherwise. So I don't mind."

Krell stopped and kneeled before Gerrard, grasping him by the shoulders. He looked at Gerrard seriously.

"This was not a bargain, Gerrard, bringing you back. You owe no obligations. There were no conditions. ReckNor didn't do it for you, he did it for me, because that's what I wanted. That's why I made Olgar do it. I wanted that because you are my friend. More importantly, ReckNor values choice, which means you're free to choose whatever you want." Then Krell grinned, and straightened. "But, if you've no other god to worship, I can put in a good word for you with mine!" He turned and resumed following the three young adventurers.

"Wow, he's annoying," said Tristan.

"So are you!" snarled Kraven.

"Seem competent enough," said Dorn, watching the three young women. "They at least know how to track. You thinking of hiring them, like you did with her?" He gestured at Lily.

"Less hire, more convert, I think," said Krell. "They didn't seem entirely against the idea of the faith of ReckNor, and he's always looking for converts. I got the sense they'd made no vows, like most people. Plus, ReckNor was interested enough to pay attention when I talked to them yesterday. We'll see."

Lily looked vaguely offended.

Dorn laughed. "ReckNor tell you to follow and help them?"

"Nope."

"So this is all your bright idea then?" said Tristan.

Krell glanced at him. "Afraid so, Tristan. You're up early and walking through the woods because that's what I wanted. No treasure, no reward, no fame, nothing but what I wanted." Krell grinned at him.

"I do what I want, Krell, not what you tell me to do!"

Krell's grin widened. "So, you *do* follow ReckNor's teachings after all!" Tristan glared at him.

Up ahead, the three of them stopped. Sheana readied her shield and drew her sword. Dahlia drew an arrow lightly on her bow, and they moved into a triangle formation, with Sheana taking the forward point. They moved cautiously forward.

Krell readied his own shield and conjured a blade.

"You thinking they'll need help, then?" said Dorn.

"I'd rather be ready to help and find they needed none, than to need to help and not be ready," said Krell.

Kraven drew his axe, and Dorn readied his shield as well. They closed the distance, staying back far enough to not interfere, but close enough that they could rush forward quickly if necessary. Verbena noticed and glared at Krell. Her eyes carried a message in them, and he could hear her voice saying *do not interfere.* She then focused on what was ahead of them.

Krell shook his head. It was actually her thought, sent to him somehow using magic. He shook his head and felt the sense of her voice fade away.

They were approaching a narrow cave, set in a rockfall on the side of the hill. As they approached, Krell felt more than heard a growl, a deep thrum he felt in his bones. Then the beast charged from the cave, directly toward them.

It was enormous, shaped like a bear, but bigger than any bear Krell had ever heard of. Its face was covered in feathers, like an owl, and instead of jaws it had a massive beak, stained with blood. It was also swift, covering the ground between the cave and the young women very quickly. Sheana readied her sword, and Dahlia sank an arrow into it.

Krell frowned. "They're too close together. Sheana needs to concentrate on defense and distract it, while the other two kill it."

Dorn and Kraven nodded.

As the beast closed, Sheana struck, dealing a slight wound to its forearm. The beast's claws raked at her, knocking her shield aside and slamming into her shoulder and chest. She collapsed to the ground.

Dahlia let out a scream of rage and shot the beast with another arrow. Krell started running toward them. Kraven let out an excited grunt and started forward as well.

The beast turned on Dahlia and pounced. Dahlia screamed in agony this time as its claws slammed into her torso, and the beast flung her to the side. She landed and sprawled on the ground, lying still.

Verbena turned to run and locked eyes with Krell.

The beast caught her from behind, shattering her shoulder, nearly tearing her arm off. She collapsed, blood pouring from her body.

It had taken less than five seconds for the beast to cut them all down.

Krell yelled a challenge to the beast as he closed on it, Kraven close behind him. It turned and reared up, and only then did he realize it was *much* larger than a bear. With a quick prayer to ReckNor for power, he wreathed his blade in lightning and struck, dealing a wound that echoed with the crash of thunder.

A bolt of fire slammed into it, passing narrowly over Krell's shoulder. Kraven took a swipe from the claws, turning to avoid the worst of it, but still getting four bloody furrows across his chest and shoulder.

Its beak came toward him, and Krell uttered a sharp word of magic, causing a shield of force to spring into existence. The beak crashed through it as if it were not there, shattering it. Krell's sword was brushed aside as he attempted to parry or deflect the strike.

His vision exploded in pain, as the beak-like mouth slammed into his shoulder. There was a crack he felt throughout his body that came with a sudden sickening weakness. Then he was airborne, landing hard a short distance away and rolling once. He coughed, and blood spurted from his mouth. His arm wouldn't move, and he watched as his blade turned to mist and disappeared. Pain thrummed through his body, and he clamped down on a scream.

He could already feel ReckNor's grace mending his shoulder, and he was close to Sheana. He reached out and dragged himself closer with his uninjured shield arm, though the shield made the motion awkward. He flung his injured arm forward, which nearly made him black out from the agony of it. His hand flopped down, just reaching her boot.

ReckNor's grace flowed sluggishly, the jagged edges grating on his senses as he felt it restoring Sheana. He could hear his companions shouting and the beast roaring, but it seemed to come from a long way away. Sheana's eyes opened, and her gaze locked on his.

Time stretched for Krell. He felt like he was falling into two emerald pools. He wondered if he passed out, whether he would ever awaken again.

Then her eyes flicked to the side, where Dahlia lay sprawled on the ground, an area of the earth around her damp with blood. Her gaze came back to Krell, imploring. She didn't move at all. Perhaps she was more seriously hurt than he thought.

The beast roared in the background, and Kraven shouted in rage.

Krell staggered to his feet and stumbled over to Dahlia. He tried to kneel, but instead fell, landing atop her, his wounded shoulder slamming into her body. He lay there for a moment, gasping for air. He tried to focus, to force the grace of ReckNor to move, but it was already in motion. It felt like shards of broken glass, and his shoulder was on fire, but Dahlia sucked in a breath and coughed.

ABIDE A MOMENT, KRELL. IF YOU MOVE AGAIN, YOU WILL PASS OUT.

Krell nodded, listening to the sounds of battle. That sounded like good advice. He wondered who had said it.

Tristan was uttering words of magic, that unmistakable cadence that called forth power. The ground trembled with the weight of the beast as it lurched about. The roar changed, now laced with pain, and Krell sighed and hauled himself to his feet. His vision was blurry, and he wasn't sure whether he was standing straight or not.

The bear creature was over twenty feet away from him, and he wasn't sure he could cover that distance, or what he'd do when he got there. Dorn took a massive swipe from its claws, his armor saving him from the worst of it. Kraven lay on the ground, bleeding profusely. Tristan was well back, and Krell wondered if he was going to run or not.

Gerrard and Lily, though, had circled behind it. While the creature focused on Dorn, they struck. Gerrard cut at its hind leg, which collapsed suddenly as he hamstrung it. Lily leapt atop it and nimbly ran up its back. When she got close to the neck, she fell forward, her daggers flashing as she embedded both.

Lily held on as the beast reared up in pain and rage. It turned and struck at Gerrard, who rolled back away from it, avoiding the strike only because its lame leg slowed it. Dorn stabbed it in the back with his blade while it was distracted. Tristan shot another bolt of fire into it, and it stumbled, its foot coming down on Verbena with crushing force. She didn't react at all.

Krell snarled, and without thought spoke his own words of power and gestured at the beast with his wounded arm. A trident made of spectral energy leapt from his hand, flew across the distance between them, and sank into the chest of the beast, vanishing immediately while leaving a strange wound. His vision swam as pain from his wounded shoulder crashed into his thoughts. It turned and charged at Krell.

Krell barely noticed. He was staring at his hand in confusion amid waves of pain.

Lily jerked her daggers free and slammed them home again, and the beast crashed to the ground, sliding to a halt in front of Krell. Lily looked up, her eyes wide. Krell saw Dorn nearly fall to the ground near Kraven and call on ReckNor for aid. Gerrard ran forward to Verbena, then looked at Krell and shook his head.

Krell nodded, then passed out.

* * *

It was a sorry-looking group that returned to Watford.

Krell had wrapped Verbena's body in his cloak and carried it. Kraven was seriously hurt, as were Sheana and Dahlia, and they could barely walk. Dorn was injured, but dwarves are a sturdy folk, and it did not seem to slow him. Gerrard and Lily were unhurt.

As was Tristan.

"Well, Krell, I hope you learned something valuable about this exercise," he said, in that nasal tone of voice that Krell was beginning to hate.

Krell sighed. "I learned that I miss Orca's blade."

Tristan smiled smugly. "Well, maybe one day you'll be smart enough to do more than charge right into its claws. Probably not, though. You're stupendously arrogant." His tone became mocking. "Oh look! A beast fifteen feet tall! Let me run forward and kill it, because nothing could possibly go wrong!"

As they entered town, Gerrard and Lily took Dahlia and Sheana back to their room at the Netminder's Friend, while Krell carried Verbena up to the temple. Everyone else parted ways. Twice guards stopped him to offer assistance, for Krell's armor was covered in his own blood. He refused both times.

He trudged onward, up the hill and alone, except for Verbena's body over his shoulder.

"I feel like I failed you, somehow," said Krell. "You were totally unprepared for that thing, and then absurdly unlucky. So was I, for what it's worth. It caught me right at the edge of the breastplate and used that as handle to throw me aside. Nearly killed me, I think."

Krell walked in silence for a minute.

"I'm sorry you died. I don't think you liked me very much."

There was a strange noise from behind Krell, something like a crackle of wood burning in a fire, combined with the hissing of a kettle just coming to boil. Krell turned.

The little dragon from the ship was perched on a rock, not ten feet away, staring at him.

"Hello, little one. Have you been leaving the dead animals on our doorstep?" Krell wondered if he had lost too much blood. He probably wasn't thinking straight.

The dragon nodded his head, then cocked it sideways, and looked at the body he was carrying.

"Well, could you stop it, please? Every morning I have a dead animal that we're not interested in eating to throw away. I appreciate the effort, don't get me wrong, but we've enough food. As for her, she died trying to be a warrior. I'm taking her up to the temple. I suspect Olgar — he's the one who lives up there — will make me dig the grave to bury her." Krell shook his head.

The dragon chirped at him, cocking his head to the other side.

"Not sure what you're doing here, still, my little friend, but I can't stand here talking. I feel like I owe her more than what she got. I said I'd help." Krell shook his head, looking down at the blond tresses matted with blood and dirt. "Guess I failed, huh?"

He turned and continued walking up the hill. Olgar saw him coming and came out. He looked at the bundle of Krell's cloak, with a mop of golden hair spilling out one end. "One of those girls you told me about, my boy?"

Krell nodded.

Olgar said nothing as he came forward and took the burden from Krell.

"You know there's a tiny dragon, not ten feet behind you, right?" said Olgar, as he walked easily into the temple. "I'll give her a funeral, and we can bury her tomorrow. Clean yourself up." Olgar's face grew dark and stormy. "And no crying! I'm not your father, and I don't want to hear you whining about what a failure you are! Go down to town if that's your plan!"

Krell slumped to the ground and sat. He stared at nothing for a moment, absently stroking the dragon's head and neck as it curled up in his lap.

Suddenly, the enormity of what he was doing dawned on him.

"I didn't mean — why are you here?"

The dragon looked up at him, and a sense of loneliness and fear came to Krell, then switched to a feeling of warmth and happiness, as it nestled into his lap. Krell looked at the dragon, marveling at its beauty.

"Do you have a name? You seem really clever and smart, more so than a mere animal."

The dragon let out a little snort of disdain and stared intently at Krell. Krell felt like he was falling and shook his head. How could he fall if he was sitting on the ground already?

"Fortis?" he said.

The dragon let out a chirp that had a distinctly affirmative tone to it, then nestled back into Krell's lap.

"You — can understand me, that's clear. How do I understand you?" Krell's thoughts whirled in his head.

Not just his thoughts, he realized. The dragon — Fortis — his thoughts were there, too. He was vaguely hungry, but not enough to go hunt for something. He didn't like crowds of people, because it made him nervous. He was lonely, terribly lonely, having been captured and caged until Krell freed him.

He was lost. His home was elsewhere, and he didn't know how to find it.

"I get it. I'm the same. I might have a home somewhere else, with a family. I don't know. What I do know is that I've made a new home, here. Found a new family. Olgar taught me that. Home is where you make it."

Krell sat there for some time, letting the warmth of the dragon soak into his legs. He could feel ReckNor's grace continuing to healing his hurts, restoring his strength. He must have been hurt far worse than he thought to still be weak after the long walk back to town. He wondered why the power didn't hurt at the moment.

IT IS BECAUSE YOU ARE NOT FORCING IT, KRELL. WHEN YOU LET IT FLOW ON ITS OWN, IT DOES NOT CAUSE PAIN. CURIOUS, ISN'T IT?

Fortis let out an alarmed hiss and leapt into the sky, fluttering around Krell in agitation.

Krell looked at him in shock. "You heard that?" he asked Fortis.

OF COURSE HE HEARD ME. HE BONDED WITH YOU, SO HIS THOUGHTS AND YOURS HAVE JOINED, TO A DEGREE. OF COURSE, I SPEAK DIRECTLY TO YOU, SO FORTIS WILL HEAR AS WELL.

"Wait, you know what he is, don't you?" asked Krell.

OF COURSE.

Krell waited a moment, and Fortis landed on the ground in front of him and sat. Even when completely still, Fortis looked like a majestic dragon.

"Well?" said Krell. Fortis cocked his head sideways, questioningly.

WELL WHAT?

"Are you going to tell me what Fortis is, what's happened to us?"

ReckNor's grace quivered with amusement.

NO, I DON'T THINK I WILL.

"You know, ReckNor, there are days when you really are the worst."

The amusement within Krell strengthened. Fortis made a rasping cackle that sounded like laughter.

Then he butted his head into Krell's hand.

Krell smiled and began stroking his neck again.

* * *

Krell walked into the Netminder's Friend.

It was early in the afternoon. Krell had spent hours cleaning his armor, then eating with Olgar. Krell kept cutting bits of meat from his meal and tossing them outside. Olgar never once commented on this.

Verbena was covered in a sheet on the altar. Olgar had cast the same spell Dorn had used on Gerrard. Her hair draped over the side, but where the sheet touched her torso, blood had seeped through. Krell's cloak was almost a total loss.

As he entered, the room was mostly empty. Only five people were present.

Marlena, of course, looking tired, sat at the bar. She looked up at him and smiled, then gestured behind her.

Gerrard and Lily were sitting close to one another, talking quietly. In the corner, at the table they first sat at when they arrived, Sheana and Dahlia sat. They both wore fine quality clothing, but the bandages over their wounds were obvious. Equally obvious, they had both been crying recently.

Krell walked over to Marlena.

"Their friend died today?" she asked. Krell nodded, then sat beside her.

"I feel like it's my fault, somehow."

Marlena looked at him, then glanced back at the two young women. "They came down just recently. I think, if they hate anyone, they hate Captain Gijwolf the most at the moment," she said. "He paid out their charter, you see."

Krell shook his head. "I don't follow."

Marlena smiled sadly. "They just lost their friend, and now they feel like they traded her for fifty golden sovereigns. If you listen to them talk, you'll learn they think this is a terrible trade."

An idea began to form in Krell's head. He nodded.

Marlena put her hand on his shoulder. "It's not your fault. You know that, right?"

Krell smiled, then leaned forward and embraced Marlena. She went rigid with surprise, then relaxed into the hug.

"Mmm, that's nice. You are a handsome one, you know that, right?" she said. "Muscular, too." Her smile became something more than just a smile.

"You've been good to me, Marlena. But this is, if not wholly, at least partly my fault." Krell stood.

Marlena grabbed his arm.

"Elias told them, and now I'll tell you. That thing was almost certainly a magical beast of some sort. Elias told them that if he'd sent a squad of guards, as he normally would have, then he'd have *lost* a squad of guards to it. I think he's a little surprised you and your friends killed it."

Krell gestured with his head toward Gerrard and Lily. "They're the ones who actually killed it. If not for the two of them, I'd be dead." Krell took Marlena's hand in his and held it for a moment.

"Why don't you wed Elias?" he asked.

"Krell! What a terrible thing for you to say!" she said in mock outrage.

"I'm serious, Marlena."

"And give up on all the handsome young men like you in town?"

"Marlena, I've been paying attention. You flirt, but nothing else. I can't think of a single man you've taken to bed. But I *have* seen the way you look at Captain Gijwolf."

She sighed. "It's not me, Krell, it's him."

Krell pulled her hand up and gently kissed her knuckles. "ReckNor works in mysterious ways, Marlena. Offer prayers, and see what happens."

Her mouth dropped open in surprise, and Krell turned away, walking over to Dahlia and Sheana. He grabbed a chair on the way, put it down at their table, and sat without being invited.

Sheana looked at him. Her face was blotchy, her green eyes bloodshot and streaked with tears. Her hair was a tangled mess, still crusted with blood. Dahlia's hair was slightly better, in that it looked like she'd at least made an effort to brush it.

"I suppose I should thank you," Sheana said, her eyes tearing up again. "Without your help, we'd all be dead."

"Captain Gijwolf said it was some sort of magic beast. It nearly killed me. It nearly killed my friend Kraven. It was fearsome."

"And we walked right up to it, and now Verbena is dead!" said Dahlia, looking at him. "She said she was going to die soon, but this sounded so harmless and easy! Kill a bear! How hard could that be?"

Sheana nodded, fresh tears streaking her face. "But at least we got fifty gold coins in exchange," she said, bitterness coloring her voice.

"What do you mean, she said she was going to die soon?"

Dahlia waved her hand toward Sheana. Sheana shrugged. "Doesn't matter much now, I suppose. She sometimes sees a bit of the future." A tear streaked down her cheek. "She sometimes *saw* a bit of the future, I mean."

Krell decided.

"What would you give to get her back?" he asked.

They both turned to him, staring at him.

"That's not funny," said Dahlia.

"I'm serious. What would you give to get her back?"

"Almost anything," Sheana said at once. Dahlia nodded.

Krell cocked his head sideways. "*Almost* anything?"

Sheana sighed, closed her eyes, and leaned back. "For Verbena," she said, starting to undo buttons on her shirt. Krell's eyes widened in alarm, and he grabbed her hand.

"No, ReckNor's balls, not that. I mean, most people would have said anything, but you said almost," said Krell, as Sheana put a hurt look on her face. "I'm not trying to cheat you here, okay? This is a good faith offer. I just want to understand you both more. Button your shirt, okay?" Krell was blushing and looking very hard at Dahlia.

"How do we even know you can bring her back?" Dahlia asked.

Krell met her eyes. They were a deep brown color. They stared at each other for a long moment.

"I could say it's because I'm a paladin and I don't lie, except that's a lie. I lie all the time. I could say it's because ReckNor does what I say, which is also a lie. Quite the opposite, actually. I can't explain it, but it's possible. I'm not *certain*, but it's possible. As for proof, well, that's easy."

Krell leaned back and looked over his shoulder at Gerrard and Lily, who were watching him. "How long ago were you dead, Gerrard?"

He snorted in laughter. "Why, a few days last week, you know what I mean, right, Krell?" Gerrard turned to Dahlia, who looked at him curiously. "Krell is intense, right? He's like this single-minded wave of determination that'll do whatever he wants. If he wants your friend back, then she's coming back." Gerrard waved and turned back toward Lily. They leaned close to one another.

Krell watched them for a moment, then decided it was none of his business. He turned back to Dahlia.

"You can really bring her back?" she said, her eyes shimmering with tears.

"I can. Well, Olgar will, if I ask him to. Maybe. What I want in return is simple. Pray to ReckNor every day, offering thanks for Verbena's life. That's it."

They turned to look at one another, then back to Krell. "That's it?" asked Dahlia.

Krell nodded, then stood and walked to the door. They watched him go.

He opened the door, then turned back and looked at them. "Coming?"

They both stood at once and joined him.

* * *

"You're certain this is what you want?" Olgar asked.

"ReckNor's balls, Olgar, for the fifth time, yes!" said Krell, growing angry.

"Why should I?"

"Listen to me, you sack of shit, in this terrible moment of loss, those two girls are willing to offer prayers to ReckNor for the rest of their lives to get their friend back. So shut up, make the magic work, and bring her back to life." Krell was angry.

"Control your temper, Krell. One day it'll get you killed if you're not careful." Something about Olgar's tone of voice gave Krell pause, but he decided he didn't care about that.

"Olgar, it's been a long day. First, I had to listen to Tristan whine and complain the entire time we were heading out, then I watched that bear thing kill Verbena. I *saw* it, Olgar. I saw it in her eyes the moment she died. For the first time, that made me desperately sad. I said I'd help, and I screwed that up. *Then*, as if the day were not shitty enough, I had to listen to Tristan berating me the entire way back after nearly being killed by some stupid magic beast. I'm tired, I'm hungry, I'm hurt, and I'm angry. So just do it, okay?"

Olgar gave Krell a concerned look and put his hand on his shoulder. Krell's hurt shoulder. He winced.

"ReckNor hasn't healed that yet?" he asked.

"I think ReckNor's grace is kind of like a bucket," said Krell.

Olgar looked at him in silence for a minute. "Lad, you're going to need to elaborate."

Krell gave a frustrated wave of his hand. "I don't know, like a bucket. There's power in it, and I empty it out when I use it. But I can empty it faster than it refills." Krell looked at him. "I can't explain it better than that, but I'm empty."

"Oh, okay. I get it. Terrible analogy, though," said Olgar, grinning at him. "It's the same for me, for what it's worth, but only a good night's sleep fills me back up."

Krell sat on the bench and looked at the altar. "Just get on with it already. I'm tired and I want to go to bed."

Olgar's tone became teasing. "Oh, well, forgive me, Lord Krell, most favored of ReckNor! My apologies for how long it'll take me to locate her spirit and wrest it back from whatever heaven or hell her soul has fled to, while simultaneously bringing her body back to life! Apologies that this massive feat of magical might, that very few of any faith in this kingdom are capable of, is so boring for you to watch!"

Krell rolled his eyes, intentionally trying to emulate Verbena.

Olgar burst out laughing, drawing dark looks from Sheana and Dahlia. "Who taught you to do that? Wasn't Marlena, that's for sure!"

Krell nodded toward the altar. "She did."

"Verbena?"

"Yes."

"Ha! Well, lad, if you were looking for a way to motivate me, you couldn't have done anything better! I like her already!" Olgar walked up to the pulpit next to the altar, and reached inside. He pulled out a flask, which he set aside, and a small bag. He dumped the diamonds into his hand, and placed them on Verbena's body.

Olgar looked at Sheana and Dahlia. "Oh, stop looking at me like that. It's all his doing anyway," said Olgar, gesturing at Krell, who was sitting on a bench at the back of the temple near the door, glowering at Olgar. "Even if he *is* sulking."

Olgar smiled at them. "ReckNor, though, ReckNor likes him. He's stubborn and somewhat dense, and brave to the point of stupidity. He never says he's sorry, either," said Olgar. "But, young ladies, that is possibly because that stubborn jackass never does anything he's ashamed of. Now, I need quiet while I do this. It'll take a little more than an hour, then you'll have your friend back."

Sheana looked at him. "What are the diamonds for?"

"Who knows?" Olgar shrugged. "The magic requires them for some reason, eating them up. No idea why, but there it is." Olgar looked at them, drawing their gaze with his suddenly stern expression.

He spoke quietly, so Krell would not overhear. "That young man is spending a year's worth of skilled labor in just diamonds alone to bring your friend back. He ask you for anything?"

Dahlia shook her head. "Only that we give thanks to ReckNor, nothing else."

Olgar smiled. "See, that's what I mean! He just doesn't do anything he needs to apologize for. It's damned irritating, is what it is. Any more questions before I start?"

Sheana looked troubled. "She's — she's going to be *her*, right? She'll be okay?"

Olgar looked at her and nodded. "Lots of stories about those that come back from the dead, how sometimes they're not the same. Sometimes they're pure evil, or some evil spirit that only pretends, riding around in the body. I'll ask you this, as you think on those stories. How many of them involved a true priest bringing someone back?"

Sheana and Dahlia thought about it. "I can't think of any," said Dahlia.

"Me either," said Sheana.

"There you go then. It'll be her, and she'll have a shitty week ahead of her as she settles back into her body. Weak as a kitten and just as useful. But she'll mend fast, and when she does, she'll be completely fine."

Olgar walked around to the other side of the altar. "No more questions now, and be quiet. Best if you go back there and sit by that petulant little boy, maybe cheer him up a bit. When I'm done, you'll know it. Does someone who's just come back a lot of good to see the faces of those they love, first thing, so don't go anywhere and pay attention, right?"

They nodded, and Olgar began calling on ReckNor for aid. They quietly moved to the back of the temple and sat next to Krell.

Dahlia leaned over. "Are you and Olgar always like that?" she whispered.

Krell shook his head and put his finger on his mouth, gesturing at the door. He got up and left the temple. Sheana and Dahlia followed.

"Olgar said we shouldn't leave," said Sheana.

Krell waved his hand dismissively. "It takes an hour or so. We've got time if you want to talk."

He walked over to the cliff edge and breathed deeply. The sea air always smelled so clean and fresh up here. Dahlia and Sheana approached, but stood a little away from him.

A few minutes passed.

"Why are you helping us?" asked Sheana.

Krell thought about that.

"I'm an orphan. At least, I think I am. It's sort of the same thing, even if I'm not."

Dahlia looked confused.

"Uh, okay?" said Sheana.

"I was lost at sea when I was young. I don't remember much from that time, but I washed up on an island alone. I wonder if ReckNor was responsible for that or not. Can't say, but knowing how his mood can change, he probably was. I lived there, alone, for years."

Krell breathed deeply. "I always loved the smell of the sea. It's a myth, you know? It's really the smell of the shore. The sea itself, the deep sea, it doesn't smell like this at all. But then, so few people drift around on debris, most never know it. The smell stays with the ship, you see."

Sheana and Dahlia looked at each other. Krell noted they were holding hands.

"Well, a ship saw smoke from the island and investigated. I saw the ship and ran down to the beach. I was saved. I'm pretty sure that when that ship was lost in a storm, that was ReckNor's doing as well. I guess he wanted to make sure if he was going to bother calling a paladin, that he'd have a good one. A survivor."

Krell shook his head. "Made *my* life really hard, but then, the gods use us mortals as they will. Still, I can't really complain much. I was cast into the sea twice, and twice I was saved. Another ship happened on the debris a few days later and scooped me and one other survivor out of the water. The next port of call was here in Watford. That was maybe six months ago, maybe a little longer."

He waved his arm at the temple. "Olgar was on the docks that day. He almost never does that, comes down from the temple, I mean. His leg, it hurts for him to walk." Krell gestured with his head toward the path leading to town. "Walking on a hill is even worse for him."

"This — doesn't answer my question," said Sheana.

Krell gave her a grin. "I'm getting there. Wow, I sounded just like Olgar! Ha!" Krell's grin turned to a grimace of pain, and he rubbed at his shoulder.

"Anyway, aside from Olgar, I didn't have anybody. He trained me, taught me what he knew of arms and armor, combat tactics, religion, and a host of other things besides. Still, I always feel like I know next to nothing. Doesn't bother me. But Olgar, he's family. Really, he was the only family I ever had. At least that I can remember."

Krell looked from Sheana and Dahlia toward Watford.

"Then Olgar told me I was ready, and the timing was good. The town issued a charter, and warriors were being recruited. So, I went down. They made me take a test to see if I was good enough, and I guess I passed. That's when I met Gerrard, Tristan, Orca, and Kraven."

Krell turned back toward them. Dahlia huddled closer to Sheana, as if trying to hide in her shadow.

"Why do you do that, Dahlia? Try to hide, I mean?"

She flinched, then took a deep breath. Stepping beside Sheana again, she looked Krell in the eye. Krell thought he saw her trembling. "Answer her question first, then I'll answer yours," she said.

"Fair enough," said Krell. He turned and looked out to sea. The night was clear, and the stars were being mirrored across the water. "I love the sea, despite the trials I've faced there. I don't know why. Well, that group of us ventured into some caves a group of dwarves nearby found. A bunch of them had gone missing, and they asked for warriors."

Krell rubbed his hand through his hair, looking at them intently. "You probably know what I mean, right? Someone you'd give your life for, standing next to in the raging tides of battle?" Sheana and Dahlia both nodded, looking meaningfully back at the temple before returning their attention to Krell.

"Thought so. I thought that those warriors, that they were my new family. You've met them. Dorn and Gerrard, and Kraven? Yes. Family. Ones I'd give my life for. Maybe Max, if he hadn't died. Orca? Lily? *Tristan?* No. I've learned over the last few weeks that there is a difference between having comrades, and having comrades who matter. Comrades of *quality.* I thought anyone would do, would be worth it. I have learned that I was wrong."

Krell shook his head and breathed in the scent of the sea again. He turned to face the two of them.

"Now, I cast a wider net. I am looking for companions that are not just comrades in arms, not merely friends, but those I would lay down my life for. Companions that *matter.* Does this make sense?"

Sheana nodded thoughtfully. "You think we might be like that? Worthy of spending time with you?"

Krell threw his head back and laughed, then cut it off for fear of disturbing Olgar. Still chuckling, he looked at them again while rubbing his shoulder.

"ReckNor's tears, this hurts. Worthy? No, that's not the right word. I'm a barely educated peasant that an angry and chaotic god is using to screw up the world in ways nobody understands. Nobody is safe near me, *especially* me. Paladins often die young, and for stupid reasons. No, what I'm offering is, at the moment, a lifetime of saying thanks to ReckNor for bringing Verbena back, and nothing more."

"Then, I don't understand," said Dahlia. "Why do this?"

"I think — well, no, ReckNor told me — you've got potential. All of you. I'd wager Verbena has already figured hers out. Have either of you?"

They looked at him blankly. "Potential?" said Dahlia.

Krell nodded. "Olgar thinks maybe as many as one out of every ten people have it — the potential to hold and direct power, to work magic." Krell held out his hand at an angle, and a dark blade materialized in his grasp.

"I have it. Olgar has it, obviously. Kraven and Gerrard have it. Tristan also obviously has it. Verbena has it, or, well, had it? Will have it again? This being dead thing is confusing. Whatever. When Olgar is done, she'll have it. ReckNor thinks both of you have it as well."

"Have what?" asked Dahlia. "The ability to, what, work magic?"

Krell nodded.

"That's insane," said Sheana.

Krell nodded again. "People often say that about ReckNor. He thinks that's unfair, but he's so erratic that it's hard to see the truth."

"Kraven does not seem to have any magic," said Dahlia, doubtfully.

"He stands there, wearing no armor, and absorbing blows that might tear the arm from my shoulder. Yet he doesn't break or falter. You think he doesn't have magic he uses every time he's in battle?" Krell said. Dahlia looked thoughtful.

"So, what are you saying?" asked Sheana.

Krell shrugged. "Well, I figure if you're going to pray to ReckNor for thanks for Verbena's life…" He paused. "You want to be warriors of skill and renown, right?"

Dahlia and Sheana nodded.

"Well, why don't I teach you how to stay alive? I can teach you about ReckNor at the same time, see if I can't help you see the truth."

Krell turned to Dahlia and met her gaze for a moment. She visibly forced herself to remain where she was and return his gaze.

"Your turn. Why are you afraid?"

Dahlia closed her eyes and swallowed hard. "Let's say that each of us had to develop a way to defend ourselves from men who would have taken us. Sheana grew strong. Men who try to take her end up beaten and bloody, though at times she does too, but someone has always come along at the noise and we've been able to escape. Verbena, she's developed this incredibly cruel and heartless way of acting that makes people so angry they stop thinking clearly. She outsmarts them and escapes that way, often with her magic."

Dahlia let out a breath. "I just hide. They can't attack me or try to rape me if they can't find me."

Sheana clenched her hand around Dahlia's, bringing both their hands up to the side of her face. "I won't let anyone do that to you — to any of us," she said. Dahlia nodded.

"I think I understand," said Krell.

Dahlia laughed, and it was a hopeless sort of laughter that had no joy in it.

"No, Krell, you don't. You have no idea what it's like to see every man, even you, as a threat. To always have to be wary, alert, on guard. Always fearful of being raped and murdered, just because we tell some man we don't want him between our legs."

Krell thought about that. He thought about Orianna, and Marlena, and their advances on him. He thought about Captain Gijwolf, and Captain Voss, and others. He shrugged.

"Perhaps you're right. So here's my offer. Stay with me, travel with me, *fight* with me. I'll train you and make you stronger. Nothing else. Then, when you think you're ready, you can leave."

"In exchange for what?" said Sheana, a challenge in her voice.

"Your friendship. And who knows what you'll teach me?"

Several seconds passed in silence, as Krell just looked Sheana in the eye.

"Nothing more?"

Krell grinned. "Oh, you never know, you might be such horrible people that I'll find I can't abide the sight of, but we'll never know unless we try, now will we?"

Dahlia gave Krell a small smile, and Sheana laughed.

"Good. Now, let's go back in and be quiet and bored while Olgar brings your friend back to life."

Chapter Seventeen

Verbena was angry.

The three of them stood outside the temple, Verbena being supported by Sheana. Dahlia and Sheana were smiling, though they'd also been crying. Their friend was back, even if she was furious.

Olgar and Krell stood inside the temple, watching Verbena berate them.

"We agreed, nobody else! How do we know we can trust him?"

"Verbena, you're being unreasonable," said Dahlia. "He's a paladin, and he asked that we learn about ReckNor. That's pretty much it!"

"What about the training? What about the traveling with him? I won't be a slave to anyone!"

Olgar leaned over to Krell. "I like her. She's got spirit."

Krell nodded, vaguely concerned. He was wondering if his plan to get a few capable followers of ReckNor was collapsing into ruin in front of his eyes. Olgar noticed his expression and grunted.

"Relax, my boy. Unless you somehow developed the ability to lie convincingly, you've already won some new followers."

"I'm not a good liar, Olgar."

"Ha! I know, my boy, I know," Olgar said, grinning at him. "Paladins are often terrible liars, at least in the stories."

Krell snorted. "The stories are mostly about Hieron's paladins. They *can't* lie, their god forbids it."

Olgar nodded. "Probably why they're so bad at it then, isn't it? They've no practice."

Krell pinched the bridge of his nose. "Olgar, you're making my brain hurt. Are you saying I should learn how to lie?"

"Shush, lad, looks like they've come to a decision."

The women walked over.

"You said you'd train us," Verbena said, not as a question but as a statement.

Krell nodded. "I did. I will. At least, to the limit of my abilities. That bear thing nearly killed me also."

Verbena started. "Wait, you almost died?"

Krell smiled slightly and nodded. "Did they tell you I warned them it's dangerous to be around paladins? We, apparently, often make stupid choices that lead to meaningless deaths. The stories don't go into it, but I bet those around the paladin also end up dead. I'm not offering safety. I'm not your owner. I'll teach you what I know. If you hate me, then leave."

Verbena was looking at him differently now. Still with disdain, but there was an appraising look to her eye. Sheana looked triumphant, grinning at Krell. Something had happened here that Krell did not understand, but at once Verbena's hostility seemed to diminish.

She nodded and leaned heavily on Sheana. "How long is this weakness going to last?" she asked. Even the act of talking seemed to be draining her.

"Lass, it varies, but no longer than a week," said Olgar.

"I need to sleep," she said.

"You're welcome to sleep here. Olgar is old and grumpy, but you can have his bed if you want. It's a nice night, we can sleep outside. Or if you want help getting down the hill, I can help you get back to the Netminder's Friend, since I think you've got a room there," said Krell.

Verbena gave him a slight smile, but it didn't touch her eyes at all. "Thank you, no. Sheana can get me back to our room." A vaguely disgusted look crossed her face, as if she just stepped into something foul. "Thank you, Krell, for my life."

Krell nodded. "Direct your thanks to ReckNor and we'll call it even."

She stared at him for a long moment. Krell had no idea what she was thinking. He just returned her gaze. He felt like he was in a contest of wills and didn't understand why. She nodded, then turned her head to Sheana.

"Can we go?" Sheana nodded, and reached down and picked Verbena up, cradling her in her arms. Sheana looked at Krell, smiled, then started down the hill.

Dahlia walked up and embraced Krell. It was so unexpected that Krell tensed up, and before he could react, she stepped back, out of reach. She smiled at him, then turned and walked after Sheana.

Olgar sighed. "I'm not sure what the future holds for those three, Krell, but you gave them a magnificent gift."

Krell snorted. "Not me, Olgar. ReckNor."

A minute passed in silence, broken only when Olgar took a drink from his flask. He suddenly turned his attention to the doorway. A warmth came into Krell's thoughts.

"Relax, it's just Fortis."

"And who, by ReckNor's baleful gaze, is Fortis?"

A tiny dragon peered around the corner and let out a chirp.

Krell smiled and spoke for the two of them. "Olgar, we're hungry."

* * *

Krell woke with a warm weight on his legs.

He looked down and met Fortis's gaze. "Good morning, my friend. You're warm. My thanks for that," said Krell. Fortis led out a contented cackling purr, then stood and stretched. His talons extended, poking gently into Krell's skin. He grunted.

Fortis jumped off Krell, landing on the floor, then stretched again. Then he sat, his tail coiled around his legs, his wings furled behind him. He looked regal and majestic. Krell gazed at him with open admiration.

"You're hungry, aren't you? Me too," said Krell. "I feel like I'm always hungry. I wonder if Olgar has any food left around here, or if we need to go into town. Wait, never mind. Let's go to town."

There was a plaintive hiss from Fortis.

"Nonsense. You'll be perfectly safe with me. If anyone tries to hurt you, I'll use this," said Krell, summoning a longsword of dark metal into his hand. Krell looked Fortis in the eye. "If you're going to stay with me, and I really want you to, you're going to need to learn how to be around people, and learn that I'm going to protect you if I need to."

Fortis cocked his head sideways in a gesture that reminded Krell strongly of the many cats he had seen in town. A new feeling came over him. The sensation was strange, like a completed thought arriving all at once.

"I don't know, but I'd like to see them, if we can," he said. "I suspect that Verbena feels like a wagon ran over her."

Krell rose off the bench, letting his sword fall away and disappear. Olgar wasn't in his room, which was unusual. When he glanced outside, the sun was just about to rise, based on the color of the sky. His stomach rumbled at him.

Krell stretched his arm and shoulder, moving it freely and without pain. He grunted in satisfaction. "My thanks, ReckNor, for the gift of your grace!"

There was a feeling of warmth and approval from within him. Krell smiled, then went outside to the privy to relieve himself. When he came back in, he donned a new set of clothes. He looked at his armor and shield, then decided against it. Normally, when he woke, he was fully refreshed. This morning he just felt worn and wanted a day of rest.

Olgar was nowhere to be found, which was exceedingly strange. Krell shrugged and walked down the hill toward Watford. He'd need a new cloak and some replacement clothes. His cloak and clothing from the previous day were a blood-soaked mess, still lying in a pile outside the temple.

The weather was going to be pleasant today. There were no clouds visible, and the breeze was gentle. Watford was alive with activity, with multiple boats still visible as they departed the harbor. On the horizon, Krell could see a sail from a larger ship.

Fortis landed on his shoulder, and his talons dug in a bit as he flared his wings, seeking balance. Krell grunted at the pain, but then Fortis settled. Krell wondered if he was bleeding.

"We'll have to work on that," he said. Fortis gave him a hiss that came with thoughts of agreement and apology. As Krell descended, Fortis constantly had to readjust his perch and Krell felt dozens of tiny wounds on his shoulder. ReckNor's grace closed them almost as fast as they appeared, but they were still unpleasant.

Worth it, though, by Krell's way of thinking.

In town proper, everyone who saw him stopped and stared. In many cases, their mouths literally dropped open. Many looked at Krell in fear, although a few gazed at him in wonder. Krell thought maybe they were just looking at Fortis instead. A young boy in ragged clothes ran up to Krell.

"Can I pet your dragon?" he asked, his eyes shining.

Krell glanced at Fortis, whose thoughts roiled in his mind.

"What's your name, lad?" he asked.

"Duncan."

"Well, Duncan, this mighty dragon, who has graciously decided I am worthy of becoming his friend, is still a little nervous about being around all these people. I tell you what, though, I am often in the Netminder's Friend, so if you go there in a few days, he might be willing to let someone else touch him. For now though, no."

Duncan looked crushed. "I can't go into the Netminder's Friend. Marlena keeps chasing me out whenever I do."

Krell raised an eyebrow. "Why is that?"

Duncan grinned. "I steal drinks and food!" With that, he turned and dashed away.

Krell shook his head, then resumed walking to the Netminder's Friend. He looked at Fortis as he walked. "Well done, my friend." Fortis still looked anxious.

As they approached, there was a shout of anger from the docks. Krell felt a nudge from ReckNor and abruptly veered toward the sound. Fortis grew agitated as the shouts became clearer, many voices raised in anger.

"Up top, on the roof, Fortis. You'll feel better and can watch my back," said Krell. At once, Fortis spread his wings, and with a leap, hurtled upward. Krell caught himself staring in awe at the majesty of watching a dragon in flight.

The shouting grew more intense, and as Krell rounded a corner, he could see what the disturbance was. A group of sailors had surrounded a pair of dwarves and were hurling insults at them.

"Watford is a human town and we'll not let you take over!"

"Go back to yer hills, ya dirt-grubbing thieves!"

"Trying to ruin us, you are, to seize our boats!"

"Taking over, that's what they want! Soon it's to the mines for the lot of us!"

Krell walked forward and grabbed one sailor by the arm.

"What is happening here?" he demanded.

"And who are you to be asking?" snarled the sailor.

Krell gave him a dark look, and the sailor's anger began changing to fear. "Don't play that game with me. You know who I am," said Krell.

"Yer that paladin that everyone's talking about." His eyes suddenly brightened. "Good! ReckNor protects his own, and a champion arrives to set these dwarves in their place!" He turned to the crowd and shouted, "A paladin of ReckNor!"

The crowd settled, and Krell walked forward. The two dwarves were standing back to back and looked calm. Krell nodded to them, and turned, looking at the sailors, trying to figure out who was leading the mob.

He gave up. "Who's speaking for the sailors? Come forward, and let ReckNor hear what you have to say!" he said.

There was some muttering and a lot of looks down at the docks. Krell shook his head and pointed. "You'll do, then. Step forward and tell ReckNor your name."

The sailor he was pointing at looked a little ashamed and afraid, but stepped forward. "Floris, my lord," he muttered.

"Tell me, Floris, what is it these dwarves have done?"

"They're coming to take Watford from us, that's what!" he shouted. "I'll not toil away in a mine, under the whips of the dwarves, while they steal my boat!"

Krell looked at him blankly for a moment, then burst out laughing.

"Floris, you're an idiot!" said Krell, wiping tears from his eyes. He looked around at the shocked and angry expressions on the sailors' faces. "You all are!"

Krell shook his head, his laughter subsiding into chuckles. Everyone was looking at him now, their anger turning toward him.

"First, what, by ReckNor's fury, would a dwarf want with a fishing boat? Look at them, do they look like sailors? I'm not saying there aren't dwarves who know the beauty of the sea, but these two? I've met them for less than a minute and can tell for certain they are not sailors."

There was some muttering from the crowd.

"You said a paladin of ReckNor would sort this out, so shut your mouths while I do!" yelled Krell, letting fury color his voice. The sailors quieted at once, some of them stepping back.

"Second, why, by the Forge Father's skilled hands, would a dwarf want a human in a mine?" He looked around at them, contempt on his face. "Do you think, for even a moment, that the dwarves actually need a human to dig a hole in the earth? That's their nature and, for the most part, their home. They're as comfortable there as you are on your boats. Would you take a totally untrained sailor aboard and expect to get a good result?" Krell laughed.

"Third, if you think the dwarves want Watford, you're daft. They live underground. You know what happens if you dig down, here in Watford?" Krell looked around, seeing the anger on the crowd changing to confusion. "You get a hole filled with water! Do dwarves breathe water?" he asked. As Krell looked around, he noticed Hilam and three other guards standing back and watching.

There was some grumbling from the crowd, but Krell shouted over them. "No, they in fact do *not* breathe water, any more than you do!"

Krell put a stern expression on his face. "Finally, starting a riot and assaulting citizens are crimes. Walk away before the guard over there comes forward and takes action." Krell conjured a long blade in his hand. The crowd gasped and stepped backward. "If you try to harm those who've done nothing wrong, it might compel me to take action. ReckNor doesn't fear these dwarves. So neither should you. Now, go away."

The crowd began to disperse, slowly at first, then all at once. Krell nodded and let his blade drop, watching it turn to mist before it hit the ground. He turned to the dwarves.

"My apologies for that," he said.

"To being fair, was not you that did the fault," said the dwarf. The other was standing patiently.

"You reside in the Consortium headquarters?" asked Krell.

"That is to being our home for the now. I am being Skazlim Earthfoot. This is being my friend, Khoundal Flatrock. May we be knowing the name of you?"

"I am Krell, paladin of ReckNor," he said. Hilam was walking over with the guards. Krell recognized Logruff, Torvald, and Jarmins.

"Skazlim, I've told you, have I not, that walking the docks is going to cause trouble?" asked Hilam. He nodded to Krell.

"Hilam."

"Krell."

"But the boats, they are being strange and pretty to our eyes!" said Skazlim.

Hilam looked up and spent a long moment breathing in through his nose. The other guards looked amused, more than anything else. Logruff eyed Krell and winked.

Hilam let out his breath slowly, and then looked at the dwarves. "I know you like looking at the boats. I know you mean no harm. Yet the people here, they are afraid that you are invaders, and in their fear they act stupidly."

"Perhaps by the familiar sight of a dwarf who does not do wrong they become less of the afraid, no?" said Skazlim.

Hilam turned to Krell. "Every morning, we have the same argument. Today was worse than yesterday. I saw you with the crowd. Why'd you stand up for them?" said Hilam, gesturing at the dwarves.

Krell grinned. "I just do what I'm told, Hilam. The power of ReckNor interceded. Not, I think, on behalf of the dwarves here, but on behalf of those sailors. Look at them," said Krell, gesturing at Skazlim and Khoundal.

"They're all solid muscle, and likely have spent more than one human lifetime swinging hammer or pick. Strong, extremely precise and tough, as all dwarves are. I'm pretty sure ReckNor had me intercede to keep his followers alive. If they pick a fight with this pair, I bet you'd need to wash human blood off the docks."

Hilam looked at Krell, and Jarmins whistled.

"You really think this was the other way around, Krell?" asked Logruff.

"I do. Skazlim, Khoundal, stop trying to pick a fight with the people here. If you kill followers of ReckNor, I'll probably have to kill you." Krell's stomach rumbled. A thought came into his head.

"Oh, Hilam, you need to meet someone," said Krell, turning toward the guards. "He's my friend, and he's not likely to hurt anyone unless they try to hurt him. Stay calm and don't panic, or I'll break your nose." Krell met their eyes, giving them a hard look.

Then he held out his arm, and suddenly Fortis landed on his shoulder.

They, as one, jumped backward. Logruff drew his sword.

"I said, stay calm!" Krell yelled, looking directly at Logruff.

"That's a ReckNor's damned dragon!" he shouted.

"He is. Very good, Logruff. As I said, he's my friend, and I'll not have anyone in town hurting him. Do I make myself clear?"

Hilam nodded, turning to the others. "Logruff, put up your sword."

Beside Krell, Skazlim tapped him on the elbow. Krell looked down.

"Much credit and honor to you, Krell, ReckNor paladin," he said. "Being made dragon friend is for stories rare, and I am being grateful for the gift of it here." Skazlim and Khoundal both gave Krell a courtly bow. Krell was a little unsure what was going on.

"We will be spreading news that Krell is dragon friend among dwarves," said Skazlim. He turned to Hilam. "Paladin Krell intervened for us, he has. He is dragon friend. To the docks we will no longer venture unattended by guards, as you wish. We have no desire to cross blades with dragon friend. We go." Skazlim and Khoundal turned at once, and headed toward the stone building that housed the Smithforge Mining Consortium headquarters.

Hilam shook his head, a bemused expression on his face. "Udar's broken blade, Krell, what a morning! Where in the hells did you find a dragon?"

Krell looked at Fortis and smiled. "I'm pretty sure he found me."

* * *

Marlena dropped the bowls, spattering cooked oats over the floor.

Everyone stopped and stared as Krell entered the Netminder's Friend. Fortis was on the edge of panic, looking at the closed room, but Krell thought reassuring thoughts toward him. *Courage, my friend. No harm will come to you while I live.*

Fortis subsided, relaxing slightly, though his eyes were darting around the room.

Krell cleared his throat. "This is Fortis, a friend of mine. He's not a pet, and he's not for sale. He won't hurt you if you don't hurt him. Don't try and touch him — he's still a little nervous around people. If anyone hurts him, I'll kill them."

Krell looked over at the table they usually sat at, seeing Kraven, Gerrard, Lily, and Dorn sitting there.

"Especially you, Kraven!" said Krell, grinning as he walked over.

Kraven laughed. "Look at you, you're intense! Walk in and threaten a whole room full of people with death! That's why I like you so much. What did you do last night, I wonder?" Kraven was eyeing the dragon warily, though he had a grin on his face.

Krell sat down. "Fortis, these are friends of mine. Kraven, Dorn, Lily, and Gerrard," said Krell, pointing at each in turn. "Everyone, this is Fortis, he's sort of chosen me to be his friend. He's a little nervous right now, so give him some time to get used to you all."

"We've met," said Kraven. Fortis glared back at him.

Lily eyed the dragon. "Is it dangerous?"

"He, not it, and yes, he's dangerous. He's a dragon," said Krell. He looked around, spotting Marlena cleaning up the mess she had made. His stomach rumbled.

"I hate waiting. Ah well, it's probably my fault for bringing you in without announcing anything, huh?" said Krell, looking at Fortis.

He turned to his companions. "So, what news?"

Gerrard spoke up. "Pretty sure you're the one with news, know what I mean?" His eyes were fastened on Fortis. "He's magnificent, Krell. Look at him! He's like a little king, sitting on your shoulder, right?"

Krell grinned. "His talons make it a little less pleasant than you might think. I should have worn my armor!"

His friends chuckled.

"What the hells is that, Krell? Where did you get it?" said Tristan. He was approaching the table, his eyes fixed on Fortis. "Is that the one you let go before?"

Krell nodded. Fortis became agitated, and Krell reached up and stroked his spine. The little spikes along his back didn't hurt if he ran his fingers from head to tail. Krell had no interest in trying it the other way.

"Tristan, this is Fortis, a friend of mine."

"He's worth thousands of golden sovereigns, Krell. *Thousands*," said Tristan.

Krell shook his head. "He's not for sale. I don't sell my friends."

Gerrard laughed. "Good to know, am I right?"

Tristan sat, staring hard at Krell. "That's thousands of golden sovereigns that you stole as treasure from the rest of us, Krell. No wonder Orca left!"

"Tristan, I will not become a slaver! He's not for sale. Wait, what do you mean, Orca left?"

Kraven gave him a sad look. "Said he couldn't stand you, so he left. He said there's lots of coin to be made in the world, and he could do it without... how'd he put it, Gerrard?"

Gerrard grinned. "Without a loud-mouthed nobody who refused to listen to authority!" Dorn and Lily laughed.

Krell slumped. The thoughts of Fortis focused on him, as a crushing sadness flowed out from Krell's heart. The laughter trailed off.

"Wow, Krell, you're taking this way too hard. Orca's an ass," said Gerrard. He looked around, and Kraven nodded at once.

"Forget him, Krell. We don't need him with us. If he wanted out, then he's out. Took his gold and left." Kraven went back to his meal.

Marlena approached tentatively. "Krell, is it dangerous?"

Krell looked up and smiled at her. "Not unless you try to hurt him. Fortis, this is Marlena, another friend of mine. Marlena, this is Fortis."

"Friend?" said Marlena in mock outrage. Kraven burst into laughter, and Krell shot him a look. Kraven held up his hand and shook his head as he laughed, then went back to eating.

"Marlena, we're hungry," said Krell, turning back to face her. Fortis raised his head and gave Marlena a happy chirp.

"You're always hungry, Krell." She looked troubled for a moment. "Those girls. I thought one of them died."

Krell grinned. "ReckNor decided otherwise."

Tristan turned to face Krell, his expression turning to anger. "You had her raised from the dead? Good gods, *why*? You're spending wealth and time on all these useless sacks!" he said, gesturing to Lily. Her expression darkened.

"Tristan, I know this is hard for you to understand, but Lily can actually hear you, since she's sitting right there," said Kraven. "If you're not careful, she's gonna gut you like she did that bear thing."

"It was a *kulukunari*, you illiterate thug!" snarled Tristan.

Kraven bristled.

"So, Fortis, as you can see, Tristan is an ass, but has a lot of magic power. It practically oozes out of him, which is why we keep him around. Kraven is angry all the time, but decent enough. Gerrard is, I think, just happy to be alive, because last week he wasn't. Lily is very dangerous. I think I might be a little afraid of her. And Dorn is a true priest of ReckNor. He's also probably insane, because he's a dwarf that loves the sea."

Dorn opened his mouth to object, then paused and shrugged. He went back to eating.

"See, Fortis, this is why I like Krell," said Kraven. "He's intense!"

* * *

Krell heard a gasp behind him and turned to look.

Verbena, Sheana, and Dahlia were standing there. Verbena was standing on her own, though she looked exhausted, her shoulders slumped. Sheana and Dahlia looked fully restored, and all of them had their hair tied into elaborate braids.

As one, they were all staring at Fortis in wonder.

Krell smiled and turned to Fortis. He was sitting in the center of the table, steadily eating a chunk of roast pork that Marlena had brought out for him. He was, Krell noted, a particularly messy eater. Bits of meat were scattered across the table. When Krell turned his attention to him, his head came up, and he looked back.

"Fortis, these young women are my friends. Verbena, Sheana, and Dahlia. Ladies, this is Fortis." Krell stood as he gestured, and then held his chair out for Verbena. "Here, sit, before you fall over. Being brought back is really hard on you."

"I'm fine."

Krell gave her a hard look. "You are not. Don't be stupid and prideful. Sit."

Their eyes locked, and a battle of wills commenced. Krell wondered how long he would have to wait. He could feel the grace of ReckNor within him bubbling in laughter. Krell wondered about ReckNor, not for the first time. So many people thought of him as a destructive god of nature, yet Krell found that ReckNor took delight in moments of people interacting with one another.

Perhaps it's lonely being a god.

Kraven and Gerrard made a wager.

After half a minute, Verbena made a disgusted noise in her throat and sat on the chair. Sheana stifled her laughter, and Dahlia gave him a smile. He winked back at them. Sheana turned and grabbed a chair for her and Dahlia, and Krell shoved Dorn over on the bench and sat. Gerrard grumbled and handed some coins to Kraven.

Marlena came over and took food orders from everyone. Her eyes kept darting to Verbena, who wasn't interested in food. Sheana overruled her, ordering enough food for four.

Verbena frowned at her, but her attention was on Fortis. She and Fortis engaged in another staring contest. Krell idly wondered if this was just the way Verbena was or not.

"Can I touch him?" she asked.

Krell shrugged. "Ask him. I don't own him, he's my friend. It's like asking me for permission to run your fingers through Dorn's beard."

"You've never felt anything so luxurious, I'd wager," said Dorn, grinning.

Krell smiled at Dorn. "I wager you're right, and yet!"

Dorn laughed. "Your loss then!"

Verbena held out her hand to Fortis, and he moved forward and sniffed it.

Then he ran his head and neck along her hand in a gesture of affection, and looked at Krell.

"Huh. He likes you."

Verbena lifted her head so she could almost look down her nose at Krell. Quite a feat, since she was shorter than him, but effective nonetheless. "Of course, I'm amazing."

Krell turned slightly, a feeling of being watched coming over him. He met Dahlia's gaze.

She'd been staring at him the whole time.

* * *

Captain Gijwolf came into the common room and walked directly over.

"So that's when I shoved him down the stairs!" said Dorn. Kraven, Gerrard, Sheana, and Lily all burst into laughter, while Krell and Dahlia smiled. Verbena frowned.

Captain Gijwolf stopped, staring hard at Verbena. Then he smiled ruefully and shook his head. Krell looked over.

"Morning, Captain. Come join us?" he said.

He nodded. "Hilam told me about a friend of yours, Krell, and it sounds so unbelievable that I came to see for myself," he said, looking around.

Kraven pointed up. Captain Gijwolf looked up and spotted Fortis, who was curled up on one of the braces on the beams running the length of the common room. He looked sound asleep.

"Bloody hells, Krell! That's a dragon," he said.

Krell smiled. "I noticed that, but thank you for confirming it for me."

"It's sleeping?"

Krell shook his head. "No, but he wants you to think that he is. He's watching everyone in here. Pretty intently, from what I can make out. Fortis, this is Captain Gijwolf. Captain, that is Fortis." Krell gestured for him to join them.

Captain Gijwolf grabbed another chair from the nearly empty common room, and sat close by. Marlena came over. Captain Gijwolf's focus shifted at once to her, and he smiled.

"Elias, good morning! Anything for you?" The smile she gave him was, as far as Krell could tell, reserved for him alone.

"Nothing for me this morning, Marlena, thank you. Here to satisfy my curiosity and to talk to these fine folk here," he said, gesturing at the table where Krell and his companions sat.

Marlena tilted her head down so she could look up at him, despite him being seated. Krell had no idea how she managed to do that.

"Pity," she said. "Well, if you think of anything you want from me, let me know!" She turned and walked. Krell watched Captain Gijwolf watch her as she left. Krell smiled and drank his water.

Captain Gijwolf turned his gaze from Marlena back up to Fortis. Fortis raised his head, looking back at him.

"It's smart, then?"

"*He's* smart, and yes, very."

"Probably smarter than you, Krell," said Tristan.

Krell nodded. "No 'probably' about it from what I can tell, Tristan."

Kraven laughed. "You know he's going to keep doing that until you react properly, right, Krell?"

"Doing what?"

Gerrard looked at Tristan, then back to Krell while Kraven chuckled. "Krell, you know, you're intense and all, but people try to insult you, right? And you don't even notice. It's like, you agree right along with them." Gerrard shook his head and smiled in admiration. "It probably angers Tristan, you know."

Krell grinned at Gerrard, then turned to Tristan. "Yeah, I know," he said.

Kraven and Dorn roared with laughter.

"You are such a jackass, Krell!" said Tristan.

Krell's grin widened, and he shrugged.

Sheana snickered.

"So Verbena," said Tristan, "I hear you've got some magical power. I'm a powerful sorcerer myself. Perhaps I could give you some pointers?" His eyes roamed over her body. "Perhaps somewhere more private than here?"

Sheana kicked Krell gently under the table, and when he looked at her, she grinned and whispered, "Watch this!"

Verbena leaned back and looked at Tristan. Despite being taller than her, she managed to look down her nose again. Krell thought it had something to do with the tilt of her head.

"As attempts to get me into bed go, Tristan, that was clumsy. Clumsy and vaguely offensive. I'll pass on that, thank you. As to the pointers, from what I've gathered, you focus your magic through willpower, correct?"

"I'll have you know I have lots of success with women, Verbena, and I can guarantee you'd enjoy yourself," said Tristan.

She sighed. "Okay, look, you're pretty, I'll give you that. Fey-touched always are. That scar looks new, and gives you a rugged and strong look. But you're also *petty*. Petty, and small. Too small for my desires."

Kraven burst out laughing. "She called you small! Tristan the Tiny!"

Krell couldn't help himself and laughed with the others. Tristan's face darkened in anger. Verbena remained calm, keeping eye contact with him the entire time.

"As for your offer of magic guidance," she said, "can you explain the interlock of divination runes designed to sense the presence of magic, and calculate the power required to flow through them?"

Tristan looked at her blankly. "I'm sorry, what?"

Verbena nodded to herself. "Look, I understand. In terms of raw power, you probably outclass me. You might even outclass everyone at the table put together. But you're a sorcerer, by your own admission. You take the ability to channel power, and you *will* it to be so. But you're doing it with no understanding whatsoever. You're like a child playing with fire. You know what fire is, you know how to set things alight, but you haven't the faintest idea how fire really works."

"I know how fire works," said Tristan indignantly.

"Excellent. What are the requirements for fire to exist, then?" she asked. Sheana kicked Krell again, a wide grin on her face.

"What do you mean?" asked Tristan, his indignation turning to confusion.

"I mean, without using magic, how do you start a fire?"

"Why wouldn't I use magic for that?" he asked.

"Humor me, Tristan. How do you make a fire without magic and then keep it burning?"

"Well, you need wood, and you need a way to start it. Normal people without my power use a flint and steel to strike sparks onto kindling, then tediously build up the fire from there," said Tristan.

"That's all?" asked Verbena.

Tristan looked at her quizzically. "Yes?" he said.

Verbena nodded. "That's what I thought. You don't understand at all. Or rather, your understanding is limited, because you just will things into being with your power, instead of investigating how it actually works. I am a *wizard,* Tristan, not a mere sorcerer. I may not have your raw power, but what I can do is likely much more flexible. You see, I learn *why* magic works, not just how."

"So, what does that have to do with the fire question?"

Verbena gave him a sweet, yet at the same time entirely condescending, smile. "Fill a bathing tub with water and then start a fire at the bottom of that bathing tub."

"You can't start a fire underwater without magic, Verbena. Everyone knows that. Well, maybe not Krell," said Tristan, as if explaining things to a child.

Verbena nodded. "Exactly, Tristan. Yet you didn't include that in the requirements. Fire needs air to work, the wood can't be completely saturated with water, and you'd be well advised to have a place for the smoke to escape. You listed none of those things. You also assumed only wood as a fuel for the fire. You don't *think* about things." Her smile abruptly faded, giving him a stern look.

"That, and the pettiness of that shot against Krell, are why you have nothing to teach me."

Kraven grunted. "Krell, I like this one."

Krell smiled at Sheana, then turned to the rest of them. "Yeah, me too."

* * *

Captain Gijwolf cleared his throat.

"As fascinating as this is, there is business to discuss, as it pertains to your charter," he said.

"About that," said Krell. "What happened with Orca?"

Captain Gijwolf frowned. "He said that you drove him out, Krell. Is this not the case?"

"Krell drives everyone away eventually, Captain Gijwolf," said Tristan. "It's that enormous ego of his. There's simply no room for anyone else to exist next to him."

Krell let out a breath in frustration, ignoring Tristan. "No, Captain. He said nothing to me. The last time I saw him was after we got back from the dwarven mining camp, after trading some gemstones. I don't understand what happened, but I know that I missed his blade fighting that bear monster."

Captain Gijwolf nodded. "He's a firm hand with the blade, no doubt. Well, he wanted to be a leader, and you lot seem to be impossible to lead. Perhaps that's it, and he's just off looking for less stubborn people to fight beside."

Kraven laughed, and Dorn said, "I am the nicest and most agreeable person I know!"

Krell looked at Dorn, then turned his attention back to Captain Gijwolf. "So, he left the charter then?"

Captain Gijwolf nodded. "I struck his name at his request. He's free and clear, and then left town, taking the road inland. Didn't say where he was going. But that isn't what I wanted to speak to you all about."

He reached for a small wooden case on his belt and opened it, pulling out a scroll. He handed it to Verbena.

"I'm glad to see you recovered from your wounds, young lady," he said. "I, uh, thought they were more severe than this."

She nodded, unfurling the scroll and placing it on the table, arranging cups to hold the edges. It was a map of the coast, with Watford near the center.

"Blame him," she said, slumping back into her chair and pointing at Krell. "He's the one who saved me." Her face took on a bitter expression. Sheana looked at her, and the sadness and joy mingled in her expression struck Krell. He felt someone watching him, and his eyes snapped to Dahlia, meeting her gaze. What felt like a long moment passed, then she looked away.

Krell turned and examined the map. There were three red markings on it, but aside from Watford and the fortress city of Heaford, there was nothing he could make sense of.

"The markings here are locations where a fisher spotted something strange. You can imagine how many false reports we've received, but three in particular stand out."

Captain Gijwolf pointed at the first. "Here, Lars, a fisher you've not likely met, saw what he thought was a fish with arms and legs. He was already making back for Watford after pulling in his nets. Otherwise, I wonder if he'd have lived or not. Assuming it was a sea devil, that is."

He pointed at the next one. "Here, another fisher, Unter, found an abandoned boat belonging to Cardiff — with bloodstains aboard. Cardiff has not been seen since his boat was found. I suspect the worst. The nets were out, so the boat was largely immobile as a result."

He pointed to the last one, tapping it with his finger repeatedly. "Finally, and most importantly, a man named Mog was about to cast nets here when he spied another vessel in the distance, making for shore. He was certain that whatever was aboard was not human and the boat was moving without the sail being up."

Captain Gijwolf sat back. "What do you make of that?" he asked.

Krell thought about it, trying to piece things together.

"It means the sea devils have established a base of operations ashore, along the coast between here and here," said Verbena, tapping her fingers on the map.

Everyone turned to look at her, and she blushed a little.

"Huh?" said Krell, clearly confused.

Captain Gijwolf smiled, and gave Verbena a tip of his imaginary hat. "Precisely so, young lady. Though I will say we struggled with this for some time before finally calling in Karaback, who deduced the same conclusion in roughly the same amount of time, though he was more precise. They've almost certainly moved into the ruins of Swamp Hold."

"I'm not familiar with that place," said Kraven.

"It was destroyed thirty years ago in a sea devil invasion," said Krell. "Olgar lost his leg there."

"Yes," said Captain Gijwolf. "Olgar and I fought them there, as did Hilam, if you want to talk to others that know. More importantly, the council paid Karaback to do some magic, to make sure. He spotted at least twenty ashore, building defenses. Under the command of a much larger one that towered over them."

"Shit," said Krell. "You're going to tell us to go raid the place, aren't you?"

Captain Gijwolf nodded. "Scout, or outright assault, as you see best. What is important is that we get some solid information. With the guard already spread thin out to the mining camp, and the time spent recruiting and training, I don't have anyone available. Not that being a town guard prepares you for battle with the sea devils. You have fought them on the fishing vessel you found and emerged victorious, despite being ambushed."

Krell nodded. "Not likely there's anyone better for the job nearby, is there?"

"No. I've also sent word that we're going to need proper soldiers to man the defenses that Petimus and his clan are building. I don't know when they'll arrive, or even if they'll arrive. So in the meantime, that leaves you. Based on the reports I've received from you on previous battles you've fought, I'd say your tactics amount to a run-forward-and-hit-it-in-the-face sort of strategy, correct?"

Kraven's brow furrowed. "What's wrong with that?"

Krell was nodding in agreement with the captain.

"If this is a large lair, then there could be dozens present, maybe more. I'd advise against running in and starting a fight without more of a plan than that."

"So, Captain, what's the reward, then?" asked Gerrard.

He grinned at them. "Five hundred golden sovereigns to be split among the survivors if you return with detailed information about their encampment. An extra two *thousand* if you can drive them out, plus full recovery rights to whatever you find."

Krell let out a low whistle.

"That's a lot of money, am I right?" said Gerrard, his eyes wide.

Captain Gijwolf grinned. "It is! It's almost like someone disrupted a major smuggling operation that left the town coffers overflowing with coin!"

"Recovery rights?" asked Tristan.

"Salvage rights are typically around four percent of the value, which is what you ended up with from that haul in the smugglers' cave. Recovery rights mean you get to keep whatever you find."

Tristan turned to Krell. "I think Krell should forfeit his share, because of him," he said, pointing up at Fortis.

Captain Gijwolf shook his head. "Let me stop you right there, Tristan. Even though I was there when Krell set him free, I agree with him. If Fortis is smart, then that's slavery, which is a crime. Or to put it another way, since the town council won't take slaves, the council would have assessed the value of Fortis as being worth precisely zero coins."

Tristan muttered under his breath. Krell couldn't catch all of it, but it sounded like he was grumbling about finding the right buyers. He looked up and met Fortis's eyes. He tried to push the thought that anyone who took him would have to do it over his dead body.

Captain Gijwolf gave Tristan a hard look, then looked at Krell.

"Lily has not signed the charter, so would be entitled only to payment as one of your hirelings. What of these three?"

"We're right here," said Verbena.

"Yes, young lady, you are, but you are not signatories to the charter. To add additional names means unanimous agreement from the current signers."

"No, I don't think so," said Tristan at once.

Captain Gijwolf smiled ruefully and gestured. "There you go, then. Yet Krell took on Lily, meaning he's responsible for paying her wages, as it were."

He turned back to Krell, then let his eyes circle the group of them. "Are they going to be taken on by anyone else here?"

Krell nodded. "Yes, if they want to come along, I'll hire them as warriors."

Tristan rolled his eyes, and Kraven grunted.

Captain Gijwolf turned back to the three of them. "Well, ladies? What say you?"

Sheana grinned. "I'm in."

Dahlia nodded.

Verbena watched both of them, then made a disgusted noise in her throat. She turned to Krell. "*Fine.* We're all in."

Krell met her gaze, seeing the challenge there. Long seconds passed.

ReckNor's laughter bubbled up within him.

Chapter Eighteen

Krell and Kraven rowed.

Captain Voss had put *ReckNor's Bounty* close to Swamp Hold. They had put the longboat over the side and clambered in. It was after midnight three days later, and they were rowing quietly to shore. Once dawn arrived, they would be able to scout properly. Krell could see clearly in the nighttime darkness — to a point. Whatever strange gift he had from ReckNor's power only let him see for around a hundred feet. Then the darkness resumed.

Fortis, of course, could see clearly without any issue. Dragons were famous for their incredible senses.

ReckNor's Bounty would look out for Fortis. He'd agreed to carry a message if they needed a pickup. Otherwise, they'd maintain readiness in the harbor at Watford. If Fortis returned without a message, they would assume the worst.

Krell sensed eyes watching him. He turned, looking at Verbena. She was staring into his eyes. She gestured at her own, then at him, a questioning look on her face.

Krell grinned at her and kept rowing.

Voices carried a long way over the water. Nobody talked.

Eventually, they reached the shore. There were a large number of cliffs, but there were sandy areas at the base. Krell and Kraven steered along the coast, moving away from the ruins of Swamp Hold, until they found what looked like a relatively gentle ascent to the top, with a beach they could pull the boat onto.

As they approached, and the boat hit the sand, Sheana jumped out, her sword and shield ready, and marched forward. Gerrard gave Krell a smile, nodding toward her, and followed.

Soon they were all on the beach. Kraven and Sheana grabbed the boat and hauled it up onto the sand, then overturned it, ensuring the oars were stashed safely beneath it. Krell inspected the surrounding ground, ensuring he could spot no tracks anywhere. Fortis circled above, a dark shape in a dark sky, only visible when a star was momentarily blotted out by his passage in front of it.

Fortis gave Krell a feeling of safety. They started to climb.

The hill was steep, and Sheana, Verbena, Gerrard, Lily, and Dahlia all needed help, since they couldn't see in the dark like orcs, fey-touched, or dwarves could. Or Krell, with his strange gift. Eventually, with some muffled curses, they crested the rise.

At the top, they were still too far to see the ruins of Swamp Hold, but Krell set a confident direction toward it.

Verbena caught his attention. "What happened to your eyes?" she whispered.

Krell shook his head. "What do you see?"

"They're black, like a pair of voids of nothingness in your head." She shuddered. "It's very disturbing."

Krell shrugged. "A gift from ReckNor, to let me see in darkness," he whispered back. "Mind the tree branch on the ground, there. Let me help you." Krell reached out and grasped her arm. She was trembling under his touch.

"Are you okay?"

She bit her lip and nodded. Now that he was paying attention, she looked exhausted. Krell motioned for the others to stop.

Quietly, they gathered around. Verbena slumped to the ground, leaning against a tree. Sheana sat next to her, putting herself between Verbena and the rest of them. Dahlia sat on the other side of Verbena, protecting her from anything that might come through the woods.

Krell turned to the others, keeping his voice low. "We've got probably three miles to cover before we get to the edge of Swamp Hold. I doubt the town was named randomly, so we're likely to hit some rough terrain. We'll rest here for a few minutes, then head out. Everyone partner up with someone who can see clearly. We need to stay quiet."

Tristan snorted with disdain. "Five can't see in the dark, only four can."

Krell waved his hand. "Fine, Dahlia and Verbena can come with me then. Dahlia knows how to move quietly, even when she can't see clearly."

He crouched down in front of Verbena. "Do you think you can make it?"

She nodded. "Give me a moment to gather myself. I won't flag or falter."

Krell smiled, even though they might not see in the darkness. "You haven't yet, not once."

Krell looked over. Lily was next to Kraven, and they were talking quietly. Gerrard and Tristan huddled together. Dorn came over and nudged Sheana, who nodded to him.

The pace Krell set was slow, both to allow people to move in silence, but also to make it as easy as possible on Verbena. She was pale and soaked through with sweat by the time Krell called a halt at the edge of what looked like the beginnings of a swamp. The sky was lightening as the dawn approached.

"We'll rest here for an hour and see what we see then," said Krell. He led everyone back into the treeline and up the rise slightly, then spread his cloak on the ground and sat, leaning against a tree. Verbena sat at the same tree, around to one side.

"Thank you," she said. Her voice had lost its usual edge. "I know you set a slower pace after you noticed my weakness."

"I've never been dead before, so I don't exactly know how it feels. If you need to rest, it's a great excuse," said Krell, grinning but not looking at her. His eyes tracked around and he saw that Sheana and Dahlia were sitting side by side, watching him.

As soon as their eyes met, Dahlia looked away. Sheana gave him a grin and kept staring at him.

"Krell, we need to discuss our plan," said Tristan quietly as he walked over. Krell looked up at him.

"You're right, of course. I don't know enough about what we're going to face. Any ideas?" he asked.

"Finally, you're going to let me plan? You're growing wise with experience!"

Krell closed his eyes and breathed in deeply.

He heard Sheana laugh quietly.

* * *

The sahuagin did not appear to be fools.

As the dawn began to break, a patrol set out from the remains of Swamp Hold. From their perch in the branches of a tree, Krell and Dahlia watched it form and depart to the north. With the sun rising behind them, they were unlikely to be spotted, but Dahlia still worried over Krell's metal armor.

Krell climbed down, and everyone gathered around.

"Dahlia and I saw maybe twenty form into a patrol, including one that was easily a foot taller than the others. They're organized and disciplined. Not sure what they're doing in there, but they're clearly building fortifications to defend against land attack. Which makes no sense to me," said Krell.

"I think we should jump the patrol," said Tristan.

Kraven grimaced. "I hate to say it, but I agree with Tristan."

"How many did you see in the village?" asked Verbena.

Krell shook his head. "Fifty, maybe more. We don't have a good angle to look at the village from here, though."

She nodded. "Do we know if there are any other patrols out?"

Tristan shrugged. "Why would that matter?"

"Well, if they have more than one out, and we don't know where it is, then we might find them ambushing us, not the other way around."

"Well, the other issue is that Swamp Hold is west of us, but the patrol went north. We lost sight of it," said Krell.

Tristan snorted. "Typical."

"I hear you, though, Krell. You think we're gonna have to swing north around Swamp Hold to find the patrol, am I right?" asked Gerrard.

"If we decide we want to ambush it, it's easier to take out a patrol by itself. Without the rest of the fortress they're building coming out to fight as well. If that's what we decide, it'll be dangerous." Krell gestured toward Swamp Hold. "The trees thin out, so unless we go all the way around, which will take close to two days, we'll need to risk the edge of the bog."

"If we spend that long going around, we won't know if there's another patrol out or not," said Kraven.

"If we cut it close, we'll be spotted," said Dahlia. "I love Sheana, but she can't move quietly, and her armor glitters in the light. In this case, the noise and reflections are likely to get us noticed, and attacked."

"So that's the question then," said Dorn. "Do we go the long safe way around and hope for another opportunity, or do we take the short dangerous path for a certain confrontation with the patrol?"

Krell thought about their options. If ReckNor had anything to say, he was being quiet. He thought either path would work, but the short path felt best. At least if they were spotted, another patrol would come for them, and they'd have the fight, anyway.

Krell was, however, curious to see what the others would think.

"If I remove my armor, I can be much quieter," said Sheana.

"No offense, but it takes minutes to properly don armor, and life and death fights are measured in minutes. You'd be going into one unarmored," said Dorn.

"I say we take the safe path and wait for another patrol," said Tristan.

"The goal here is to kill the sea devils, Tristan, not to hope we can find and kill them later!" snarled Kraven. Krell noticed that Kraven and Tristan were sparring with one another almost constantly, and that Kraven was increasingly aggressive and angry when they did.

"Kraven is right," said Verbena. "The goal is to kill the sahuagin. That means the only logical choice is the short path."

"Why's that?" asked Tristan.

"Because either we get past without the fortress lookouts spotting us and ambush the patrol, or the fortress sees us and sends a force to attack us. In both outcomes, we have a fight with sea devils, but only some of the sea devils," said Lily. She shrugged. "It makes sense to me." Verbena nodded in agreement.

Krell nodded as well. "I agree. It should be the short path."

* * *

The bog stank.

Krell missed the smell of the sea as he trudged through yet another ankle-deep patch of slimy mud. It was tedious and difficult, but they had little fear of stumbling into a patrol, since the terrain was so difficult to traverse.

After five hours, the sun was well above the horizon and the advantage they had of it being behind them was gone. They'd covered most of the ground they needed, and it was already firming up.

Krell felt like he was covered in mud. His boots squelched when he walked. Cleaning his armor would be difficult, though the breastplate was vastly easier to clean than the chain mail would have been. He looked at Sheana to see how she fared.

She was almost perfectly clean. Her hair was still in an elaborate braid. She met his gaze and cocked her head questioningly.

Krell looked at once for Verbena and Dahlia, and found them in the same state. It was as if the mud refused to stick to them, and the grasping branches refused to scratch at their hair and clothing.

He turned back to Sheana. "How are you so clean?" he whispered.

She smiled at him. "You know how few people notice that?" she said. She gestured at Verbena, walking behind her. "She cheats, using magic all the time. It's pretty great."

Krell looked at Verbena, who raised an eyebrow and gave him a slightly mocking smile.

"I'm… wow. I want to know how to do that. Can you teach me?" he asked.

Verbena met his gaze, and she and Krell stared at one another until Tristan moved past.

"Stop staring at each other like cats and keep moving," he said.

Verbena smiled, though it didn't touch her eyes, and moved past him. She looked like she was going to collapse at any moment, her shoulders slumped, and her breathing coming somewhat erratically.

Sheana nudged him, and Krell turned to face her. She met his gaze, a serious expression on her face. "She's strong, Krell. Strong enough for this. I think she might be stronger than me."

"I don't doubt her," said Krell. He turned and followed Verbena.

The ground was indeed rising, and the mud fell away as the trees grew more frequent. There had been no shout of alarm from the direction of the fortress.

"I think we're clear, at this point," said Dahlia, looking behind her. "If they were going to raise the alarm, they'd have done so.

I didn't see a patrol leave and head in our direction, so we're probably safe."

Krell nodded, then pointed. "The patrol went this way a few hours ago. What do you think, Dahlia?" She came over and looked at the terrain in front of them.

"Yes. It looks like a path they've worn into the ground. We should move farther along it." She looked behind her, at the fortress barely visible through the trees. "Preferably put a hill between us and the fortress."

Krell cocked his head sideways. "Fortis says he's found them. About four miles away, coming toward us. There are thirty-six of them, and they look tired."

Everyone turned to look at Krell.

"He's communicating with you telepathically?" asked Verbena.

"Less like he's telling me, more like he's showing me." Krell looked around at everyone staring at him, then shrugged. "If we want a hill between us and the fortress, we'd better get moving. I think this was less a patrol, and more a scout party or something."

Nobody moved for a moment, then Dahlia nodded, and went forward. Krell turned to follow her. As he did, he thought he glimpsed Sheana and Verbena looking at one another.

Verbena was smiling.

* * *

The sea devils paused, almost as one, lifting their snouts into the air and sniffing.

Dahlia had shot a squirrel, hitting it on her first try with an arrow from extreme range. They had placed it partly beneath a rock just off the path, in a narrow ravine with no exits. Bait for their trap.

The smell of blood attracted their attention, just as Verbena had suggested. They began to turn toward it, but the leader, a hulking brute easily towering over the others, shouted something in the strange guttural tongue they used and they subsided. Then they split into three equal groups.

One went to one side of the ravine, where Krell, Kraven, Dorn, Lily, Gerrard and Sheana were hiding. Another went to the other side, which was impassable. Dahlia, Verbena, and Tristan had walked all the way around the far end of the ravine, and were atop the rocky bluff.

The third group remained on the trail, not moving.

Kraven shot Krell a look, hefting his axe. Krell nodded. The plan looked like it was falling to pieces.

Then the sea devil plan came apart. The leader of the group had stayed on the trail, and once the other two groups started moving away, the scent of blood overwhelmed whatever commands had been given. They abandoned their strategy of searching for an ambush and merged back together in front of the entrance. The hissing and croaking noises from the leader became strident, but about fifteen still turned and went into the ravine, while nine remained, staring at the leader as he hissed at them.

Kraven grinned at Krell, then turned his attention back to the pack.

The plan was simple. Catch them in the ravine and trap them in there, killing all of them. The sea devils were only partially cooperating. Still, there were only nine small ones at the entrance.

Krell caught Dorn's eyes and nodded. His blade of dark metal sprang into existence in his hand. Dorn reached out and clasped his forearm, a warning look in his eyes. Krell gave him a wave of his hand.

The sound of voices came to Krell's ears. Tristan and Verbena, chanting words of power. There was a hiss of an arrow, taking one of the sea devils at the entrance to the ravine in the neck, dropping it at once.

The sea devil leader exploded in a series of guttural croaks and hisses, gesturing around. The scent of blood from the wounded sea devil hit the remaining eight standing near it, and they turned on their fallen comrade, biting and tearing.

Five of the sea devils from the other group ran toward the fortress. The leader gathered the rest, and they charged the entrance to the ravine. Krell could make out the sound of Tristan's bolts of fire raining down on the sea devils in there, as well as the hissing of arrows through the air.

Distantly, Dahlia's voice, raised in panic, reached his ears. "Now!"

Kraven charged from the brush, Krell, Dorn, and Sheana right behind him.

The sea devils reacted at once, turning to face this new threat. Any sort of battle strategy was lost on both sides, and the sea devils came on in a chaotic wave. Krell's voice raised in a prayer to ReckNor, and his blade crackled with lightning. He stood between Dorn and Sheana, their shields forming a short wall.

"Death to the sea devils! For ReckNor!" he shouted, striking at them as they came into reach.

The sea devils crashed against their blades and shields, and recoiled away wounded, leaving two dead.

Kraven had rushed forward and was surrounded. The large one had pounced on Kraven, but he avoided its bite and claws. One of the smaller ones slashed Kraven from behind, leaving four bloody furrows on his back.

The sea devils fell into a frenzy.

They swarmed at Krell; he tried to hold position, but only managed to foul Sheana's sword arm with his shield, and then knock Dorn off balance as he tried to give her space.

Formation fighting was not his strength. Olgar had taught him how to be a knight, not how to be infantry. Krell charged forward, shouting praise to ReckNor as he went.

He took one blow to his shoulder and another to his leg, but cut down two of the beasts. He sensed Sheana and Dorn behind him and trusted them to do their part.

Krell cut another one down, deflected some claws on his shield, and attacked the larger sea devil from behind. The sea devils had covered Kraven in wounds and he was roaring in anger, his axe a blur. His strategy seemed to be to ignore the big one and slay the smaller ones around him.

Krell struck, his blade wreathed in lightning, dealing a wound that let loose an echoing blast of thunder. The big one turned to him, slamming an attack into his shield, knocking Krell back and nearly causing him to fall. Its claws raked at his sword, and its jaw slammed shut right in front of his face, only his shield holding it back far enough to avoid being killed.

An arrow came out of nowhere, flitting over Krell's shoulder, and took the sea devil in the shoulder.

Krell struck at once — a prayer to ReckNor wreathing his blade in lightning — and hit it in the leg. He shoved forward, and the sea devil's leg collapsed. It fell to the ground, though its claws found Krell, cutting his leg nearly to the bone. Crippled, Krell hobbled backward.

Kraven spun at once, and his axe fell directly into the skull of the beast on the ground. It abruptly went still.

Sheana and Dorn were both wounded. Lily and Gerrard darted out from hiding and slashed the sea devils in the back, killing them before they knew they were in danger. The sound of battle from the ravine reached them.

That was not a good sign.

ReckNor's grace had been working, and Krell's leg was mending, but not fast enough. Dorn and Sheana charged into the ravine while Krell hobbled over to Kraven. Lily and Gerrard finished the last of the sea devils on the ground, then darted into the ravine after the others.

Kraven was breathing heavily and fell to one knee. He was covered in wounds and was losing blood fast. Krell tried to drop to one knee, but his leg refused to cooperate and he fell onto Kraven.

Good enough. ReckNor's grace began to work on Kraven. Now that he was forcing it, it felt like shards of glass being dragged through his guts. ReckNor was right.

Kraven sucked in a breath as his wounds began to close. He looked at Krell, then grabbed him and raised him to his feet as he stood.

"Looks nasty," he said. "Can you walk?"

Krell shook his head. "Only a little, and not far. Go. I'll be healed through the grace and power of ReckNor soon enough."

"Ha! You're intense!" Kraven clapped him on the shoulder, nearly knocking Krell over, and then charged into the ravine.

* * *

Tristan, it turned out, was the hero of the battle.

The fifteen sea devils had swarmed into the ravine, and instead of being trapped as they came under attack, simply started to climb. Where Krell would have had no chance at ascending, they simply dug their claws into fissures in the rock and hurled themselves up at tremendous speed.

Tristan had summoned webs to cover the top of the ravine, and the sticky mess stopped them in their tracks. Dahlia and Verbena took advantage of the easy targets and slew many before they broke free. Dahlia defended them with her blade until Dorn and Sheana charged in.

"Well done, Tristan," said Sheana. "Seems your power slew most of them here, today."

"Naturally," said Tristan.

ReckNor's grace had healed Krell's leg enough to walk, and he caught everyone's attention.

"I found something. You should all see this," he said.

The large sahuagin had worn a leather satchel, and while Krell waited for his leg to heal, he inspected it. He showed the others the papers he had found.

"Impossible," said Sheana, reading. "Nobody is suicidal enough to deal with sea devils!"

Krell tapped the paper. "It would seem you are wrong."

"And what, exactly, is the Betterment Society, and why are they working with the sea devils?" asked Tristan.

Krell shrugged. "Excellent question, to which I have no answer."

"What do they say?" asked Dorn, gesturing at Sheana.

"That in exchange for the supply of metal weapons and armor, the sea devils promise to destroy the towns and cities along the southern coast of Baltorc on the Harackeena Sea." Sheana shook her head. "It explicitly lists Heaford here. Heaford is a fortress. I've been there. It's impregnable."

"Gods be damned, good enough then," said Tristan. "We should get back to Watford and let everyone know."

"We can't," said Krell.

"Oh, and why is that? You're not the leader here, Krell, you don't get to tell us what to do!"

Krell shook his head. "You misunderstand. The five that ran have arrived back at the fortress. Almost immediately, a force of more than fifty, with five big ones that Fortis can see, left. It looks like they nearly emptied the place. They're coming this way. Fast." He looked around. "We have to move."

"This makes no sense," said Gerrard. "I mean, who deals with sea devils? They're insane! Stories say you have so much as a nosebleed and they'll try to eat you. How do you cope with that?" Gerrard shook his head. "It's insane, am I right?"

"Insane or not, we have to move," said Kraven.

They left the ravine and the trail. Dahlia took the lead, trying to find a way through the untracked forest so they could lose them. Krell looked at his wounds and at the smears of blood all over the ground as they left.

"They'll have no trouble tracking us — our path is pitifully easy to spot," said Krell. Kraven, standing next to him at the rear, grunted in assent. He looked up, his eyes unfocused for a moment. "They're moving faster than us, and not wounded. Pass word to Dahlia. We'll need a place to hold up and fight."

"Don't think we can hide?"

Krell shook his head. "They'll smell us, smell the blood."

Chapter Nineteen

Krell could hear the sahuagin approaching from behind.

They'd been moving as fast as they could, trying to escape, for the last two hours. The sahuagin were still in pursuit. Now they were close enough that Krell could hear them croaking and hissing at one another as they followed their tracks.

"They're coming, Kraven. We need to get ready to fight." Krell looked around. The terrain offered nothing promising for them to use, and the trees meant that they'd have little use of ranged attacks before the sahuagin were close enough to use their claws.

"Bad place for a fight," said Kraven. "They'll get around us easily."

"Yeah, but they're going to run us down and kill us one by one if we don't." Krell hurried forward, toward the others.

"They're coming and we're out of time. Find a place for us to stand and fight."

Dahlia nodded, then pointed off to the side. The hill they were on fell away to the rear, and the brush looked impassable to one side. She turned and headed in that direction.

They gathered up, and Kraven used his axe to fell a few small trees, clearing some space nearby. Krell, Sheana, and Dorn arranged themselves a little farther apart, leaving Tristan, Dahlia, and Verbena in a pocket behind them. Gerrard and Lily looked at each other, then melted into the treeline, vanishing from sight.

Then they waited.

They did not have to wait long.

Dahlia struck first, an arrow disappearing into the brush, eliciting a hissing shriek. More croaks and shrieks could be heard, an angry tone to their speech.

They came forward in an enraged wave.

Magical webs sprang up, catching a large group of them in the strands, but leaving a few for Dorn to deal with. Grudgingly, Krell conceded that Tristan had timed that perfectly. He spotted one of the larger ones hanging back as the smaller sahuagin rushed forward, snarling.

A blue streak of light shot from Verbena, missing. Tristan's bolt of fire caught one, blowing a hole straight through it. Then they were within reach, and he didn't have time to think anymore.

Krell marked the passage of time through the wounds he took, and how quickly they healed. The flood crashing against them seemed unending, and they were savage and fierce. There was no regard for their own safety. They threw themselves forward to attack with reckless abandon.

Kraven was ahead of Krell and his axe swung in large arcs around him, occasionally killing one of the beasts, but driving the rest back. They flowed around him to assault Krell and Sheana, who were standing back to back.

An arrow took one as it leapt toward Krell, and he batted the corpse aside with his shield. The ground was getting treacherous as the blood began turning it into a vile mud, slippery under his feet.

Sheana crashed into his back, and he turned, taking another wound. Three of the devils were clawing at her as she collapsed to the ground. Krell lashed out with his foot, kicking one in the head as his sword took another. He stood overtop of her, trying to avoid crushing her, but also striving to keep them back.

A blue ray struck the one attacking him, frost forming over its arm and torso. Krell took its head from its shoulders, but felt claws digging into his back. He spun, and a bolt of fire caught it, setting it alight. Krell cut it down and shoved, and it fell backward...

Into a group of seven more.

Dorn was there, and reached down to Sheana.

"ReckNor isn't done with you yet, lass, so get up and keep fighting!" Krell sensed more than saw the power flow from Dorn into her, and she gasped in a breath, then fumbled for her sword as she stood.

"Kraven needs help, Krell. We've got to shove forward!" said Dorn, pointing.

"Little busy, Dorn!" Krell's armor let out a metallic shriek as claws scored across it without penetrating.

"Stop whining and get moving!" Dorn cut at one clawing at his shield, then stepped forward, giving Sheana room to rise in relative safety. "If Kraven goes down, we've all had it!"

Krell nodded and threw away caution, charging forward into the group of them. He hoped the charge would catch them by surprise, but they were so maddened by the smell of blood that they largely ignored it. Instead of defending himself, Krell struck at one that was going to leap for Kraven, his slash carving a deep wound across its hunched back.

Then he was surrounded and had little time for thought. Someone shouted his name, but he took a wound on his head, and the blood was dripping into one of his eyes. Their breath smelled like rotten fish, and their bodies looked vaguely scaly.

Their eyes were wide with bloodlust.

Krell's vision was dimming, the grace of ReckNor beginning to run out. He focused, only seeing the attacks coming for him, losing sight of everything else.

With no warning, a towering sahuagin crashed into him, knocking Krell to the ground. It loomed over him and let out a croaking roar as its bone spear came hurtling down.

It shattered on his breastplate.

The sea devil pulled back the haft of the spear and stared at it. Krell did not hesitate, and shoved his sword upward, burying it almost to the hilt inside the beast. He let it go and rolled away, rising to his feet, and for the first time in minutes took stock of what was happening.

Sheana was down again, two sea devils raking at her armor with their claws as her arms tried to shelter her head from their blows. Gerrard was trapped, having climbed a tree, but with four of the sahuagin coming up after him. Lily was nowhere to be seen. Kraven and Dorn were still standing, and Krell could hear Dorn chanting words of power, pouring the strength of ReckNor into Kraven. He counted over thirty of the sea devils dead on the ground in front of him.

He turned and saw Dahlia fighting for her life. One of the large ones and several smaller ones had plowed through the underbrush and attacked her from behind. Verbena and Tristan were moving away, raining magic down on them.

Krell rushed toward Sheana, slamming one away with his shield and catching the other with his gauntleted fist. He looked down at Sheana, and she met his gaze. He nodded, then summoned his blade again. The two sahuagin recovered quickly, attacking.

"Get up! Dahlia and Verbena need you!" He killed one of the sahuagin and shoved the other back with his shield. Sheana stood, grasping her sword as she did so, unsteady on her feet. She stepped forward and took the one Krell knocked back across the chest. It fell, whimpering in pain, and Krell stabbed it in the eye.

"Almost there, Sheana, almost through," murmured Krell, grabbing her shoulder to steady her. The grace of ReckNor moved within him, almost spent, but closing some of Sheana's wounds. He met her gaze. "You're strong enough for this. Let's go save Dahlia."

She gave him a grim smile, and Krell turned and charged. Dahlia's leather armor provided scant protection from their claws, and Krell watched the larger one bite down hard on her shoulder. She screamed, which muffled the sound of Krell's approach, and he drove his newly conjured blade through the beast's torso.

The sahuagin let Dahlia drop and let out a choked croak, and as it fell, it yanked the blade from Krell's hand. Two were approaching Verbena and Tristan, and without thinking, Krell spoke words of power and gestured, a trident of magic coming into existence and slamming into the one nearest Verbena. She gestured, and daggers of magic energy struck the beast, cutting it to pieces that fell to the ground. She turned to aid Tristan.

Sheana had cut one of the small ones down, but was being overwhelmed. Krell called a blade and attacked, killing one from behind. He moved forward over the corpse and slashed the arm of one about to attack Sheana.

"Flee before ReckNor's power!" he shouted.

They hissed, eyes wide with madness, and came for him.

* * *

Krell and Sheana sat back to back. Fortis was curled up in his lap.

The sahuagin had stopped attacking, but Krell could hear them croaking in the distance, along with strange crunching noises. They had dragged off some of their dead. It sounded like they were eating.

Dorn was heavily wounded, his beard dripping blood as he walked over. Krell's face was a red mask. The wound on his brow had healed thanks to ReckNor's grace, but his face was still covered in his own blood.

The rest of him, too. He felt like he was dripping gore whenever he shifted, though most of it was disgusting green instead of red. The smell reminded Krell of a rotting carcass in a bog. He wondered how Fortis felt about the smell.

"Think they've got us?" Dorn asked, then groaned as he sat down next to Krell. He gave a smile and nodded to Sheana. She closed her eyes and leaned back, her helmet clanking against Krell's again.

"What worries me more is that they could've sent for more reinforcements. We slew, what, forty? Maybe more?" Krell shook his head. "We're nearly spent. Only got two of the big ones, so there's at least three still out there. If more show up, we're done for sure."

Kraven, lying on the muddy ground nearby, looked at Krell. "So, what do we do then?"

Krell shook his head. Lily was gone, and Krell feared the worst. Gerrard had broken his leg, though ReckNor's grace had partially healed it. Still, he could barely walk, let alone fight. Dahlia was injured, still bleeding from deep wounds to her stomach and shoulder. Tristan was hurt, savaged across his arms and legs. Verbena was hurt, her leg still oozing blood from a nasty bite wound.

Krell had done what he could. Nearly everyone's wounds had stopped bleeding. He was so tired, he just wanted to sleep. ReckNor's grace would not let him. It demanded action.

Tristan hobbled over. "We don't have a choice, you know that, right?" he asked.

Krell looked up at him. "What's your plan?"

"Attack," said Tristan.

Dorn snorted. "And how do you suppose we do that? By hopping forward and bleeding all over them? We've barely any strength left!"

Kraven rolled off his back, then stood up, hefting his axe. "Gods curse me for a fool, but Tristan's right," he said. "We wait here, and they'll come for us for sure, with numbers that will overwhelm us. We fight, and maybe we kill them and make our escape. Maybe we die taking a few of those big ones down with us." He shrugged, then glanced at Krell.

"Don't feel like you've done anything stupid yet. Thought you said paladins died stupidly. Do you think that means we're going to live?" He gave Krell a savage grin, then held out his hand. "If we're going to do it, better to go now, while they're eating, than to wait longer."

Fortis leapt clear as Krell grasped Kraven's arm and let himself be hauled to his feet. Sheana gave a sigh and rose, as did Dahlia. Krell had done what he could, but the grace of ReckNor only flowed so much.

He looked around. "Fine. Let's go kill them, then we can sleep." Kraven grinned, and Krell turned to Fortis. "My friend, if we fall, can you return to Watford? Olgar will understand what it means." Fortis nodded, then with a thrust of his wings, was into the branches and out of sight.

"If, you know, I can, I'll just lie here then, right?" said Gerrard.

Krell walked over. "I'd reach down to clasp your hand, my friend, but I'm afraid I'd fall on you. We'll be back in a bit." Krell's expression darkened. "Or we won't, and we'll meet again in ReckNor's halls!"

Kraven nudged Sheana. "See, that's the positive attitude that makes me like him so much!"

She giggled. The sound was so out of place that Krell turned to look at her. Her eyes were bright with laughter. He raised an eyebrow at her.

"What?" she said. "You *are* intense!"

Krell looked around at his companions. They were all watching him, laughter in their eyes.

"Come on, let's go kill them," he said. Sheana giggled again.

Everyone rose to their feet, nodded to Gerrard, and readied themselves. Krell reached out and touched Dahlia on her elbow. She flinched away from him, startled.

"One last effort. Let me try, before you bleed out," he said. She nodded, and Krell reached out, grabbing the tiny scraps of ReckNor's grace from deep within himself and forcing them through to heal Dahlia. He could feel the power scraping him raw.

YOU COULD TRY RUNNING.

Krell shook his head. The headache exploded in full force in his thoughts as ReckNor's voice crashed into him like a thunderstorm.

"Can't run. They're faster than us, and the wounds let them track us."

"True," said Kraven, "which is why we're going to attack."

YOU COULD TRY RUNNING, BUT WON'T.

"Something about running feels wrong to me."

Kraven gave him a weird look, then shrugged. He turned to Sheana. "I think he's not talking to us."

I HAD PLANS FOR YOU.

"Great," said Krell, "I look forward to learning all about them. But first, I've got some sea devils to kill."

"Yeah, definitely not talking to us," said Sheana.

THE ARROGANCE! IT IS ONE OF MANY REASONS I CHOSE YOU. DO YOUR BEST TO LIVE. I SHOULD BE DISPLEASED IF YOU DIE.

"If I die, it'll be on a pile of dead enemies, shouting your name," said Krell, conjuring a blade in his hand. The crunching noises were louder. "But for now, shut up. I've got work to do." The remaining traces of ReckNor's power shuddered in laughter, then focused on him. Krell could tell that ReckNor was watching.

Krell broke into a trot and entered a small clearing. The sahuagin all looked up as one, and let out a collective hiss of rage and hunger. They leapt from their grisly feast and surged forward.

Krell could feel a trickle of ReckNor's power within him, and he pulled on it, clutching for more. Something gave way, and a brief flow of power crashed into him, along with waves of agony. Krell promised himself he'd worry about that later, if he survived.

He felt the power within him twisting like a raging river. He needed an advantage in this fight.

THEN SHOW THEM THE TRUE COLOR OF MY DOMAIN.

The magic within him warped again, and he uttered some words of power. There was a vivid feeling of magic coming together and interlocking, only through the force of his will. As he concentrated on holding the magic together, an inky globe of darkness grew out of him, hiding everyone from sight. His companions stopped in alarm, but the globe moved with Krell as he continued his charge.

Krell could see through the darkness clearly. It was also obvious to him that the sahuagin could *not.*

"Praise ReckNor!" he shouted, as he darted among them, passing by the smaller ones who flailed wildly, and struck the head from the body of one of the larger ones. The blood stank of rot.

Three of the small ones had moved out of the darkness, and suddenly able to see, had turned to assault his companions. Their combined might easily overwhelmed them while the others flailed about in darkness, striving to find him and cut him down.

"Krell, what's happening?" shouted Kraven. He made no move to enter the darkness.

Within, the sahuagin were raising their snouts and sniffing, trying to find him in the darkness. As Krell moved, he slashed at them. The two large ones issued a series of hisses and croaks, and grasped one another's arm. Then they turned and fled.

Krell charged after them. "ReckNor is not done with you!" he shouted. As soon as he ran, the darkness moved away from the remaining ten sahuagin.

At the sound of his companions engaging the sahuagin behind him, Krell dropped his sword and lashed out with some of ReckNor's power. A trident made of magic leapt from his outstretched hand and caught one of the large ones in the leg. It hopped and croaked at the other, grabbing for support. The unhurt one shook off its hand and ran into the trees. Krell moved closer, and darkness fell over the wounded one. It turned and slashed its claws through the air, though Krell had not closed the distance yet.

He paused, then sent another magic trident crashing into it before darting to his left. It surged forward, claws slashing at the air where he'd been. Then it closed its eyes and breathed in deeply, turning to face him.

Krell conjured a blade in his hand and cut it across the sea devil's shoulder. It spun at once, claws and teeth coming for him, but the darkness shielded him as much as his armor and skill, and he escaped harm from the attack. The sahuagin hissed in rage and charged.

Krell's blade slid into its throat as it came toward him, even as he pivoted to the side. It fell, gurgling, at his feet, yanking his sword from his hand. Without pausing, Krell conjured a new weapon, a hammer, and slammed it down on the back of the sahuagin's skull, shattering it.

The sound of battle diminished behind him, and Krell spun in the direction the escaping one had taken. There was little chance he could catch it in the woods. He didn't know where it had run.

Thoughts from Fortis reached him. Krell had a feeling from him he could best describe as smug and self-satisfied, urging him onward. After a minute following the tracks of the sahuagin that escaped, he found it lying on the ground, unconscious but alive. Fortis perched on a tree branch nearby, looking majestic and regal.

"What happened?" he asked, quietly.

Fortis moved his tail around and held it up. The bulbous tail, with a protruding sharp spike on the end of it, was soaked in green blood. With a flick, Fortis let a drop of some fluid fall from the tip. He then began licking the blood from his tail, cleaning himself.

Krell shook his head in wonder as he walked over and killed the helpless sahuagin on the ground.

* * *

There was no sign of Lily, or anything that looked like halfling remains. After a brief search, they started walking.

The assault had worked, much to everyone's surprise. Now they took the opportunity to move away from the carnage and find a safe place to rest. It was five hours later. Everyone was exhausted, and the sun was getting closer to the western horizon.

Kraven carried Gerrard, who couldn't walk. Almost everyone had a limp in their stride, and people fell often as they navigated the forest floor.

Verbena collapsed.

Dahlia was at her side quickly. She was struggling to rise.

"Enough," said Krell. He staggered to a halt, leaning against a tree to keep from falling over. Kraven set Gerrard down, then slumped against a rock.

"We're stopping here. Fortis says they have not pursued us. Yet. We need to rest. At least an hour, maybe more." He shook his head. "I think we got all of them, and they don't know we've escaped."

Tristan sank to the ground, saying nothing. Krell knew that was a sign of just how exhausted they all were.

Kraven looked at him. "I'll take first watch. Sleep, Krell."

He wanted to argue with Kraven, but couldn't muster the ability to do so. The ground was coming closer as he slid down the tree. His last thought, before sleep took him, was one of warmth from Fortis.

Fortis would protect him.

* * *

Krell woke to the sound of angry voices.

He sat up, feeling less pain than he would have expected. It was deep in the night. Clouds had moved in while he slept, and he couldn't see any stars. Most of his companions were still asleep, but Dorn, Tristan and Kraven were awake.

Tristan and Kraven were arguing, their arms waving about even though their voices were low.

"We need to retreat, to get out of here!" hissed Tristan, emphasizing his points with hand gestures.

"I think we should charge in and attack. The small ones die pretty easy, and we've slain, what, six bigger ones? Over fifty smaller ones? How many more could there be? Krell said they emptied the place out. Best to root out the nest completely, instead of having to come back and start over."

"Are you stupid?" said Tristan. "We almost *died* back there. Lily may already be dead! We're all hurt — our magic, while replenished, is not up to the scope of this task. We need reinforcements!"

Krell reached out, gently touching Dahlia while she slept. He felt the grace of ReckNor moving, and her face relaxed as she slept, a visible cut on her cheek healing as Krell watched. He moved to Verbena next.

"Don't be such a coward, Tristan. We were hired to kill sea devils. Well, they're in that abandoned town just over there. Let's go kill them."

"Don't call me a coward!" said Tristan.

Krell watched the wound on Verbena's shoulder mend through the tears in her shirt. He turned and found Gerrard close by.

"I get it, Tristan," said Kraven in a low tone of voice. "You've got magic. Like all magicians, you think that makes you special. Well, one day it might, but you'll die pretty quick with my axe in your ribs, so shut up. *Shut. Up.* We're going back."

"You don't get to threaten me, Kraven."

Gerrard met Krell's eyes as he kneeled beside him, then gestured at the argument. Krell nodded, placing a hand on Gerrard's shoulder. It vaguely nauseated Krell to see the leg bone, still only partially mended and somewhat crooked, straighten. Gerrard sucked in a pained breath that came out as a relieved sigh.

"Oh, wow, thanks, Krell. That's much better. Know what I mean?"

Krell smiled at him. "Don't thank me, Gerrard, thank ReckNor. It's his power. I'm just his minion here." Krell lifted his head, spotting the shock of red hair that marked Sheana, and walked over, padding quietly.

Kraven and Tristan both had valid points. Certainly, the sea devils were dangerous, and in greater numbers than they had realized. If this was a major incursion, then the importance of getting word out was vital. Yet, if it was merely a foothold, there was a chance to cast them back into the sea.

Krell sat near Sheana and placed his hand on her boot. The grace of ReckNor flowed into her, healing her wounds.

"Fine! Be like that! Dorn, what do you think?" snarled Kraven.

"I think we should ask Krell. Krell, what do you think?"

Krell grinned at them in the darkness. "I think we should ask Verbena, since she's smarter than the rest of us put together."

"So what, we're letting your nobody hirelings decide our fate now?" Tristan looked like he was going to pull his hair out or cry.

Krell shook his head. "You're an ass when you're like this, Tristan. No, I want to know her thoughts because she thinks both faster and deeper than any of the rest of us. I want to know what she thinks because it'll probably be the most logical thing to do. And besides, she might agree with you, so what's your problem?"

"Just remember, Krell, they don't get a share of the reward. You pay them out of yours!"

Krell looked at Tristan, expressionless.

"You can stare at me with those black eyes all you want, Krell. Makes no difference. Captain Gijwolf will back me on this!"

"I… you know what? It isn't worth it." Krell turned to Kraven. "Have you slept?"

He nodded. "A little."

Krell reached forward and forced the power of ReckNor through himself and into Kraven. He grunted.

Krell pointed at the ground. "Sleep now, I'll watch." He turned to Dorn and reached out. ReckNor's grace flowed smoothly and easily, even when he tried to force it. Dorn smiled, then walked a few paces to his bedroll and lay down. Almost at once, he began a gentle snore.

Krell turned to Tristan, who held out his hand. Krell sighed and reached out, trying to force ReckNor's power to move again. It had replenished itself while he slept, but he was in danger of completely depleting it again.

ReckNor's grace flowed from him into Tristan smoothly and easily.

"Huh," said Krell.

Tristan raised an eyebrow.

"It's just… the power hurts to use sometimes, and I can't figure out why."

"Want me to look?"

Krell shrugged. "Do you know how to look at something like that?"

Tristan grinned and reached forward, putting his hands on Krell's temples. His fingers pushed unpleasantly on Krell's head, and he felt a spear of Tristan's power trying to push into his mind. It deflected off of ReckNor's grace and fell apart.

"Huh," said Tristan.

Krell smiled slightly and raised an eyebrow.

Tristan gave him a small smile. "Normally, my magic doesn't fail like that."

"I think it was ReckNor's doing."

Tristan drew his hands back and sat against a tree. Krell thought he had fallen asleep. Krell walked around the camp, listening for any noises that did not belong.

"You're going to want to attack, aren't you?" Tristan asked quietly.

Krell turned to him. He was still sitting with his eyes closed. He looked like he was asleep.

"I think it's the best way forward. At best, we cast them into the sea. If there are too many, we have a good sense of their numbers, and we retreat. Worst case, well, it isn't likely you're going to ReckNor's halls, so if we die you'll never have to bother with me again."

"Stop, Krell. I'm not joking."

Krell walked over and squatted in front of Tristan. "Neither am I. We're all mortal. If I die fighting sea devils, well, I can think of worse ways to go. If you want, though, you and any others who will go can set off to Watford. Kraven and I will go and poke the nest, to see what can be learned."

Krell stood and stepped back. "Either we push them back now, or we come back with more people and push them back later. No matter what, we have to push them back. If we do it now, a lot fewer people are going to die."

"Gods, you're arrogant," muttered Tristan.

Krell surveyed the camp. His eyes fell on Verbena, and his eyes met her cool and appraising gaze.

He walked toward her and kneeled while she sat up.

"Hmm, that did not hurt nearly as much as it should have," she said, rolling her shoulder. "Your doing?"

Krell nodded.

"I thought as much. I overheard. Your plan is to attack?"

"Yes. We've killed at least two full patrols. It's a good opportunity. Unless, of course, I'm totally wrong and we're walking into a nest of two hundred or more."

"That makes sense. You said your magic hurt to use. I've never heard of anything like that before." She bit her lower lip absently, her eyes unfocused in thought. "Can I try to look?"

Krell shrugged and shuffled closer. She moved to her knees and placed her fingertips gently on Krell's temples. Krell stared at her eyes. They were green, but had streaks of gold and brown in them.

"That's really creepy, you know that, right?" she said.

"Huh?"

"Your eyes. It's unnerving if you're not ready for it. It isn't that they're black, it's that they're absent, like a void of darkness that light cannot penetrate."

Krell felt Verbena's power. It was much more precise than Tristan's, but also much less powerful. Krell wondered if this was what ReckNor was talking about when he told him to keep Tristan around. Certainly, her power was moving much more slowly. Less a crashing wave, more like a gentle current.

The tendril of magic moved forward and brushed the edge of ReckNor's grace. Krell felt it harden, and with an effort of will, gradually he softened it. It was strange how her left eye had more gold streaks than her right. Her power flowed deeper into him.

Suddenly, she gasped and fell backward. Krell caught her wrist, keeping her from toppling over.

"What did you do? You… I don't even know how to describe it. You *shattered* your power! It's leaking all over the place within you! It was agonizing to brush against it, like shards of glass being dragged across my hands. How do you bear it?"

"I suppose you get used to it, and it doesn't hurt all the time," Krell said. He released her arm.

A long moment passed.

"I think, if we live through the attack, I should look again. Now that I know what to expect, I can be ready for the pain."

Krell nodded, then realized she couldn't see him clearly in the darkness.

"That would be fine. I'd like to know what happened as well, if possible."

"This isn't something ReckNor did?" She looked startled.

"No, this was my doing. I sort of grabbed it and pulled, and it shattered. But then I could do different things with it." Krell stood. "I'm supposed to be watching. See if you can get more sleep."

She nodded and lay down, turning away from him at once.

Only an hour later did Krell realize she agreed with him and Kraven.

They would attack.

* * *

"This is a stupid plan," said Tristan, for the seventh time.

Dorn smacked his fist into his palm. "If you have a better plan that doesn't involve running away like a coward, by all means share it with us!"

"It's not cowardice, it's prudence, Dorn!" Tristan was agitated. "You're talking about charging into an unknown number of them with nothing more than a cut-them-to-pieces plan in place!"

Krell grinned. "Nonsense! The distraction should lead a bunch away, so we can fight only some of them, not all of them."

Tristan put his hand on his face as he looked down and sighed.

Kraven clapped him on the back, startling him. "Relax, Tristan! It'll be fine! If anything, the diversion group is the one in real danger!"

"You mean the group that's going to shoot some arrows until they come out and start chasing them, then run away and lose them in the forest, and *not* the one that's going to assault them directly?"

"That's the one!" Kraven grinned at him, then turned to Dahlia. "Since they're faster runners, they're probably going to catch you and eat you. You know that, right?"

"Why do you think I don't want anyone else in the diversion group?" she said. "You're all competent enough, I guess, but I'm faster in the woods alone, and my tracks will be harder to spot than the forest-crushing path you'd leave behind, Kraven."

"Ha! I like this one!" She stepped back as he raised his arm to clap her on the shoulder. Kraven frowned.

"No offense, Kraven, but I need my shoulder to work to shoot arrows." Dahlia smiled at him while hunching down a little.

He shrugged and turned to Krell. "When do we go?"

"Dawn. One more day of rest for us. I think these things see in the dark just fine, so let's have some daylight to eliminate that advantage. We approach from the east, so the sun will be behind us. Dahlia attacks at range, to draw them northwest. We begin when she starts running. Fortis will stay with her and let me know. Then we run in, and if it's a sea devil, we kill it."

Tristan shook his head. "Like I said, this is a stupid plan."

"Like I said, Tristan, if you have a better one, speak up now!" yelled Dorn.

"Quietly, Dorn, quietly," said Krell, touching his shoulder. He looked at Tristan. "I know you don't like it, but it's the best plan we have. We'll all be, by ReckNor's grace and power, fully healed by the time we go. One more day should see their worry over the lost patrol either grow worse or subside. If they come out searching for it, we jump the patrol as we did before."

"Oh, yeah, that was a good idea," said Tristan. "Let's ask Lily how well that went, shall we?" He looked around theatrically. "Oh, wait, we can't, because she's dead!"

Krell put out a hand, grabbing Kraven's arm as he moved forward, growling. He stopped at Krell's touch and glared at him.

"We're swimming in circles here, Tristan. Come with us to fight, go with Dahlia to distract, or walk back to Watford. I'm through worrying about how happy you are." Krell turned away, catching Kraven's eyes as he did so. "The sea devils are enough. No fighting with Tristan."

Kraven turned and met Sheana's eyes. They both laughed.

Chapter Twenty

Krell crouched in a ditch.

The sun was rising behind him, and there was a scant hundred yards of open ground between him and a rough wood-and-stone barricade. Three small sahuagin hunched down behind it, trying to avoid the sun. Beyond, he could see dozens of them running about in town.

The remains of the town were as Captain Gijwolf described. The burned stone foundations of Swamp Hold were visible as outlines of where buildings used to stand, with the occasional tumbled remains of a stone chimney. A large stone tower sat in the center, the former guard house.

Strange pits filled with water had been dug all around the former village, and makeshift structures that resembled tents made of seaweed were chaotically distributed among them. Dozens of sahuagin could be seen beyond, moving about quickly.

While Krell watched with his own eyes, he was also concentrating on Fortis. Impressions and vivid images came from him sporadically as Dahlia took careful aim and loosed, the arrow striking at extreme range. Occasionally Fortis could see a sahuagin drop; sometimes Krell could directly. Unless the sahuagin were being managed by one of the larger, more intelligent ones, they quickly swarmed the victim, savaging them. This made them easy targets for Dahlia.

It was disorienting having two different perspectives, but Krell persisted.

She had over forty arrows remaining and planned to use all of them. Larger sahuagin were visible now, ordering the smaller ones around, getting them behind cover, and forming a large group of over forty led by six bigger ones.

At a brisk trot, they departed, immediately angling across the swampy ground toward Dahlia. She shifted fire to that group at once, wounding two of the big ones, before shifting back to the settlement. Fortis kept his attention on the approaching group. When they were halfway across the swampy ground, she turned and ran into the woods. Fortis followed.

"She's running. We'll go in one minute," said Krell quietly. Fortis kept sending images of Dahlia. Krell shook his head. She was substantially faster than the rest of them as she ran through the woods. He hoped she'd be able to outrun the sahuagin.

Krell brought his focus back to the ground in front of him. Several groups of sahuagin inside were almost rampaging around, either wounded or assaulting the wounded, while three larger ones were trying to gain control, often through force.

Krell counted forty, mostly smaller ones. He looked at Kraven and Sheana, who nodded back at him.

Krell stood and began a fast trot toward the barricade.

* * *

Moving as quietly as he could, Krell killed a sahuagin.

The three huddling behind the stone barricade were inattentive, focused more on the interior of their encampment than they were on watching the approach. That changed the moment the scent of blood and the gurgling cry of the one Krell killed reached the other two, and they let out hisses of rage, flying forward to attack.

Kraven and Sheana each took one, making quick work of them, but the advantage of surprise was gone. Nearly sixty sahuagin turned to look at them. With a chorus of croaks, they rushed toward them, threading between tents and the stone chimneys. Krell dropped his blade, and with a word of power, flung a trident made of magic at one of the sahuagin, killing it.

"Come, enemies of ReckNor, and die!" he shouted.

The larger ones croaked in rage, and the sahuagin came forward in a wave.

"Gods damn you, Krell! Stop provoking them!" shouted Tristan. He muttered some words of power, and strands of magical webs appeared, falling atop a group of nearly ten of the sahuagin. Their charge faltered as Krell, Sheana, Kraven and Dorn stood in a loose line and cut them down as fast as they arrived.

The larger sahuagin had stayed back, and the charge ended as they forced the smaller ones away from the scent of blood, retreating toward the stone tower. Krell cut the last one near him down and watched as Tristan and Verbena finished killing the ones stuck in the webs. One broke free and charged, but Kraven and Dorn killed it.

That the sahuagin would fall back was not something Krell was prepared for.

"If they're falling back to protect the tower, let's go get it!" he shouted.

Kraven let out a yell, and without waiting, charged forward. Krell grinned at Sheana and charged after him, avoiding a pool and letting his sword fall away. He flung a trident of magic toward any sahuagin that he could see, missing as often as he connected, now that they were running around to the other side of the tower.

Kraven ran forward around the tower, yelling incoherently as he pursued them.

As Krell rounded the tower, he heard a shout behind him. The scene in front of him, though, took his full attention.

Kraven was engaged with six smaller sahuagin. Beyond were at least ten large ones, hefting metal spears in their hands as they approached in a tight group. Dozens and dozens of smaller sahuagin were squatting behind them, not moving, but staring intently in their direction.

There was a huge one standing among them.

It towered over the others, nearly twelve feet tall. It had four arms and held two massive spears. It wore metal plate armor, a sight Krell had never seen before. It let out a croaking laugh that echoed across the remains of Swamp Hold, then slammed the butt end of a spear into the ground. A pulse of power flowed out from him.

The sahuagin surrounding him stood in unison and began charging forward. Krell heard a strange noise to his right. The nearby pond was thrashing, and a sahuagin crawled from it, followed by another. Then three more. The water roiled with activity as another came out.

All of the ponds — dozens of them — were disgorging sahuagin the same way.

"Shit," said Krell.

* * *

Krell struggled to defend the doorway.

Even Kraven had retreated into the stone tower. There had been ten small sahuagin within, but Gerrard, Sheana, and Krell made quick work of them, while everyone else ran inside.

Three of them were clawing at Krell, slamming attacks into his shield. He was concentrating on defense, blocking the only entrance. His sword deflected claws, or made jaws recoil to avoid harm. Countless claws raking at his shield and armor left them both dented and battered.

The group of ten large spear-wielding sahuagin stood arrayed behind the ever replenishing rank of small ones. As Verbena, Dorn and Tristan struck with magic, slaying the ones assaulting Krell, they used their spears to skewer any sea devils that fell, and hurled them clear of the doorway.

The enormous sahuagin stepped into Krell's field of view.

"So, little land-things, you seek to resist the red tide?" Its voice was raspy, guttural, and low-pitched.

Krell nearly took a cut across his face, he was so surprised that it spoke to him. Verbena shot one of those blue rays over his shoulder, hitting one of the larger spear wielders. It hissed in pain as frost formed on its chest and shoulder.

"If your red tide means you coming up onto the land to kill us all, then yes!" shouted Dorn, who promptly cast another spell. A pillar of white fire flashed for a moment, burning the same spear wielder. It retreated from view.

Krell was breathing heavily. His will was strong, and he'd had lots of practice over the last few weeks with his sword and shield. Yet there were so many. It was only a matter of time before he began to slow.

"Why fight the inevitable? My god devours all and will consume your gods in the end! Surrender to his jaws, find peace in death, and become part of him when he consumes you!" The giant sahuagin let out a croaking laugh, which was picked up by many of the sea devils surrounding him.

A bolt of fire from Tristan shot toward him. He moved one of his massive spears with fluid grace, intercepting the bolt of fire and deflecting it away.

Claws scored along Krell's helmet, and he almost took a step backward. He stood firm, taking a minor wound. His shield caught one in the face, knocking it prone. Leaving the doorway would be certain death for everyone.

"You are skilled, but surrounded. Does your weak and puny god command you to eat, as mine does? Perhaps you should convert before the end. All things eat. This is the way of things. Eat and grow, or be eaten and die. My god is pure, simple and powerful! Surrender and become part of him!"

The sahuagin leader turned, his spear lashing out and spitting a small one in a single blow. He held it up before his face, the sahuagin on the spear hissing in panic and rage.

Then he bit its head off. Green blood spurted from the wound, covering his face. His expression was impossible to understand. The crunching noises as his jaw shattered the skull echoed across the area, heard clearly over the sound of the hissing rage and slashing claws of the sahuagin battering at Krell.

"He's using magic to make the noise carry! Ignore it!" shouted Verbena, who promptly shot a blue ray at one fighting Krell. Frost covered its head and torso. Krell risked a strike, cutting the head from its shoulders. It was replaced almost at once.

The plate-clad sahuagin leader brandished the spear with the body impaled on it. "This is the way of life. This weak one exists as part of me now. All life eats." He moved the spear, and his massive jaws opened and bit off a dangling arm. The sound of shattering bone again echoed within the base of the tower.

Krell could feel himself slowing slightly. The shield was getting heavier.

"There is no escape. You have trapped yourself in our larder. Still, you are skilled. I will offer you the chance to bow in worship to BranLagNos and honor you by devouring you myself. This generous offer will not be repeated!"

Krell shook his head. "BranLagNos? The mad god of devouring? His followers are cannibals and worse. They are put to death on sight by anyone with any sense." He ducked his head to avoid slashing claws while his blade threatened another, forcing it to pull its face back as it attempted to bite.

"BranLagNos consumes all!"

Krell laughed. "It makes perfect sense to me that you'd worship a lunatic! ReckNor laughs at your puny god of eating!" His sword slashed a bloody wound on the chest of the one in front of him.

Tristan blasted one of the spear wielders with a bolt of flame. Verbena gestured and magical darts of force flung from her hand.

They changed direction as they flew, avoiding the smaller ones and striking the one clad in plate. It let out a hiss of rage.

"Then you will be devoured by lessors! Lessors who will end without being eaten in turn! I will see those that devour you are burned in sacrifice, to end you forever!"

Krell laughed again. "ReckNor laughs at your feeble threats!"

There was a series of croaks and hisses, and the remaining nine spear-carrying sahuagin strode forward.

"Gods damn you, Krell! Can you *please* stop making things worse?" shouted Tristan.

The spear points flashed at Krell.

* * *

"Done!" said Gerrard.

Krell was concentrating hard on defense. Only three of them could stab at him with their spears through the doorway, but it was taking everything he had to fend them off. Their strikes were precise and fast, and his armor saved him more than once. It was dented and scored, and he was taking wounds, mostly to his arms and legs.

He sensed Dorn behind him, muttering a prayer to ReckNor, then felt him reach out and touch him. Soothing power flowed into him, and his wounds began to close up.

"Be ready, they're almost up," he said.

Krell nodded, his sword moving as fast as he could, his shield angling to deflect the spears harmlessly away. Another cut to his arm. A point grazed his leg. A blow punched him in the chest, denting his armor.

"When I slap you, jump backward at once," said Dorn, loudly enough for Krell to hear. He began muttering words of power. A blast of flame shot past Krell, hitting one of the large sahuagin in front of him.

Dorn's voice rose in a crescendo, and he slapped Krell on the back. Krell flung himself backward, taking two cuts from spears as his defense collapsed. Dorn's spell finished, and a thunderous booming crash knocked the three sea devils away, causing them a moment of hesitation.

That moment killed them, because they were not the target of Dorn's spell.

The wall of the keep collapsed, rocks crashing down. It caught the three larger sahuagin in the collapse, green blood spurting out from under the stones as they crashed down. The whole side of the tower then broke free as Dorn and Krell retreated away, both holding their shields up and feeling rocky debris slam into them. Krell looked up, seeing cracks form in the ceiling above him.

"I told you, relax. I know stone!" said Dorn. "It'll only fall on the one side!"

They both hurried to the opposite wall, where Gerrard had been stringing a knotted rope for them to climb. Kraven had been smashing a section of the ceiling out while Krell held the doorway, and everyone had ascended to the next level. Dorn looked up and glowered at the rope.

"I hate climbing."

Krell doffed his shield and grabbed the rope. He immediately began climbing. "Tie yourself up with it, then Kraven will haul you up when I get up there!" As soon as Krell was high enough, Kraven reached down and grasped his arm, nearly wrenching it from his shoulder as he pulled. Krell collapsed onto the floor, gasping for air.

He lay there for a moment, listening as Dorn was hauled up, cursing in Dwarvish the entire time. His thoughts wandered as he simply concentrated on breathing, feeling ReckNor's grace struggling to close his wounds. Maybe he would learn Dwarvish, to learn how to curse like that. It sounded impressive to Krell.

"Get up, Krell. We aren't done yet," said Verbena.

Krell sighed and rose slowly to his feet as Dorn ascended. Kraven shoved him aside, then began pushing a large wooden cabinet, causing the rotten wood to fall across the hole, blocking it off.

"That won't stop them if they try to climb up," he said. "The wood is soft with rot."

"Only a handful are smart," said Verbena. "We kill them and the rest might kill one another if we give them wounds here and there."

The room they were in was an office of some sort. Arrow slits in the walls were closed off with vegetation, though some small amount of light filtered through. The remains of a wooden desk and a now toppled-over cabinet of some sort were the only objects in the room, though the floor was covered with a thin layer of grime and animal droppings. A ruined door was hanging lopsided from its one remaining hinge.

Krell stepped into the next room. Gerrard was carefully climbing the wall next to what looked like the remains of a rotted wooden ladder. There was a hole in the ceiling, leading to the floor above, and beyond that, a patch of clear sky.

"I'll get this secured up here," said Gerrard, "then maybe Dorn drops this whole level down onto the ones below us, right?"

Tristan came into the next room. "And how will we get down?"

Gerrard gestured to the rope he was carrying. "Climbing rope is good for you, Tristan!" he said happily.

Tristan turned to face Krell. "So, we're trapped inside a stone building with no way out. Our plan is what exactly? Because the part of the plan where we realized there were too many and we run away has not worked out very well."

Krell had to agree with that. He shrugged. "I don't know, really. Focused on keeping us alive for the next few minutes, then we'll see if we can come up with something better."

Sheana and Verbena came into the room, with Dorn and Kraven right behind. Gerrard vanished through the hole at the top of the ladder, then a rope snaked down.

"Looks okay up here, and there's more light," he said. Sheana took the rope and climbed. When she reached the top, she rolled out of sight, and Tristan began to climb.

Dorn examined the stone farther in. "I figure this is the center of the tower. I wouldn't move much past this point." He gestured at a doorway on the far side of the room, the door swollen shut in its frame. "I wouldn't be surprised if that opens to the sky now. Probably lots of sea devils out there."

Kraven looked at Krell, meeting his eyes. "This might be that stupid and arrogant part you were talking about."

Krell grinned. "What, charging a fortress full of our enemies?"

Kraven gave a sharp laugh. "Yeah, that part. Think they've got us?"

Krell's grin faded, and he looked at his companions. Verbena and Dorn were watching him. "I'm not sure. ReckNor won't say, but then, it was our choice, and he's big on consequences of your choices. I do know this. I'm not dead yet, and I'm certainly not going to just let some stupid servant of a god of eating kill me without a fight!"

"Devouring," said Verbena.

"What?"

"BranLagNos is the god of devouring, not the god of eating," she said.

"Are you serious?" said Tristan from above. "We're arguing about which god is what right now?"

Krell's grin returned. "Doesn't mean she's wrong!" He gestured at the rope. "After you!"

Kraven laughed. "I like that one, Krell."

Krell nodded, then cocked his head sideways.

"Why aren't they attacking?" he asked.

Dorn went back into the office, walking to the exterior wall. He removed his helmet and put his ear against it. Seconds passed.

"I don't hear or feel them on the stone outside," he said.

Krell looked at the swollen door in the frame and hurled a magical trident at it. It ruptured and collapsed into shards of wood, and sunlight flooded the room.

Beyond, it looked like another office of some sort, but only half the floor was visible. The rest was gone, sheared off as the outer wall fell. The sahuagin camp was clearer from above, with dozens of sahuagin visible to him outside. They were squatting, watching the tower. Several of them croaked and hissed when they saw him.

Kraven glanced at Krell, then looked out at them. "What are they doing?"

Looking down from the hole above, Verbena said, "What do you see?"

"They're just sitting there, doing nothing," said Krell.

"Maybe they're giving up?" said Tristan.

Verbena shook her head, her blond braid falling over her shoulder. "No, otherwise they'd have left. I bet they're waiting for night." She disappeared back into the level above.

Kraven and Krell looked at one another. "ReckNor's balls, she's right," said Krell.

Kraven nodded. "They either know some of us can't see in the dark, or they fight better in the dark, or both." He looked around at the tower. "I bet if Gerrard can climb the walls in here, they can climb the outside walls."

Krell nodded. "Or they'll just hammer at the tower and make it collapse. Kill us that way."

"Stop trying to cheer me up!" said Dorn, as he grabbed the rope, closed his eyes, and began to haul himself upward.

"Works better, Dorn, if you keep your eyes open," said Krell.

"Shut it, paladin!"

Krell chuckled and looked up as Sheana peered down at Dorn. She smiled, then grabbed the rope and began hauling it up. Dorn ascended slowly, then rolled out of sight above them. The rope snaked back down.

Krell climbed up next and took Sheana's outstretched arm when he was close. When he stood, he saw what looked like the remains of weapon racks on the walls and rotted beds scattered throughout the floor. The wall on one side was cracked and broken, the bottom parts fallen away. Sunlight flooded in through the hole.

Dorn pointed at it. "Everyone stay away from that," he said.

Kraven climbed up without apparent effort. He pulled the rope up behind him, coiling it.

Krell looked around, then up as a shadow darkened the room slightly. Gerrard poked his head over the remains of the trap door. "Battlements up here, and the floor looks solid. Don't want to test it without Dorn's say so, though, know what I mean?" He tossed a rope downward.

Krell grabbed it and climbed. He reached the top and rolled out of the gap, crouching and walking to the side of the tower that should be secure. He peered between the merlons on the battlement.

Nearly three hundred sahuagin were arrayed forty feet below him. As he watched, listening to the others climb up, he saw them moving methodically. They were each taking a turn to vanish into one of the water pits. From above he couldn't see below the surface as they roiled in constant agitation.

Kraven crouched down beside him, peering out. "Well, there's certainly enough of them! No need to share, huh?" He flashed Krell a savage grin.

"What I find interesting is that they know there are spellcasters among us up here, yet they're sitting there in range of our magic," said Krell. "It's like they want a bunch of them to die, for some reason. Makes no sense to me."

Tristan approached, crouched down as well. “Well, if we focus, we can kill them one at a time, then, right?”

Krell shook his head. “There are too many, and they’ll just fall back. I think Verbena is right — we need to kill the smart ones. Notice how they’re all well back. Think you can hit them from here?”

Tristan shrugged. “Only one way to find out, I suppose. Can you?”

Krell grinned at him. “Only one way to find out! Closest one on three?” Tristan nodded.

“One, two, three!” Krell raised up slightly, and uttered some words of power at the same time as Tristan. A trident made of magic and a bolt of fire shot forward, striking one of the larger ones toward the rear. It let out a hissing shriek.

Krell didn’t wait, and summoned another trident. It struck the same sahuagin as it attempted to retreat, slamming it to the ground as Tristan’s bolt of fire blew a hole in its chest.

The other larger ones fell farther back.

“Look!” said Verbena, gesturing down. Krell looked, but didn’t see anything other than swarms of smaller sahuagin.

“What am I supposed to be seeing here?” he asked.

“When they moved back, the ones closer in became more agitated. Less controlled. Shoot one of them below us, closest to the tower,” she said, absently chewing her bottom lip.

Tristan shrugged and shot a bolt of fire nearly straight down. He caught one of them, and it croaked in fury as it caught fire. As it leapt to its feet, the ones surrounding it did the same. They fell at once onto their wounded companion, tearing it to pieces.

Then they began eating, even as the next ring of surrounding sahuagin began edging closer, trying to get some of the kill. A fight broke out, both combatants wounding one another. They were promptly attacked by those surrounding them.

Verbena grinned delightedly and shot a blue ray at a different nearby group.

A silver spear slammed into her shoulder, hurling her backward. The plate-armored sahuagin strode forward, establishing order while watching above, his other spear clutched in one of his hands, ready to be thrown.

Krell jerked the weapon out of Verbena's shoulder and put his hand on the wound. Blood coated his gauntlets, pumping rhythmically. She was looking at him in panic, but the grace of ReckNor began to flow into her, and the wound ceased bleeding at once. He held the pressure there until the wound was closed.

"Well, at least we got one of his spears!" she said in a weak voice. With a gesture, she used magic to clean the blood from her shirt and knit the torn garment back together. She rolled into a crouch, rotating her arm, then looked Krell in the eye.

"Thank you," she said. Her expression was flat and blank.

Krell nodded and watched as she used magic to get errant strands of her hair back into her braid. She then absently brushed the dirt, mud, and bloodstains from her clothing, leaving herself perfectly clean. She went forward toward the battlement again.

Krell whistled softly, and she turned, looking at him.

"That is really useful," he said. "Can you *please* teach me how to do that?"

She gave him a small smile that did not touch her eyes. "Perhaps, if you're smart enough to learn it." Her smile vanished. "And if we live through this idiocy. Otherwise, no." She crept over to the battlement, peering cautiously over the edge.

Kraven hefted the spear with two hands and grunted. "This thing is solid metal, Dorn."

Dorn nodded, then ran his hand along the haft. "Yup, though it isn't steel. I wonder what it's made of? It's a magnificent weapon, though it's more of a pike than a spear for us."

Krell and Tristan crouched at the edge of the battlement. The plate-clad sahuagin was looking up, and moving in a circle toward Krell. His eyes were fastened on him as he moved, and he errantly stepped on or kicked aside the smaller sahuagin who did not get out of his way fast enough.

His other spear was poised to throw the entire time he was moving.

He reached a point directly in front of where Krell and Tristan were perched, and held out his hand. Krell's eyes widened.

Dorn grunted in surprise, and Kraven shouted. Krell shoved Tristan hard, knocking him sideways, as the spear wrenched itself from Kraven's grasp, cartwheeled across the stones as if trying to descend, and narrowly avoided Krell as it shot past him. It flew through the air and returned to the hand of the sahuagin below.

Krell looked at Tristan, who was staring back at him with equally wide eyes.

"Okay, that was a good trick. Do you know how to do that?" he asked.

Chapter Twenty-one

The sun was setting, and the sahuagin were growing agitated.

The patrol that went out to capture Dahlia had returned, further bolstering the numbers surrounding them. Krell reached out to Fortis to learn whether Dahlia had escaped or not, but received nothing in return. Verbena and Sheana were worried.

Krell and Tristan had moved from one side of the tower to the other, striking at sea devils until the large plate-armored leader could make his way around. They had easily slain over fifty by doing this, yet the numbers before them only seemed to grow every time they looked.

Kraven nodded toward the sunset. "At least it's a pretty one."

Krell nodded. They were in for a terrible night. Verbena had talked about lighting up the walls, but she couldn't do it everywhere at once.

"Think they'll come up the walls, or up from inside?"

Krell looked at Kraven. "Both. They've the numbers for it, so why bother choosing?"

Kraven let out a growl. "What's the plan then?"

Verbena looked over. "Kraven, Krell, and Dorn fight to keep them from coming over the walls. That won't be possible, but it will buy time and kill several of them as they climb. You can all see in the dark, so that shouldn't pose a vision problem. Sheana, Gerrard, and I are one level down, defending the hole in the floor. I can light up the lower level so we can see them as they approach.

Tristan stays up here, next to the hole in the roof, and blasts the ones that get past you until you can't hold them anymore. Then you come down."

Everyone turned to look at her.

"It's the best way to last the longest," she said.

Kraven turned to Krell. "I like her! Pity we're all going to die here," he said.

Krell slapped Kraven on the shoulder. "I'll die when ReckNor tells me it's my time, and not before. In the meantime, BranLagNos is going to lose a lot of followers!" He turned back to watch the sun continue to set.

"Okay!" said Gerrard.

Krell stood at once, summoned a magical trident, and hurled it at the largest sahuagin he could see. It caught it in the shoulder and vanished, leaving a bloody wound behind. Two smaller ones made as if to leap at it, but it croaked and hissed, and they settled back down. Krell ducked down as the plate-armored one walked quickly to the same side of the tower, spear still held at the ready.

It croaked a laugh that was picked up by many of the other sahuagin below.

"You kill, but do not eat! You deny the wisdom of BranLagNos! For this, you end in fire!" He turned to face the horde of sahuagin, croaking and hissing at them. As one, they rose to their feet.

Krell turned to the others. "Here they come." Sheana nodded and dropped down the rope into the darkness. Verbena and Gerrard followed, while Tristan stood near the hole. Krell, Kraven, and Dorn spread out.

"Remember, don't get too close to the edge, or you'll get that spear. Kill them fast," said Kraven.

"If you start to get overwhelmed, shout. I've got some of ReckNor's power I can spend to help," said Dorn, rolling his shoulders. He drew his rapier and nodded to them. "If ReckNor has decided we're to die, let's die bravely, so he'll be happy with our choices!"

Krell nodded and turned to the battlement. The hissing and croaking of the sahuagin language was rising in volume. The last rays of the sun disappeared behind the horizon.

The sound of them climbing signaled the beginning of a long night.

* * *

The first one that reached the top near Krell was enormous.

Its clawed hands grasped the battlement to haul itself up and over. Krell didn't hesitate, and his shield crashed into it as it tried to do so, his sword cutting at the hand. It fell into the darkness beyond the wall with a hiss of rage.

A small one started to pull itself up and Krell struck it in the neck. It gurgled and fell from sight. Three more crested the wall nearby, including a larger one.

Krell charged, leading with his shield, and crashed into the bigger one while it was still climbing up. It croaked in anger, its teeth catching the edge of his shield even as it released the wall to slash at him. The sudden weight as it fell nearly dragged Krell over the edge.

Krell saw a flash of silver as his shield came free and the sahuagin fell out of sight. He threw himself backward in a panicked roll, bringing his shield up as he did. A silver spear crashed against his armor, deflected upward. Krell watched as it arced up into the air, then abruptly reversed direction and flew back down.

"I like that trick," he muttered, as he rose to his feet. The other two had clambered over the walls, one coming for him, the other heading for Kraven. Krell darted forward, caught its slashing claws on his shield, and gave it a wound with his blade. As he watched, four more reached the top and started over the edge.

Tristan was suddenly next to him as he fanned his hands out, thumbs touching, while he cast a spell. A thin sheet of fire flowed from his fingertips, catching all four of the sea devils climbing up and setting them alight. They shrieked and fell from the wall. Krell felt the claws of the wounded sahuagin strike his armor, and he turned and hammered at it with his blade, killing it.

Without waiting, Tristan turned and did the same thing to another section of the wall. Three had already climbed over, and two burned to death immediately in the torrent, though one ducked down and survived. The sahuagin smelled surprisingly good when burned, like grilled fish.

Kraven was roaring in rage as his axe swung in broad arcs, and if the force of the blow didn't kill a sahuagin, then it was enough to knock them back over the edge.

Dorn stabbed quickly, his blade catching the sahuagin in the eyes or throat as their head came into view. Regardless of whether the wound was fatal, it often caused them to lose their grip, and they fell.

Krell turned back to his section of the wall and surged forward. There were three fully up and over the side, but Krell put faith in his armor as he cut at the one just reaching the top. He slashed it across the face, knocking it backward. Krell heard it strike others as it fell and hoped that they were knocked off the wall.

The hissing and croaking was endless. His armor took a blow from behind, knocking him forward. He hit the battlement and stabbed downward, taking a larger one in the shoulder and knocking it from the wall, then ducked quickly as a silver spear shot through the space he had just been in. Green blood sprayed over him from behind, and Krell grinned.

He rolled sideways as the spear bounced off the stone and flew back down to its master's hand. A sahuagin standing behind him had been slain, but now there were eight. Krell shook his head, then Tristan was there, another fan of flames catching most of them from behind.

Another big one climbed to the edge, and Krell struck it with the pommel of his sword, shattering something in its face and causing it to lose its balance and fall. He turned to face the ones atop the tower already, knowing they were barely stemming the tide. There was a clatter of metal hitting stone behind him.

Then, with a booming crash of thunder, Dorn let loose a spell, and a section of the tower slid away and fell. Krell threw himself backward, away from the collapsing stonework. Dozens of sahuagin fell, and many more were crushed below.

"ReckNor!" shouted Dorn, who reached down and grasped his sword from where he had dropped it, then began to fall back. "Kraven, close in!" he said.

Kraven was covered in claw marks and he was drenched in blood, much of it green. Krell dropped his sword and reached out to grasp him by the shoulder, letting ReckNor's grace flow into him.

The sahuagin seemed to pause, almost, as the echo of the collapse died out. Three larger sahuagin came over the wall, marshaling others around them as more came up and over the side.

"Tristan, get below!" said Krell. Without waiting, Tristan sat on the edge, grasped the other side, and swung himself down to the lower level.

"Dorn!" Dorn nodded and dropped down. Krell hurled a magical trident at one of the large ones, missing. Kraven didn't wait and dropped below. Krell hurled another trident and stepped backward into empty space.

His fall was interrupted by Kraven grabbing and pulling hard, keeping him from plunging to the level below. One side of the room was open to the night sky.

"Now, Sheana!" shouted Verbena. Sheana lifted a wooden table up, holding it across the opening. Verbena cast a spell at it, hurling a sparkling dust into the air. There was a flash of blue surrounding the wood, and Sheana cried out as it slammed tight against the ceiling, crushing her fingers.

She screamed and fell. Her hands jerked free, and Dorn caught her. Her gauntlets were crushed, and blood dripped from them. Krell let some of the grace of ReckNor flow into her, to try to heal, but there was resistance. He started to push harder, the power becoming jagged against his thoughts. ReckNor's grace resisted his efforts.

Verbena kneeled next to her, her hands hovering without touching. "No, no, no, I didn't mean to hurt you!"

THE GUANTLETS ARE CRUSHED AND MUST BE REMOVED BEFORE MORE CAN BE DONE.

Krell winced, then started unfastening the gauntlet straps.

"Careful, we don't want to pull her fingers off if they're crushed as badly as they look," said Dorn. There was a thud from the wood panel that was affixed to the ceiling.

Krell nodded. "Yet the gauntlets need to come off," he said, continuing to work at the straps. Sheana looked at him, tears running down her face, her expression pained but calm. She nodded.

Krell tugged as gently as he could at the metal, and Sheana sucked in a breath in agony. As he pulled, he forced the power of ReckNor to flow. The gauntlet slid off, and the ruined mess of her hand reformed as they watched. Krell moved to the other gauntlet.

Kraven let out a yell, and Krell heard the croak of a sahuagin from behind him. A quick look showed one with Kraven's axe embedded in its head, falling back through the hole to the next level down. As soon as it was clear, another one started trying to climb up.

Krell turned back to Sheana, who was slumped against Verbena, her face a mask of pain.

"How long will that last?" he asked, gesturing with his head toward the wood fastened over the hole to the roof.

"Forever, unless they break the wood or the magic," Verbena said. Krell grunted as he began to pull the gauntlet slowly from Sheana's hand.

Her breathing became easier as ReckNor's grace flowed into her, and she flexed her hand in front of her eyes. She looked at

Krell and smiled. Verbena let loose a little sob and clutched at her, burying her face in Sheana's hair.

"Hush, I'm fine. We're fine. Help me up," she said. Verbena helped Sheana rise, and she donned her shield.

Krell stood and spun in alarm as he heard scrabbling from the open section of the wall. A sahuagin hand reached up and gripped the edge, then the stone gave way and fell with a crash. Without pause, another clawed hand came over the edge.

Verbena spoke, and a blue ray shot from her hand, striking it. There was a croaking hiss that ended in a crashing noise.

There was a loud thump on the wood from above, accompanied by the sound of wood breaking.

Verbena looked at it, then back at Krell. "I have a better estimate. Probably about ten minutes before it breaks." Krell nodded, then hurled a conjured trident at a sahuagin who was climbing over the edge. The force of the strike knocked it clear, and it plummeted out of sight.

Kraven was working tirelessly at the hole in the floor. As a sahuagin climbed partway up, his axe flashed down, killing it. Sheana and Gerrard stood on the opposite side, ready to aid when necessary. Krell spun to face the open wall.

Joined by Dorn, Verbena, and Tristan, they rained magic strikes against any that tried to climb up. Krell moved so he could observe Sheana and Kraven while also throwing magic toward the sahuagin who climbed over the edge.

The crash against the wood from above was becoming more rhythmic.

It was only a matter of time.

* * *

With a crack, the wood panel gave way, and a sahuagin fell into the room.

Sheana took it as it fell, but the force of the falling body jerked her sword from her hand. Kraven roared as a spear stabbed down, catching him in the shoulder. As the spear withdrew, another sahuagin leapt down from above.

Krell stepped forward, conjuring a blade in his hand. He struck as the sahuagin landed and turned toward Sheana, who was pulling her sword from the corpse of the one she killed. Kraven killed another that dropped from above, but took another spear wound as he did so.

A sahuagin dropped from above and bit at Krell's face. He slammed his shield into it, knocking it away, and killed it with a thrust into its chest. Sheana stood, her blade lashing out at one that tried to climb up from below. Gerrard drove his sword into its neck.

A larger sahuagin with a spear dropped into the room. Kraven swung, but it caught his axe by the haft using its free hand and bit at his face, forcing him back. Sheana stabbed it in the back, and it spun its spear around, catching her across her body with the haft, knocking her aside. It stepped forward toward Kraven, shoving him away while twisting his axe from his grasp.

Another large one dropped directly behind it. Gerrard stabbed it in the back of its leg, and it croaked in rage, backhanding him and knocking him across the room to the far wall.

Magical webs appeared, and the two thrashed in place as they were restrained. Krell yelled and thrust his sword into the back of the newest one, but it caught on a bony spine, inflicting only a minor wound.

Verbena's blue ray flashed, and the one pressuring Kraven hissed in pain and rage as frost formed across its arm and chest. Kraven grappled with it, trying to gain control of his axe.

Which left Dorn facing the opening to the night sky alone, as the plate-clad sahuagin leapt onto the floor.

The stone beneath its feet began to crumble at once, and it needed to hunch a bit in order to fit in the room, since the ceilings were only ten feet high. One spear lashed out, catching Dorn's shield as he spun, deflecting the strike. It hurled the other spear, catching Tristan across the shoulder, knocking him prone.

The spear spun through the air and returned to its hand. A half dozen sahuagin began to climb up behind it.

Dorn didn't hesitate. He dropped his blade and gestured while speaking words of power. A crash of thunder slammed into the sahuagin, but it simply crouched and slid backward a few inches. It looked at Dorn and let out a croaking chuckle.

Dorn grinned back, stepped forward, and stomped his foot down. Hard.

The stone floor groaned, then abruptly gave way. The sahuagin fell from sight with a surprised croak of rage. Dorn leapt backward, trying to get clear of the collapse, as the whole side of the tower failed. Verbena helped Tristan move farther from the edge, blood drenching both of them from the wound on his shoulder.

Krell let his blade drop and dove toward Dorn, reaching out. Dorn grabbed his arm, his grip closing like iron on Krell's wrist.

"Shit!" shouted Krell as Dorn's weight began to pull him over the edge. He felt a weight on his legs, and his fall stopped. He strained, but couldn't lift Dorn. "Kraven!"

Kraven was suddenly next to him. Sheana was yelling in the background, and Krell saw flashes of magic, blue from Verbena and red from Tristan. The crackle of fire reached his ears.

Kraven reached down and grabbed Dorn's wrist, heaving. Dorn shot over the edge, releasing Krell as he did so. Kraven fell back onto the floor, and Dorn landed atop him. They rolled to their feet at once.

Krell's eyes widened, and he rolled to the side. The silver spear flashed firelight as it hurtled past him, slamming into the stones of the ceiling. Krell rolled again as it skipped downward, narrowly avoiding the return strike.

As Krell stood, he saw the webs largely burned away, the two large sahuagin lying dead on the ground. Kraven retrieved his axe, but a spear from above traced a wound across his back. Dorn gestured, and silvery fire was visible through the hole above.

With a loud snap, a crack formed across the stone ceiling, and it began to fall.

"Back! Back!" shouted Dorn, rushing away from the collapsing side of the tower.

Krell's footing shifted, and he was suddenly trying to run uphill as the stone floor beneath him tilted. Sheana yelled something as he sprang backward. He saw Verbena falling and dashed toward her. He threw himself prone and grabbed her by her braid. She shrieked in pain, but stopped sliding.

He felt hands grab his shield and turned to see Sheana pulling him away from the collapse. The pain in his shoulder was enormous, as his arm bent painfully. The roof gave a low groan, and the stone gave way and collapsed. Krell heaved, and Verbena was pulled clear of a large stone that crashed to the floor.

Verbena rolled and grabbed his armor, pulling herself up and over him. When she was clear, Sheana heaved, and they both fell away from the collapse.

Fully half the tower shuddered and gave way, and the roof section broke off entirely, tilting downward into the room. It slid, and the entire edifice fell off the side, crashing to the ground. Dozens of sahuagin were carried with it.

A large stone struck Krell on the shoulder, and dust obscured his vision. Another rock slammed into his helmet. He heard Verbena cry out nearby and leapt toward her. He fell over her and braced his arms as rocks slammed into the backplate of his armor.

After a moment, the rockfall stopped, and an eerie silence descended.

Krell looked down and met Verbena's eyes. She had a cut on her head, which was bleeding red into her gold hair. She arched an eyebrow.

"Krell, your knee is between my legs. Get off me."

Krell nearly jumped upward, his face flushing red, and reached down to help her stand. She slapped his hand away, then pressed on her wound. She looked at him. "See to Tristan, he's hurt far worse than me."

Krell turned and found Dorn hunched over Tristan, a blue light wreathing his hands. "Dorn's got him, it looks like."

The tower was a ruined shell of what it was. Barely a quarter of the floor they were on remained, with a partial wall rising behind them. Everything else was gone, fallen below. Krell hoped each rock crushed a sahuagin on the way down.

"Who else is hurt?" he said.

"I can't… I can't feel my legs, you know?" said Gerrard, his voice laced with pain.

Krell moved at once, and saw a large stone had landed on his back, pinning him in place. Krell grabbed it and lifted, straining. Gerrard cried out in pain.

Kraven reached over with one hand, grabbed the stone, then grunted. The rock lifted off Gerrard and was hurled over the edge. There was a series of hisses and croaks from below as the stone crashed down that rapidly quieted. Krell kneeled down and felt ReckNor's grace moving into Gerrard, but slowly. He gasped, and his legs twitched.

Krell was weary.

The silence stretched on for a minute. Dorn sat next to him.

"Sheana's unconscious, but alive. Took a rock to the head." Krell looked over. Sheana was lying on the ground, Verbena sitting next to her. She was hunched over, whispering something, while she attempted to bandage herself. There was a croak from below.

Dorn gestured at the floor and remaining wall. "This section's weak now. Won't stand up to too much more if we have a fight," he said, quietly. "Not sure if it's better to break free and run, or to stand and fight. If we stay, we're fish food. If we run, we're probably fish food, but take a lot fewer of them with us."

"You think they've got us, either way?"

Dorn nodded his head, his shoulders slumped in exhaustion. The croaking and hissing were growing more frequent. And louder.

"Well, if a dwarf gets tired, you know you're in trouble!" said Krell.

Dorn looked up at him, and Krell grinned back.

"No, we can't win, but that doesn't mean we have to lose. Verbena is right. We don't need to kill them all, as satisfying as that would be. We need to kill the big ones. How many of them have we seen, and how many have we killed?"

Dorn looked at him, his expression unreadable. "You think we can survive?"

"Of course he does. His arrogance makes it impossible for him to see any other outcome," said Tristan. The usual venom in his voice was absent, replaced with exhaustion.

Krell looked at Tristan, his smile fading. "Better to die fighting than to run, stinking of blood, into the midst of them. Better still, Tristan, to slay the smart ones and survive the day, and live to see that princely reward we were promised."

He looked around at all of them. "The leader here — the one in plate. It needs to die. Any other big ones, them too. Ignore the smaller ones as best we can. We've all seen it, the sea devils turning on one another without a strong leader. They eat each other without one, right?"

The croaking and hissing from below was growing louder.

"Now, they're coming for us. Tristan, Verbena, Dorn, and I will focus on killing the larger ones. Kraven, you keep the small ones off us. Gerrard, you're still too hurt, and Sheana's out. Stay by her and keep her safe."

Kraven chuckled, looking at Tristan. "He thinks we can survive."

Tristan nodded. "Yes, the arrogant fool thinks we can survive." His voice was resigned, defeated. Exhausted.

Kraven laughed as the croaking and hissing grew louder. "He's only an arrogant fool if he's wrong!" He hefted his axe, and stepped forward, looking at Dorn. "How stable is this?"

"It isn't," he said. "The whole thing could go any moment."

Krell reached out, pouring the last bit of ReckNor's grace into Kraven. His wounds began to close, and his shoulders straightened.

Kraven smiled. "Good. Nothing I need to worry about then." He set his feet and raised his axe.

* * *

They came at them from every direction.

Kraven roared in fury as their claws slashed at him. His axe was a blur, killing any that got close.

Krell and Verbena stood to one side, their magic blasting any that tried to come up over the edge. Opposite him stood Dorn and Tristan, doing the same.

They were all gathered in close together. There was no room for retreat. Gerrard leaned against the wall, his sword held ready. Sheana was next to him, still unconscious.

"How long till the bigger ones show up?" asked Verbena.

"No clue." Krell created a blade in hand and stepped forward as the sahuagin came up faster than they could be blasted off with magic. He cut at one with his sword, while hammering another in the face with his shield.

Kraven was engaged, fighting four of them. Every time his axe took one, it seemed two more were there to take its place. As he fended them off, four larger ones climbed up.

Verbena and Tristan targeted them at once, and Krell had no more time for thought. There were six in front of him, and more climbing up every moment.

He slashed with his blade, killing one before him but taking a jagged wound to his leg. His shield hammered another, knocking it off the ledge, taking a wound to his sword arm. Two grabbed his shield, wrenching at it as they leaned forward. Their breath stank of rot.

A large one climbed up in front of him.

Gerrard shouted, and Krell risked a glance. A sahuagin had dropped from the top of the wall above him. He cut it, but not fatally. Two more were coming over the top of the wall.

Dorn sprang backward, crashing against the stone wall. He rebounded as the wall heaved, collapsing. He shoved Gerrard toward Tristan and threw himself over Sheana. The wall collapsed, crushing the sahuagin and casting more of them back to the ground below.

Tristan yelled as three of them slashed at him. He recoiled away, wounded. Gerrard cut at one from behind, his sword slicing up into its torso. Two more slashed at him, and his legs gave way. Gerrard fell, stabbing one on the way down.

Krell met Verbena's eyes. They were being overwhelmed, and the plate-armored one was nowhere in sight. He'd need to go find it if the others were to have any chance of survival.

Something of what he planned must have shown on his face. Her eyes widened, and her voice drifted into his thoughts — *Don't!* Krell smiled back sadly at her, trying to convey an apology as best he could.

Verbena gestured, and a wave of magical darts shot from her fingers, moving around Krell and slamming into the large one that had just got its feet under it. Krell turned and sprang forward, knowing he was leaving at least five behind with nobody between him and Verbena.

His shield crashed into it, and they both went over the edge.

They hit the pile of rubble from the collapsed lower levels, the sahuagin softening Krell's landing. Krell heard its bones snap as he bounced off, rolling down the rubble, crashing through multiple pairs of sahuagin legs, taking wounds from their claws as he went. He managed to control his roll enough to come to his feet.

He brought his sword up in a sweeping parry, narrowly deflecting the silver spear from his face, taking a ringing blow to his helmet. The next strike was a beat behind, catching him in the shoulder, and then the large sahuagin's foot lashed out, catching him dead center. His sword flew from his hand, and he flew backward ten feet into a group of smaller ones.

Convenient that I don't have to look for it, thought Krell.

He sprang to his feet, his sword reforming as he cut upward, taking the arm off one and burying the tip in the neck of another. The silver spearpoint flashed toward him and he ducked, narrowly avoiding it. The second attack came fast and precise, a glancing blow that still drew blood.

"ReckNor says you're all about to die!" he shouted. Then he dropped his blade and spoke words of power, even as he retreated away from the larger one. Claws and teeth raked at him, his arms taking multiple wounds. With a gesture, he finished his spell.

Darkness rushed out from him. The sahuagin paused in confusion, hissing in alarm. Krell struggled to hold on to it, the spell squirming in his mind, trying to fall apart.

His will prevailed. The darkness persisted.

"I send you to ReckNor's depths!"

Krell formed a new blade of dark metal, and leapt forward, springing upward as fast and high as he could, as quietly as he could. The plate-clad sahuagin thrust with both spears toward where he had been when he shouted, but only one strike grazed Krell's leg.

He buried his sword in its mouth.

It let out a gurgling croak, then thrashed to the side. Krell hung on with his last remaining strength, and his weight on the blade caused it to pivot, carving a bloody furrow in the neck and head of the sahuagin leader. It fell to its knees, and Krell regained his feet. A set of sahuagin claws scored along his back. Something was wrong with his leg. A quick glance showed a sahuagin with its jaws clamped down hard. The darkness shattered as the magic flew apart in his mind.

He jerked his sword free, then cut sideways as it dropped the two spears. His blade caught in its throat, stopped by some protrusion of the armor. He pulled, but it did not budge. The one on his leg clawed at him, leaving bloody wounds.

His legs were not working correctly. Krell fell to one knee, punching his fist into the face of the one biting him. He rolled onto his back, creating a small dagger in his hand, and thrust it into its eye.

A big one loomed in his vision, even as clawed hands grabbed at his shield. A silver spear, wielded by new hands, raised over Krell, ready to strike.

An arrow buried itself in its throat. It dropped the spear, clutching at the fletching, and fell forward atop Krell.

He felt himself falling into the depths, as if sinking through water. Vile green water that stank of rot. His last thought was that the grace of ReckNor seemed pleased with him.

* * *

"ReckNor clearly likes you!" said Kraven in admiration.

Krell nodded. Everything hurt. The sun was coming up, giving him a sense of how many hours had passed.

Kraven looked spent. His shoulders were slumped, and one arm dangled uselessly at his side. His axe was resting on the ground. He'd just rolled the big sahuagin that fell atop Krell off him.

Krell tried to talk, but nothing came out. Gerrard was suddenly in his field of view, his face bloody and bandaged. He pressed a waterskin to his lips and squeezed gently. Krell choked, then managed to swallow.

"Took you long enough," he said.

Kraven let out a bellowing laugh, which echoed off the shattered remains of the stone tower.

Krell glanced up at it and then looked at Gerrard. "Remind me to never make Dorn angry."

Gerrard's concerned expression broke into a smile. "Well, you know what, if you're okay enough to make jokes, I think you're going to be okay, right? Am I right?"

Krell closed his eyes and let out a sigh. "Of course I'm going to be okay. Paladins only die when they do something stupid. Turns out, this was heroic." Kraven laughed harder.

"Gods damn, Krell. When you jumped over the edge, I thought you were dead for sure!" Krell heard him turn and walk away.

"Gerrard?"

"Yes, Krell?" Krell heard him sit down next to him.

He opened an eye and turned his head. Gerrard had a set of four parallel slashes on his face, and his arm sleeves were tattered ruins and coated in blood. He sat against the dead sahuagin leader, its plate armor covered in green blood.

"What happened?"

Gerrard chuckled. "Hey, you know, I was going to ask you that, right?"

Krell closed his eye and let his head fall back to the ground.

"The others?"

"Alive, right? Dorn and Sheana are both hurt bad, Verbena is worse. Tristan is hurt, but should live. Kraven is a machine, still moving somehow. I can barely walk. You?"

"I'll be okay, I think."

"Good," said Dahlia. "I'd hate to think I spent all day running through a swamp, then circling back to save you, only for you to die now."

Krell's eyes snapped open and looked at her. She was covered in mud and scratches. Her quiver was empty. He'd never seen anyone look so beautiful before. Some of that thought must have come through his gaze. She blushed.

"Thank ReckNor, you're alive! We didn't know," he said.

"Fortis didn't tell you?" she asked.

Krell set his head back down, then shook it.

Fortis dropped onto his breastplate, chirping, then rubbing his face against his chin. Krell reached up and stroked his neck. He let out a happy cackling purr. A weight in Krell's chest he hadn't realized was there suddenly lifted. He could feel a tear running down the side of his face.

"I'm glad you're okay, my friend. I need up," said Krell.

"You should probably lie there a little longer," said Gerrard. "You're covered in your own blood, right? You really think you should move?"

Krell shook his head. "No, but you said only Tristan would probably live. At worst, I need to get Dorn up to help the others. At best, I can help everyone. Besides, I bet ReckNor is pleased with us, so might be willing to help."

He held up his arm, and Dahlia reached down and grabbed it, hauling him to his feet.

He nearly fell at once. He looked at his leg, seeing a massive cut on it.

"Is that, uh, my leg bone?" Blood was dripping down his leg.

Gerrard nodded. "It is. I think that's your blood on that silver spear over there, right?"

Krell closed his eyes. "I thought he just grazed me." He opened them and looked down. As he watched, the wound closed slightly. Very slowly. He looked at Dahlia.

"You're going to have to support me."

She nodded and turned to put his arm over her shoulders. Together, they staggered over toward the remains of the tower. Krell could see Kraven walking in an ever-widening circle, his axe occasionally flashing down.

"He's tracking down wounded sea devils," she said. "They kept coming for a while. Now, they either try to eat the dead, or come and try to eat us. He's tired of it, so he's putting them down."

As they approached the debris, Krell could see Tristan, sitting on a large rock.

"Too arrogant to die? Gods, I knew I couldn't be so lucky," he said.

"I'm pleased to see you too, Tristan."

Dahlia ignored him. Fortis flew past and landed behind the rock Tristan was perched on. He muttered some words of power, and a bolt of fire shot from his hand, hitting a sahuagin as it padded forward, sniffing at the air. It let out a hissing shriek and collapsed. Kraven dashed over, and his axe flashed.

Behind the rock, Dorn, Sheana, and Verbena were laid out. Sheana looked much the same. Dorn was out of his armor, which was laying nearby, severely dented. His breathing sounded wet and labored.

Verbena was covered in deep claw wounds. She was very pale and still.

"Dorn first," he said.

Dahlia frowned, but helped him over the uneven terrain. He tried to kneel, but instead collapsed beside Dorn, dragging her down with him. She helped him sit so his leg was straight, and he put his hand on Dorn.

YOU WILL DIE IF YOU TRY TO HEAL OTHERS.

Krell winced, a headache exploding into his thoughts as ReckNor's voice crashed like thunder.

"If I don't," he said, "then the three of them will die."

THAT IS LIKELY, BUT NOT CERTAIN.

"They all follow you, do they not?"

DORN IS A TRUE PRIEST. THE OTHER TWO HAVE RAISED VOICE IN PRAYER.

"Well, am I their paladin, or am I not?" said Krell.

I WOULD PREFER YOU TO LIVE.

"I will not sacrifice them to save myself! Why is that so hard to understand?" said Krell, letting anger tinge his voice. Dahlia sat before him, looking at him calmly.

"Tell him I want him to help, Krell. ReckNor, help my friends." A tear coursed down her cheek. "Please, ReckNor. Help Verbena and Sheana and Dorn. We were brave. Please help us!"

Nothing happened for a moment. Krell listened to Dorn's breathing, wet and rattling. It sounded like his body was full of water.

"ReckNor?" he said.

I AM DWELLING ON WHETHER I SHOULD HELP OR NOT. MORE THAN I ALREADY HAVE.

"Time presses, oh Lord of the Seas and Skies."

Dahlia looked at him, then looked up. "Choosing not to choose is a choice!" she yelled.

Krell looked at Dahlia. "He's thinking about it."

Her face filled with fury. "What's there to think about? We're followers, we need help, and we have a paladin here, right now!"

Krell looked at his hand and tried to marshal some grace. He felt a flicker flow into Dorn. His leg flared with agony and began to bleed. He stopped at once, drawing a hissing breath between his teeth.

"Dahlia, do you have any bandages?" She looked at his leg and shook her head. Krell looked up at Tristan. "Tristan, toss down your cloak!"

"I'm using it!" he said.

"For what?"

"It's pillowing my ass on this hard rock!"

Dahlia made a noise that sounded like a snort of disgust mixed with a chuckle. She scaled the rock, pushed over Tristan, and stole his cloak.

"Hey, harpy! Give that back!"

Dahlia unfurled it. It was grimy, but intact.

"I'll buy you a new one, Tristan," he said. Turning to Dahlia, he nodded. She pulled a dagger and cut it into strips.

"Bandage the leg above the cut as tight as possible. Take the rest, and stuff the wound. I need to avoid bleeding to death while I help Dorn and the others."

YOU ARE STUBBORN.

"Look, if you wanted to help, you would, but you won't. Or maybe you can't? Either way, shut it. It's my choice!" said Krell. Dahlia looked at him in surprise, tensing up.

He chuckled. "Not you. ReckNor," he said, waving his hand in the air.

She nodded and tied his leg tight. She looked him in the eye. "It would be a shame to watch you die now, when you're surrounded by the corpses of your enemies."

Krell grinned. "I suppose that depends on how tight you make that bandage."

Dahlia nodded, looking serious. She stood. "Kraven!" she called. "Come over here. I need you to tie off Krell's leg!"

Krell chuckled. "That's clever," he said.

"Don't die." She turned as Kraven trotted up. "I need you to help me tie this as tight as possible."

Kraven set his axe down and leaned over with his one good arm. He and Dahlia pulled the makeshift bandage tight. Dahlia tied it with her free hand, placing a stick into the knot. Then she twisted it. Krell gasped as the pressure on his leg exploded in searing agony. Kraven's hand slammed into him, holding him down.

After a moment, the pain subsided to regular agony, and Kraven released the pressure. Dahlia helped him sit up. "I don't know if you'll keep the leg or not, Krell," she said, looking at his wound.

"If ReckNor wants me to bring about his will, I'll need two legs. I expect I'll keep it," he said, his voice coming out heavy with pain. She glanced at him.

"You okay?"

"The pain is, to use Kraven's word, intense." Krell closed his eyes and reached out for Dorn, groping. He felt Dahlia take his hand and set it on Dorn.

"By ReckNor's grace, be healed, my friend," he said. A tear trickled from his eye. He could feel it running down his face.

For a moment, nothing happened. Then Dorn sucked in a breath, turned on his side, and vomited. There was a lot of blood. He crashed back down, gasping. His breathing smoothed out, and he sat up.

"Oh, wow, that's much better," said Dorn. He looked at Dahlia, then down at Krell.

His face had gone gray, and he was unconscious. Blood seeped from his leg, pooling on the ground.

Dorn snorted. "Oh, no you don't. You led us into this mess — you're going to lead us out!"

Dorn cast a spell.

Chapter Twenty-two

The rest of the day was spent lying very still.

Krell was sorry it wasn't raining. The stench was horrible. Rain might have washed some of it away.

ReckNor's grace trickled into him, and it was spent as soon as it arrived. Between him and Dorn, everyone's hurts were patched enough to make sure they lived. Dorn and Krell made sure Kraven and Tristan, the least hurt among them, were fit and healthy once they had power to spend on injuries that were not life or death.

Verbena had been savaged by the ones Krell left behind him, as he feared. They had been on the verge of being overwhelmed, with two of the larger ones remaining.

Then the sahuagin battle plan had disintegrated when Krell slew their leader. The two surviving larger ones had apparently turned and run. Without guidance, the smaller sahuagin descended into madness, biting and tearing at one another, or feasting on the dead. With the pressure off the survivors, Kraven, Gerrard, and Tristan were able to fend them off, until they dispersed into the surrounding area.

They were still creeping back in, drawn by the scent of so much blood. Kraven had spent time hauling corpses away from the tower to buy them some peace. Tristan spent most of his time blasting bolts of flame at any that ventured close.

Twice, while Krell slept, Kraven, Tristan, and Dahlia had fought short battles with a group that formed, drawn to the living. Dorn helpfully explained that BranLagNos encouraged his followers to eat those that still lived or were recently dead, as opposed to carrion.

When Krell was more rested, and his leg wound healed enough that he wouldn't die, he forced the grace of ReckNor to flow into the others. Sheana awoke with a pounding headache. Verbena's cuts healed, restored by ReckNor's power as if they had never been, though she was weak from blood loss.

Kraven had explored the remains of Swamp Hold and outlined what he had found. It wasn't much.

"One big cache of weapons and other tools. That's it," he said.

"What sort of weapons?" asked Dorn.

"Spears and daggers."

Krell grunted. "Useful when you're in the water. And the tools?"

"Looks like stuff to work stone. Not sure, though," said Kraven.

Dorn stood. "Show me." Kraven nodded, and they walked away.

"There's also the stuff the big one was using," said Tristan. "Do you think any of it is magical?"

Verbena shook her head. "I already checked. None of it. Though the metal isn't silver or steel. I'm not sure what it is."

"Probably valuable, whatever it is," said Sheana.

"Something, then, for this idiocy." Tristan stood and walked toward the remains of the tower.

Dahlia and Verbena shared a look, then turned back to Krell.

"So what now?" asked Dahlia. "We walk back to Watford? Or do we take one of those?" She nodded toward the collection of fishing boats that bobbed in the harbor.

"No, we wait for our ride," said Krell.

"What ride would that be?" asked Verbena.

"*ReckNor's Bounty*. Captain Voss will probably get here — assuming they aren't attacked on the way — sometime in the next few hours. I sent Fortis with a note describing our victory as soon as I could write."

Verbena looked at him, her expression unreadable. Dahlia looked impressed.

"Clever," said Sheana. She leaned back against a rock and closed her eyes. "Wake me when they get here."

Dahlia sat next to her and rested her head on her shoulder. Sheana moved her arm around her, and she closed her eyes as well. Verbena was watching them, a small smile on her face.

"You really do love one another, don't you?" asked Krell.

She nodded, turning to make eye contact.

Gerrard coughed, then stood and walked away. Krell watched him head toward Kraven and Dorn. When he turned back, Verbena was still looking at him.

"This was arrogant and stupid, you know that, right?" she said. "Attacking a fortress full of them? Then that leap from the tower!"

Krell nodded, then closed his eyes and leaned back against a rock. His leg was throbbing in agony.

A moment passed in silence.

"That's it? A nod?"

Krell nodded again. "Afraid so."

"That is… I don't even know what to say about that." She sounded disgusted.

Krell opened his eyes and looked at her. "I'm going to keep my word, Verbena. I'll teach you whatever I can. But I am ReckNor's paladin. His sword. He tells me to go, and I go. I don't question. I obey."

ReckNor's grace exploded in mirth within him. Krell looked up, confused.

YOU QUESTION EVERYTHING. YOU ARE STUBBORN AND ARROGANT.

Krell winced. "Wish he had a voice that didn't sound like thunder all the time," he muttered.

"What was that?" said Verbena.

"ReckNor is calling me a liar. He told me that I argue about everything, and that I'm stubborn and arrogant. On that, at least, you and he agree. If it matters, I agree also." Krell looked back at her. "Though I might phrase it differently."

"Does ReckNor often speak to you directly?" she asked.

Krell nodded. "All the time, it feels like. He doesn't call many paladins, according to Olgar. I guess he doesn't have a lot of people to talk to, so he talks to me. A *lot*."

"And he tells you that you're a liar? Forgive me, but if paladins are supposed to be champions of their god, you seem to have a strange relationship with him."

Krell shrugged. "Never been a paladin before, nor have I ever met another one. I'm just stumbling around trying to learn before I do something stupid and get myself killed." Krell waved his arm broadly toward Swamp Hold. "Stupid, like this. This was a trap, and we walked right into it."

She arched an eyebrow at him. "A trap? How does that make sense?"

"Think about it," said Krell. "Karaback used magic to spy on the town, but saw only twenty or thirty. We saw fifty in the patrol, and maybe another fifty wandering around. As soon as we were in deep, close to the tower, that big one sprung the trap. There had to have been, what, four hundred? More?" He shook his head.

"No, they knew we were coming. They were waiting for us. This trap was *made* for us. For *me*. And I walked right into it." He grinned ruefully. "Makes me a little sad to know that Tristan is totally right about me sometimes."

"How would they know we were coming, though?"

Krell shifted, reaching into his magic bag, and pulled out the satchel they had captured. He tossed it to her.

"Whatever the Betterment Society is, they're hardly working for something better. Unless this is a ruse, they sold us out. I think

I want to track Halpas down and ask some questions. Assuming he survived his swim."

Verbena furrowed her brow. "Who is Halpas?"

"He's a true priest of ReckNor. Also, a smuggler and probably a pirate. He was aboard the ship that we seized."

"*ReckNor's Bounty?*" she asked.

"Yes. We fought, and I let him go. It was dark, and the ship was some way from the shore."

"Wait, you fought?" Verbena asked. "I think I need some clarification about ReckNor's faith here. We fight one another?"

Krell grinned. "See, this is why ReckNor is the best. We fight one another only if we want to. If we don't, then we don't. Freedom of choice, Verbena. He wants you to choose. And he *demands* that you deal with the consequences of your choices. Halpas had to do a dangerous night swim as his consequence." Krell grimaced. "I nearly died along with the rest of you here, as consequences for mine. Probably why ReckNor is angry with me."

I AM NOT ANGRY, KRELL. IF ANYTHING I WOULD SAY I AM DELIGHTED.

"Wait, really?"

"We need some sort of code, Krell, to let me know when you're not talking to me anymore," she said, her voice cross.

"You always know, so this isn't a problem. ReckNor is telling me he's happy." Krell shook his head. "I can see why lots of people think he's insane. I don't understand him."

YOU CHOSE TO ACT. YOU USED MY GIFTS BASED ON YOUR WILL, ALIGNED WITH MINE. MY GOAL IS TO PRESERVE MY FOLLOWERS AND MAINTAIN MY POWER. BRANLAGNOS WOULD DEVOUR MY FOLLOWERS, YET MINE LIVE AND HIS LIE DEAD AROUND YOU. YOU WERE FAITHFUL, KRELL, BUT MORE THAN THAT, YOU UNDERSTAND AND ACCEPT THE CONSEQUENCES OF YOUR CHOICES. YOUR FAITH PLEASES ME.

Krell clutched at his temples, hissing in pain. "Okay, thank you my lord ReckNor. Please no more talking, especially that much at once, until this headache goes away."

The grace of ReckNor bubbled in amusement within him.

* * *

Krell stood in Amra Thort's dining room.

His companions were arrayed around him. Tristan and Gerrard were finishing the account of their expedition. It was not a terribly flattering depiction of their actions, even if it was accurate. Krell noted that he received most of the blame for poor decision-making.

Aldrik's eyes were wide. "Thank you, Gerrard, Tristan. So let me see if I have this right. You saw a fortress full of sea devils, and you attacked it and killed all of them?" His grin made him look younger.

Krell shrugged. "A lot of smaller ones ran off into the woods or back to the sea, but pretty much, yes."

"Remarkable," said Daylan. "Just remarkable. Who in their right mind would trade with the sea devils? Would trade *weapons* to the sea devils?"

"Not a few, either," said Captain Gijwolf. "Sixty spears, one hundred daggers, and masonry tools that could be used to build a stone fortress. That's an army large enough to raze Watford itself. The town guard would be overrun in short order with those numbers."

Amra cleared her throat. "It would seem then that we are in their debt, are we not?"

Daylan snorted. "Of course not. They had a charter, and they fulfilled it. That's the end of it. If they want more, I'm sure another charter can be drawn up." He turned to Tristan and Gerrard. "The town of Watford expresses its thanks for your heroic actions, and will gladly pay the terms specified on your charter."

"Plus recovery," said Captain Gijwolf.

"Yes, yes, and recovery. The town has assessed the value of the goods recovered. Any you wish to claim are yours. The rest are of use to the town, and we will purchase them at the discussed valuation," said Daylan.

"Who did the assessing?" asked Tristan.

"I did, mostly," said Petimus. "The weapons, the smith tools, and the strange metal items you found. The boats with no next of kin were assessed by Daylan and Amra."

"Sorry, but next of kin? I thought we got recovery rights on whatever we found, you know?" said Gerrard.

"Ah, you are correct. However, there are only two boats that have remaining family here in Watford that they can be returned to, so..."

"Then assess them and pay us fair value," said Tristan, interrupting, "exactly like it says in the charter we signed."

Amra shrugged and slid a paper toward Tristan. "This is the full accounting of value for the items found." Tristan picked it up and read it, a grin crossing his face. He handed it to Gerrard.

"Per the charter, five hundred golden sovereigns to do a raid, and an extra two thousand if you drive them out. They were driven out. The reports from Captain Voss and his crew spoke of well over a hundred dead sahuagin littering the ground of Swamp Hold. They've more than earned this reward," said Captain Gijwolf.

"No, Captain, they earned precisely that reward and no more, per the terms of their charter," said Daylan.

Captain Gijwolf sighed. "Try not to sound so grateful, Master Plintform. In any event, the recovered items. Sixty spears, of high quality, at two golden sovereigns each. One hundred daggers, of high quality, at one golden sovereign each. Various masonry supplies, valued at forty golden sovereigns. A suit of massive plate armor, sized so nobody can wear it and of bizarre design, valued at five hundred golden sovereigns. Two enormous spears, pikes really, made of silvery metal, valued at eighty golden sovereigns each. That totals nine hundred sixty additional golden sovereigns.

"As to the boats themselves, of the seven recovered, they have been assessed at a total value of two thousand four hundred golden sovereigns. In addition to the total value of the charter, this means that the reward to be paid by Watford to you is five thousand, eight hundred twenty golden sovereigns." Captain Gijwolf paused.

Krell was in shock. Split five ways between Gerrard, Tristan, Kraven, Dorn, and himself, that was over three years of income for a skilled laborer. The others were also quiet.

Gerrard spoke first. "I'm thinking that is totally acceptable!" His grin was enormous.

The grace of ReckNor moved within Krell, prompting him to action. "Anything we want to keep, we can, right?" he asked.

Tristan turned on him at once. "Absolutely, as long as you reduce your gold earnings by whatever you keep! If you want one of those spears, then eighty gold less for you! I'm not buying you gifts here, Krell."

Krell nodded. "That's fair. The total for each of us is what?"

"One thousand one hundred sixty-four golden sovereigns," said Verbena, at once.

Krell smiled at her, then turned back to the council. "That's more than enough, then. I want the armor and both spears." It surprised Krell when Petimus suddenly tensed up.

Amra smiled. "Easily done. They're in the foyer. You can cart them away at your leisure."

Krell was counting on his fingers. "So that means I end up with five hundred and four gold, right?" Amra nodded. Krell turned to Verbena. "How does that split four ways?"

"One hundred twenty-six," she said, her eyes widening.

"Perfect. That's how I want my share."

Sheana gasped. Dahlia stared at him, her mouth dropping open slightly.

* * *

"This is still too generous," said Sheana.

They were standing outside, trying to figure out how to move the enormous plate armor. It wasn't heavy — it was lighter than Krell had expected — but made of many small parts. It was proving impossible to carry.

"Nonsense, you earned it. More than earned it," said Krell. He looked up from his crouch near the armor. "If you hadn't been there, I'd be dead. I think I'm an idiot for leaving my bag up at the temple. If we put the pauldrons and greaves and whatever these are supposed to be inside the clamshell, and Dahlia and Verbena each take vambraces and gauntlets, you and I can carry it. What do you think?"

"And the spears?" asked Verbena.

"Well, crap. Spears." Krell looked at them. They were each easily eight feet long and made of solid metal.

"Maybe slide them through the armor, make a set of handles?" said Sheana.

"This is ridiculous. Wait here," said Verbena, who opened the door to Amra's house again. Petimus Smithforge was standing right there, as if to open the door to leave.

"Ah, young lady, excuse me and please, after you!" Petimus glanced at Krell, took a large step backward, and gave a flourishing bow to Verbena as she passed. She murmured something to him, then began speaking with Godun, who had been escorting Petimus out.

Petimus closed the door and walked over to Krell. He and Sheana tried to put a spear through the bundle. There was a clatter of metal on cobblestones as the armor came apart. "Might I have a word with you, Krell?"

Krell nodded, a disgusted look on his face.

"I think I'm just going to buy a cart! What can I do for you, Master Smithforge?"

"I'd like to make you an offer for the armor and spears," he said.

"I see," said Krell. He stood perfectly still, looking at Petimus.

After a moment, Sheana stirred. "Uh, Krell?"

"I'm thinking," he said. "Master Smithforge here understands."

"Indeed."

A minute passed, then another.

"I am afraid I shall have to decline, Master Smithforge. May I ask, though, about your interest in this armor?"

Petimus let out a heavy sigh. "I, well, to put it bluntly, I may have made an error. I have a doubt, you see. I assessed the armor as if it were plate, but cut the value sharply because of its ridiculous size and idiotic construction. Yet, I wonder about the metal it is made of. Lighter than it should be, based on the thickness. I am planning to send word to an expert in such things, who resides in Talcon. She, perhaps, as a master smith, would know more."

Krell grinned. "Ask her to come here, so she can forge it into armor that I can wear," he said.

Petimus smiled, and to Krell it seemed forced. "I'd say it's unlikely that one of our masters would travel to see anyone, especially to perform their craft. A forge is more than just tools, it's a home. Familiar. Their craft is elevated when they know the details of how everything works, the place where everything goes."

He pulled in a breath. "Well, if I've erred, then so be it. What is done is done, as you humans say. Still, if I hear word back, I will let you know what I learn. Good day to you, Krell. Ladies." Petimus bowed, and started to walk toward the mining consortium headquarters.

"Master Smithforge, one last question," said Dahlia. "What is it you suspect?"

He turned and gave her a small smile. She hunched slightly, moving so Sheana partially obscured Petimus's view of her.

"We dwarves like certainty, young Dahlia. The certainty of stone. The certainty of metal. There is a comfort to it. I dislike speculation." He looked at Krell. "Keep that safe." He nodded to them, then turned and left.

"Well, that was strange," said Sheana.

Krell looked down at the armor and wanted to scream in frustration. If it was a connected set of pieces, like normal armor with straps, they could have lashed it together. Instead, it was crafted to slot onto the spines that a sahuagin had all over their back. Verbena suspected it was made of so many individual parts because sahuagin constantly grow.

Verbena and Godun came around the side of the building, Godun pulling a small cart behind him.

Sheana and Dahlia looked at each other, then turned to look at Krell. The look of consternation on his face caused them to burst into laughter.

* * *

The cart made everything easier.

Krell carried two spears, and Sheana pulled the cart. The ground was uneven on the ascent to the temple of ReckNor, but Dahlia was able to keep it balanced enough to prevent the cart from tipping over. Fortis circled overhead, enjoying the weather.

The three of them were chatting idly about buying a property in town. They sounded excited at having a substantial amount of money of their own for the first time. Verbena talked of opening a jeweler's shop in Watford.

"Wait," said Krell. "A shop where you make jewelry?"

Verbena turned to him, her smile fading and her expression becoming guarded. "Not precisely, more like a trade in gemstones. I know how to cut them and value their worth. I don't have the skill to work metal to make jewelry, though."

"Yet," said Krell, smiling at her. "It sounds as if you plan to remain in Watford?"

She nodded, and Dahlia murmured her assent.

"Good." Krell turned and looked at the temple. The cloudy sky made the lighting a little ominous, and ReckNor's stern visage was staring down at them as they approached.

"Good?" said Verbena.

Krell nodded without looking at them. "Yes. Without you, I'd have died in Swamp Hold. I promised to teach you what I know, but I already know I have nothing of magic to teach you, Verbena. Nor can I teach you anything about the bow, Dahlia. I'd wager both of you can teach me a thing or two. Sheana, you and I both use the blade. I wonder what we'll teach one another."

"You're still going to train us?"

Krell turned to them and smiled. "Of course. You're followers of ReckNor. I'm his paladin. That makes me *your* paladin. ReckNor teaches that we are free to choose, and you choose to be competent. *Dangerous.* I approve. As, I'm sure, does ReckNor. And if he doesn't, I don't care, and will teach you whatever I know of value anyway, because that is what I choose."

Verbena looked confused, but smiled. "You're *our* paladin?"

Krell stopped, his smile fading, and regarded them seriously. "Yes. Whatever else ReckNor may want from me, one thing is clear. When his followers pray for aid, whether from a storm or from sea devils, he needs a way to respond. That is what paladins do. I am here to be his sword, to keep his followers alive, and to slaughter his enemies."

They were all looking at him with wide eyes. Sheana was smiling a little, her eyes bright with excitement. Verbena's mouth had dropped open slightly, and she looked vaguely panicked. Krell couldn't read Dahlia at all.

Krell turned and continued up the hill.

Olgar came out of the temple when they approached and walked over to Krell.

Then he embraced him.

Krell went rigid in surprise.

Olgar chuckled and squeezed, lifting Krell off the ground for a moment. Then he released him and stepped back, one hand on his shoulder.

"I'm glad your idiocy didn't get you killed, my boy!"

Krell laughed. "It was a near thing!"

Olgar turned to the others. "Ladies," he said, "what is that in the cart that I see, but do not understand?"

"The armor of the sea devil leader," said Sheana, "the one Krell killed."

Krell felt embarrassed hearing it described like that, and blushed. He caught Dahlia staring at him, a slight smile on her face.

Olgar saw none of it, his eyes locked on the armor. He pulled up a piece, running his hands over it as he turned it. Then he hefted it up and down, as if testing its weight.

"They let you walk away with this?" he asked.

Krell cocked his head sideways, his confusion written on his face. "Yes? I mean, it's part of the reward I claimed. Why wouldn't they have let me take it?"

"Because if they knew what it was, they'd never have let it go," said Olgar. He held out his hand for one of the spears. Krell handed it to him.

Olgar grunted as he hefted it. "Lighter than it should be, for its size," he muttered. He slammed it down, point first, into a stone set in the path. The stone broke in half. He inspected the point closely.

He looked at Krell and grinned. "Mithral, unless I miss my guess," he said.

Krell's eyes widened. "I thought that was a myth," he said.

"Oh, no," said Olgar. "It's real enough. The myths are all about how it's formed. I wager Verbena here has some theories about it."

"My favorite one is that it's solidified magic. Magic that condensed into a metal somehow," she said.

"Yeah, that's a good one. But if this is mithral, and I'm not saying it is, then it's possibly worth more than the town."

Krell looked at Olgar, not understanding. "The town?"

"Yes, Krell. The town. All the buildings, possessions, and money, plus all the boats, plus the land, and more besides. You'd probably be best to keep this conversation secret, understand?" Olgar looked at them all seriously. "I don't like having to kill people that break into the temple late at night to rob me, and who will probably try to kill me while they do it."

Olgar grabbed the cart, gently nudging Sheana aside. "If you young ladies will wait here a moment, I need to let Krell in on a little secret. We'll be back in a moment. It's a ReckNor thing." Olgar took the cart and walked into the temple. Krell followed him in.

"Krell, close the doors."

Krell turned and gave a confused smile to Verbena as he closed the doors.

"This way," said Olgar, wheeling the cart to the rear wall behind the altar.

"How *did* you move that altar, Olgar?" asked Krell. "It's got to weigh, what did you say, seven thousand pounds?"

"Magic. Now, look here," he said, gesturing at the back of the altar. The images of the sea flowed together to ReckNor's symbol, a trident piercing a wave. Olgar reached out and touched the two outside points with his fingers.

After a long moment, there was a strange *click*, as if two stones had been knocked together. Olgar turned around and shoved on the back wall.

It pivoted open, revealing a small narrow room.

"Olgar, what is this?" asked Krell.

"It's a secret room. If people measured outside, they'd know my room, which is right on the other side of this wall, wasn't big enough to account for the space. This, though, this is where things too dangerous to leave lying around are kept. Don't touch anything," he said. Then he began unloading the armor, stacking it as neatly as possible in the corner.

Krell looked in wonder. There was a crystal orb the size of a small apple. It was filled with thunderclouds, and lightning flickered from within. A withered hand sat on the shelf next to it. Beyond that was an axe, and when Krell looked at it, he felt a wave of cold and dread, coupled with a strong desire to reach out and take it.

Olgar slapped his hand hard, then punched him in the face. Krell stumbled backward, crashing into the altar. He hadn't even realized he was reaching out for the axe as the compulsion to grab it faded.

Olgar gave him a stern look. "Yeah, you felt it, right? That thing is deadly. Don't touch it. Anyone who picks it up becomes a fierce warrior, but with no ability to stop fighting or any ability to tell friend from foe. Give it to a peasant in town, and they'd kill a hundred people before they were put down. Then some idiot would pick up the axe, and the death would continue. *Never touch this.*"

Krell straightened and nodded, rubbing at his jaw.

Olgar grinned at him. "Learn to throw a punch, my boy. You'll never know when you need the skill!" He glanced at the spears. "You going to keep those in hand, or want me to stash them?"

Krell eyed them and shook his head. "Stash them for now. I prefer the longsword, and these are too heavy for me to use."

Olgar put them in the room and took a book off the shelf.

"There's writing implements on the pulpit there. Fetch them for me?"

Krell walked to the pulpit and found a quill and inkpot next to a flask. He brought all three over.

"Ha, clever boy, no need for another trip, hey?" Olgar took a drink, and passed it to Krell. He sniffed and took a sip. The liquid was fiery and burned as he swallowed it. His eyes began to water.

"How do you drink that?" he gasped out.

"With my mouth. Now, come here and look at this," said Olgar.

Krell shook his head, feeling ReckNor's grace working within him. The kick from the drink vanished.

The book was a detailed account of the items in the room, Krell saw. The page currently opened described the orb, which was named Storm Sphere. It was an item created with a singular purpose, to create a storm. The longer it was held, the more power it stole from the one holding it. It took that power and fed it into a storm.

There were some notes on when it was used, but the dates were so far in the past that they meant nothing to Krell. None of the places listed were known to him.

"So you see, if anything happens to me, this is the list. You need to keep these things out of the wrong hands." Olgar looked at Krell. "This is important, Krell. Listen carefully. Those wrong hands are your hands. They're also my hands. I don't trust myself to use anything in there. I don't trust Dorn with this information, either. He's too erratic, too young in his faith. The cost is too great, the consequences too severe. I'm only telling you because I trust ReckNor to stop you from being an idiot."

Olgar tapped the page. "Some of these notes are not clear enough. The sphere drains the life from you, and powers a storm of such fury it would wipe Watford from the map. Probably kill you if the sphere didn't suck you dry first."

Krell nodded. "I understand, Olgar. I won't try to touch them, nor will I tell anyone about them."

"Good," he said, spinning the book back in front of himself, flipping to an empty page. He opened the ink pot and proceeded to write a detailed description of the spears and armor. He stoppered the ink and returned it to the pulpit.

"So, what happened to Lily?"

Krell's expression fell. "I don't know," he said.

"I see. What's your guess?" asked Olgar.

"That the sea devils caught her and ate her."

"Probably the most likely guess. Sorry, Krell. I hate those bastards. All they do is kill."

"Devour," muttered Krell.

"Ha! Yeah, BranLagNos is an ass. You ever see a human follower of his, put him to death. He's already a cannibal if you can catch him in the worship of BranLagNos." Olgar took a drink from his flask.

A moment passed in silence.

"What's your plan now?" asked Olgar.

Krell looked up, his face deep in thought. "I don't know, exactly. Now that the sea devils have been defeated, what's left for me to do? Wait for ReckNor to say something, I suppose. Maybe learn Dwarvish." Olgar was looking at him strangely.

"What?" asked Krell.

"You really think that's it? One little encampment, and they're going to run back and tell BranLagNos that it was too hard to eat the surface dwellers?" Olgar shook his head. "That fortress they were building on land would have been bad. We'd be seeing raids inland. Like those little halfling farming communities. They'd start disappearing, one by one. Oh, the buildings would still be there. But the people would be gone, with enough spilled blood to make it clear none of them would ever be seen again."

Olgar took a deep breath. "But stopping that, good as it is, just means that the main fortress, the one underwater, will need to be found and purged. There may even be a settlement of them. You think they're dangerous on land? It's our home, where we have every advantage over them. They dry out, get slow and weak. Underwater, it's the reverse. We're meat in a nice metal can being served up to them," he said, tapping Krell on his breastplate. "Not only are they faster while you're slower, not only can they see and hear better than you while you thrash around trying to swim and fight at the same time, the scent of blood carries. For *miles*, Krell."

He shook his head. "No, this isn't over." Olgar took a long drink from his flask.

"It's barely even begun."

* * *

Krell stood with Sheana, Verbena, and Dahlia atop the cliff.

The stone base of the tower was behind them, still unoccupied. Watford and the temple to ReckNor could be seen below and to the west. The clouds were heavy with rain, dark and foreboding, casting everything in a dim light.

Dahlia breathed in deeply, her hair blowing in the breeze. "It's a fine view. Do you know what you're likely to do?"

Krell shook his head. "I can't remember ever owning a house before. I mean, living in one. Not sure what I should do." He turned to them. "Any thoughts?"

Verbena smiled and took Sheana's hand. "I think we're going to get a place in town, for us."

"Good," said Krell. "I just… what should a house *be*? I don't actually know. Should I just copy Amra's house?"

Verbena looked at him, then at the view of Watford and the sea. She gestured.

"Whatever you do, keep this. You'll want to be able to see this view from any room in your house. Otherwise, Amra's house is nice, but awfully big for just one person." She shook her head. "Costly, too. And you'd need to hire staff, who may need a place to live, since town is a bit of a walk. There are a lot of factors to consider."

Krell smiled. "That's why I'm asking you. You're smarter than me."

Sheana laughed, and Verbena smiled at Krell.

For the first time, it reached her eyes.

Epilogue

"It would appear that Ingelnas has failed, my lord." Brelmo stood rigidly, waiting for a response.

Marden nodded, staring out the window at the people moving about on the street below him. No noise from the crowd intruded. There was merely the ticking of a clock, perched atop an elaborate writing desk. The walls were unadorned, but the wood was polished to a high shine.

Marden sighed. "Well, setbacks are to be expected. Particularly when dealing with the sahuagin. Do we have details on what happened yet?"

"The smuggling operation was detected and eradicated. Watford apparently has a new strike team they employ, and they were used for this purpose. Cor escaped the assault on the tower they were using, but could not notify Captain Sohleal before he approached. The strike team apparently found the signals and deciphered them."

Marden turned and stroked his chin with his hand. "I see, and *The Glorious*?"

"Taken, my lord, and now renamed *ReckNor's Bounty*, pressed into service to Watford."

"Obviously Ingelnas did not survive, or he would have warned him. What of Sohleal?"

"Slain, my lord. Halpas, however, did escape and has returned to us."

"Did he now? And how did he manage that?"

"Released. Apparently, ReckNor has called a paladin in Watford, and this paladin decided that a true priest should be set free."

Marden raised an eyebrow. "Truly? Well, that is completely unexpected. Unexpected, and frustrating. We will issue some new orders to Cor, to have him observe and avoid contact for a bit." He strode over to his writing desk and sat, reaching for a quill.

"There is more, my lord," said Brelmo.

"Oh?"

"The base the sea devils were constructing, to use to raid inland, has been neutralized for now."

Marden sat back in his chair, his hands resting on his lap. "Explain, please." His voice was very quiet. Brelmo took a moment to collect himself.

"Apparently, this same strike team was dispatched to scout the remains of Swamp Hold. Instead, the team assaulted it and killed all the leadership caste that had grown, driving the rest into the sea or dispersing them into the countryside."

"This strike team *assaulted* the sahuagin base?" asked Marden, his eyes widening slightly.

"They did, my lord. From what our agent reports, they did so largely without loss, and after slaying nearly two hundred of the beasts."

Marden steepled his fingers, lost in thought.

"My lord?"

"Mmm?" said Marden, bringing his attention back to Brelmo.

"It is likely that our involvement trading weapons to the sahuagin has been discovered."

Marden sighed. "Paladins. What a bother. Okay, there's little to be done about it now. Certainly, we never used names of people in our organization on any written document. What's important is that we stop antagonizing this… man?"

Brelmo nodded. "Krell, of no last name. Found adrift at sea and put ashore in Watford. It sounds like Olgar was waiting for him on the docks. This lends a lot of support to the argument that he is indeed ReckNor's paladin."

Brelmo looked down at the papers he was holding. "We're still establishing profiles for the others he travels with. So far, we've got Dorn Ironbrow, another true priest of ReckNor. Orca, of no last name, an orc warrior. Tristan, of no last name, who is employed to one degree or another by Karaback, the crown's agent in Watford. Kraven Atka and Gerrard Riverhopper we know little about at the moment, nor do we know anything about the various warrior women Krell has hired."

Marden nodded. "Okay then. Move operations to an entirely passive mode in Watford. Have Cor keep a low profile. It is likely that Daylan Plintform has lost all of his value to us, so we'll ignore him for the time being. I'll write up orders for Cor."

Marden bent down and picked up a quill.

Brelmo waited patiently — and quietly — for Marden to finish.

When he finished, he set the letter aside. Marden looked at Brelmo.

"This is sufficiently important that I want you to go to Watford yourself. Pose as a minor messenger, and deliver these orders. Make sure you read and understand them first. Then remain in Watford and keep an eye on Cor. If memory serves, he does not take failure well, does he?"

Brelmo went a little pale. "Remain in Watford?" he asked.

Marden nodded. "I know. It's a risk to you personally. I apologize for that. The impression I have is that the sahuagin invasion has been blunted. Likely, the paladin will confront them under the waves, ending the threat for another generation. This aspect of forcing Baltorc to make ready will doubtless fail now. However, I could be wrong."

Marden took out a new piece of paper and wrote out new orders. Brelmo again waited patiently.

"Take this downstairs to Garm. He'll assign you a squad to act as escort and bodyguard, including a spellcaster so we can stay in touch and to help you locate Cor. If I'm wrong and the sahuagin do attack, you are to retreat inland at once with the guard force. No heroics. If Cor is with you, feel free to bring him along. Otherwise, cut him loose."

Marden gave Brelmo a stern look. "Cor is replaceable. The guard force is replaceable. You are not." He handed the first letter to Brelmo now that the ink had dried. He leaned back in thought as Brelmo read, then reread, the orders.

"I wonder, Brelmo, if we shouldn't adjust the entire axis of our campaign against Mavram and Fideon. Certainly stirring up the sahuagin and getting them to attack was always high risk. Perhaps encouraging a martial response against the sea devils can lay the same foundation we need for the upcoming war."

Brelmo looked at Marden. "If it means we don't have to let the sahuagin murder scores of innocent people to mobilize the armies of Baltorc, that would be better, I'd say."

"Well, regardless, the paladin will upend our plans no matter what we do. Keep an eye on the temple of Hieron as well. No, I'll send separate orders and a full team. If ReckNor called a paladin, I'm wagering that Hieron is going to do so again, and probably in Heaford. Let's plan for the worst." Marden began writing again.

"I thought we *were* planning for the worst?" said Brelmo.

Marden looked up and gave him a small nod.

"The Black Theocracy must be stopped. At any price."